THREE SISTERS RESORT

Complete Series Box Set

Morris Fenris

Table of Contents

Book 1: Marianne

Prologue

Marianne looked out the window as the car ran smoothly along the black, paved road. She and her younger sisters, Sue and Lynn, were headed to their new home.

Never in her life had Marianne suspected such a thing could happen to the Wright sisters. Sudden wealth had dropped into their laps, and they were expected to hobnob with the bigwigs.

Marianne smiled to herself. The three sisters hadn't been raised poor, but the wealth their Uncle Nathan had left them was beyond anything they could have imagined.

The inheritance came with a lot of responsibility, however, which was something the three girls would have to get used to as quickly as they could. Uncle Nathan had left the three of them in charge of his vast resort in the eastern-most part of Georgia, ridiculously close to St. Simons Island. Their uncle had always boasted about how many customers it brought to his resort. That's why it thrived, he said. He also said he would never have a bad word to say about the place.

It had made him rich.

Now it made the three sisters rich. None of them were able or willing to let the thriving business fail. They would keep it up and running, build on it, expand where they could, and make it better and better as the years passed; just like their uncle had.

There was a small village just down the hillside from Emerald Resort called Queen Anne. It was quaint and small, making it feel like you had been transported back in time when visiting. It was the perfect tourist attraction. The Wright sisters were now owners of the entire village; at least, the land it stood on.

In his will, Uncle Nathan made sure to put in a clause that ensured the rent could not be raised on the residents in Queen Anne; not on their businesses or their homes. Expansion would be at the girls' discretion, but he did not want the village to be too large or too modern.

Mari and her sisters had no plans for expansion. Not in the village anyway. Sue had been bubbling over, as much as her serious nature would allow, with excitement and new ideas for the hotel. She wanted to make it more family-oriented, or at least have an area where families would have the most fun together.

The resort was, undoubtedly, a place for adults, the way it was now. Built in the late 1800's, the only modernization completed was appliances, water, and other luxuries created in the past hundred years. Otherwise, the original layout remained the same, having been restored to its original glory about every twenty years.

Mari's idea for running the resort had been excitedly accepted by her sisters. They agreed that it would be fun to put their combined skills together, and open the resort to weddings and grand ceremonial balls. The elite would flock to the place to hold their events, and the girls would make more money than they could handle.

Mari was glad it was already a working business. She knew anyone her late uncle had hired was trustworthy; otherwise, Emerald Resort wouldn't be making money hand-over-fist.

She felt a bubble of excitement growing in her chest when the driver turned to speak over his shoulder to the three girls. Sue had to turn around when he spoke, because she was facing her sisters in the short limousine.

"The resort is just up here around the corner, ladies, if you'd like to see how it looks as you're driving up. I just want to tell you all that it's always been such a pleasure working for Nathan, and I'm sorry he's gone. He was a great boss."

His voice sounded a bit sorrowful, for which Mari was grateful. Her uncle was always a kind man; good at business, but also personable enough to do things with a gentle hand. He made friends and had a successful business at the same time. He was never shady and treated everyone with respect, from the highest CEO to the street cleaner. Anyone who got out of bed and went to work in the morning had his respect.

And, much to Sue's pleasure, he compared motherhood to a job. He enjoyed being productive with his days, and respected anyone else who held that same work ethic. He had no tolerance for laziness. It was his opinion that everyone had a worthwhile skill they could be using.

"We're all human beings," he had told the girls, just a few months before his death, when he visited for Christmas. "It's important that we treat each other as such."

The heart attack that took him, at the young age of 45, had devastated an entire community of people. Mari had never seen so many people at a memorial service, graveside service, or funeral.

Mari, Sue, and Lynn turned their heads, to look out the window as they rounded the corner.

Mari heard Sue and Lynn gasp at the same time. She couldn't gasp. Her breath was caught in her throat. The tree line receded to reveal one of the most beautiful places Mari had ever seen.

She was in awe of the grand building in front of her. The shrubs were trimmed to spell out the name "Emerald Resort", and the bright green flowers that dotted those shrubs looked like emeralds. The place was alive with action. It had not shut down after the death of its owner. They were all expecting the sisters, and had kept the place running in the interim.

Today, the Wright sisters would meet the group of people that kept the place running. There was no real committee to speak to. Somehow, Uncle Nathan had made all the business decisions himself. He had no board of directors.

The driver turned into the driveway that would take them around to their portion of the hotel; their large cottage, set apart from the hotel but joined by an enclosed hallway.

To their right, they saw two large, fenced rectangles, where tournament-sized tennis courts offered the guests plenty of exercise. To their left was a wall. On the other side of the wall, a raised pool stretched for what seemed like a mile. The girls couldn't see that it was a pool until they were almost to their cottage.

White walkways made squiggly lines all across the landscape, allowing people to get from one place to another without always walking on the grass. Tall, black, old-fashioned lampposts lined not just the road going up, but the walkways as well.

In between the walkways was the most beautiful, healthy-looking grass Mari had ever seen. Her sisters oohed and aahed in amazement. She herself was speechless. She could see the other amenities the resort had to offer across the land in the distance. It would take her a couple of days to explore everything, if not longer.

And it all belonged to her and her sisters.

Thank you, Uncle Nathan, she thought, gazing over the landscape.

"When we get up there," the driver said, "I'd be glad to show you where you'll need to go. From there, Linda will show you around. Don't worry. You'll get used to it real soon. Everyone does. Most people don't want to leave once they get here, even if only for a vacation. You'll love the employees. All of them are real nice people. This is a great place to work."

Mari smiled. "I'm glad you think so, uh…"

"Oh, sorry. The name's Hank Miller. I'll be your driver. Anytime you need to go anywhere, if I'm available, I'll drive you. And I only say 'if I'm available' because there was only one Nathan Wright, and there's three of you. I can't be in three places at once, you know?"

The girls laughed. "I suppose we'll have to hire a few more drivers."

Hank nodded, looking through the windshield again. "Yeah, I suppose you will."

"You know a lot more about what it takes than we do," Mari said. "Feel free to recommend some people to us, if you like."

Hank smiled at her in the rearview mirror. She returned the smile.

"I'll do that, Miss Mari. Thanks."

Mari laughed. "You don't have to add the Miss. It's just Mari."

Hank nodded. "Will do. Mari."

Mari chose to ignore the look Sue gave her. She was probably thinking she'd want everyone at the resort to call her Miss Wright, or something like that. But that's not the way Uncle Nathan ran his business, and it wasn't the way Mari intended to run it now. She held the majority stock, with her sisters both having 33%, while she had 34%.

Hank pulled the limo up to the cottage and turned to them again. His twinkling blue eyes lit on each of them, his white teeth making his smile flash.

"Well, you're home."

Chapter 1

The girls gathered in the middle of the large study. They hadn't had to do any decorating since moving in. The only thing they had done was triple everything they needed, such as desks to sit at, filing cabinets, and other office equipment. Each one had an assistant hired for them, just after the will was read. Uncle Nathan had suggested they do so, and they took his advice.

Otherwise, just being there felt like home. The only other thing they had changed was their individual "chambers", as Uncle Nathan had liked to call their suites in the cottage. Each of those had been decorated in their own style.

Mari's rooms were now decorated in deep green and gold colors, from the long drapes to the quilts on the King-sized bed. Everything was modernized, so she could press a small button on her remote control to make things close and open, such as the cabinets on her built-in entertainment center.

She laughed when she discovered that the entertainment center held mini-versions of every game system she could have wanted, with joysticks, and even guitars for Guitar Hero, if she felt like going old-school.

Sue's room was decorated in deep brown and tans, and heavy leather furniture abounded. Even the paintings and pictures she'd chosen for the walls were dark in nature, giving her room a rather gloomy feel, in Mari's opinion, though she didn't say so. She kept her thoughts to herself.

Lynn's room reflected the bright, sunny nature of the girl, with yellows, oranges, reds and bright colors all around her. Brightly colored flowers in vases decorated every table. The pictures on the walls were classic renditions of floral arrangements.

And just like her room, Lynn was dressed that morning in a bright yellow dress made of flimsy material, that practically draped from her slender shoulders down to her shapely ankles. Her hair was up, in double French braids along the side of her head that met in the back, and had yellow flowers weaved in with the braided hair.

It wasn't a new hairstyle for Lynn. She had gone to beauty school to learn to create hairstyles. Her plan had been to be a hairstylist to the stars.

Now, she found herself in an excellent position to use her talents at the resort. Designing fancy 'do's' for the Elite ladies would put her name out there. She no longer needed the money. She just wanted to be known for her skill.

Despite her flouncy, happy-go-lucky nature, Lynn was surprisingly smart. Sue, the most serious sister, often asked her how she could possibly maintain such a positive attitude, when most of the world looked so bleak.

Lynn's answer was almost always the same. The words might change, but most of the time, she simply shrugged and said, "Not in my world. There's just too much beauty to only see darkness."

Mari tried to maintain an optimistic attitude like her sister. She had often failed at it, dismissing her own abilities and despairing at the smallest flaw. But when that happened, she just picked herself up and remembered what Lynn liked to say.

"Life's too short to dwell on the negative."

And she was right. Mari was determined to live by that motto as much as she could.

Sue was standing in front of her desk, looking down at the blotter in front of her. She was the only one who had insisted on keeping track of things that way.

"If I don't write it down," she said. "I'll forget it. I have to have it right in front of my face."

"But you can set notifications, so that any reminders you need come to you," Lynn said. "That's what I do."

"I don't always have my phone with me," had been Sue's response, which made Lynn give a wide-eyed look. The look made Mari laugh.

"So, we're supposed to see those two brothers in twenty minutes," Sue said, almost to herself. Her sisters looked up at her from their desks.

Lynn was seated at hers, browsing a website of trending hairstyles of celebrities. She was propping her head up with her fingers, her elbow on top of the desk. The other hand was resting on her mouse, and her index finger repeatedly reached up and scrolled with the button on her mouse.

She turned to look at Mari, and smiled. "Our first customers. Can't wait. I hope this goes smooth."

Mari nodded. "Me, too. It's kind of weird to be dealing with the grooms instead of the brides, though, isn't it?"

Lynn raised her eyebrows and shrugged. "I don't know. This is my first rodeo."

Mari grinned wide. "Mine, too."

"Well, I've planned weddings before, as you both know," Sue said firmly. "And you're actually mostly right, Mari."

Mari looked pleasantly surprised. "Mostly right? What does that mean?"

"The majority of clients that approach wedding planners are women, but there's a growing number of grooms that have become interested in the planning stages of their wedding. Men are getting to be more open with their feelings."

"Yeah, but…"

Mari held up one hand, stopping Lynn's words. "No political debates right now, sisters. Let's talk about the brothers. What are their names again, Sue?"

Mari had to stop Sue and Lynn from the discussion they were heading into. The two were staunchly opposite when it came to politics, and though Lynn was mostly mild-tempered, she could be fiery when it came to her feelings on the political realm. She had no problem expressing those feelings, either.

Mari had quickly grown tired of their bickering, from the

moment they were each able to express a voice on matters of society and government, and told them, in no uncertain terms, that she wouldn't tolerate it.

"Let's see..." Sue took her cue from Mari, looking back down at the monthly planner. "Brian and Dexter Scofield. They're the sons of that oil magnate who still lives in Texas with his fourth or fifth wife. I can't remember. They're loaded."

"Well, of course," Mari said. "Only the best for Emerald Resort, right?"

"We should lower prices," Lynn said. "Or open up an area for lower-income families, so they can afford to come here."

Mari looked at her sister with a soft look in her eyes. Lynn was always thinking of the underdog. She smiled at her. "We can't. There are plenty of places for people like that, Lynn, but we happened to inherit a place that caters to the elite. And now we're part of that elite. So, we have to act like we know what we're doing."

Lynn giggled. "I can't act like I know what I'm doing. I don't know what I'm doing. I'm stuck in the hot dog, grilling out, paying rent frame of mind."

Mari knew exactly how her sister felt. She was fresh out of her nursing job, knowing she would never need to worry about working again. Not in that field, anyway. Not unless she wanted to. She was already considering giving emergency services courses to all the employees of Emerald Resort. She would hold classes. They could attend of their own volition, and get to personally meet one of the Wright sisters, as she had heard them called earlier in the day. She liked the sound of it.

"I understand, but we still have to try."

She turned back to her computer screen and saved the short list of questions she was writing, that she needed to remember to ask the Scofield brothers.

"What more do you know about these brothers?" she asked Sue, without looking at her. "Besides the fact that their father made them rich, and he's had a lot of wives?"

She looked up when Sue responded. Her sister's voice had gone soft in a way Mari had never heard before. She was always brash and brazen. "They don't live off daddy's money," Sue said, breathlessly. Mari watched her sister stare at the computer screen.

"They are rich in their own right. They did borrow money to start their companies, but it   looks like Brian, the one who's getting married, started a chain of restaurants that have brought in customers from all over the world. He's apparently some kind of amazing chef. Wonder if he knows Gordon Ramsay?"

Mari and Lynn chuckled softly.

"The other brother, Dexter, he's the best man," Sue continued, still gazing at her screen. "He's a... whoa, he's a computer genius and owns stock in Apple, IBM, all those high-tech companies, cell phone giants... wow. And before you say 'all rich kids own stock', he apparently came up with a computer program that can compute algorithms in advanced animatronic engineering, and it's being used in every movie and television studio around the world."

"Good God Almighty," Sue and Mari breathed at the same time.

"He's brilliant." Mari suddenly felt intimidated. She might have as much, or close to as much, money as the brothers did in the bank, but she wasn't raised with it. What if she made a fool of herself from the get-go?

She tried to calm her beating heart. Waiting for the men to arrive felt like an eternity to her. Finally, there was a knock on the door and Sue went to answer it.

Mari watched her pull in a deep breath before she opened the door. She glanced over at her sisters and Mari nodded. They were both nervous.

Sue opened the door and stepped back.

Two men came through the door, both wearing smiles that beamed at the sisters.

"Hello!" The first man who came through had dark brown

hair, swept back, and brown eyes to match. He held out his hand, which Sue shook. "I'm Brian Scofield. The groom. You're the Wright sisters?"

Mari and Lynn stood up, approaching the two men. They all shook hands and introduced themselves.

Brian turned to the other man, who was the opposite of his brother on the color scale, with bright blond hair and sky-blue eyes. "This is my brother, Dexter." He looked at the three sisters. "Don't worry. He's not a serial killer."

Mari laughed, as Dexter rolled his eyes and Lynn gave her a confused look.

"What..." Lynn's voice trailed off. Mari just shook her head, glancing at her.

"It's a television show. I doubt you've seen it. Don't worry about it."

Lynn turned a smile to the men.

Dexter shook their hands and Mari invited them in to sit down.

The sisters had created a meeting area in the middle of the study, where a large round table allowed up to ten people to sit; twelve if they squeezed together. The group sat to make a half circle around the table.

Sue set a notepad in front of her and held her pen at the ready. Brian looked at her, scanning the notepad and pen. "You're going to write it all down?"

Lynn opened her small laptop in front of her, and held her fingers over the keyboard, ready to fill in the online questionnaire form.

"I just like to take notes," Sue responded with a smile. "I find that it helps to write down little keywords that people say. That way, I can pinpoint little things, later, that they might not even remember saying."

Brian raised one eyebrow, looking amused.

Mari looked at the two brothers, impressed with their overall demeanor so far. Dexter seemed to be the quiet one, though Mari suspected he was only letting his brother take the reins because it was his wedding. He was a handsome man.

She flushed when, at the moment the thought slipped through her mind, Dexter's eyes slid over and met hers. They were warm, and for the first time in her life, Mari felt a tingle slide up her spine.

Chapter 2

An hour later, Brian and Mari had hammered out all the details, with the rest of the group chiming in with ideas every now and then. Brian had chosen the festivities he wanted included at the reception, which would be held directly after the ceremony. He booked one of the three ballrooms for the entire weekend, and asked to rent out an entire floor in the hotel.

Mari's heart raced as she calculated the charges, according to the prices their uncle already had in place. Brian didn't bat an eye when she quoted him the six-figure bill. He pulled a wallet from his back pocket and took out a card.

He flapped it in the air in front of him.

"You take plastic, don't you?"

Mari smiled. "Of course, we do, Mr. Scofield. Sue will take care of that for you."

Brian dropped the card flat on the table and slid it to Sue with his fingers. "Here you go, darlin'. Add a ten percent bonus onto that for the three of you, for being so easy to deal with. No, make that twelve percent, so you each get a four percent bonus."

A chill ran through Mari as she listened to his words. She looked at Lynn, hoping she didn't look too shocked. She noticed Dexter was looking at her again, with that same amused grin on his face. She didn't know how to take it.

She had to be making it obvious that this was all new to her. She knew she was blushing, and when she felt her cheeks become hot, she blushed even harder. She looked away, not wanting to betray herself any further.

Sue got up from the table and went to her desk.

"You girls need assistants," Dexter finally spoke up. "This has got to be a lot of work."

Mari nodded, letting herself look back at him again. The amused look was gone, and he just gazed at her in a friendly way. He had his hands clasped together in front of him on the table, and he was leaning forward in his seat. His suit fit him well, but was somewhat casual. He didn't wear a tie, and the top two buttons of his shirt were undone.

Mari noticed the cuffs of his sleeves were not buttoned, and he wore no cuff links. She almost asked if it was "Casual Wednesday", but stopped herself just in time. What a silly thing that would have been to say.

"Our uncle did it all himself," Lynn replied in a soft voice, obviously overwhelmed by the sheer luxury the two men represented. "I guess between the three of us, we can handle it."

"Actually," Brian said, as he signed his name with his left hand at the bottom of the contracts Sue was handing him. "It's a well-known fact that your uncle did have an assistant, and that he thought of him as invaluable." He looked up at the girls one-by-one. "Surely he told you about him?"

Mari pulled her eyebrows together. "I don't remember Uncle Nathan ever mentioning an assistant."

Brian raised his eyebrows, looked nonchalant and shrugged, going back to reading through the documents, and signing them. "Well, I'm sure... right here? Yes? I'm sure his name will come up when you talk to the people who work here."

"We have a meeting with them in an hour," Lynn said. "I'm going to ask about him. This assistant was never mentioned before."

Brian nodded, turning to ask Sue a question about a clause in the contract. Mari didn't quite hear the question. Her attention had returned to Dexter, who was staring at his fingers, picking at one of his fingernails. He looked up at her and caught her watching. The smile that came across his face made Mari instantly feel nervous.

She smiled back.

"I guess you had to uproot yourselves completely to come to Georgia, didn't you?" he asked her.

She nodded. "Yes, we were living up in Virginia."

"Do you miss it?"

Mari glanced out the window, thinking about the rolling hills she had left behind, the co-workers at the hospital where she worked, the men she either was dating or wanted to date. She smiled at Dexter. "Sometimes. I mean, we lived there from the time I was twelve. That's fourteen years. I was practically raised there."

"Well, at least you've got some southern in you," Dexter said. "You can't live in Georgia and not have southern in you, to appreciate it."

"I'm worried about bug season. It was bad in Virginia. I can only imagine what it will be like here."

Dexter laughed, a pleasant sound that sent an equally pleasant feeling straight through Mari. "It can get pretty bad, but we have ways to work around it. I might have time to show you a few tricks. Do you have a lot of friends down here?"

Mari shook her head. "No. We've only been living here for a month. I mean, here in Georgia, not here at the resort. We've only been here a week, but we didn't know anyone before that."

"Well, I'll introduce you to some of my friends, then, at the wedding. I'm sure they'll all be delighted to meet someone as brilliant and beautiful as you."

Mari was enveloped in a warm feeling, that spread from the top of her head, all the way down to her toes. Dexter moved his eyes to Lynn, and then to Sue.

"All of you. I'm sure you'll make lots of friends."

Mari struggled not to sigh like a love-struck teenager. She had to admit that she was attracted to Dexter, and it had nothing to do with the money in his bank account. He had a smooth, friendly voice, an attractive smile, and he wasn't an arrogant rich kid with a spoiled attitude.

Neither of them were arrogant.

Mari was grateful that the Scofield brothers were the first clients for her and her sisters. It seemed like it was going to be a smooth transition into their new careers; into a new world for them.

"Thank you so much for that compliment, Mr. Scofield," she said. He shook his head at her.

"Dex. Please. You can't call us both Mr. Scofield. It will confuse everyone."

Brian finally gave them his attention. "Oh. Yes, just call me Brian. No need to be so formal. Mr. Scofield…"

"…is our father." They both ended the sentence at the same time and laughed together.

Mari and her sisters couldn't help smiling at the comradery of the brothers. Mari could see the similarities between them when they laughed. They both had the same narrow eyes, perfectly shaped lips, straight white teeth and a dimple in their chin.

Mari ignored the thumping of her heart. She certainly couldn't be thinking along those lines every time handsome grooms and best men came through the resort. She'd be forever falling in love.

The thought made her giggle. She lifted one hand and pretended to cough into it.

Mari stood up when the men did, signaling their time for departure.

"I'd like to bring my fiancée back and show her the place, as soon as we get the opportunity, if that suits you," Brian said, holding out his hand to Sue once more. She shook it, nodding.

"Come back anytime. Just give your name to the front desk clerk in the hotel, and you will be given a pass to go anywhere you'd like on the property."

"Thank you so much for your cooperation. It's going to be wonderful working with you," Mari said, holding her hand out to Dexter. He took it. When he wrapped his hand around hers, she had a sudden vision of him pulling her toward him, wrapping one strong arm around her waist and kissing her firmly on the lips.

But that didn't happen, and the thought was gone as quickly as it came.

She pulled in a deep breath, letting go of his hand quickly.

The brothers said good bye to the sisters, saluting them with two fingers in exactly the same way, just before turning toward the door. The girls looked at each other, sharing amused looks.

They waved and nodded, when the brothers reached the door and glanced back one more time.

"Good bye!" Brian called out, and they closed the door behind them as they left.

Mari looked at her sisters.

At the same time, they all let out a collective sigh. Still in sync, they turned away from each other and headed back to their desks.

"Well, I think that went really well," Sue said. She dropped into her office chair and pushed it back a little so she was facing the ceiling. She stretched her legs in front of her and let her arms dangle over the sides of the chair's armrests.

Mari nodded, sliding into her chair and moving her mouse slightly to wake the screen up. She immediately typed in Dexter Scofield's name in the search engine, and hit search. She wanted to find out as much as she could about that man. He intrigued her.

She had always believed that the people in the upper classes were snobbish and arrogant. He didn't seem like he was either, even with his accomplishments. She liked that about him. She liked a lot of things about him.

As she read through the pages and pages of short news clips about his accomplishments, his family, their business dealings and relationships with various people in the upper elite classes, she was even more taken in.

The man had met with presidents.

She shook her head. She had no idea she would be

immersed in such an atmosphere. The hospital in Virginia was low-key for the most part; a small hospital nestled in the mountains, just outside Montgomery County. They'd had a total of two celebrities in their hospital, and both of them were in the 80's, long before she was around to enjoy their fame.

She thought about the friends she'd left behind to move to Georgia, and the question Dexter had asked her. Did she miss it? She missed them, but they were all on her social media pages anyway. She could keep up with their lives and not have to be completely apart from them.

Thank God for the technology age, she thought with a smile.

She did miss Virginia, and suspected she would miss it more when the weather in Georgia turned humid. She'd really miss Virginia when there was a chance of hurricanes, floods, or some other natural disaster she hadn't even thought of.

No matter how much she tried not to think about it, she knew there was one thing she was dreading more than anything else. She'd mentioned it to Dexter, and he had waved it off as if it was nothing.

But humidity brought one thing that Mari disliked more than anything else.

Bugs, she thought and lifted one hand to hide a giggle.

Chapter 3

Brian didn't return for a week. It was exactly seven days later, on a bright Saturday afternoon, when Mari ran across him and his fiancée, Laura Smithson. She was the daughter of a state representative and one of the prettiest, shortest women Mari had ever seen.

She was on her way to check the front gate, to make sure they had the updated list of guests who were expected to attend. It was too pretty to stay inside and call people all day. The same calls would come to her cell phone anyway. So, she decided to take a walk.

Brian and Laura were walking toward her, passing the tennis courts, where they had apparently stopped and chatted about the merits of the sport, in between passionate kisses.

Mari lifted one hand and waved at them.

"Hello! How has your visit been? Have you been down to Queen Anne?"

Laura nodded, holding out her hand. "You must be Mari. Brian described all of you to me, and I know you just have to be Mari."

Mari nodded with a smile. "I am. I hope they were friendly reviews."

"Oh, yes, definitely. He says you each have your own unique style." As she repeated her fiancé's words, she looked up to the sky and tapped her closed fingers in the air with each syllable. She laughed and took Mari's hand in both of hers, shaking it a second time. "It's so nice to meet you. This is so beautiful. And Queen Anne is such a… a unique little quaint town, isn't it, Bri?"

Brian nodded, leaning forward and smiling at Mari. "It certainly is. Mari, as you have probably guessed, this is Laura. Her maid of honor, Karen Beasley, is in the hotel lounge with Dexter."

Mari looked into Brian's eyes when he said his brother's name, hearing a strange tone in his voice. Laura didn't react to it, but Mari could have sworn she saw the corners of Brian's eyes crinkle with amusement.

She couldn't decide if he was laughing at her or not.

She decided she had misinterpreted the look, and turned to walk back toward the hotel with them. If Dexter was on the property, Mari felt like the front gate list could really wait a while.

She listened to Laura, as she admired the beauty around her, nodding and agreeing when appropriate, but her mind was somewhere else.

It was in the hotel lobby with Dexter. She wanted to meet Karen Beasley, who was often in the newspapers, and even some tabloids. She was always linked to some movie or TV star. Mari didn't know what she'd done to deserve getting introduced to those people, but there she was, in the limelight for some reason or another.

She didn't ask Laura how Karen came to be a friend of hers. She couldn't think of a polite way to phrase the question. So, she didn't ask, figuring if she was meant to find out, she would, eventually, throughout this process.

Mari walked behind Laura and Brian when they went in, allowing them to take the lead, as a proper couple should. She smiled at Dexter, who was on the other side of the lounge, leaning against one of the load-bearing pillars around the room. Each pillar was artfully sculpted into a menagerie of exotic animals.

Mari admired the one he was leaning against as the three of them approached. Her eyes moved to Dexter's, when she sensed he was still looking at her, and had not looked away to greet his brother. She smiled at him, and basked in the one he returned to her.

"Good afternoon, Mari," he said in a smooth voice.

She tried to act calm, but her heart was racing a mile a minute. "Good afternoon, Dex. How are you doing today?"

"I'm doing good, thanks for asking. You?"

She nodded. *Better now that you're here*, she thought.

She dared not say it.

"It's been a good day. Really productive. I like to stay busy."

Dexter nodded. "That's a good way to be."

"What would you know about that?" Karen asked. Mari looked around Dexter, at the woman who'd spoken, lifting her eyebrows in surprise. Karen was looking at Dexter through narrowed eyes. Mari looked back at Dexter, and instantly knew what was going on.

There was no mistaking the look of disgust Dexter gave Karen when he glanced back at her.

"Excuse me, Karen?" he asked, his voice suddenly turning dark.

Karen made an exasperated sound and rolled her eyes. "You wouldn't know the first thing about being productive. So, you created a computer program. Now all you do is sit around and socialize, and go on vacations." She grunted. "So productive with your days."

"Look, Karen…"

"You two stop it right now." Brian stepped toward the two, stopping when he was in between them. He looked back and forth at each of them, holding up one finger in front of them. "You're not going to ruin this for Laura and me. I wish I'd known you two knew each other, before we asked you to stand up there with us. But we are committed to having you there because you're our best, oldest friends. Put your differences aside for our sakes, got it?"

Dexter backed up immediately, nodding. Mari's only thought was that he was closer to her now. She took in a deep, silent breath, breathing in the scent of his cologne. She didn't know what kind it was, but it was breathtaking.

He turned slightly and looked down at her. His face was still sullen. "Sorry about that," he mumbled.

Mari shook her head. "Don't apologize. I've known plenty of people that completely rubbed me the wrong way."

26

Dexter looked at Karen's retreating back as she walked away, with Sue next to her, talking rather rapidly. Sue seemed to handle the woman just fine, so Mari didn't say a word. She didn't like confrontational people, and Karen seemed like a fine example of that type of personality. She didn't blame Dexter for his dislike.

She didn't even know her, and already she disliked her.

"Is she always like that?" Mari asked.

"She's always like that when I'm around," was Dexter's response. He settled his sky-blue eyes on her, and she felt a chill run down her thighs. "Maybe if we hang out enough, I'll tell you about it sometime."

"Okay. I'm always up for a bit of gossip." She giggled. "Actually, I'm not much on gossip at all. It kind of makes me feel bad. But if you ever want to tell me about your... past relationships and how you..."

"No, no," Dexter stopped her, waving one hand and shaking his head. "She's not a previous relationship. We never dated. No, nothing like that. This goes back to college." Dexter chuckled. "It's actually not a big secret. It won't have any relevance at my brother's wedding. I'll just tell you."

Mari felt privileged that Dexter had changed his mind, and his attitude, so quickly with her. It was a sign of trust that Mari recognized.

"Okay, I won't say a word."

Dexter grunted. "When I was at the university, I was studying for my engineering degree, and I always used the same desk in the library every day. I mean every single day. And one day, I was asked into the dean's office, where he told me that he suspected I was cheating with another student. That is, allowing someone else to look at my tests and giving them my answers, the right ones. My scores were always exceedingly high, and the person who was cheating off my tests was getting the exact same answers wrong that I was."

Mari listened with fascination. Dexter lifted the plastic bottle of Coke to his lips and took a swig, his eyes looking straight

27

across the room, staring out the window on the other side.

"Was it Karen who was cheating off your tests?" Mari asked.

He glanced at her, shaking his head, as he pushed himself from the post with one shoulder. "No. It was her boyfriend."

"Oh."

"Before you wonder why I'd be mad at her for what her boyfriend did, he's not her boyfriend now. She was the one who put the hidden camera over my study hall table. They watched me take all my pre-exams and copied all my answers. I almost got kicked out of school, and my reputation in the business community would have been ruined."

He shook his head. "I never would have amounted to anything. And her saying that I'm not productive?"

Mari frowned, also shaking her head. "Wow. I can't believe that. She could have done a lot of damage. How did you get them to see the truth?"

Dexter began to walk across the lounge, gesturing with the Coke bottle for her to come along. She complied, falling into step next to him.

"Well, my family has a really good reputation. My brother was there two years before me, and knew the Dean really well. Plus, my dad and the Dean's cousin play golf together. So, there's been talk about our family on their side, and about their family on our side. There wasn't any favoritism. It's just that we have a reputation for being trustworthy. You know, honest."

"That's what I gathered," Mari said, softly.

He gave her that handsome, amused look, lifting his eyebrows slightly along with the corners of his lips. "What you've gathered?"

Mari chuckled. "I have to confess, I ran your name through a search engine. I did like what I read. I noticed that your family is very well-liked among a lot of different circles."

Dexter nodded. "Yeah. None of us are politicians."

Mari laughed with him.

"Do you think you'll ever try your hand at something like that?" Mari asked, genuinely curious.

When they reached the other side of the lounge, Dexter reached forward and pushed open the glass door in front of them. He held it open, sweeping his other hand through the air to indicate she could go before him.

She stepped out on the deck and walked to the edge, where she could look out over the vast golf course in front of her. It was one of three; two of them were on opposite ends of the resort, and the third was closer to Queen Anne village.

She narrowed her eyes, focusing on the little specks of people on the course, who were inspecting their tees, checking the wind ratio, choosing which club to use next. They were all relaxed and happy. She was grateful to be a part of it.

Dexter stepped out from behind her and stood by her side, also looking over the waist-high railing. He rested one hand on it. He gazed down at her. She couldn't help looking back at him, with an adoring look she hoped he didn't recognize.

"I think it will be a cold day in Hell before a Scofield gets into politics, to be honest with you. I won't be encouraging my children to do that, and I know Brian won't either. The only other one is our sister, Lilith, but I don't think she ever wants to get married. She's perfectly happy being daddy's little princess for the rest of her life."

"Do you really think so?"

"I really think so." He tapped one finger to his temple. "She's got a few bats in the belfry, you know."

Mari's eyebrows shot up. "Bats in the belfry? I haven't heard that in... well, ever. Not from a single living, breathing person."

Dexter chuckled, pleasantly. "I don't mean any disrespect. I love the girl. But I have to say, she's not quite all there. Sweet as can be, though."

Mari laughed. "I look forward to meeting her."

Chapter 4

For the next half hour, Mari and Dexter talked on the deck, barely noticing anyone around them. Mari was about to ask him what he might like for lunch, when he said, "You know, I'm starving for some chicken. Does your kitchen serve chicken wings?"

Mari smiled wide. "It does. You like chicken wings?" For some reason, she had never envisioned the upper class enjoying a good batch of hot wings.

Dexter rested one hand on his stomach. "What I wouldn't do for a big batch of chicken wings with buffalo sauce. I also enjoy them with barbecue sauce, or hot sauce. Spicy hot sauce, with maybe some habanero on there."

Mari blew out through pursed lips. "Whew! Too hot for me." She waved one hand in front of her mouth. "I can take the hot wing sauce, but nothing more than that. Those peppers... I don't want to have it so hot I don't enjoy it anymore."

Dexter shook his head. "You're right about that. I like them really spicy, but if that ruins the taste for you, we'd better stick to the regular hot sauce. Don't worry, you probably don't want hair on your chest anyway, right?"

Mari laughed abruptly. "Uh, no, I'd rather not."

Dexter nodded. "Good. That's really good to hear."

"Well, what do you say we go get some?" He held out his arm in a formal manner, bent at the elbow, and she circled her hand around it.

"I think that's a grand idea," she said in her haughtiest voice. She was only able to keep up the façade for a few moments before collapsing in a fit of giggles.

"Awww, you ruined it," Dexter said, laughing with her. "I was totally trying to be, you know, serious and all."

Again, Mari laughed. She was blessed to have met Dexter. He was loads of fun, good-looking, and a great conversationalist.

He had such a witty sense of humor. She wanted to listen to him every day, all day.

She hoped she wasn't acting like a school girl with a crush, but at the same time, she wanted to enjoy the feelings she was experiencing. He was so *attractive*.

"I'll get you the biggest batch of wings ever," she said, as they made their way back to the lounge. "But we'll have to go back to the kitchen. Would you like to meet the head chef? He's the best!"

Dexter nodded. "Sure. I'll meet him. You think he's as good as my brother?"

Mari's eyebrows shot up, and she gave Dexter an innocent look. "Oh, I couldn't say. I've never eaten your brother's food."

"You've never eaten at any of our restaurants?" Dexter sounded surprised.

Mari giggled, wondering what Dexter would think when he realized he was talking to a nurse, who had only made $45,000 dollars the year before coming to the resort. She couldn't imagine his tax return would show any less than seven figures, as hers now would.

But she didn't have to worry about any of that. Accountants would take care of it now.

"No, I've never been able to afford to eat at a place like that."

Dexter clucked his tongue. "Well, that's a shame. You are officially invited to dine with me, along with your sisters, at the restaurant my brother is cooking at this coming Friday. How does that sound?"

"I like the sound of that," Mari replied. "But I'll have to find out if my sisters are available."

Dexter's face lit up with his smile, the corners of his eyes crinkling in that adorable way, and he said, "Well, we could have them come another time, and just the two of us go this time, if you'd like."

Mari felt a shiver of pleasure run down her spine. He was asking her out. Wasn't he? Maybe he wasn't. Surely, he was.

She grinned at him. "Are you asking me on a date, Dexter Scofield?"

His grin matched hers. "I think that's what I'm doing, Mari Wright."

"I would love to go with you to the restaurant. My sisters can enjoy their night here, or wherever. I don't care. I mean, it doesn't matter. I mean, not to be mean to them but..." Mari stammered over her words, stopping midsentence to choke on a laugh. She covered her mouth with her hand. He couldn't see that behind her hand, she was biting her bottom lip.

"Dexter!" A female voice barked his name, so close to Mari's ear that she jumped. He held out his hands to her, though his eyes were looking over her shoulder, glaring at someone.

"Whoa. You don't have to go around yelling my name, Karen," Dexter said. He looked down at Mari. "You all right?"

Mari took a few steps forward so she wasn't near Karen, who had apparently come up right behind her. If she had to hazard a guess, she would say Karen didn't like seeing Dexter having a good time, or talking comfortably with someone. Mari was beginning to like the woman less and less.

"I'm fine, thank you," she replied to his question. She turned her hazel eyes toward Karen, running one hand through her strawberry blond, shoulder-length hair. She didn't realize until after she did it, that she was subconsciously preening. Karen might be one of the worst women in celebrity society, at least as far as trustworthiness was concerned, but she was a beautiful woman.

She was immaculately dressed in form-fitting jeans, and a blue shirt made of an incredibly soft-looking material that Mari longed to touch. Her make-up was perfect, accentuating the blue specks in her hazel eyes magnificently, not too heavy, not too light, and her obviously dyed beautiful red hair fell over her shoulders in a pretty way.

Mari had no doubt that Karen had a personal trainer, and

was in perfect shape for her age.

Karen's perfect eyes weren't on Mari, though. She was staring at Dexter. Mari instantly felt the rebuff the woman was giving her. She felt a sharp churning in her stomach, as humiliation slid through her. She wasn't really one of them.

Not that she wanted to be.

But the slight made Mari feel bad, anyway. She turned away so the hurt look wouldn't show on her face. As she turned away from Karen, she caught a glimpse of the look on Dexter's face. He was looking at her, not at Karen, and he looked mortified. She stopped moving, letting her eyes settle on his face.

He turned his angry eyes toward Karen. "What's wrong with you? What do you want?"

"I've been looking all over for you. I want to go."

Dexter's face screwed up into an even more confused, irritated look. "What does that have to do with me?"

Karen dropped her eyelids, looking at him through her eyelashes. "You're my ride," she said, as if she was speaking to a simpleton. She crossed her arms over her chest, her small bag swinging out slightly.

"I'm not ready to go. Call your own driver." Dexter turned away from her, indicating he was done with her with a fling of one hand. He looked down at Mari.

Karen huffed loudly. "Dexter! I can't call my driver. He's sick. He's not working this week. That's why I *rode with you*." She said the last three words in an exasperated tone.

Dexter looked at her with disgust written on his face. "Look, I'm not leaving. Call an Uber or something. I'm not giving you a ride home. Now go away." He flicked his hand in front of her face this time, as if she was a fly bothering him.

Her jaw dropped. She was obviously stunned to be treated that way. Mari couldn't help feeling amused by the whole scene. From what Dexter had told her, she was shocked he even bothered with Karen. He must have a strong love and respect for his brother, to put up with this woman.

She slid her eyes away from Karen, though the woman was providing some excellent comedic relief for her anxious nerves. Her gaze rested on Dexter, who was looking more and more attractive to her as time went on.

He'd asked her on a date. She was going on a date with him the next Friday.

She thought it was safe to assume he was attracted to her, too. She scanned his face, wondering what it would be like to kiss him.

She pushed the thought away. It was too soon for something like that. She still needed to get to know him a little better. What she read about him in the news clippings and biography articles was fascinating, but it couldn't replace really talking to someone to get to know their mannerisms and characteristics.

To one person, a man could be a saint, and to another he could be the devil. It was all in the perspective.

She was definitely impressed with Dexter so far.

She'd almost forgotten Karen was still standing there, when the woman yelled loud enough to draw the attention of nearly everyone in the room.

"You expect me to get an Uber? Have you lost your mind?"

Her voice was so loud, both Mari and Dexter cringed.

Dexter's eyes opened wide, and Mari thought for a moment he was going to reach out and slap Karen across the face. He clenched his fist and lowered it to his side.

"If you were a man..." he said in a low voice. "You'd be eating my fist. Get out of here, Karen. Get a ride some other way. I'm not taking you home. Call daddy. Call a friend. I don't care. Just leave us alone."

Karen had lost all the color in her face. It made her make-up stand out even more. She took a step back, reaching in her purse to fumble around blindly for her cell phone, never taking her eyes off Dexter's face.

Dexter lifted one finger. "Oh. And if you ever again treat Mari like you did earlier, I swear I'll tell everyone about that time at Drake's, when you had a little too much to drink and ended up in the back of that Blazer with..."

"All right, all right!" Karen spat out, spinning around and marching away from him, her hips moving back and forth.

Dexter looked down at Mari. Mari blinked at him, not even trying to hide her amusement.

It took a moment for the anger to drain from his face, but Mari had a feeling the warm look she was giving him might make it a little easier. He grinned.

"I don't actually remember a time at Drake's," he confessed. "I just made that up, because chances are, she's got something to hide."

Mari threw her head back and laughed, covering her stomach with both hands. "Oh, no!" she said through her laughter. "You're so bad, Dexter. So bad!"

He laughed with her.

Chapter 5

It was Thursday before Mari heard from Dexter again.

The Scofield wedding was still a month away. She was glad the brothers had decided to plan so far ahead of time. It would give her plenty of excuses to call Dexter. She hadn't utilized that benefit yet. She found herself much busier than she thought she'd be.

Each day between Saturday and Thursday, when she finally heard from him, she went to her phone, clicked on his name, and stood there like a mannequin, her thumb hovering over the letters, not typing anything in.

Every time she saw his name on her message list, she froze. What could she say to him? Her mind was a blank. She would back out of the texts and put her phone away. She would wait a little longer to see if he contacted her first.

She didn't want to bother him if he was busy, anyway.

Brian and Laura visited the resort several times during that week, hammering out more details and enjoying all of the amenities the place had to offer, paying their way, each time, without hesitation. Mari couldn't help but notice that every time Brian said his brother's name, he looked at her.

It could have just been her imagination, but he seemed to smirk humorously at the same time.

Mari had a feeling the two brothers had discussed her. It made her nervous to think her name had come up in conversation. She wondered what was said about her.

"Mari?" Lynn waved one hand in front of her face. "You with us?"

Mari focused on Lynn, lifting her eyes from her phone. She blinked and smiled.

"Of course. Why?"

"You've been reading that text for about five minutes

straight. I thought you'd had a stroke or something."

Mari frowned. "That's not a funny thing to say at all."

Lynn shook her head. "I wasn't being funny. You kind of froze up. You scared me half to death. What on earth happened? What does the text say?"

Mari didn't realize how much the text from Dexter affected her until that moment. She licked her bottom lip, and moved her eyes from her sister, to her phone, and back again. "Sorry, Lynn. It's... it's from Dexter. Dexter Scofield."

Lynn raised her eyebrows. "The brother of the groom? What does he want? Is everything okay?"

Mari realized she hadn't said a word to either of her sisters about her upcoming date with Dexter. She pressed her lips together, wondering what they would think. She decided she might as well come clean. Friday was the next day, and she would be getting dressed up as nice as she could for this dinner. She would want their opinions, their help.

"Well, girls..." She looked from one sister to the other. "I'm going on a date with Dexter. The text isn't about business. It's a reminder that he's picking me up tomorrow at the resort, to go to one of his brother's restaurants."

Sue's eyebrows shot up into her bangs. She blinked rapidly. "What? You're going on a date with a client?"

She should have expected a response like that from Sue, she thought. She turned her eyes to Lynn. "What do you think, Lynn? Is that bad business."

Lynn immediately looked at Sue. "Dexter isn't our client, Sue. He's the brother of our client. She's not doing anything wrong."

"Well, it might give the wrong impression."

Mari shook her head. "No, Sue, don't be like that. Look, I'm going on the date with him tomorrow. He's attractive, he's smart, he's funny. I like him, and I think he likes me. I want to see what comes of it. You never know! Maybe we'll fall in love!"

The shocked look never left Sue's face. "Wow. You've already gotten that far?"

Mari sighed. She shook her head. "No, Sue, that's not what I'm saying. I'm just saying I have hope. There's nothing wrong with having hope, is there?"

"Yeah," Lynn added, nodding. "There isn't, Mari. You're exactly right. You have to stop being so negative all the time, Sue. Come on. Mari is entitled to find a man, isn't she?"

Sue looked like she wanted to say something, but couldn't find the words. "I… I'm not trying to make you feel bad, Mari. I'm sorry. I just don't want anyone to think we don't know what we're doing because we're women."

Mari shook her head. "Don't worry about that, Sue. Plenty of people know us, and know our uncle wouldn't have left this to us if we weren't capable of handling it. Besides, they know all the policies are still in place, and we haven't made any changes that have hurt the business. Everyone still has their job, everyone is still happy to do the work. Come on. We're blessed. Let's have a little fun, too."

Mari could see her sister struggling with her anxiety. She felt a little sorry for Sue. She was so uptight that sometimes Mari expected to see her with her auburn hair pulled back in a tight bun, with big black spectacles on her face, looking like a school marm of the old west.

She just needed to loosen up a bit. Relax and have some fun once in a while.

Mari almost felt bad for not including her sisters in the Friday night date, but she couldn't help being glad she hadn't. She wanted to have time with Dexter by herself, with no distractions.

"I'm happy for you, Mari," Lynn said, in a high-pitched, excited voice. "I can't even remember the last time you were on a date."

Mari nodded. "I know. Me neither. I won't know how to act."

Lynn laughed. "Sure, you will. I saw you two talking the last time he was here. He looked really comfortable with you, and you with him. You didn't look nervous then."

Mari lifted her eyebrows. "Really? I'm pretty sure I *felt* nervous."

Lynn glanced at Sue. "I knew Sue was steering that Karen girl away from the situation, so I offered to show Brian and Laura the spa and fitness center. They're sure to be in there, going up the rock wall, at their reception."

Mari laughed. She was relieved that Sue was laughing with them. The three sisters took their purchases to the check-out counter and waited in the short line.

Mari couldn't remember the last time she'd been able to buy a whole new wardrobe. When she cashed the bonus money from the Scofield check, she couldn't think of one thing in her closet she wanted to keep. It had been at least five years since she'd made any significant changes to her wardrobe.

Lynn was talking about something insignificant when Mari heard a familiar cackle. She immediately forgot what Lynn was saying, when her attention was drawn to Karen, who was standing at the door to the store, staring at Mari.

"I know you, don't I?" Karen asked, as if she had forgotten Mari in five days, because she was so unimportant and insignificant.

Mari gave her the same look she'd given Dexter in the resort lounge five days ago. She lowered her eyelids and looked at Karen like she was an idiot. "Why, yes. I believe Dexter was refusing to give you a ride home in the lounge of my resort last week. That was you, am I correct?"

Mari had guessed correctly, that the other two young ladies just behind Karen were with her, and were probably watching the whole scene. Both sets of eyes widened and turned to each other. Both covered their mouth with one hand.

"Never mind about that," Karen said dismissively. "I just want to tell you girls something." She took a step closer and leaned in, taking in all three Wright sisters, one at a time. "Just because you inherit something from your uncle, doesn't make you one of society's elite. You just remember that. It would take years of training for you to understand what it's like to be one of us."

Mari frowned, stepping closer to Karen, with a challenging look on her face. "Look, Karen," she said confidently. "I'm really sorry your brain got stuck and never moved past high school, but we are grown women and don't play little girl games anymore. We have a business to run and important decisions to make. Today," she held up her three bags. "the decisions are in these bags."

Karen's cheeks burned red, but Mari knew it wasn't from embarrassment. She was getting angry. The giggling ladies behind her sure didn't calm Karen down any.

"I'm sure you know a lot of people, Ms. Beasley," Mari said formally. "Now, if you don't mind, we need to get out to our driver. He's waiting for us in the hot sun."

Mari started to push past Karen, but the woman stepped in her way. She was seething, and her words came out dripping with ice. "I'm just telling you girls, now. If you mess up anything in this wedding, you'll have hell to pay. I'll make sure you're sued for everything you have. I'll end up owning the resort. And you three can go back to bumpkinville, or wherever you're from."

Mari couldn't believe the nerve of the woman. She hadn't even achieved her celebrity status by doing anything productive. She wasn't involved in any charities. She wasn't even touted as being very smart. She had nothing on Mari and her sisters.

Mari turned to look at Sue and Lynn. Sue looked ready to explode. Lynn looked confused, and sorry for Karen, at the same time.

"Girls? Should we push Ms. Beasley out of our way?" She turned back to glare at Karen. "I think the three of us can probably shove you right out of our way, Ms. Beasley, since we're such rough-'n-tumble country bumpkins and all." Mari added a thick country accent to her voice for the last sentence. She narrowed her eyes and smiled at Karen. "Right?"

Karen took a step back, but continued to give Mari a disgusted look.

"Oh, something you might like to know," Karen said quickly, her voice suddenly turning saccharine sweet. Mari stopped and stared at the woman, but said nothing.

"I know you're trying to get with Dexter," Karen went on. "I have to wish you luck with that."

Mari frowned. Lynn grabbed her upper arm and pulled gently on her. "Don't listen to her, Mari. She's just being hateful."

Mari ignored her sister. "Why do you wish me luck?"

Karen grinned.

"Mari..." Lynn said in a warning voice. "Don't listen to her. She doesn't have your best interests at heart."

Karen cackled again. "Look, I'm just trying to warn little miss wedding planner here that somebody else has his heart. She'll have to put up one helluva fight to get Dexter away from his woman."

Mari's frown deepened. She'd read about a relationship Dexter had supposedly been in, but there wasn't much said about it. So little, in fact, she couldn't even remember the name of the woman.

But when Karen said it, the article she'd read came barreling back through her mind. It was accompanied by a photo of Dexter, stepping out of a limo at some kind of an award event, clutching a woman's hand. She was smiling and holding up her long skirt so she wouldn't step on it as she got out of the car.

"Dexter is in love with Brittany Langley. You know, one of the judges on that cooking show Brian used to produce?"

The name rang a bell in Mari's mind. Everything seemed personal to the family. Mari felt an unwanted streak of jealousy pass through her. Karen had been around longer than she had.

Maybe Dexter was playing a game with her, because she was newly wealthy?

Chapter 6

It wasn't until much later that Mari realized she hadn't texted Dexter back. She didn't know what to say to him. When she thought back to their comfortable conversations, she couldn't tell whether she was being fooled by his charms, or he was being genuine in his actions. She didn't want to be toyed with.

But she'd never felt such an attraction to a man before. Her past relationships had been casual and youthful. She'd had a boyfriend all through high school, who ended up going overseas as a combat soldier, where he remained to this day. It was a friendly parting and she missed him sometimes.

She had never felt like she wanted to have something long term with someone. In two separate meetings, Dexter had made her feel that way.

She stared down at the phone and decided to make the message she sent as casual as possible. She wasn't going to let him know how much she was overthinking all of this. She sat on the couch in her sitting room and pulled her legs up on the cushion next to her. She leaned back, getting comfortable before she started tapping a message.

Sorry I didn't get back to you sooner, she texted. *I was out shopping with my sisters and ran into your favorite person in the whole world.*

Mari read back through the text a few times, her thumb hovering over the send arrow before she finally pressed it.

She waited a moment for the response and when one didn't immediately come, she backed out of her texts and pulled up a game app.

She hadn't played any of the games on her phone since she came to the resort. She just hadn't found the time. It had been a good distraction when she came home after a hard day at the hospital. She'd sit on her butt and play a game, watching Wheel of Fortune and Jeopardy, and relaxing till she made a can of soup or a pizza or something.

She got less fun out of the game than she had hoped. She couldn't get her mind off Dexter.

She pulled up her text app again and looked to see how long ago it had been since she sent her text. Dismay slid through her when she realized it had been four minutes.

Four minutes, she thought in disgust. *Four lousy minutes. Are you serious?*

She was just about to lower her phone when she saw a message pop up below hers. She snapped her eyes back to the phone, tilting it so she could see the screen clearly.

Oh God, you saw Karen, didn't you. I'm sorry. Do you need some aspirin for your headache? Crackers for nausea? Ice for bruised knuckles?

Mari burst out with laughter after reading the last question. She tapped out her response quickly.

I'm afraid I was successfully able to maintain my adult composure, and not put my hands on the girl. Maybe another time.

Mari hit send. It felt like a bolt of excited energy split through her, at the same time her thumb pressed the screen of her phone.

She felt almost giddy. Her common sense kept trying to override her happiness, but Mari figured it was a good way to keep herself balanced through these uncharted waters.

Almost immediately, though, the thought that Dexter might still be seeing Brittany Langley make Mari nervous. Brittany was famous. She was beautiful and talented. Dexter had been seen with her many times. She wanted to know the truth before she invested her feelings into a man.

Mari's mother had given her some excellent advice when she was a young girl.

"Once you give your heart to a man, you gotta be sure to guard it at the same time, because men are like horses. They're their own creatures, and you are never gonna fully tame them. You might domesticate them, but you won't tame them. So, you have to

43

be careful your heart doesn't get trampled."

Mari remembered the words and tried to apply them in her life. But at the same time, she didn't see how she could avoid the thumping of her heart, the blood racing through her veins, the desire that ached in her body.

It wasn't all sexual in nature. In fact, lust was at the bottom of the list of what she was feeling for Dexter. It was on a much deeper level.

She desperately wanted to give him her heart.

But Karen knew him better, and she seemed to think that Brittany Langley and Dexter were still together.

Her phone vibrating in her hand, a split second before the notification tone sounded, made Mari jump in her seat. Her eyes darted to the phone and she tapped on the icon. Dexter's next message opened, and she breathed a heavy sigh.

We're still on for our date tomorrow night, right? She read.

Feeling a strange surge through her body, she hastily tapped out a response and sent it to him.

I feel really bad for leaving my sisters out. Can I bring them, too?

She waited anxiously for his response. Five minutes passed. Six minutes passed. Almost ten minutes later, her phone buzzed. Dexter was finally getting back to her.

She wondered if he'd had to stop and think about that for a moment. Did he think he had misinterpreted her intentions?

She didn't want him to think she wasn't interested. It was just that she knew her sisters would not look at him the way she did. One of them was bound to notice if he was sociopathic or a psychopath. They wouldn't let her step another foot near him.

Of course, that's fine! He texted back. *I'll send the limo around to pick you all up, and feel free to come by the mansion for a night cap before going home. On me. See you at seven? I'll be waiting for you lovely ladies.*

Mari tried to read into the tone of the message. She got nothing from it but his usual friendly attitude. It made her miss him a little bit. She almost regretted insisting her sisters come. But when she looked down at her phone, remembering that his texts had her blood running hot through her veins, she knew she was already done for.

She didn't want it to get worse, especially if he was playing games with her. Being with him by herself might prove too much of a temptation for her. She would fall in love, he would use her, and she would be left heartbroken and falling apart.

For some reason, she felt like she needed to give Dexter a chance to prove he wasn't just using her. She hoped she was overthinking the charges that he didn't even know he was charged with.

She didn't respond to the text. She didn't know what to say. Mari didn't want the conversation to end yet, but she couldn't think of a thing to say to him. To her delight, her phone buzzed, as another message came from Dexter.

She read it, her spirit lifting a little.

So, how did you manage to cross paths with the foul, demon-breathed, Devil's spawn today?

She giggled, responding immediately.

I guess she rose from Hell to buy some new clothes. I saw her at the boutique in Queen Anne.

I'm sorry you had to go through that. My thoughts and prayers are with you. His response was quick to come through.

She suddenly laughed out loud, throwing her head back.

Much appreciated.

Mari didn't want to give up on this man. He seemed like the perfect man for her.

She grunted. He seemed like the perfect man for *any* woman.

And therein lies the problem, she thought. He was the

perfect guy. Good looking, money lining his pockets, lives in a mansion, isn't arrogant, and has an excellent sense of humor. There had to be something wrong with him.

There had to be. No guy could be that perfect.

Mari began to imagine different scenarios that always led back to the same conclusion. If she thought of Dexter as some kind of criminal, she dismissed it, because his character didn't show those tendencies. He wasn't greedy, he didn't want control over other people, he was more casually comedic than businesslike. He was very personable.

His resume should start with "plays well with others".

Mari grinned. She was going to have a magical night with him tomorrow night, whether it was the two of them or not.

She vowed to clue her sisters in later that afternoon, when they came for lunch. The three sisters stopped whatever they were doing, no matter what it was, to have lunch together every single day.

She wanted them to evaluate Dexter on a more personal level. If they felt he was safe, they would leave. If not, they would challenge everything he said until he was so humiliated, he would leave. She was really hoping they would find him genuine and truthful. Lynn had already expressed her desire to have Dexter as a brother-in-law. She'd said it jokingly, asking if her future brother-in-law had texted yet.

She looked sad when Mari had answered no.

Well, now she could say yes. And she was as pleased as she could be.

She didn't bother to go to any other apps on her phone. She stared at it until it buzzed again. Another message from Dexter.

So, what are you doing right now? He asked.

Mari giggled. She hadn't gotten a text like that from a boy in at least seven or eight years; not since leaving high school. She decided to play along. If he was going to have a mad, school-boy crush on her, and show it so blatantly, she was going to return the favor with her best school girl impression.

Sitting on the couch in my sitting room, with my legs up, thinking way too much about life. What about you?

She waited, smiling when his text came back.

Same! Amazing how people connect and start doing the same things all the time.

Seconds later, she received another text.

Hope you got the sarcasm in the last message. I wasn't trying to be hateful sarcastic, just funny sarcastic. Hope you weren't offended. I mean, not that there's anything wrong with me sitting on the couch with my legs up, thinking about life. Guys do that, too, right?

Mari thought if Dexter kept her laughing that way, she would develop laugh lines really fast.

At least now, she thought with new laughter in her mind. *I can afford to do something about my wrinkles.*

Chapter 7

"You know what the problem is, Lynn?"

Lynn was admiring her hair, turning her head back and forth while looking in the mirror. Instead of turning to her sister, she looked at her reflection. "Problem? What problem?"

Mari bent over to grab her boots from in front of the large closet. Lynn had come in her room to use the lights on her dressing table, which cast a softer light than the ones in the bathroom.

Mari sat on the bed and pulled her boots on, pulling the zipper up to secure the boot on her foot. She leaned over to prop herself up with her arms crossed over her knees.

"The problem with Dexter," she replied, looking at Lynn's reflection. Her sister raised her eyebrows.

"I didn't know you had a problem with him. I think your problem should be with Karen."

Mari nodded, but reluctant regret crossed her face. "Well, obviously I have a problem with her, but that's temporary. Once Brian and Laura are married, there's no reason I should ever see her again."

"I guess." Lynn's voice dropped, as her attention shifted back to fixing whatever makeup or hair problems she saw. "And if you see her when you're socializing or something, I'm sure she'll ignore you. She's that type. She might be confrontational now, but later on, she'll go back to thinking she's too good to acknowledge you at all."

Mari thought that was a real possibility. But if she really did start dating Dexter, she would be thrust into the environment he lived in. That would make the chances of running across Karen more likely.

She wasn't afraid of the woman. She just didn't like confrontation. It made her nervous for the rest of the day, even if she won the argument. Sometimes she would say things she regretted later, or felt guilty about. Mari didn't like to argue with anyone.

"I'll have to take Sue with me wherever I go," she said, trying a joke to break the tension she felt. "She loves to argue."

Lynn smiled at her. "You're silly, Mari. But you're probably right. She'd argue for you. So, what's your problem with Dexter? How come Sue and I are coming on your date tonight?"

Mari shook her head. Lynn frowned at her, a light expression that didn't crinkle her face very much.

"Don't tell me you're letting what Karen said get in the way."

Mari looked down at the white carpet under her feet. She studied it, though she wasn't really seeing it. She was picturing Dexter in her mind. "I guess I can't help it. I know he had a life before he met me, I'm just…"

"I know." Lynn turned in her seat and rested her arm over the back of it. She gave Mari a sympathetic look. "I know you don't want to get hurt. It makes sense to me, Mari, it really does. But sometimes you just have to take chances."

"That doesn't mean you should throw caution to the wind." Both women looked at the doorway, where Sue was now standing.

"Well, don't you look pretty, Sue!" she exclaimed.

Lynn grinned wide. "Do you like her hair, Mari? I did that!"

Sue was smiling, which made her normally stern face much more attractive. Mari was glad to see it.

"It looks great, Lynn. You did a good job." Mari stood up and approached her sister, circling her to look at the hairstyle, which was braided and pulled together in the back to form what looked like a heart. "Amazing, Lynn. I don't know how you do it."

Mari gave her sister a big smile. Lynn returned it, standing up and crossing her arms over her chest. "That's the point. I don't want anyone else to know how I do it. I'm not putting that online."

Mari laughed. Lynn's online blog posts about different

hairstyles had taken off tremendously since they moved to the Georgia resort.

"You're just trying to distract me from the subject, Mari," Sue said, her smile unwavering. "I think if you have a feeling something is off, it probably is. You have to trust your gut instincts."

"But sometimes that doesn't work, Sue," Lynn said, shaking her head. She went back to the dressing table and bent over to examine herself one more time. She ran her finger around her lips, seemingly removing any out of place lipstick that Mari didn't see. "You have to take chances sometimes, or you'll never have any fun."

Sue shrugged. "I just want you to be happy, Mari, but I don't want you to be hurt."

Mari pulled her lips back and smiled softly. "I guess being hurt is probably inevitable these days. But I don't want to be either, trust me. I don't expect a fairy tale life with a happily ever after, but it would be nice."

Lynn giggled, returning to her sisters. "It can happen. I know it can."

"Let's go," Sue said, pulling her phone from her bag just long enough to press the power button and check the time. "We don't want to be late. That would look awful."

The girls filed out of the room. Mari followed her sisters down the hallway that connected their three suites to the stairway.

As she went down the dark red carpeted stairs, she was amazed by how much thought her uncle had put into his plans for her and her sisters. The three of them had never known, until they arrived, that Uncle Nathan planned to give the resort to them all along. He had the cottage built for them, over the last few years, without saying a word.

It was as if he knew he would have a heart attack that would take him early.

Mari felt a painful twitch in her chest. Her heart was

aching. The sisters hadn't had a lot of opportunity to really get to know him, but he was a delight at holiday occasions, when the whole family got together.

Something Brian said, on the first day they met him, came to her mind and she halted. Sue was walking beside her and she turned to stare at Mari.

"What's wrong, Mari? Are you all right?"

The concern in her voice made Mari look at her. "I was just wondering about that assistant Brian Scofield mentioned when he came in to sign the contracts. I forgot all about it until just now. Did you two ever hear anything more about him? Did you ask anyone?"

Sue shook her head, turning her eyes to Lynn. "Not me. You?"

"I didn't think anything about it. Why shouldn't Uncle Nathan have an assistant? There was no reason for him to ever mention one to us."

The logic of Lynn's statement resonated with Mari, but she was still curious. "I don't know where the assistant went. Don't you think it's a little strange that he disappeared? That we haven't heard anything about him?"

Mari looked back and forth between her sisters, not understanding why they accepted the story of the assistant. It had no ending. It was like an open question to Mari. She wanted to know the answer.

"I want to know who that assistant was. Whoever he is, he knows everything about this resort. Think about it," She directed her eyes to Sue, who had suddenly raised her eyebrows. "Think about that, Sue. He knows this place inside and out. He probably knows all the security codes and everything."

"Good God Almighty," Sue breathed. "I didn't think about that. I have to change it all! I have to call the security companies!"

Mari pressed her palms toward the floor, urging Sue to calm down. "But if we find out who it is, you won't have to worry as much. Maybe he still wants his job. We've been talking about getting assistants, anyway. Who better than someone who actually trained under Uncle Nathan?"

Sue looked skeptical, but willing to listen.

"We don't want to be late, sisters," Lynn said. "Come on, we have to meet Dexter in twenty minutes."

"Oh, let's hurry."

The three women left the cottage behind, telling Hank to step on it. He was delighted to be given permission to speed 'just a little', as Mari said.

The drive may have only taken fifteen minutes, but Mari felt like it was an eternity. She sincerely wanted to talk to Dexter about the assistant his brother mentioned. He might at least have a name.

When the girls arrived at the restaurant, they were once again taken aback by their luxurious surroundings. So much so that Mari heard Sue lean toward Lynn and whisper loudly, "Close your mouth, we look like tourists."

Lynn's cheeks were flushed, but she nodded and plastered a neutral look on her face. Mari could tell she was trying to look like she wasn't at all taken in by what she saw around her.

Before they reached the glass doors, Mari spotted Dexter. He was talking to a man in a suit, both of them standing casually on the curb. Dexter said something that made the suited man laugh and respond with a smile on his face.

Mari couldn't help thinking how handsome he was. She wished she didn't have misgivings about the whole thing. She was only twenty-six, and her trust issues were strong. She giggled. The only psychology courses she'd taken were the ones required for her nursing degree, which were bottom level, and electives to begin with. But she'd taken three years, and realized that she had some issues to deal with.

She scanned him, trying not to look so obvious. She lifted one hand and shaded her eyes with it to see him better. He saw them and raised one arm to wave.

"There he is," Sue and Mari said at the same time. They smiled at each other, and crossed the two-lane entryway to get to him.

He excused himself from his friend with a pleasant, "I'll talk to you later, Ned. You have a great day."

Mari heard the words float across the air toward her as she crossed the narrow driveway.

"Hey, you too, Dex!" The man called out, as Dexter walked toward the sisters.

Dexter's smile was broad. He took in all three of them with his sky-blue eyes.

"Here you are, the Wright sisters. It's a pleasure to eat with you ladies tonight. There's gonna be a lot of rumors going around about me pretty soon."

He laughed pleasantly, making the sisters smile. Mari felt her heartbeat speed up. It looked like he was going to greet Sue first, but he turned suddenly and held out his hand to Mari.

"You look lovely this evening, Mari. I hope you find something on the menu that suits you."

She smiled up at him. "I'm sure I will. I'm not really picky."

Sue snorted softly, making them all look at her. She chuckled. "Sorry. I was just clearing my throat."

Dexter chuckled, holding his hand out to the other two. "It's nice to see you both. I'm glad you could come. Let's go on in and get a seat. To tell you the truth, I've been on my feet all day and I could really use a drink, and to sit down."

He held the door open and the ladies went in before him. They stayed quiet and followed behind him as they were taken to a large table for six in one corner of the restaurant. The seat was half an oval, and they slid into it with the sisters in a row and Dexter on the end. Mari noticed her sisters made sure she was seated next to Dexter.

Chapter 8

The dinner was almost finished. Desserts had been ordered and all of them were warm and comfortable, when Mari felt a strange sensation slide through her.

She'd been trying all night to think of a way to ask Dexter about her uncle's assistant, without sounding like an idiot. *Who cared who worked as his assistant?* She thought several times, only to contradict her own thoughts with the reasoning she'd given her sister. Where was he? Why did he suddenly disappear? How come no one on the staff ever mentioned him?

It was such a strange thing, and Mari simply couldn't forget about it.

When she realized that she was being stared at, she lifted her eyes from her plate and glanced around the room. Sue and Dexter were having a casual conversation about something, and Lynn was thanking the server, who was dropping off their desserts.

Once the chocolate sundae was in front of Lynn, she started spooning it into her mouth, her eyes closed. She appeared to be in heaven.

Mari continued to scan the room, turning her head further, to the end of the bar.

There was a young man looking at her. It could have been a casual glance, but she didn't know, because as soon as her eyes rested on his, he turned and moved away from the bar, taking his drink with him. He went behind a pillar and must have taken one of the small hallways to the private dining rooms in the back, because she didn't see him again.

But there was something about that moment, that millisecond when their eyes met. She instantly felt like she knew him. She combed through her memory. The light was dim on the other side of the room, but her eyes were good. She'd seen him clearly.

She looked at Dexter.

"If you don't mind, I have to use the ladies' room before we leave."

"Oh, sure, of course." Dexter pushed himself out of the round booth, and Mari followed.

"You want me to come with you, Mari?" Lynn asked.

Mari looked down at her, noticing the amusement on Dexter's face. "No, I'm good. I can find it. I'll be right back." She turned her gaze to Dexter. "I see that look. Don't even say it."

Dexter lifted his hands. "I didn't say a word," he replied, shaking his head. "Not one word."

The ladies laughed and Mari turned to hurry across the restaurant. She hoped they wouldn't notice she wasn't going in the direction of the closest bathrooms.

She got to the pillar and went around it, looking down the hallway at the rows of doors that led to the private dining rooms. One of them opened and a couple came out, laughing about something. She could hear soft music on the other side of the door and a lot of murmuring voices. The couple came down the hall, leaving the door slightly open.

They were still chattering about something, huge smiles on their faces. They glanced at Mari as they passed, nodding a friendly greeting to her.

"Excuse me," she said politely. The couple stopped, looking at her inquisitively. "Is that a wedding party?"

"It's the engagement party for Greg and Kathy," the girl said. "Greg Vanderhoff. Do you know him?"

Mari looked back down the hall. The names meant nothing to her. "I don't think I'm in the right place."

The girl leaned forward and placed her hand gently on Mari's arm. "Girl, you go crash that party. There are lots of single guys in there, if you're looking."

"Veronica!" the man said with a laugh. "You're such a match maker. Come on, we gotta be at the lake house in an hour."

"I'm coming, I'm coming," Veronica said, with as much humor as he had when he spoke. Mari could see the love in her eyes when she looked at the man she was with. She turned back to Mari and continued, as she backed away to follow her boyfriend. "I'm telling you, girl. Some really good catches in there. Go on!"

Mari wasn't looking for a love match. She was looking for a certain person she was sure she saw escaping down this hallway. She took a few steps toward the open door.

"Mari!"

Dexter's voice behind her made her halt in place. Her heart slammed against her chest and she felt a chill run through her body. Suddenly, she felt terribly guilty, as if she'd been caught committing a crime.

She turned and looked at him with wide eyes. He was coming toward her with a smile.

"What are you doing? Do you know Greg or Kathy?"

Mari raised her eyebrows and looked at him curiously. She wondered how he knew who was in the engagement party. Just as she realized it was something he would know, he tilted his head to the side and gazed at her.

"This is my brother's restaurant, hon. We know everyone that comes through here, personally. A lot of them make reservations. It's a popular place for people our age."

Mari nodded.

"So, you don't know Greg or Kathy?"

She shook her head no.

"Then why are you going in there?" He asked the question in the most innocent tone she'd ever heard. He obviously didn't want her to think it was upsetting him.

"I... I just wanted to look in and see the decorations."

Dexter's smile widened. "Is that all you wanted? Well, come on. I'll be your date for the party. Let's go say congratulations to Greg and Kathy."

He held out his arm, crooked at the elbow. She put her hand through the hole it created and he led her to the door. He pushed it open and let her go first.

Mari was impressed with the flower arrangements and the colors the decorator had chosen. Everything was beautiful. The silver utensils reflected the soft light of the bulbs behind clouded glass lamps. The party was enjoying dessert and the engagement cake had been cut.

Mari eyed the four-tier cake. The top was still intact but many pieces were missing from the two bottom tiers. She expected it to topple over at any moment, but it stayed where it was, solid as a rock.

The cake looked delicious. Despite the meal she'd just eaten, Mari felt her stomach rumble. She had a sneaking suspicion it was Bavarian chocolate cream pie, with whipped cream topping. Her mouth was watering.

Dexter leaned close to her after greeting some of the guests with a wave and a "hello" called out across the room, in a low voice.

"I think you've got your eye on a piece of that cake, don't you?"

Mari turned a guilty face toward him. "I think I might die if I don't get a piece of it," she replied in a serious voice.

Dexter widened his eyes. "Now, that we can't have. I'm sure they won't mind if you get a piece. In fact, I'm sure there are two free chairs next to each other, and we can sit and talk for a bit."

Mari instantly remembered why she'd wanted to come into the room in the first place. It had completely slipped her mind when she saw the cake. She nodded at him, putting an innocent look on her face.

"Okay, let's do that." She kept her voice low. As they walked to the cake at the front of the room, and Dexter asked for two slices of cake and two waters, she slowly glanced around the room, taking in each face that she could see.

The tables in the room were all round, and the booths that lined the walls were the same half-circles as the one she was eating at with her sisters.

Her eyes darted to the door of the private dining room. Her sisters! They must be wondering what's going on. She took Dexter's arm, looking up at him.

"My sisters. We can't just disappear. They will wonder what happened to us."

Dexter shook his head, picking up the drinks and putting them in Mari's hands. She took them without thinking about it and stood waiting for his answer, as he turned to pick up the two pieces of cake.

He gestured with his head. "Let's sit over there, where no one is. It's a small table. We won't be bothered."

Mari felt a little irritated. She didn't want to leave her sisters wondering what had happened to her.

They got to the table and she set the water down, intent on turning around and going out to her sisters. Dexter caught her arm as she started to do just that. His touch sent a jolt of excitement through Mari. She looked up at him with curious eyes, not trying to get her arm away. They were so close, that she could feel the warmth of his body washing over her.

"You don't have to worry about them," Dexter said, in a deep, reassuring voice. "I told them I was coming to find you, and maybe talk to you alone for a little while. I... I'm not sure your sister, Sue, really liked the idea. But Lynn was all for it. So, let's sit, okay?"

Mari relaxed, knowing her sisters weren't worrying about her. She slid into the booth on the side across from Dexter, and pulled one of the plates with the cake on it toward her. She unfolded the napkin and spread in on her lap.

She picked up her fork and stared down at the cake. "Dear Lord," she said quickly. "Thank you for making this kind of cake. I could eat it all day."

Dexter laughed. She looked up at him, pushing the fork into the cake for her first bite. "What?" she asked.

He shook his head. "I thought you were praying. I've never seen anyone act like that about cake before."

Mari put the first bite in her mouth and closed her eyes, relishing the deliciousness on her tongue. Once she swallowed, she opened her eyes, saying, "Not just any cake. *This* kind of cake. I can't believe how delicious it is."

She could feel Dexter's intense gaze on her as she ate, but she didn't care. It was too delicious to care.

Once again, the reason why she'd even come to the room came back to her with full force.

Damn these distractions, she thought, getting frustrated with herself. She stopped eating suddenly and cast her gaze across the room. At that moment, she saw the retreating figure of a young man. He was going toward one of the exits on the back side of the room. One would lead out to the street. The other to the hallway that led back into the dining room.

Mari jumped up and hurried after him, not realizing that Dexter was watching her with a confused look on his face.

The young man pushed open the door that led to the back parking lot, and disappeared on the other side. Mari quickened her steps, reaching the door a few seconds later. She pushed it open and went out.

She saw no one.

She scanned the parking lot, stepping forward and looked both ways. He had to be hiding. He was behind one of the cars.

This was ridiculous. What was going on? Why would he run and hide from her?

She frowned.

The door behind her pushed open and Mari turned to see a very confused Dexter standing behind her.

"What's going on?" he said.

She shook her head. Her explanation would sound too ludicrous. She didn't want to go into it.

"I… I thought I saw someone I knew. It's… it's nothing. I want to go home. Will you take me home, Dexter?"

Dexter stared at her for a moment, but quickly nodded his head. "Of course. Of course. Let's go."

He held the door open. She didn't have to see his face to know he was giving her the strangest look he'd ever given a woman in his life.

Chapter 9

Dexter stepped out of his dark blue Chevy Mustang, and felt the back pockets of his jeans for his wallet and cell phone. He felt the familiar bulge of the wallet, but his cell phone wasn't in the other one. He reached into the inside pocket of his jacket and felt it there.

He stepped away and clicked the key fob, as he bounded up the back steps two at a time. It was a shorter walkway than the front. He chuckled, thinking it was much more convenient to take the "servants' entrance", as he liked to call it, though it was mostly just for the kitchen staff. It saved him from having to go past the front desk and see all the people that wanted to stop and talk to him.

He didn't mind talking to the employees. It was always a quick conversation, because everyone had a job to do and they did it. It was one of the most efficient staffs Dexter had seen, and he'd seen plenty, having a famous chef for a brother.

He went through the kitchen, swinging his keys and greeting some of the staff he knew by name. The others he nodded and smiled at. He pushed the swinging doors and came out in the dining room. It wasn't meal time, so there were only a few stragglers sitting around. He didn't see any of the sisters.

He passed the tables, going down the wavy middle aisle to get to the entrance to the dining hall. The double doors were standing wide open. He went through, across the lobby and into the gathering room. Above the door was a white and green plaque that read "Emerald Parlor". Because of that, everyone referred to the room as the Parlor.

It had been three days since Dexter had talked to Mari, or any of the Wright sisters. He didn't see Mari in the parlor, but he did see Sue. She was talking to someone he didn't recognize. Their conversation did not seem intense, but it wasn't humorous. Sue was not smiling.

Dexter went in her direction, with the intention of asking if she knew where Mari was.

The last three days had been rough for Dexter. He'd had a lot of trouble thinking about anything other than Mari. She was taking up a lot of brain space. It was best to go at things like that head-on. If she was interested in dating him, she needed to tell him.

The way she'd run after that man at Greg and Kathy's party troubled him. It seemed there was more to Mari than he thought. She must know more people than she let on.

Of any of the sisters, Sue would be perfectly blunt and honest about her sister's intentions. Dexter didn't want to be hurt again. The trouble he was having with his ex was enough to deal with.

Dexter didn't even like to think about Brittany. She was such a…

He closed his eyes and tried to breathe normally. She was a beautiful woman with a black heart, and claws like a vicious monster. She had sucked the life out of him for so long. He had to let that go.

A week with Brittany was like an eternity in Hell. He was glad to be free of it.

But heading into another relationship wasn't going to be easy for Dexter. Even though Mari didn't seem the type to do that to him, he couldn't help being worried about it.

Sue looked across and saw him coming. The look of surprise and curiosity that crossed her face reminded Dexter of the look Mari often got. They were definitely sisters.

She excused herself from the person she was talking to, and stood up to meet him.

She held out her hand as he approached, and he shook it.

"Hello, Sue."

"Hi, Dexter. I didn't expect you to be here. Is everything okay? The wedding is still on for tomorrow?"

Dexter nodded, reassuringly. "Oh, yeah, I'm not here because of my brother or anything. They're fine. Everything's fine."

Sue looked relieved. She held her arm up in the direction of the door. "Would you like to take a walk? It looks like you have something on your mind."

Dexter raised his eyebrows, resting his hands on his waistline. "That's very intuitive of you, Sue."

She nodded. "I'm glad. I have something on my mind, too. I think we should discuss it."

He moved with her when she began to walk to the entrance of the parlor. "I have a sneaking suspicion we might want to talk about the same thing."

Sue glanced at him, a neutral but pleasant look on her stern face. Dexter admired the way her auburn hair fell around her slender, pale cheeks. She was as pretty as Mari, but he had a sneaking suspicion she would be the first one with wrinkles. He could tell she worried a lot.

"I think you have been pursuing my sister. Am I wrong about that?" Sue asked.

Dexter chuckled to himself silently. As blunt as ever.

"I am interested in seeing her, yes. I wonder if you know how she feels about me? I don't like jumping into anything with just blind faith."

Sue nodded. He walked beside her as Sue led him outside, onto the huge deck in front of the hotel. Many people were milling about, talking, relaxing, looking at their cell phones.

They walked to the railing and stopped, both looking out over the land.

"Well, she isn't that type either. I know you must have a past because... well, you're social that way."

Dexter knew she meant he had money, and was basically a playboy in the eyes of people who had just come into money. "And

I'm here to tell you, Dexter, she has a soft heart and has never experienced anything real before. The last boyfriend she had..." Sue stopped, glancing at him. "She's going to kill me if she finds out I told you this. Her last boyfriend was in her first year of her college, when she was a freshman. He was a year younger than her, and you have to remember, she went to college early because she finished school early."

Everything Sue was telling him was news to Dexter. Mari had never said a word about what she did before coming to the resort.

"What did she go to college for?"

Sue narrowed her eyes at him, crossing her arms in front of her chest. "You haven't asked her about herself? Have you asked her anything about herself?"

Dexter flushed, realizing he hadn't really gotten into that. They spent a lot of their time together laughing at his jokes.

"I... I guess we haven't had time."

"What about when you were with her at the restaurant. Didn't you talk then?"

Dexter remembered that night, how odd Mari had acted. She'd run off after that young man like it was a matter of life or death. It made Dexter wonder who the man was, and what connection he had to Mari. Was she secretly pining for someone else?

It gave Dexter pause. He stopped thinking about Mari's college past and started thinking about her relationships. Sue directed the topic when she continued.

"Mari's last boyfriend was that freshman year, and he didn't go to her college. At the time, she was taking basic courses because she was young and wanted to get them out of the way. From that point on, she went into nursing, but was really interested in psychology."

Dexter stared at Sue. He was hearing this information for the first time. "Seriously? That's amazing. She must be really smart."

Sue laughed softly. "Well, to be honest, I've seen some pretty dumb nurses. Just like many people can be dumb in pretty much any industry. But yeah, when you're talking about my sister, she's really smart. That's something she brings to our business that helps. She has good intuition."

She narrowed her eyes again and looked directly at him. "Now, you... I think her opinion might be a little skewed when it comes to you."

Dexter's eyebrows shot up. "You do? Why do you think that?" He was a bit hurt.

"Well, I'm naturally suspicious," Sue responded. "And it takes a lot to gain my trust. When I looked you up on the Internet, I saw you with that girl Brittany, and when Karen said you'd recently been seen with her..."

Dexter shook his head, lifting one finger in the air to stop her from continuing. "First of all, that's old news, and second, you can't believe anything Karen tells you. The woman has lost her mind. I'll never understand why she can't keep her nose out of my business."

Irritation split through Dexter.

"I'm sorry, Dexter. She's my sister and I want to protect her."

Dexter shook his head again. "You don't have to worry about Brittany. She isn't going to come between me and Mari... if there ever is a me and Mari."

Sue's eyes never left his. He would have squirmed under her gaze, but he needed to remain confident on that topic, so he stared back at her. He noticed she had the same eye shape as Mari, but her eyes were a deep green that any man would find beautiful and attractive.

He lifted his eyebrows, waiting for her to break her gaze. Finally, she dropped her eyes and looked out across the horizon.

"So, at the wedding tomorrow, what can we expect?" Sue

asked. "Will you be dancing with the maid of honor? An ex? The wedding planner?"

Dexter found this amusing and let out a laugh. He was surprised when Sue gave him a smile. He had caught on to her joke and it made her happy to hear him laugh. He laughed a bit longer to prolong the positive vibes.

"I don't want you thinking I'm trying to take anything from your sister. I don't want to hurt her. But that man she went after at the dinner... do you know who she was looking for?"

From the look on Sue's face, he could tell he caught her off guard with the question.

"You didn't see the guy she went looking for at my brother's restaurant?" he asked.

Sue shook her head and pulled her eyebrows together. "Guy? At your brother's restaurant? Are you saying Mari ran after some guy that was there? Who?"

Dexter shrugged. "I was kind of hoping you knew."

Sue looked completely confused, which did not help the way Dexter was feeling.

"I don't know what you're talking about, Dexter. I'm sorry."

Chapter 10

Brian and Laura's wedding ceremony went off without a hitch. The only thing that passed, in Mari's mind, as a negative was Karen's behavior. She was obviously an attention seeker, and the dress Karen had chosen as maid of honor was lavish and form-fitting. It had its own train that swept along behind her and was a crimson red.

It made her stand out more than the bride, in Mari's opinion. But she wasn't going to tell anyone that. If Laura didn't mind, which she didn't seem to, it was none of Mari's business.

Mari and her sisters sat at one of the tables in the reception room, watching the festivities. Brian and Laura cut the cake, and very respectfully put the small pieces in each other's mouths. They kissed afterward, their smiles and the squished cake shared between them. They ended up still having small smudges of icing on their lips and cheeks, which made them, and everyone watching, laugh.

"They are so happy," Lynn said in a soft voice. Mari looked at her.

"You're not jealous, are you?" She asked.

Lynn lifted one side of her lips. "Oh no. Jealousy is when you want something someone else has. I don't want Brian. I am wistful. I look forward to that kind of happiness. It's beautiful."

Mari nodded. The wedding made her think of her own future, as well. She couldn't help wondering if a wedding with Dexter would be like this. Would she be the belle of the ball, like Laura? The young woman seemed comfortable in her position; so confident in herself, where she was, what she was doing.

Mari felt like she was swimming in a pool of murky waters, not knowing where she was going or what would happen next. She worried every day that she would say something or do something that would embarrass her and her sisters. And... retroactively, her uncle. She didn't want to embarrass her uncle.

Dexter could teach her what she needed to know about

rubbing elbows with the wealthy. Surely, he knew what behaviors were acceptable and which weren't.

She lifted a glass of champagne to her lips and took a sip. She didn't care for champagne, but the only other options were punch and white wine. She didn't want either of those. She curled her nose, swallowing the dry liquid.

"Good God Almighty," Sue murmured. Mari followed her eyes to the other side of the room, in the corner near the bathrooms.

"What's going on over there?" she asked, craning her neck to see around the people in between her and the action.

Sue replied, keeping her voice down, "It looks like Karen is arguing with someone."

Mari's heart sank. Not at this beautiful wedding, Laura's big day, and the first wedding she and her sisters had put together. If anything was going to ruin it all, it would be Karen.

"Oh no," she groaned. "What are we going to do?"

Sue turned her head and gazed at her sister. "*We're* not going to do anything. It's up to the bride and groom to take care of it. It's their wedding and their friends. We aren't security, Mari. We just do the decorations and stuff."

Mari pulled in a deep breath. It felt more personal to her because of Karen's confrontational behavior outside of business. She chewed on her bottom lip.

"I don't think we can just let it happen, though. We own this place." Mari pushed back her chair and stood up. She could see better standing up, and didn't care if everyone in the room knew she was watching.

But what she saw sent a hot blade of anger through her. Karen was indeed arguing with someone outside the bathroom hallway. It was Dexter. She was almost spitting in his face. The look on his face was almost blank. He was just staring down at her.

She lifted one hand and jabbed him with her finger, saying something with a nasty look on her face.

68

Mari felt a hand close around her wrist. She looked down at Sue, who had wrapped her fingers around Mari's wrist.

"You can't go over there, Mari. You'll make a big scene. Let me do it. I'll have to send them both out though. And this isn't our job, really."

"We own this place," Mari retorted hotly. "And I don't want you throwing Dexter out. I don't think he deserves to be treated the same way as her. She's making a scene, not him."

Sue shook her head.

"Mari, we have to do this. I have to send them both out. But just until they calm down. He can come back in if he wants to. If she does, she has to be calm."

Mari pulled in a deep breath, looking over at the couple in the corner. "Doesn't look like we'll have to do anything," she mumbled.

Dexter had taken hold of Karen's arm and was directing her toward the front doors. Mari watched, a feeling of longing spreading through her. She didn't want to see him with another woman. She wanted him to be next to her. If he was going to argue with someone, he could argue with her. She would make sure it ended with a kiss.

Mari walked through the crowd, listening to their mumbling and murmuring. Among the crowd, the only ones who didn't seem to care were the bride and groom. They were still dancing in the middle of the room with some of their friends, who also weren't paying attention.

They were having fun. Mari was glad to see it hadn't interrupted their good time. She'd had enough chances to talk to Laura, to realize the young woman was a bundle of joy almost all the time. She was so short, she reminded Mari of a fragile, gentle pixie. It made Mari want to protect her feelings. She had a feeling that was one of the things about her that drew Brian to her.

They were a happy couple.

She had reached the door and pushed one open, stepping

into the middle lobby quietly. She stopped abruptly, freezing in place. Across the middle lobby between the inner and outer entrance doors, Dexter stood, holding one of the doors open.

Mari could hear every word the two said to each other.

"You know you've been thinking about it. I can tell, Dex. Come on. You know I'm right!"

She couldn't see Karen, but she could hear her voice as plain as day.

"You're delusional, Karen!" Dexter responded. "I have never thought of you that way. The opposite, in fact, has always been my way of thinking."

"I don't believe you. You want me just like I want you."

Dexter took a step back. Mari could see he had to, because the full weight of Karen had fallen against him, knocking him back into the middle lobby.

Both Karen and Dexter looked directly at Mari. She stood watching them both, moving her eyes from one to the other, before turning and going back in, letting the door close behind her.

She was only a few steps away from the door, when someone new stepped into her line of sight. Someone she had only seen in pictures. She was already in a daze. She'd had too much champagne to be dealing with this much drama.

All she wanted to do was go sit back down with her sisters and process what she'd just seen.

It was clear to her that Dexter didn't want Karen in a romantic way. At first she'd had doubts, because of Brittany. Now Karen was showing signs that he'd done something to make her think he wanted her.

It couldn't just be his good looks. He was charming, too, and wealthy, of course.

Mari tried to stretch her mind to think the way those women might be thinking. They didn't have the upbringing she did. Yes, some of them may have struggled with problems. No one got away from that. But they hadn't had to wonder how to keep the electricity on when someone lost a job, or how much was in the budget for groceries.

Those weren't the kind of problems those people had.

She couldn't wrap her mind around it.

"Are you Mari? Mari Wright?"

The woman's voice brought her out of her thoughts. She focused quickly and shook her head to clear it.

"Um… yes, yes, that's me. I don't think I know you."

The short woman gave her a look she couldn't decipher.

"No, I suppose you wouldn't know me. You don't really know anyone here, do you? Aren't you the one who planned the wedding? You and your sisters?"

Mari suddenly realized what the woman was doing. She was being condescending. It was the same tone of voice she'd heard from Karen, when they were coming out of the restaurant after lunch.

Mari braced herself, immediately on high alert. She straightened her shoulders.

"This is my hotel," she replied in a warm voice, smiling at the stranger. "I own Emerald Resort."

"You *inherited* it, you mean," the woman said, returning the smile, though it dripped with saccharine.

"Of course. But since my uncle remains in Heaven, it's now mine and my sisters'. What can I do for you?"

"I have a message for you." The woman stepped closer to her and said in a low voice, "from Brittany. You know who I'm talking about, don't you?"

Mari narrowed her eyes. That's where she remembered this woman's face from. She looked like Brittany Langley, the socialite Dexter had been seeing.

"Oh, you must be April, Brittany's sister," she blurted out.

71

They were all famous. Everyone knew them, and their faces were plastered all over newspapers and magazines on a regular basis.

The woman tilted her head to the side and looked at Mari like she was an idiot. Mari immediately resented the look and lost her smile.

"Yes, I'm April. And you need to watch your back. She has her eye on Dexter Scofield. They are meant to be together and everyone knows it. You just watch your back."

Mari frowned. Had she been transported back to high school?

She tried to think of the dumbest thing she could to respond to the incredibly childish warning.

"Oh, ok. Am I going to have some unflattering photos taken from behind, April?" She leaned forward when she said it, holding up one hand as if hiding her words from everyone else. She giggled, a sound she didn't have to force, because April immediately looked confused.

"Don't you worry now," Mari continued, waving her hand as if shooing a fly. "I'll make sure I'm watching my back." She did air quotes when she said the last three words of her sentence. She moved past April Langley, narrowly brushing her with her shoulder.

Her heart was pounding hard. She was proud that she didn't embarrass herself in front of anyone. But the drama was almost more than she could take.

Was Dexter worth it?

She got back to her table and turned around to slide into her chair.

Lynn and Sue were staring at her.

"What happened?" Lynn finally asked in an excited voice.

She looked at her two sisters alternately. "You don't even want to know."

"Oh, yes, we do," Sue said, sounding just like her sister.

72

"Come on. Tell us what happened?"

By the time Mari was finished telling them what she'd seen, she had made her decision.

Chapter 11

Dexter pushed Karen away from him with enough force to knock her back a few steps. She swayed, but he didn't reach out to help her. He was furious with her. All he wanted her to do was leave the premises, which he knew she wasn't going to do until Laura told her to leave. Laura was the only one who ever had any influence over this woman.

"You are behaving outrageously!" Dexter hissed. She came toward him and he straightened one arm out in front of her with his palm out. "No. Don't come near me. You stay out here and smoke a cigarette or something. Calm yourself down, and maybe sober up a little bit. It's a little chilly. Maybe that will bring you to your senses."

"I don't have to stay out here because you tell me to," Karen replied, slurring her words. She managed to stay on her feet.

"No, but you will if you know what's good for you," Dexter admonished her sternly, shaking one finger in her direction. "Damn, Karen, don't you see what a fool you're making of yourself?"

"I... I don't..." Karen turned around, holding one hand to her stomach.

Dexter scrunched his nose in disgust and let the door close. He didn't want to deal with her anymore. He turned around to go back into the reception hall, and almost ran over a smaller woman. She'd been standing directly behind him.

He pulled back abruptly, lifting both arms up. "Oh my God, Brittany! What the hell?"

Brittany tilted her head to the side and lifted the corners of her small lips. "Hello, Dex."

"What are you doing here?" he asked. His aggravation level was skyrocketing. Any more blows and he was leaving, whether Mari was here or not. Things weren't going the way he wanted them to. She'd seen Karen hanging all over him, and her reaction was to turn and walk away. What could she be thinking about him?

His chest tightened, thinking about all the horrible things that were probably going through her mind.

Now, having Brittany standing right in front of him, taunting him like she always did, all he wanted to do was reach out and strangle her. His love for her had dwindled to nothing in the last few months. Since they had broken up, he only thought of her with disdain.

"What is wrong with you?" he asked, when she stepped closer to him. He took a step back.

"What's wrong with me?" Brittany repeated in a high-pitched, innocent voice. "What's wrong with you? I'm here because Laura invited me, of course."

"You were uninvited. I know you were, because I was standing next to her when she called you."

Dexter enjoyed the fleeting look of guilt that crossed the woman's face.

"It doesn't matter. I was still invited and I'm here. I'm not leaving. I know Laura will want to see me."

Dexter frowned. "You must think a lot of yourself, Britt. You need to leave. No one wants you here, least of all me."

Brittany took another step toward him, forcing him to back up against the door he'd just closed. He pressed his back up against it, and held his breath when Brittany pushed her body against his. Her face came dangerously close to his, when she stood on her tiptoes to whisper to him.

"I know you want me here, Dexter. You want me with you everywhere you go."

It took all of Dexter's strength not to punch her in the face. He closed his eyes and lifted his face away from hers.

When he couldn't take it anymore, he put up one hand, placing it firmly on her shoulder. He shoved her away as hard as he could, making her stumble backward. She lost her footing and fell to the ground. She stayed there, glaring up at him, holding herself up with both hands.

"What is wrong with you?" She hissed.

"I asked you first," Dexter replied, hotly. "But I didn't need to. I know what's wrong with you. You're a self-absorbed narcissist who can't stand not having your way. You aren't going to get your way this time, Britt. I don't want you here. We're not together, and haven't been for a long time. Now please, I'm asking you nicely to leave.

Brittany held out her hand to him. When he didn't offer his, she grumbled and pushed herself up clumsily. She wobbled a little on her heels, but it wasn't because she was drunk. One of her heels had come loose.

"Look what you did, Dexter!" she cried out in dismay. She pulled the shoe from her foot and shook it at him. "You broke my shoe! Do you know how much money I paid for these?"

Dexter snorted. "No, and I doubt you do, either. You don't look at price tags. It's all on daddy's credit card, right?"

"Oh!" Brittany screeched in anger. "You are horrible!"

Dexter shook his head. "Only when I'm confronted by people like you, Britt. Now, there's the door. You know how to use it."

"I'm not leaving!" Brittany shrieked. Dexter was glad they were between the two entrance/exit doors, so no one inside heard her screaming. At least, he hoped the music in there would drown out her big mouth. She pulled up her skirt on the side where she had no shoe, spun around and hobbled in the other direction.

"Brittany!" he called after her in dismay. He would never get a chance to talk to Mari if this was the way the night was going.

She ignored him completely, swinging the door open and hobbling through, her head darting from left to right as she looked for Laura. He saw her lift one arm, a huge smile crossing her face. He remembered when he'd been intrigued by that smile, how soft and cute Brittany had appeared to him. But slowly, with the passage of time, she became more and more evil. She was snide and condescending. She looked down on people who had less than she did. People who weren't as pretty or as wealthy, or as physically fit.

She wasn't a pretty woman on the inside. She had a heart as black as coal. She would stomp on anyone to get something she wanted.

It had taken only one time for Dexter to know who Brittany really was. He'd watched her conspire against a mutual friend, with other friends, to swindle a large amount of money and take a lustrous vacation. She'd included him in the planning stages, thinking he was on board without even asking him.

Dexter had spent most of his time writing everything she said down, keeping track of the scheme until the eleventh hour. Then he sent a text to the mutual friend, warning him what was about to happen to him financially, and Brittany's scheme fell apart.

Brittany was very good at making people think she was stupid. But her kind of cleverness was the kind everyone needed to watch out for. Innocence was not always what it seemed.

He followed her into the reception hall and looked around for Mari. She had returned to her seat with her sisters. He wanted to go over immediately and explain himself, but something made him return to the bar and take a seat there.

He could see Mari from where he sat. He hadn't intended it that way, but when he realized it, he was grateful he chose that particular seat. The only problem was that he could only see her if he leaned forward slightly to look around Sue, who was in the way.

She was gazing out the window and seemed to be calm. She shook her head, responding to something one of her sisters said, and otherwise appeared fine. She didn't look upset at all.

But then, she wasn't standing in front of him, was she? Who knew what she would have to say about him after this? And what if she saw him come out right after Brittany?

For a moment, he questioned whether it was even worth it.

The next moment, Sue leaned forward and got up. She

moved away from the table, heading toward the bathroom.

Dexter gazed at Mari, who was delving into a piece of her favorite kind of cake. Dexter had requested it be made special for her; the Bavarian chocolate cream cake she loved. He could see how much she loved it, just from watching the delight on her face every time she took a bite.

He chuckled, suddenly feeling a little giddy. Too much champagne, maybe. But he'd only had two glasses. It wasn't alcohol that made his head spin. He'd been suddenly overwhelmed with a feeling of desire that he hadn't felt for a long time.

Brittany had never made him feel that way. It was more than physical. It was the desire to stand next to her, be seen with her, talk to her whenever he wanted to. It was those types of feelings that washed over him.

He couldn't think of any woman who had made him feel that way. He gazed at her face, unable to look away.

It was only when she looked up, licking chocolate cream from her fingers, and straight into his eyes, that the spell was broken. He blinked rapidly and gave her a weak smile and a nod. His cheeks had to be flaming red, as hot as they were.

His heart was pounding. He wanted to go over to her, but wasn't quite ready to hear what she had to say to him.

At first, she didn't seem to have a response. She continued chewing, just looking at him. Then she swallowed and smiled back at him. She pointed down at the cake in front of her, and then pointed at him. Then she turned her finger inward toward herself.

To him, she'd just asked if he had ordered that special cake just for her.

He nodded, hoping he interpreted her sign language correctly.

Her smile was so warm, he felt like he'd just stepped out of the rain, into sunlight. She tilted her head to the side and flattened her hands against each other. She bowed slightly and mouthed, "Thank you."

Dexter was flooded with a pleasant sense of delight. He turned back to the bar and tapped his finger, ordering a drink. When it came, he turned and crossed the room, heading for her table.

Chapter 12

"So, what are you thinking, Mari?" Sue asked. "You think he's a playboy? I mean, look at what these women are putting him through."

Mari nodded, noticing the dessert cart was making its way around the room. She was starving for something sweet. She responded to Sue, though she didn't take her eyes from the cart.

"That's exactly right, Sue. Look what they're putting *him* through. It seems to me like they're trying really hard to keep us apart."

"They probably are," Lynn said, softly. "We haven't been wealthy for very long. They're waiting for us to embarrass ourselves."

"That's not going to happen," Sue said. "We are doing just fine."

"I'm not turning my back on him, Sue. I'm sorry you don't like him…"

"It's not that I don't like him." Sue lifted one hand. "I'm sorry to interrupt you, but I am just looking out for your best interests. I don't want to see you caught up in some playboy's schemes or anything."

"I know, Sue," Mari replied in a gentle voice. She gave her sister a smile before lifting her hand to the server pushing around the cart. He made his way to their table.

"I want that chocolate cake right there," she said, pointing to what she knew had to be her favorite Bavarian cream chocolate cake.

"I am afraid this is reserved, Miss. What is your name?"

"Marianne Wright. I own the resort." Mari would have pushed her authority if she had to, in order to get her hands on that cake.

The server smiled. "Oh, then it is yours. It was reserved for you. Enjoy, Miss Wright."

Mari looked down at it when the server placed it in front of her. He lifted the glass lid from the top, and handed her a dessert fork wrapped in a cloth napkin. She took it with a thank you and a nod.

She looked at both of her sisters, who were looking at her like she had lost her mind. She gestured with the napkin and fork. "What? This is my favorite cake."

"Yeah, but you had your own favorite cake served at our client's wedding?" Lynn asked. She looked at Sue. "Isn't that kind of... inappropriate?"

Sue was just looking at Mari with amusement, as Mari unrolled the fork from the napkin. "I don't know," she replied quietly. "I've never had to think about it."

Mari shook her head, holding her fork right above the cake, ready to dive into it. "I didn't order this cake, sisters. But I think I know who might have."

She couldn't help grinning from ear to ear. For the cake to come to her tonight, Dexter would have had to arrange it weeks ago, with the caterer and bakers. He'd been working behind the scenes and Mari didn't even know it.

All to make sure she had a slice of her favorite cake.

"I've had some champagne ordered," Sue said. "I thought we could enjoy the music and the company, and talk about how we did tonight."

"Wow, that doesn't sound exciting at all," Mari said sincerely. She narrowed her eyes at her sister. "Are you sure you aren't the oldest?"

Sue grinned at her. "Cut it out, Mari. Haven't we had enough excitement tonight?"

Mari was feeling too good about Dexter right then. She didn't want to remember him with Karen crawling all over him, or watching him argue, out in the lobby between the doors, with Brittany. There didn't seem to be any love lost on either side, so her opinion hadn't changed. If Dexter was interested in her, she would say yes to a date with him.

"Actually," Mari said, dipping her fork into the first bite of her cake. "There's something I want to talk to you two about."

Both sisters looked at her, surprised. "Oh?" Sue asked. "What is it?"

Mari relished the deliciousness that flooded her mouth, closing her eyes. She didn't speak again until after she swallowed. She wanted to wolf it down, but she knew she had to take it slow to fully appreciate it. She looked at each of her sisters in turn.

"Remember what I was telling you before, about that mysterious assistant Uncle Nathan had?" She managed to get in another bite while they were contemplating it. They both nodded and Lynn shrugged.

"I remember you saying something about that. Why?"

"I keep seeing someone. A man. It's like he's just lurking around, waiting to be seen, so he can rush off again."

Lynn gave her a harsh stare. Sue looked confused. Mari continued to eat her cake, looking at them.

"Is that a joke?" Lynn asked. Mari was surprised to hear fear in her voice. She hadn't thought about whether it would scare her sisters or not. She shook her head, pointing at Lynn with her fork.

"You don't have to worry about your safety, Lynn. I don't think so, at least. He doesn't seem to be doing anything wrong. He's just lurking around, and when I try to introduce myself or ask him a question, he disappears. It's crazy the way he slips in and out of this place without being detected."

Lynn visibly shuddered. "That doesn't sound like someone who can be trusted, to me."

Sue nodded. "I agree with Lynn. That sounds shady to me. You should find out who he is."

Mari leaned forward, lowering her voice as if someone

might be listening. "That's the thing. I think he's the assistant. I think they are one and the same!" She said the last sentence triumphantly, and realized she was definitely tipsy. Her brain felt like a warm piece of fuzz.

But of one thing, she was clear. That man she'd been seeing, he had to be the assistant. Judging by his behavior, there was something wrong. He was acting suspicious. If there was nothing to worry about, why hide away? Why not walk up and introduce yourself?

She realized she hadn't been saying any of her thoughts aloud. She opened her mouth to speak when Sue dropped her napkin on the table next to her, and put her hands flat on the surface on either side of her plate. She leaned forward, her eyes directly on Mari.

"Listen, Mari, I know you've already had some wine and champagne but you're not really making a lot of sense. If this guy is the assistant, he would come up and talk to us. If not, it's a lurker, or worse yet, a stalker out to capture a woman who isn't used to having a lot of money. He's a swindler."

Mari shook her head, closing her eyes to enjoy another bite of her cake. She chewed and swallowed too quickly, in her opinion. "No, I don't think it's like that. If that was true, he would have let me come over to him. Or he would have come to me."

"Are you saying you saw each other? You looked at each other?"

Mari nodded, picking up her glass of ice water. She took a few sips. "We made eye contact at least once, that I know of. I think he's... I don't know. Something's wrong, of course, but it's more like... he's ashamed. Or scared."

Sue sat back. Mari enjoyed another bite of the cake. She was almost done.

"So, you're saying he's scared."

Mari shrugged. "I just don't get a dangerous vibe from him. I just don't. I think he's ashamed of something."

Lynn's eyes widened. She leaned forward like her sisters and whispered loudly, "You don't think he actually killed Uncle Nathan, do you? Maybe he didn't know the resort would come to us, and figured, as his assistant, he might get something from Uncle Nathan's fortune? Maybe all of it?"

Mari's eyes widened. "Oh no, we can't think something like that. That's not what the coroner's report said."

"But people can pay for things like that!" Lynn insisted, her wide eyes moving between her sisters.

Mari was so shocked by the notion, she stopped eating for a minute. She had sobered up some at the same time, the cake filling her up after the huge dinner.

"No," she shook her head after sitting, frozen, for a minute. "No, I just can't believe anyone would want to hurt or kill Uncle Nathan. He was a friend to everybody. And an assistant, someone who worked by his side, day by day? It just doesn't seem possible. He was so likeable." Mari shook her head again. "It just isn't possible."

Sue looked around at the guests remaining at the party. "Do you see him here? Has he been here at all today?"

"I have to admit, I didn't see him today." Mari sat back with a thoughtful look on her face.

"But that doesn't mean anything, does it?" Lynn asked. "Unless he's somehow acquainted with the Scofield brothers, and I don't think he is. They would have acted more like he was a friend, than someone they gossiped about."

Mari nodded. "So, you remember that conversation when they first hired us?"

Her sister nodded back. "Yes, I remember it."

"Okay," Sue lifted both hands to her sisters. "So, we've established that there is, in fact, at least one stranger lurking around, possibly stalking one of us, who may also be a murderer of our beloved uncle, who was friends with everyone. Why does that sound complicated?" Her question was asked sarcastically.

"It may sound complicated," Mari said quietly. "But no matter what, there is someone out there. We have to be on the alert. And in the meantime, we need to find out who that assistant was. Have you done any checking?" She was looking at Lynn when she asked the question. Lynn gave her a confused look in response.

"Me?" Lynn asked, pressing her fingers under her throat. "Why would I have done any checking?"

"You said you remembered the conversation when we were first hired."

Lynn lifted her head in understanding. "Oh, I see. No, I remembered that tonight, as we discussed it. I haven't thought about the assistant at all this past month."

Mari glanced at Sue, who was already shaking her head. At the same time, she was pulling her phone out of her purse. "I'm going to make a few phone calls," she said. "I'll be right back."

She pushed herself out of the chair and trotted toward the front door, holding her phone up to her ear with one hand, and her purse clutched to her side with the other.

Mari noticed she had a few bites left of her cake, and was delighted with herself for leaving some. She still had a little to enjoy.

She pulled the cake off the fork with her lips and closed her eyes, enjoying the taste as much as she could. It was always gone too soon.

She opened her eyes and was looking directly at Dexter.

He was seated at the bar, watching her. He looked so apprehensive. She guessed he was thinking she was mad at him. It was probably that way with the women he regularly held company with, but Mari wasn't like those women. She was willing to take chances and work for the best relationship she could have. She didn't expect it all to come easy. She knew that was nearly impossible.

She gestured to her cake and then at him, and finally pointing at herself. She suspected him all along. When he nodded

85

and smiled, it just confirmed what she'd thought. He'd done this a long time ago. It wasn't something he felt he had to do to "make up" for what she'd seen.

Her heart thumped hard in her chest when he got up and started across the room.

Chapter 13

Dexter couldn't tell if Mari was as nervous as he was. By the time he reached the table, he'd recovered his courage and smiled at the two of them. "Mari. Lynn. Are you having a good time?"

Both women nodded. Mari gestured to the chair next to her. "Why don't you sit for a moment, Dex? We can catch up. It's been a few hours since I last talked to you."

They both chuckled.

Lynn looked exceedingly uncomfortable, until she finally said, "I… I forgot I… had to do something. I'll be right back, Mari. You two just take your time."

Dexter smiled at Mari, as Lynn got up, turned swiftly and marched away from them.

"That was the most subtle thing I've ever seen," he joked.

"I'm a little tired of sitting here, Dexter," Mari said. "Do you want to go for a walk with me? I wanted to talk to you about something, anyway."

Dexter raised his eyebrows, wondering if they wanted to talk about the same thing. It couldn't be. That would be too good to be true.

"All right," he said, nodding. "But you go first."

She looked a little confused and tilted her head to the side. "I go first?"

"Yeah, I wanted to talk to you about something, too."

Dexter couldn't read the look on her face. It didn't look fearful, and for that he was grateful. She didn't look guilty or upset. He decided she looked curious, and it made him curious about what she wanted to say to him.

"Do you want to take a drink with you?" he asked, reaching for her champagne glass. She swiftly shook her head.

"I'll be fine. No more alcohol. I won't have you carrying me out of here over your shoulder, like a sack of potatoes."

Dexter laughed. "A sack of potatoes! You? Never!" He stood up and held his hand out to her. She took it and rose from the chair, looking directly into his eyes. He hoped they could make their way to the front door of the reception hall, that led to the outside of the facility, without confronting anyone he didn't want to see. He could think of two, right off hand.

He pulled her along relentlessly, not realizing, until they reached the door, that he'd practically dragged her over there. When he looked down at her behind him, she looked a little flushed.

"I am so sorry," he said, dismayed. "I often forget my long stride. I wasn't thinking."

Mari shook her head. "No need to apologize. I like tall men."

Her words took Dexter by surprise. He wondered if she knew what she was doing when she said that. He looked down at her and spotted that special smile. It was the same one that other girls gave him when they were flirting with him. It reached their eyes, but was so soft it was almost alluring.

She seemed to be in control and she was far from a stupid woman.

"I'm glad to hear that," he replied quickly, smiling back at her.

They stepped out into the dimming light of evening, and turned to walk around the huge veranda that surrounded the entire reception hall on three sides. The fourth side was attached to the hotel.

Dexter looked out at the scenery from that angle. "I really like this beautiful landscaping, don't you?" he asked.

Mari turned her eyes to gaze at the circular garden. It was one huge circle of bushes that made a gigantic trail up the hillside and down the other. Inside the circle ran trails of concrete flanked by multicolored flowers. A statue or fountain was placed strategically throughout the circle garden.

"Ah, Uncle Nathan's handiwork," she sighed, clasping her hands together in front of her. "It really is lovely, isn't it?"

"Not as lovely as what I see in front of me."

Mari turned to look into his longing eyes. Dexter was looking directly at her.

"That's a very sweet thing to say," she said softly.

"When they start playing the music again, I would love to step on the dance floor with you." He dropped his eyes to her hands, lifting one of his to entwine a finger through one of hers. "You do know how to dance, don't you?"

His eyes snapped back up to her face. "Not to imply there's any reason you wouldn't know how to." He felt guilty for a moment. When she giggled and looked up at his eyes again, he could feel a pleasant warmth flowing over him.

"I haven't danced in a long time," she said. "But I'm willing to get out there if you are. What kind of music is it going to be? I didn't handle that part of the planning at all."

"It's a lot of booty shaking music," Dexter laughed. "If I know my brother's wife." He felt wistful for a moment, his eyes growing soft. "I can't believe ol' Brian is married. And I'm happy for him, don't get me wrong. I'm really happy for him, as a matter of fact. I'm just thinkin'... I don't know. I guess I'm waiting for something like that, too."

He looked down at her. She was smiling at him as they walked the trail that took them to the circle garden.

"I know how you feel," she replied, stepping up the small stairway to the trail at the beginning of the circle.

"Have you thought about getting married?" Dexter asked. "I notice that you or your sisters have never been married."

"Oh, we're too young for that," Mari said, dismissively, waving one hand. "None of us have dated seriously enough to consider something like that."

"That surprises me," Dexter replied, sincerely. He held out his hand so she would go in front of him. She stepped up and waited for him in the clearing. He closed the gate behind him.

"Why does it surprise you?" she asked. He wondered if he'd offended her with the statement. If he did, he didn't intend to.

"Because you are all really pretty, and smart and have a lot of good qualities and skills. Plus, you're all friendly. You do business really well. Shall I go on?"

Mari stood frozen, seemingly stunned that he could list off the top of his head so many qualities he saw in her. She looked away from him, her cheeks turning red in the lamplight. The sun was down enough for them to have automatically turned on. The light was a dull yellow, making her face paler than usual. When she blushed, it stood out like a stop sign.

Dexter chuckled. "I didn't mean to embarrass you, Mari."

"Didn't you? You can't say those kinds of things without expecting someone to be embarrassed."

"Don't be embarrassed," Dexter insisted. "Be flattered. Be grateful. Anything but embarrassed."

Mari gave him a long, sincere look. "That was a nice thing to say, Mr. Scofield," she said formally. "I think I will take those suggestions."

"Glad to hear it."

Mari was quiet for a minute, then spoke in a low voice, making Dexter lean over to hear her better.

"I want to ask you something, Dexter. I'm hoping you can help me with something."

Dexter was surprised. She did have quite an inquisitive look on her face. He felt a bit of a thrill flow through him. If she proved to be adventurous and mysterious, as well as smart and beautiful, he would have hit the jackpot.

"Go ahead. Ask."

"When you first came to the resort and hired us, your brother said something about an assistant."

Dexter nodded. "You said something about this before. Why, do you have new information about him?"

"I don't have any more information than I did before," Mari admitted. "But there's something else. "Do you remember coming after me, when I followed that man in your brother's restaurant out the back?"

"I remember." That was an incident Dexter wasn't likely to forget. He wanted to know who the man was as badly as anyone else. Just thinking about that night made him annoyed.

She stopped walking and turned to him. "I think that was him," she said urgently.

"The assistant?"

She nodded. "Yeah."

"How can you be sure?" Dexter asked, thinking back to the last time he'd had a reason to think of the assistant. The last thing he remembered was seeing both Nathan and the assistant at the airport, getting ready to take off overseas. They did no more than exchange pleasantries, before both were off to their prospective destinations.

"I can't. That's why I might need your help. If you will."

Dexter smiled, gently taking her shoulders. "You don't have to even ask, Mari. You know I'll help you out however I can. But what if there's danger involved? Maybe this man is stalking you. There's no way for you to be sure that this man and the assistant are one and the same."

Mari nodded. "I know. I've been trying to think of the best way to go about finding out who he is, without alerting him. He might run. He looks kind of skittish."

"You know if he hasn't done anything wrong, we can't just do with him as we please. This is America after all."

Mari giggled. "I know, Dexter. But if he's here, he's an

uninvited guest, and if he is invited, we can find out what his name really is."

Dexter sighed. "Alright. I have a feeling if I don't go along with you on this, you're going to do it anyway, and then something might happen to you. Do you know how bad I would feel if something bad happened to you?"

Mari smiled up at him. "Aw, that's sweet, Dexter. Because I put together such a great wedding for your brother?"

"More like suddenly found the love of my life," Dexter mumbled softly. Mari stared at him. He wondered if she'd heard exactly what he said. He was grateful when she didn't ask him to repeat himself. He flashed a sudden grin at her. "Well, do you have a plan, miss detective? You must have a plan or you wouldn't have brought it up tonight. When was the last time you saw this guy?"

Mari remembered the last time she saw the stranger. It was the evening before. "I was walking down the trail from the hunting cabin, just below the tree line, and I was coming back. I saw him as I was heading toward the tennis courts. He was watching two people play."

Dexter furrowed his brow. "Do you know who was playing? Did you recognize them?"

Mari retraced the memory, but once she noticed the stranger, she completely ignored the people playing. She shook her head reluctantly. "No, I can't say I do. I guess I was so preoccupied seeing him, I didn't even look at who was playing, who he was watching. Wow, suddenly I feel really stupid."

"Don't feel stupid," Dexter said. "We'll figure this out. I have an idea."

He looked back toward the reception hall. "Listen. Do you hear that? They started the music. Let's go dance off some of this cake we've consumed." He said with a laugh, pulling on her hand.

She allowed him to hurry her down the path, telling him he was just too horrible, in an "I love you" kind of way.

Chapter 14

Dexter danced across from Mari, his body gyrating gracefully around her. She had to admit it was fun dancing with him. She laughed several times when he did something fancy with her, sliding her between his legs once, but sticking mostly with modern dances.

When a slow dance finally came, Dexter gathered her in his arms, and she let herself fall into him. She closed her eyes, and instead of having her arms around his waist, she had her hands resting against his chest. Her cheek was also against him and she listened to his beating heart. Both of their hearts beat excitedly, that was for sure.

She wondered, if they were together enough, would their hearts beat in sync, and they wouldn't even know it? Was that love? Or was she a psychopath?

She giggled. He lowered his head, swaying back and forth, his arms around her with his hands clasped behind her back.

"Are you having a good time?"

She looked up at him. "Obviously." She smiled. He lowered his head a little more. She was sure he was about to kiss her. She closed her eyes and heard another voice ringing in her ears.

"What's this, then?"

Aggravation flowed through Mari. Her eyes flew open and darted to her right, where Karen was standing with her hands on her hips. She was staring at Mari with pure disgust. When her eyes turned to Dexter, Mari saw a look that could only be taken as pure hatred.

"Dancing with the help, are we? That's going to look fine splashed across society's papers."

Mari flushed with hot indignation. She instinctively pushed away from Dexter and faced Karen.

"I'm sorry, did you just call me the help?" she asked.

Karen flashed a sweet, fake smile at her. "Well, you are the wedding planner."

"I own this resort, Karen. And I can have you thrown out of here." Mari made sure to keep her voice down. She didn't want to cause a scene at someone else's wedding. And it wouldn't look good on the resort as a whole, either. She had to think about Uncle Nathan's reputation.

"You were given this place. You don't know anything about running it." To her credit, Karen had sobered up enough to also keep her voice down. Instead, she hissed in Mari's face. "And I would like to see you throw out the maid of honor at the first wedding you ever put together. That will look wonderful on your resume."

"I don't..."

"Ladies, can we not do this on the dance floor? Better yet, Karen, take yourself off the dance floor. You aren't dancing with anyone and you're keeping us from having fun."

Karen moved her vicious eyes to Dexter. "Telling me what to do again, Dexter? Those days are over. You don't get to do that anymore."

Mari's eyes darted to Dexter's face. She'd been convinced there wasn't anything between Dexter and Karen from the beginning. Was she wrong? The look of confusion and rage that crossed Dexter's face was obvious.

He looked at Mari, shaking his head. "There was never anything between us."

Karen gasped, acting offended. Mari thought she really looked hurt, until the words spilled out of her mouth. "You lying bastard," she breathed. "How could you forget our love?"

The words were so insanely cheesy, even Mari didn't believe them. They sounded stolen from an old soap opera.

She opened her mouth to say something, when Dexter stepped in front of her. By this time, they were being noticed by others on the floor, but no one had stopped dancing to watch. Mari was grateful. She was sure she saw one or two of the other guests take a look at Karen and roll their eyes. They would follow up by saying something to their dancing partner, who would also roll their eyes.

Karen had a reputation that Mari was just beginning to suspect wasn't as bright and shiny as she liked to portray.

"Everyone knows you and I have never been together, Karen," Dexter said, breathing angry words in Karen's face. "You need to leave me alone. Once this reception is over, there's no need for me to ever see your face again. I wish to God my sister-in-law had chosen someone without a black heart to be my companion tonight."

Karen scoffed. "*Your* companion? You are my companion."

"And you are a child!" Dexter stormed, forgetting himself. "I am sick and tired of your behavior."

Most of the people dancing around them had stopped or moved away from them, giving them a wide berth. Mari wondered if they thought there was about to be a cat fight. Well, there wasn't. She wouldn't humiliate herself like that, for anyone or anything.

She stayed back, letting Dexter deal with the woman. She crossed her arms over her chest. She didn't want a scene, but Dexter wasn't holding back anymore. She was surprised he'd been able to hold his temper as long as he did.

He reached out and grabbed Karen's upper arm. "You are leaving."

Karen looked like she was about to start screaming. He got in her face and mumbled, "Don't you dare scream, Karen. I've asked you nicely to leave several times. If you want to be forcefully removed, you will be."

Mari's eyes looked around the room at the guests who were watching. She could see her wedding planning business drying up, at least with the people in this room. She hoped there weren't any reporters or reviewers in the room.

At that moment, all she wanted to do was shrink into the background. She wanted to dance with Dexter, but it was too much of a hassle. She was beginning to feel the spotlight on her, and she didn't care for it.

She took a step back, still watching Dexter and Karen argue. He was pushing Karen, step by step, off the dance floor. She was going backward and slipped once, Dexter keeping her on her feet with a hand on her arm.

Instead of going in the same direction, Mari was moving away from them, toward the other side of the room. There were two double doors that led to the inside of the hotel, in the direction she was going. She thought she might go lay down and see if the smashing headache she was expecting might not come as a result.

Dexter was oblivious to where Mari was at that moment. She was willing to bet he thought she was right behind him. She felt a little guilty for not going with him to show her support, but she was worried about the resort, how it would look on her sisters, Uncle Nathan and the whole business.

She looked around again to see the rest of the guests. Some had stopped watching Dexter and Karen. Others were watching with open curiosity. She examined their faces, wondering what each one was thinking about the ongoing situation.

There was someone in the back she could barely see. He was standing against the wall, his eyes fixed on the couple on the floor. She squinted, but he was in the shadow and she couldn't see him well.

A chill ran over her arms. It was the stranger. The stalker. She was sure of it.

Mari suddenly wanted Dexter right by her side, so he could see there really was a mysterious stranger in the place, always appearing the last place you'd expect.

She glanced at Dexter, her heart slamming inside her chest. "Dexter," she called out. When he turned to look at her and saw she was not right behind him, he looked shocked. She waved at him frantically.

He turned back to Karen and pushed her away. "Get away from me, Karen. And leave us alone. Just leave us alone. I'm telling all of you..." He looked around at the guests who were watching. "I'm asking this woman nicely to leave me alone. You all heard it." He looked back at Karen. "You bother me anymore and I'm pressing whatever charges I can think of."

He turned his back on Karen, who gasped and stomped off, shoving other guests out of her way.

Dexter sneered at her retreating back and moved to where Mari was waiting.

She had tried to keep her eye on the stranger, and still watch what happened with Karen. She was relieved when the other woman stomped away in a furious rage.

Dexter was by her side in moments. "What are you doing? I thought you were behind me."

"I'm sorry I didn't back you up, Dex. I thought you could handle it. Look. In the distance over there," she moved only her eyes. "The stranger. He's standing over there." Again, she moved her eyes in the direction of the man, but left her head facing him. She even tilted it in the right direction.

Dexter turned and peered across the room. Mari looked over, when his eyes continued to scan the aisles. She was dismayed to see the stranger had once again disappeared.

"Oh, this isn't possible!" she exclaimed. "How is he doing that? I don't understand it!" She looked up at Dexter with pleading eyes. "You have to believe me, Dexter. He was there! I swear it!"

"Well, if he was," Dexter replied. "He couldn't have gotten far. I'll help you look for him. Give me a general description to go by."

"He's about 5'7", not very tall, I guess, black and white suit, and red tie. Curly brown hair around his head. Haven't seen his eyes. I'm gonna say brown because of his hair."

"Okay, I'll go looking on that side and you on this side. I'll keep looking for signs from you. If you see him, whistle as loud as

97

you can."

Mari nodded. "I understand."

He gave her a strange look. "You know how to whistle loudly enough?"

Mari laughed. "What a funny question to ask. I do know how to whistle, actually. Like a hummingbird, mom always said."

"What a nice analogy. Okay then. Whistle for me if you see him."

"What if I don't see him?"

Dexter grinned. "You can just come back in here and find me. I won't go far if I do leave. Maybe to the bathroom but…"

She laughed. "All right, be listening because I know I saw him."

Mari walked around the darker side of the room, looking at each face to see if the man was there. She came to a corner and was astounded to notice the screws for the large air conditioning vent were laying on the floor. The vent popped off when she grabbed hold of it. She set it aside gently and looked inside. There was enough room for someone to crawl through. She bent over and ran her finger along the edge of the vent. It was clean of dust, where the sides and top of the vent were covered in at least an inch.

She stood up straight and looked through the crowd to find Dexter. She didn't see him. She whistled, but still didn't see him. Her whistle was faint, only because she realized whistling would bring a great deal of attention to herself, and she was trying to be discreet.

She ducked down into the vent, regretting that her dress would get dirty, but it was a sacrifice she was willing to make and, thankfully, could now afford.

Chapter 15

It was dusty in the vent. She crossed through only one pipe before it came to the other side, where the vent had not even been replaced. She hurried, hopeful that she was right behind the stranger. She couldn't believe her stroke of luck, but did wish she had Dexter there, just in case she needed his strength.

She slid out the other side and looked to the left and right. She recognized the room as one of the grand ballrooms attached to the resort. It was also used for large wedding groups, and events thrown by charitable associations and the like.

It was a long room, a huge rectangle. A rush of adrenaline ran through Mari when she spotted a retreating figure in the distance, jogging down a long hallway toward the cloak room. She took off after the man, holding up her dress so she wouldn't trip. Her soft shoes made no sound as she crossed the floor.

She was in the hallway in enough time to see which room the man disappeared into. He'd dashed into Coatroom B, one of the larger ones, with family rooms. She hurried, but slowed her pace some, not wanting to catch up and be suddenly confronted by an angry stalker. He had to have known she'd already seen him, or he wouldn't have gone running again.

The door to Coatroom B clicked softly to a close, just before Mari got to it. She wanted it closed. She approached it as quietly as she could and pressed her ear against the door. She couldn't make out the sounds she heard on the other side.

She frowned in confusion. What was he doing in there? It sounded almost like scratching on wood at first, then wood sliding across wood, a door opening. She was suddenly covered in chills. Was there a hidden door in there? What could possibly be stashed behind it? Was there enough room for him to hide in it?

If she went busting in there, there was no guarantee he might not come bounding out of some hidden space, conk her on the head with a heavy, blunt object and leave her for dead.

Again, a chill of fear ran over her body. She couldn't leave.

If she did, he would get away.

She tried to think quickly. She looked around her. Along the walls, in between doors and under windows, were many different small tables with decorations adorning them. She ran her eyes over them all, looking for one she could use as a weapon if she needed to.

She spotted a gold-plated baseball bat hanging above a fireplace not far from the Coatrooms. She ran softly to the fireplace, snatching the bat from its pedestal display.

"Perfect," she breathed, hurrying back to Coatroom B.

She put her hand on the doorknob and pulled in a deep, quiet breath. Her heart was racing a mile a minute. She felt like ice was sliding through her veins, but it was just the finger of fear toying with her.

You're gonna be fine. Just go in and introduce yourself.

Even as she thought the words, she scoffed at herself. Introduce herself? While carrying a gold-plated baseball bat?

Before she could talk herself out of it, Mari turned the knob and stepped inside the room.

She wasn't overly surprised to see Coatroom B was empty. But she knew better. She knew he was in there somewhere. She made as little noise as possible. She moved to her right and peered through the jackets and coats hung up on the racks. While she looked for a person, she was also examining the walls behind the racks. They were smooth and they were wood. One of them had to be fake.

Her heart hammering in her chest, Mari tightened her grip on the baseball bat and crept around the room. When she decided one area looked particularly disturbed, she went toward it slowly. She narrowed her eyes and bobbed her head back and forth, looking in between the jackets.

She got to the wall and knocked on it lightly to see if it was hollow on the other side. She compared it to other places nearby. It didn't sound hollow to her.

Disappointed, Mari continued her search of the room, looking for any sign there might be a door. There had to be one. There had to be something. There was no vent large enough for a human to go through in this small room. If there wasn't another door, the stranger must have vanished into thin air.

No matter what else happened, Mari refused to believe there was a ghost in the resort. If someone else didn't spot the stranger soon, Mari thought her sisters and Dexter might start thinking she was losing her mind; that she really thought she was seeing someone she wasn't. That wouldn't be good.

Mari lowered the bat and turned in a circle, examining once more. She noticed there was a sharp indentation in the wall she was facing. It seemed unnecessary, though it did provide a few more racks for hanging coats.

She went closer to it and knocked on the side closest to her.

It sounded hollow. She raised her eyebrows. Her anxiety had returned, and her heart resumed its thumping. She tried to breathe normally, and not be afraid.

She ran her hand down one side of the wall and then the other. It was smooth, except in two places. Both of them seemed to be in the same place on opposite sides. Intrigued, Mari set the bat down next to her and pressed her fingers into the two small buttons at the same time.

There was a grinding noise from inside the wall. The panels in front of her began to fold in on themselves, opening a doorway in between the walls. There was a corridor just wide enough for a human to get through, if they weren't too big.

She immediately reached for her cell phone in the small bag she was carrying with her. She opened the flashlight app and directed it down the hallway. There was a small switch to her right but she didn't dare flip it. It might alert the man that she had found the passageway.

She stepped into the darkness and cautiously moved forward. There was nothing impeding her path, and it never narrowed or became wider. It was just a long passageway. She realized she hadn't closed the door behind her. She didn't know how to close it anyway. She looked behind her, flashing her phone in that direction. The door had slid silently closed behind her.

Fear slipped through her. The only thing she'd seen on the inside of the walls was the light switch. She wouldn't be able to go back that way if she didn't find a way to open it. She turned back and hurried down the narrow hallway, her heart beating harder the further she got.

Just when she thought she'd made a terrible mistake, she saw a door in the distance. Relief flooded her when she spotted the doorknob, flashing bright in the light from her phone.

She sped up a little more, anxious to get out of the hallway. It was so closed in. She felt the pressure on her chest and needed some fresh air. As she got closer to the door, she heard the sound of music playing on the other side.

She slowed down a little, recognizing the music. The Scofield wedding was the only event they were having that day, at that time. It had to be the reception room.

The thrill of realization swept through her. That's why she hadn't seen him come into the reception room. There was another way in. The vent led to a circle coming back to the same room. She hadn't realized she was even going in a circle.

Astounded by her discovery, Mari was even more curious than ever. When had this passageway been put in? Did her uncle know about it? If the stranger was the assistant, and he knew about it, what kind of schemes was he up to while her uncle was alive?

Many questions whirled through her mind. She got to the door and pressed her ear against it, trying to guess by the sounds what was around her. She grasped the knob in her hand and tried to turn it, but it was locked. Panicking, she looked down.

Her shoulders slumped in relief when she saw the lock was on her side. She turned it and tried again.

It turned smoothly, as if it had just been used. She grinned. Of course, it had just been used. The spark of humor gave her a little more courage. She pushed open the door and peeked through the crack.

She was almost confused by where she was until she realized what was going on. The music she heard was coming from the reception room, just outside the kitchen in front of her.

There were servers and caterers working smoothly around each other. She stepped out of the door and closed it behind her casually. No one looked at her. They were all concentrating on the jobs they were there to do.

She felt a sense of pride as she walked through. The quality of the employees would boost the ratings of the resort, and their sales along with it. She pushed open the double doors and went out into the reception hall. The bride and groom's final dance had just begun.

She saw all the other groups involved in the ceremony on stage, dancing. But not Dexter.

She remembered she'd left him in that room without telling him where she was going. Her heart thumped in apprehension. She didn't see the stranger walking around anywhere either.

She hurried through the crowd of spectators, all smiling and clapping for the new husband and wife. She excused herself several times, pushing through people to get to the other side of the room. She wanted to go back into the lobby of the hotel, and go out front to see if anyone was leaving the resort.

Mari came to a skidding halt as soon as she went through the front door of the lobby. She heard the sound of bickering voices, on the other side of a tall shrub placed neatly in a pot next to the front door. She stood frozen in place, wishing she wasn't, but needing to eavesdrop when she recognized Dexter and Brittany.

Chapter 16

Dexter didn't see where Mari went before Brittany ambushed him. She put herself directly in his path and wouldn't move. The frustration that had been building all night had tightened every muscle in his body, and it was taking everything he had not to let it out.

He looked down at her, shaking his head. "Now is not the time, Brittany. You need to get out of my way."

"Doesn't someone look like he's on a mission." Brittany said in her cutest voice. He felt a measure of disgust.

"Please, get out of my way," he growled. "I don't have time for this right now. I thought you'd left."

Brittany shook her head, a sickeningly sweet smile plastered on her face. "No, you just wanted me to leave, but I told you I was going to stay and support Laura. I've been talking to her and she is very happy. Your brother is a good man."

She closed the few inches between them and pressed herself against him. He felt revulsion pulse through him. He stepped back, allowing her to lose her balance. She grabbed at him, pulling herself back up to her feet.

"I know he's a good man," Dexter said sternly, as if speaking to a child. "Go talk to Laura some more. I don't have time for you."

"I can't." Brittany's voice was weak. Dexter wondered if she'd been drinking before she came to the reception. "She's getting ready for the speeches and all that stuff. I'm not in the wedding party, so I don't have to give a speech. But you do." She raised her glass to him, putting emphasis on the last two words. She giggled. "You got something prepared, right?"

Dexter narrowed his eyes at her. He didn't know it was that close to speech time. He searched through the crowd, trying to spot Mari. He had to tell her. He didn't see her, and felt Brittany tugging on his arm.

"I think they're calling your name now, Dex. You better go!"

He did hear his name being said over a loudspeaker. He hurried to the front of the crowd, running his speech through his head. It was all experiences and memories he shared with the two, and he would have no trouble remembering it.

But as he spoke, he searched the crowd for Mari and didn't see her. She had disappeared from the room. Along with the stranger.

He smiled at Brian, mentioning a time or two when he and his brother had a scuffle, as boys, that ended up with one or both being punished in a variety of ways. He had the crowd laughing several times.

Once he was done, everyone was clapping, and he hugged his brother and new sister-in-law. He finally felt free to find Mari. He thought she might have gone outside to look through the parking lot. That would be something he would do.

Just as he made it to the door, his anger returned when, once again, he heard Brittany's voice. He scowled and grunted angrily.

"Dexter, the dances are…"

"Brittany!" he barked at her. "You're like a little dog, or better yet, a parasite attached to me. You have to leave me alone. I'm busy!"

"But the dances are going to start in a minute. People will expect to see you out there with Karen."

Dexter yelped a loud laugh. "I won't be dancing with Karen tonight, Brittany. Don't worry about that."

Brittany smiled that familiar smile that Dexter had come to detest. "Okay. I won't worry about it."

Dexter recognized the flirting, and was feeling a bit sick to his stomach at that point. He shook his head at her. "You've got to leave me alone, Brittany."

He pushed through the front doors, and hurried across the front porch to look through the parking lot. He didn't recognize any more cars than he thought he would. He was down at the bottom of the steps, turning in circles, scanning the area around him, when Brittany came through behind him.

"Dexter! I told them you would be right back in! What are you doing? What are you looking for? Are you looking for that wedding planner?"

Dexter turned on her. "Will you stop calling her that? You don't know her at all. You shouldn't judge her. She owns this place, whether she inherited it or not, and she's a good woman. She's nice to people. That's more than you can say. You treat everyone like dirt!"

Brittany shook her head. "You don't really mean that, Dexter." She turned away from him and stomped to her right, stopping with her hands folded over her chest. Her dismissive attitude infuriated Dexter, and he went up the steps in two angry bounds. He crossed the porch and came up behind her.

"You have no place judging anyone, Brittany. Not after the heartless schemes you've been involved in. Just for money's sake. Greed. It's disgusting. I don't want anything more to do with it. That means you have to leave me alone. From now on. Completely. You got that?"

"I understand, Dexter!" Brittany replied, in a voice that implied her throat was clogged with tears.

Dexter frowned. Her voice didn't sound angry. She was suddenly defeated and looked broken hearted. She turned to face him. His anger receded a little. He unclenched his fists and spoke in a softer tone. "You've got to understand. You and me... we aren't a couple. We never will be. I know you aren't stupid."

"But we had something, Dex! It was so good! What more do you want? I'm everything you ever dreamed of in a woman."

The claim took him off guard. She was far from everything he wanted in a woman. "If you're talking physically, sure. You're gorgeous. But I'm not interested in what's on the outside. I'm more interested in what's on the inside. The soul. And I don't like yours. I don't think we have anything between us." He moved his hand between them in a straight line. "Am I making sense?"

"Well, it's funny that you should say that, Dexter," Brittany said, looking up at him. "Because there is something between us now."

Dexter frowned in confusion. "What are you talking about, Brittany?" His voice expressed the alarm he felt. His body tingled in anticipation. He knew what she was going to say before she said it.

"I'm going to have your baby."

He could feel tiny explosions of rage bursting in his head. He closed his eyes and balled up his fists. It was almost impossible for Brittany to be pregnant. They had not been together for months. She was not showing, and was her normal slender self. No one had mentioned it to him, and he knew it would have been the talk of the town.

This was a ploy and he wasn't falling for it.

Pushing himself to stay calm, he said in a low voice, "What makes you think it's mine?"

Brittany put on a hurt face. He didn't care whether she was hurt by the question. He was a thousand times certain, even if she was truly pregnant, that it wasn't his.

"I just know it is. It can't be anyone else's."

He dropped his eyes to her belly. "You're still pretty small for what... going on four or five months? Aren't you supposed to have a bump or something?"

Brittany smiled the fakest smile he'd ever seen. "I'm just naturally small."

Dexter shook his head. "I don't believe you, Brittany. I'm going to fight you with everything I have. You aren't going to ruin me and my brother."

Brittany stepped close to him and gave him a kiss on the

cheek before he could pull away. "Don't you worry, Dexter," she whispered in his ear. "I'm going to get everything that's mine, and more."

Dexter stood rigid as she moved away, and walked down the steps to the parking lot. She crossed to go down the patio to the gazebo. He turned slowly. His body was tense, his nerves were tingling and his breathing was shaky.

He pictured the hassle it would be to go through legal proceedings to prove any child she bore wasn't his. He knew, from medical reports of his past, that the chances of him having a baby were slim. He hadn't thought about it at all until he saw Mari that day. Now the prospect of having a family with her felt more like a possibility.

But the chances were still small, and some medical procedures might need to be performed for his future wife to get pregnant.

He looked up at the ceiling and spoke aloud, "God, please don't play a joke on me. I'm sorry for whatever I've done. Amen."

"I don't know if He's gonna respond to that prayer," Mari's voice came from behind him. He spun around and stared down at her. His face was hot. He knew it had to be beet red.

"Did you hear all of that?"

Mari nodded. "I sure did. I heard it all." She took a few steps toward him, gazing into his eyes. "What are you going to do? Do you think she really is?"

He shook his head. "Your guess is as good as mine, honey."

It was the first time he'd used a term of endearment for Mari. He saw a look of pleasure cross her face. He was glad what she had heard didn't seem to dampen her resolve. She looked as determined as ever to stand with him.

"I have something to tell you," Mari said, closing the distance between them quickly.

"I'm sure you do. You completely disappeared from the

reception hall. Where did you go?"

"I found out how the stranger got out of the reception hall without you seeing him. I really thought he vanished into thin air. But I found a vent."

She used heavy emphasis on the last word, raising her eyebrows.

"A vent." He repeated. It seemed, by the look on her face, that she was surprised by that, so he wanted to be understanding.

"Yes, one of those big air conditioning vents that runs through the whole place."

Dexter nodded. He'd seen the vents when examining the rooms. Every room the size of a ballroom or event room had large enough vents for someone to climb into to repair one, if needed, in a hurry. "Let me guess. You went after him."

Mari nodded. "I sure did, and guess what else? I found a secret passage way! In a coatroom off the reception hall!"

"What? That's lunacy!" Dexter looked astonished. He took Mari's arm and gently pulled her back to the front doors of the lobby.

She turned back, pulling her arm away from him. "Wait, I wanted to see if anyone was leaving…"

"There hasn't been anyone in this parking lot since I came out with Brittany, Mari. There's no sense in searching from car to car. There's nobody out here but us."

Mari uttered a deep, heavy sigh. "It just doesn't seem possible, Dexter. He keeps disappearing. It's like he knows everything about this place. It's starting to give me the creeps."

Dexter put his arm around her shoulders and pulled her into a hug. "Don't worry, Mari. If you feel scared, I'll stay with you, and we'll stay up all night talking in front of the fireplace. Or watching the stars. Your choice. Both wonderful ideas."

Mari looked up at him. "I suppose I could use a night to enjoy myself. Are you asking me on a date, Mr. Scofield?"

Dexter laughed. "I think I'm officially asking you on a date, Miss Wright."

"I accept your offer."

They grinned at each other.

Chapter 17

The next morning, Mari's head was pounding. She sat to eat breakfast, dropping into her chair as if she were a sack of potatoes. She groaned and leaned forward, resting her head in her hands.

Sue and Lynn were already at the table eating. Neither of them looked as worse for the wear as Mari, but they were both swollen and tired-looking. They were slowly eating the meals they'd ordered from the kitchen, taking small bites and letting a long pause grow between each bite.

"Don't anybody say anything," Mari whispered.

"Don't plan to." Sue's voice was just as soft.

"Where's the ibuprofen?" Mari looked at Sue. Her sister moved her head slightly in the direction of the door. "You mean the bathroom, don't you." It wasn't a question.

Sue pressed her lips together, as if Mari should know the answer. Mari grunted, but it came out as a whimper. She pushed herself to sit up straight. She'd already put her order in with the server, and was just waiting for her breakfast. She decided to go light. She didn't want anything heavy on her stomach.

"I think I had too much wine and champagne," she murmured.

"I think there was clearly too much alcohol consumed altogether last night."

"And so much drama!" Lynn shook her head. "It was a little shameful, if you ask me. The first time we hold an event like that, and it turns out to be an episode of Dynasty. What do you think they'll be saying about this resort if those women start lying about everything?"

"You know they're going to lie to make themselves look better," Sue said. "They're known for that kind of thing. We can already assume that's going to happen." She turned to look at Mari. "What kind of impact do you think this will have on our business, Mari?"

Mari didn't want to think about the business. "I don't know. I'm not thinking about that right now."

"I saw you and Dexter were involved in some of it," Sue said. "And I never got a chance to update you on what I found out about the assistant."

Mari felt interest cut through her hangover. She excused herself to get something for her headache, telling Sue to hold her thought. When she returned with the pills, she took them with water and squinted at Sue, pushing through. "Tell me now. What did you find out?"

Sue leaned forward. She used one finger to emphasize important points, by jabbing it toward the table. "There *was* an assistant that worked for Uncle Nathan, and it *was* kept under wraps by almost *everyone*. There are some people here *now* who knew about the assistant, but they never ask about him or speak about him, and I can tell you why."

Mari narrowed her eyes. "Tell me why, then."

"Because they were all made to sign privacy documents." She folded her arm over her chest, after stabbing the table with the last four words.

Mari sat up straight again. She frowned. "Why would they have to do that?"

"I have no idea. But they can't talk about him to you."

"I… I mean, we must have some legal way to speak to them," Lynn said. "If the man worked here, and now that we have a suspicion there was something shady going on, we should have a legal right to question him."

Mari raised her eyebrows at her sister. "You're right about that, Lynn. There must be a way we can force the information out of someone."

"Well, unless you're thinking of bribing someone with a lot of money, I don't see a legal way for those people to break their vow of silence."

Mari shook her head. "I just don't get it. I just don't. I mean, why would they keep an assistant hidden from us?"

"And who is the 'they' to begin with?"

"That's a good question, too." Mari looked at Lynn.

"There must be some other way we can find out. No one around here is going to tell us anything," Sue said. "I even tried asking a few."

"What reaction did you get?" Mari sat forward again, this time more out of interest than for comfort. Her headache had retreated to the back of her head. She hoped the ibuprofen would work for that. She was anxious to hear what her sister had to say, and to tell them both she saw the man stalking them at the wedding and reception.

"Stone faced silence," Sue replied, shaking her head. "Even from the ones who are typically friendly. From the housekeeper in the main facility to the chef in kitchen 3. You all know how friendly he can be." She tilted her head and gave them both a sarcastic look. Mari chuckled.

"Yes. So, nothing from them, then. I'm going to talk to Dexter. I think we have a real problem on our hands. Last night, I –"

"Wait a minute," Sue cut her off, leaning forward. "You're going to talk to Dexter? About what?"

"About all of this going on. About the assistant. It's because of him that we know about it in the first place."

"No, it's because of Brian Scofield that we know about the assistant. He's the one who mentioned him."

Mari nodded. "I know, but I've been talking to Dexter about this since it started bothering me; since I told him about seeing that man around the resort. He just seems to come and go as he pleases. I don't like it, and I'm convinced he's the assistant. I wish I could get a picture of him. I wish I could draw it for you."

"I wish you could, too." Sue said in a low voice. Her arms were still crossed over her chest. "Eventually, we're just going to start thinking he's a figment of your imagination. I can't believe you involved Dexter in this. You barely even know him."

Mari frowned. "All right, Sue, I don't know what problem you have with him, but you need to set it aside. I'm going to date him. We've already decided that. We had a wonderful time together last night, and he made me feel safe and at ease. I don't feel like I'm in danger with him."

"But you don't know what he'll do to your heart." Mari didn't think Sue sounded all that convinced that Dexter would hurt her. Then again, she had already made up her mind Dexter that was just caught in a web of deceit he was trying to disentangle himself from.

"No matter who a person is, there is always a possibility someone will get hurt," Mari reasoned. "I'm not going to stop myself from taking chances that might better my life, just because I'm afraid of getting hurt. I have to take risks. That's our nature. We're all like that. Admit it."

She raised her eyebrows at her sister. Sue sighed and sat back hard against her chair. Her arms were still hugged around her. She had a sulking look on her face, but it wasn't very pronounced. Mari felt like she might be giving in to the urge to trust Dexter.

"So, I'm going to talk to Dexter and see if we can find a way to draw this assistant out in the open. He might have some connections that will let us dig deeper into the workings of this resort, before we came along."

"What do you think he'll be able to do?"

"I don't know, yet. I'll talk to him, and tell him what you told me." She replied to Sue. "But I need to tell you what happened to me last night." Mari thought for a moment, and then stood up. "Actually, the story is too ridiculous. Let me show you instead."

Her sisters looked at each other curiously, pushing their plates forward and getting up to follow her through the door. The walk to the reception hall, where they had been the night before, would take about five minutes. It was in the front wing of the building, while the kitchen where the sisters were eating was all

114

the way in the back.

Hurrying, Mari cut that time in half and they were in the reception hall a couple of minutes later, watching the final clean up. Mari led her sisters through the empty room, all the way to the back corner where she'd gone through the vent.

She stopped in front of it and turned to her sisters, who were staring at her inquisitively.

"What's going on?" Sue asked, looking from Mari, to the vent, and back.

Mari pointed at it and said, "I went through here last night. You two need to follow me through it so I can show you where it leads." Mari thought twice about it, and shook her head. "You don't have to follow me through it. Let me take you to the Coatroom and show you that passage."

"Passage?" her sisters repeated in sync. They all looked at each other.

"Yes, follow me." Mari hurried away from the vent, glancing down at it as she went. The screws had been replaced.

The sisters followed Mari to the Coatroom down the hall, and watched in astonishment as she went straight to the hidden hallway, pressed the buttons and the door opened up. She'd prepared her cell phone, so she waved at them, turning the flashlight on.

"I'm not going in there," Lynn said in a firm, deep voice.

"It's just a hallway, Lynn," Mari reassured her sister. "There's nothing scary in here at all, no holes in the walls or anything. It's just a hallway to the other side. I want you to see where it comes out. It's a bit fun, after you've done it the first time. Come on."

She waved the light again. "Turn on your light if it makes you feel better. It's a straight shot. No worries."

She didn't mention that it was kind of a big circle or arch. Lynn didn't need to know that. She only needed to feel safe. After a few more words of encouragement, both sisters complied and followed Mari into the long corridor. Lynn whimpered a few times, but halfway down, she realized there really wasn't anything to it.

"You can't get locked in," Mari said. "Because this door only locks from the inside."

"Then how do you keep people out?"

"Because where you come out isn't noticeable, and people in the room are always busy."

"I don't understand." Mari heard Lynn call out behind her.

"You'll see. There's the door, up there. Watch where we come out."

Mari hurried to close the space between them and the door. She was feeling apprehensive, even though she knew everything would be fine. She reached for the doorknob and turned it. It was locked again. She had time to wonder who locked it, before turning the latch and then the knob.

It opened easily, just as it had the first time. Mari breathed a sigh of relief as quietly as she could. She didn't want her sisters to know she'd been doubting the safety of their journey, either. She pushed the door open and stepped out into an empty kitchen. It was clean and sparkling, ready for another event. She stepped to the side to let her sisters come out, feeling satisfied. She smiled at her sisters.

"Is that amazing or what?" she asked. They both had looks of shock on their faces. Sue turned to her.

"You followed the stranger through here? Did you see him again?"

Mari shook her head.

Lynn's eyes widened. One hand went to her mouth. "Maybe he's a ghost!" she said, breathlessly.

Mari frowned. "What? Why would you say that?"

"Because you never catch up with him, and he's showing you parts of the house you didn't know about."

Mari felt a bit of amusement slide through her. She shook

her head. "The man I saw was solid, not a ghost. And a ghost wouldn't need to go through a vent to show me a secret passageway in another room. He was trying to get away from me."

Lynn visibly shivered. "I don't know, Mari. I just don't know."

Chapter 18

Later that day, Mari had plans to meet up with Dexter. She and her sisters had a few business meetings to tend to. Mari couldn't concentrate on any of them. Sue ended up taking over, giving orders to her sisters as to what their part in each wedding would be.

They had already decided on a set routine for work, so Mari didn't expect more, less, or different than what Sue assigned her. It was best to split up the management into three sections. It made everything much more efficient and organized.

She came out of her thoughts as she was walking through the lobby, going toward her office. As she approached, she noticed her office door was open.

A jolt of fear split through her. She stopped where she was, staring at the open door. It was only cracked, but she always locked her door when she left. She kept personal items in there she didn't want anyone to steal.

With her heart slamming against her chest, she proceeded forward, clutching her handful of papers to her chest. She was gripping them so tightly, they were crumpling under her fingers. In her state of mind, she didn't think to relax them.

She got closer to her door and heard shuffling from the other side. She stopped just before she got to it, trying to see inside as much as she could. She heard the sound of her desk chair squeaking and one of the drawers sliding open.

Gathering all her courage, she braced herself and stepped forward, pushing her door open wide. She turned and glared at the person leaning down, looking in one of her drawers.

She almost fainted when Lynn looked up at her.

"Hey, Mari, I need a form for the… what's wrong?"

Mari was shaking from fear. She had completely expected the stranger to be in her office. She had no idea what she would have done if it had been him, but she was eternally grateful it

118

wasn't. She exhaled sharply and put one hand over her heart.

"You scared me to death, Lynn. I thought you were…"

Lynn raised her eyebrows and looked back at her sister, sympathetically. "I'm so sorry, Mari. I didn't mean to scare you. I was just looking for that form to give to the caterer, with all the options we have for them…"

Mari held up one hand. "I know where they are. Here, get up and I'll get a couple for you. I have everything filed according to my own system."

"That's smart, but if me or Sue needs something, we won't be able to find it."

Mari smiled. "Just making sure it's as hard on you guys as it can be, when I meet my maker."

Lynn gasped with a smile and swiped her hand at her sister's arm. "I can't believe you can say things like that, Mari! God, forbid!"

Mari laughed as she switched places with her sister. She leaned down and pulled out a file from the drawer Lynn had been going through. "Here you go." She pulled out three pages, with yellow and pink sheets attached underneath. "Make sure they fill out every service they offer, and that they know what we're looking for specifically."

Lynn nodded. "I know what to do. This will be the fifth one I've set up in the last week. Things are really picking up. I hope we don't get any blowback from the Scofield debacle."

"It wasn't a debacle, and it's too early to tell." Mari set her bag on her desk and opened it to remove her laptop. "I've got work to do, but if you hear of anything going around town about last night, or the wedding, let me know. Good or bad. Okay?"

Lynn nodded. "Will do, Sis." She turned to walk back to the door. Once there, she turned back and asked with a sly smile. "When do you see Dexter again? Have you talked to him?"

Mari looked up from her laptop. Lynn bit her bottom lip, her smile remaining.

Mari chuckled and shook her head. "I've been in contact with him all day, Lynn. What do you think?"

"You're going to date him, aren't you?"

Mari nodded. She couldn't help gazing into space, picturing his handsome face in her mind.

"Aw, I'm so happy for you, Mari. Just think, maybe we'll be planning a wedding for you!"

Mari almost choked. She coughed a little bit, her eyes widening as she stared at Lynn. "Whoa, you just took me from first date to my wedding day. Slow down!"

Lynn laughed and left the room, shaking her head.

Mari stayed behind her desk, thinking how accurate Lynn actually was. Mari couldn't help thinking that Dexter was the perfect man to marry, if he ever asked her. And she knew there was no chance she wouldn't accept.

She told herself it really was too soon for such thoughts. But it wasn't like they'd just met. It wasn't like they hadn't already had an adventure or two. The mysterious man they were hunting was sure to bond them in ways no dating ritual possibly could.

Pleasure slid through Mari. She was truly happy. She sighed and stared down at the papers in front of her. After a moment, she realized she was still looking at the open folder of caterer acquisition forms.

She closed the folder with a chuckle, and returned it to her desk drawer. She closed the drawer and looked down at her laptop. She typed in her password and clicked on email as soon as the wallpaper loaded successfully.

She double clicked on the icon to bring up her email messages. She read the first two and dismissed them. The third drew her interest immediately. It wasn't from a familiar address, but the subject matter drew her attention.

It said, "Assistant to Nathan Wright".

She ran the mouse up to it and clicked it hurriedly. Her

finger twitched and double clicked on it, bringing up the title, as if she wished to change it. She groaned. "Don't do this to me now. Just open up the dang email."

She clicked away from it and clicked it again to bring it up on her screen.

It flashed up and she read through the letter intently.

To whom it may concern,

In the time before Nathan Wright passed on, about a year ago, he was involved in a few legal problems that required a heavy-handed lawyer. In using that lawyer, he became involved with a certain young man who wormed his way into working for Mr. Wright.

Something happened to Mr. Wright that made him fully dependent on this assistant. If you find the assistant, you will discover there was a lot more going on in Mr. Wright's life than he let on.

I urge you to look into Mr. Wright's personal and financial records from last year. I think what you will find there will surprise you. Put what you learn to good use. You'll find all your answers if you ask the right questions.

Mari stopped reading. Her mind was already whirling with questions. She scrolled down, reading more of the same, until she got to the bottom. It was signed, *A Friend.*

The letter seemed so cryptic. It was such a gentle and confusing warning.

Mari frowned. That was not as helpful as she thought it would be. A friend. They didn't do anything but warn her. And she couldn't tell if they were hiding something about the assistant or her uncle. Her uncle was known to be an honest man, so anything he got involved in, illegally, had to be unintentional. He wasn't the kind of man who broke the law to get ahead.

She knew because of the way he was talked about by colleagues and business associates, as well as the employees he'd hired, and even the way she and her sisters had been treated by him over the years.

When she and her sisters took over the resort, everything, business-wise, was running smoothly. The resort was not in debt, she and her sisters had been left with a small fortune just to live on, and the place was generating high returns daily.

The one glaring thing she noticed about the letter was that it failed to mention the assistant's name. In fact, though it was the subject matter, the assistant was barely mentioned at all.

The whole thing left her feeling confused. She printed off a copy of the email. As she got up to retrieve it from a few feet away, she glanced out the window behind her desk and stopped abruptly, her hand outstretched to grab the paper from the printer.

Out on the tennis courts, which she could just see clearly, was a tall, handsome man playing tennis. She couldn't see who he was playing tennis with, but whoever it was, they were good. Dexter kept smacking the balls back to the other side, not missing, running back and forth to get in front of them.

"I'm never playing tennis with you," she mumbled, a feeling of longing spreading through her. She wanted to be out there playing tennis with him.

She grinned at her silliness. She would play tennis with him eventually.

She picked up the printed copy of the email and stared down at it. Since she knew where Dexter was, she might as well go talk to him, and show him the email she'd received.

She hoped she wouldn't get down to the tennis court and see Dexter playing with Brittany or Karen. Thinking of him playing against Karen was actually quite funny, and made Mari chuckle. There was no way *that* was going to happen.

She went back to her laptop and scrolled through the

remaining unread messages to see if the one in her hand was the only one she'd gotten.

It was.

She had a feeling she would be receiving more, though. People who bothered to send one letter, were bound to send another.

She closed her laptop and slid it back in the case. She zipped it around so it was closed, and left it on the top of her desk, before rethinking and hiding it under the file folders in her bottom drawer, where there was plenty of room.

She got up and glanced once more out to the tennis court to make sure Dexter was still playing.

He was. She watched for a moment, admiring his grace and skill. Finally, she broke herself away.

Chapter 19

Dexter slammed the ball back toward his brother with every bit of force he had. He and Brian had trained together, and were almost equally matched in skill. He grinned when his brother stumbled and still managed to make a wobble-handed hit back toward Dexter.

"There ya go! Get that!" Brian yelled out, nearly falling face first. He got himself under control and bounced back and forth on his feet, his racket held out in front of him.

Dexter held a hand up, holding the ball as if he was about to serve, when his eyes moved to the side of the court. Mari was walking toward them. He felt a warm, pleasant sensation slide through him. The sight of her brought a smile to his face and he lowered the hand with the ball in it.

Brian turned to see what he was looking at, and relaxed his tennis stance. He turned his head back to his brother. "I think you're wanted, bro," he said.

Dexter gave him a satisfied grin. "I sure hope so, Bri."

Brian lifted his eyebrows. "First time I've ever seen a look like that on your face, Dex. You like this one a lot, do ya?"

Dexter nodded. The two brothers were walking toward each other, and soon had just the net between them. "You mind if we take five?" Dexter asked.

"Of course not. Go talk to your girl. Mine's waitin' over there anyway. I'm sure Laura would love for me to take a break, and use it talking to her."

"Well, you're married now," Dexter teased him. "So, now you have to concentrate on actually getting alone time."

Brian chuckled. "Yeah, when you're single, you don't want alone time and struggle to find companionship. You get companionship, and struggle to find alone time."

Dexter shared his brother's amusement. He nodded. "Yep. It's the truth."

"Well, go look for your companionship. You've got my blessing. She's one of those smart, pretty ones."

Mari was nearing the court. Dexter lifted his racket to his brother. "See you back here on the court in ten, then."

"Oh, you need five extra minutes?" Brian asked sarcastically. He winked.

Dexter snorted. "Go on, Bri."

Brian walked to the other side of the court, where a small gate gave him access to the gazebo that sat on the hill just beyond. Laura was there, waiting for him, her eyes on a small book in front of her.

Dexter walked toward Mari. "Hey you. You're lookin' pretty this afternoon."

Mari smiled at him. "That's awfully sweet of you, Dexter. Thanks. You're looking pretty good yourself, I gotta say."

"Back atcha with the thanks."

Dexter felt like an idiot but he said it anyway. He hated that now he was suddenly nervous around her. There hadn't been a moment wasted on being nervous the night before. They sat and talked, relating and opening up to each other. He'd never had an experience like that before. It was what he assumed girls' slumber parties must be like.

Thinking of having a slumber party with Mari made Dexter chuckle.

"I'm glad you're happy, Dex," Mari said, coming close enough to stand on her tiptoes and kiss his cheek. He wanted to grab her and kiss her directly on the lips, but he refrained. He wasn't sure what she would do if he did. He thought she would probably kiss him back, but he wasn't quite ready if she rejected him, or thought he was being too forward.

She had turned her head away by that time anyway, actually dropping it to look down at the papers in her hand.

"I have to show you something, Dexter. I was checking my

125

email and I got this." She pulled it out and handed it to him. He skimmed through it, reading quickly.

"Okay, so what does this have to do with the assistant? And what dealings could your uncle possibly have that had to do with the law? There's no way he did anything illegal. I would be stunned if that was true."

Mari nodded. "That's how I felt, too. I never knew my uncle to be anything but honest and true."

"Everybody liked him," Dexter said, drawing his eyebrows together and reading the email again. There had to be more to it. "I don't understand why they would name the subject title that, and only speak vaguely of the assistant. This is more like a jab at your uncle than the assistant."

"It seems to me," Mari said, as she walked down the sidewalk next to him. "That someone wants me to know about Uncle Nathan's legal trouble last year. Maybe he filed a lawsuit. Maybe it has something to do with the assistant."

"But why put that as the subject, when that's not what it's about?"

Mari thought about it for a moment. Then she snapped her fingers and looked up into his eyes again. "They wanted to make sure I opened it. I've been asking around. I know my sisters have, too, and you have. They sent it to me because I'm the oldest."

Her eyes widened. "Do you think it's a warning? Are they telling me to back off?"

Dexter's eyes narrowed as much as hers had widened. After a moment, he shook his head. "You know, I don't really think so. I think they are just trying to tell you more about your Uncle Nathan. And yes, it has to be someone who knew about the assistant, and your interest in finding him. I don't see how urging you to look into your uncle's past could be a threat."

He handed the paper back to her. She held up her hand. "You keep it and study it. Maybe something will occur to you that I've missed."

Dexter looked down at the paper, nodding. He folded it up in two quarters and shoved it in the big pocket of his tennis shorts. He immediately took it back out. "Maybe you should take it and hold it for me. It might come out while I'm playing. I don't want to miss a shot chasing after it."

"Are you joining me for dinner tonight?" Mari asked. The look in her eyes sent warmth through Dexter's body. He smiled at her, leaning over and daring to put a soft kiss on her lips. She responded with a soft one in return. He was amazed by how kissable her lips were. He kept himself from going full on with the kiss. It was too soon.

He wanted to be on his first date with her before he went that far – well, second, if you counted the night he'd just spent with her. He hadn't kissed her the night before; not for the whole night. He was amazed at his own restraint, and could only hope she knew he was doing it out of respect for her, and not because she wasn't wanted.

She never gave him any indication he was doing something wrong. She seemed as enamored with him as he was with her.

"Of course, I'm coming to dinner."

"Yay." Mari used a small girl voice, and clapped just her fingers together. He chuckled, running one hand down her cheek. They stared into each other's eyes for a moment, before Brian's voice finally broke through to them.

"Dexter! It's been ten minutes. Let's play!"

"You're too anxious for a game of tennis, bro. I'll be over there in a minute."

"Ah!" Brian lifted his racket and swung it at Dexter, shaking his head. Dexter knew he wasn't serious by the relaxed look on his brother's face. Brian turned around and headed back to the gazebo.

Dexter looked back down at Mari. The desire for him danced like flames in her eyes. He was overwhelmed with passion and lowered his head to press his lips against hers.

127

She responded with just as much warmth. They kissed until they couldn't breathe, and had to come up for air. When he did, Dexter's heart was pounding so hard, he knew she would be able to hear it.

"That was very nice," she said, her eyes burning with a craving that made his body ache.

"Just nice?" he teased, whispering against her lips. He was cupping her face in his big hands, holding her so she could not pull back even if she wanted to. And she didn't want to. Of that, he was sure.

"I said *very* nice," Mari repeated, emphasizing the very. "And it was. I'm so… so glad you finally did that, Dex. I've been waiting for it for so long. All night last night, I hoped you would kiss me, but you never did."

Dexter shook his head. "You were almost full-on drunk last night, Mari. I could never take advantage of you like that. I have too much respect for you. But trust me, I wanted to. I really did."

Mari smiled. He could feel her breath against his skin when she spoke, and it gave him chills up and down his spine.

"I really wanted you to, too," she said, quietly.

He pressed in for another kiss, wrapping his arms around her and holding her to him. They were broken up once more by the sound of Brian's voice, and the rapping of his racket on the net.

"Hey! Break it up or get a room! Come on, Dex!"

Dexter was annoyed with his brother at that point. He glared across the court at him.

"Do I interrupt you during important business, Bri? I can just leave, you know." He used a threatening tone. Brian's eyebrows shot up.

"You're gonna leave and not finish our set? That's not like you. You never want to miss the last set."

"Oh, is this the last set?"

Brian smiled. "It is if you say it is, bro. Come on."

Dexter sighed. His brother was right. He hated to leave the court with unfinished games. It stuck under his skin until he could rectify the situation. At times, in the past, he was calling his brother at 2 am, telling him to get to the court, they were going to settle whatever game they had left undone.

"I do hate to miss the last set. We didn't get to finish our game."

Mari nodded. "I would love to stand back here and watch you finish the game, Dexter. Then, maybe, we can have a late lunch or an early dinner. You don't have to come to a formal dinner with my sisters tonight. It could just be the two of us."

It was the first time Dexter had heard that Sue and Lynn were even supposed to be at the dinner. He grinned. He should have realized his mistake, when Mari asked him if he wanted to have dinner at the resort. She hadn't specified whether her sisters would be there, but Dexter assumed they wouldn't. He began to question whether she thought of the dinner as a real date or not. Perhaps she just said that to get him to help her find this mysterious assistant.

Dexter shook his head, clearing his thoughts. He was definitely overthinking things. He leaned forward and pressed his lips firmly on hers. "You can stay right out here, or go on over there to the gazebo and sit with Laura. You might as well." He looked directly in her eyes. "You'll probably be seeing her a lot more now."

Mari grinned at him.

Chapter 20

In all the excitement of getting the email, Mari had almost forgotten about the confession of pregnancy from Brittany. She thought about it as she watched Dexter play two more games with his brother. She'd been immensely relieved when she came out to see that it was Brian he was playing against.

She chided herself for the moment of jealousy and anxiety she'd felt. The budding relationship between the two felt like unexplored land to her. She wasn't used to putting her trust in a man. No one other than her father, who was an upstanding individual that she respected, loved, and looked up to. She and her sisters were raised by a man with loving hands, who allowed them the freedom to try new things, but warned them of consequences should they make a mistake.

Their mother had been somewhat firmer with them, but she was proud that she grew up in a functional homelife, instead of some of the traumatic experiences she'd heard from friends growing up.

Mari watched Dexter moving gracefully across the court, pounding back the tennis ball almost every time. He and his brother were very skilled. They could have the ball lobbing back and forth for almost ten minutes on a good run, if not longer.

She was about to leave when Laura plopped down on the bench next to her. She flashed a brilliant smile at Mari.

"Hey, honey!" She said, right before wrapping her arms around Mari's shoulders and giving her a hug. "I didn't see you sitting over here until just now. You should have come to sit with me."

Mari gave the young woman a warm smile. "I just thought I'd rest here. It's a long walk from my office to here. I needed to rest my feet."

"I understand. Well, I've been doing nothing but sitting around all afternoon. I didn't mind walking around. I hope it's okay that I sit with you."

Mari was astonished by the tone Laura was using with her. She came from one of the richest families in Queen Anne and the near town of St. Simons Island. Most of the women in her elite class looked down on Mari, as if she was paid help.

Laura must have recognized the look of surprise on Mari's face, because she straightened her arms and grasped the bench under her with both of them. She leaned over and tapped shoulders with Mari.

"I know what you're thinking. I know you are trying to get together with Dexter. I don't blame you. I would, too, if I wasn't already in love with his brother."

Mari didn't know how to take Laura's words. From her tone, she meant no malice. But taken in another context, she might be suspicious that Mari was only in it for Dexter's prestige and money. Mari licked her lips, debating how to take it. She was about to respond when Laura cleared it up for her. The woman turned her head and stared out at her husband and his brother.

"Dexter needs a woman like you in his life, Mari," she said, thoughtfully. "He is such a good guy. Underneath that tough exterior is a hurting man. Yes, he's really hurting."

Laura sounded sad. Mari was immediately curious about where this conversation was going. She leaned over so she was pushing Laura back with her own shoulder. Laura giggled and pushed back so they were rocking back and forth.

"What do you mean, he's hurting?" Mari asked. Laura gave her a sorrowful look.

"I suppose he hasn't told you anything very deep or personal yet, has he?"

Mari shook her head, her eyes focused on Laura's. If she heard anything derogatory about Dexter's past, she might be hurt. She would rather not know. She didn't stop Laura, though, and the woman continued.

"I won't be able to go into much detail. I'm sure when he's comfortable, he'll tell you all about his past. He's been hurt, honey, and you have to remember that, if you're going to love him."

Mari glanced out at Dexter, who had just noticed them sitting together. He was about to serve and lifted his racket up to wave at them. They both waved back.

Mari turned her eyes back to Laura. "Tell me what happened to him," she said. "I have to know, now that you've mentioned it."

Laura shook her head. "I can't tell you his life, Mari. You need to hear it from his perspective; not from a friend's. I can tell you that it left Dexter feeling pretty raw when it comes to relationships. So, if he's willing to get close to you and tell you about himself, you've gotten over that wall, and that's pretty amazing."

Mari had no idea Dexter was so reserved. He'd been friendly and funny whenever they were together. His charm and his good looks were all he needed to get by in life. Thank God he had a good heart, too. And from the sound of Laura's opinion, it was a sensitive one. Dexter didn't want to be hurt.

Realizing this made her heart grow larger with warmth for him. She didn't want to admit it was love beating in her heart. It was too soon.

Or was it?

Maybe she could risk it all, just like she told her sister she would do, and admit that she loved him.

The thought was daunting. She felt an overwhelming sensation of fear. He would turn tail and run if she told him how much she adored him, and wanted to spend all her time with him; how she thought of him nearly every minute of the day and relished every moment they had together.

Now she was convinced she should keep it to herself, for now. She would know when the time was right.

"I don't know what to say in response to that," Mari said, bluntly. She turned her head to the side and smiled at Laura.

"Well, do you have feelings for him? It certainly looks like you do."

Mari thought about the amazing kisses Dexter had given her, before rejoining his brother on the court. Her cheeks flushed and she bit her bottom lip.

"Oh, I see that look," Laura said, knowingly, nodding her pretty blond head. She pointed a finger at Mari, before turning it down to tap on Mari's leg. "You are in love with him already." Laura laughed delightedly. "Oh, what joy! I am so glad. You are perfect for him."

Mari's eyebrows shot up. "Why do you say that?"

Laura pulled back a little, giving Mari a look of surprised amusement. She held her arms out wide, taking in all of Mari. "Well, look at you, girl! You're amazing! You've got that pretty hair and those eyes, a nice little body, and a cute little tush, I gotta say." Mari laughed aloud when Laura winked low at her. Laura joined her laughter and continued.

"Why, you have all the money you need, so you won't have to rely on a man to keep you going. You have a head for business and stuff like that. Girl, you have what you need and don't need a man. That's the kind of woman Dexter needs. The kind he deserves. Plus, he feels the same way about you."

The kisses flashed through Mari's mind once more. So passionate and warm, so full of desire. Even though they were so loving, hearing the reassuring words of Laura made it even more real to her.

"I... I hope we get together. We have a dinner date tonight."

Laura's delightful laugh filled the air once more. She squeezed Mari's knee joyfully. "That's wonderful. Do you know where you're going?"

"I don't think we're going anywhere. We're eating here. We were going to have a family dinner, but I think I'd rather just be with Dexter. You know?"

Laura nodded vigorously. "Oh, yes, I do, honey. You bet. I

would want to be with the man of my dreams, all alone, whenever possible." Laura lifted her shoulders and giggled. "And now I am! It's so wonderful!"

Mari felt instant affection for the little blond woman in front of her. She was such an adorable little pixie woman. "I'm so happy for you, Laura. Married one day. Amazing. You'll be blessed for many, many more to come, I'm sure of it."

Laura grabbed her hand and squeezed. "What a sweet thing to say, Mari. You truly are a sweetheart. I'm glad to know you, and I'm glad Dexter found you. It's wonderful. It really is."

"Thanks, Laura. You're a really sweet girl."

Laura swung her arm around Mari's back and held on to her shoulder. "We're going to be good friends, you and I," she said in a confident tone. "I can see it now, you and me, fighting battles for our husbands, keeping our kids safe. Can you imagine it?"

Mari laughed. "It's kind of hard not to," she said. "Every time I mention anything about me and Dexter these days, people have us married or married with kids already. We haven't even had our official first date yet!"

Laura lifted her eyebrows in surprise. "You haven't? Well, what would you call last night? I know he stayed in your suite."

"Yeah, but he slept on my couch. It's a great big thing. Incredibly comfortable."

Laura shook her head. She lowered her voice and leaned her head closer to Mari. "I didn't imply you slept together, Mari. Surely you don't think a date is only official if you do *that*." She clucked her tongue in a motherly way. "Either that, or you think that's the way *I* would take it." She sounded, but didn't look, offended.

Mari shook her head back and forth as she spoke. "No, no, Laura. I just thought. I mean, he was there last night to pro…" she stopped. She hadn't mentioned the mysterious stranger to Laura. She hadn't seen a need to speak to either Brian or Laura about anything on their first day of being married. She sure wasn't going to throw in anything to muck up their happy honeymoon.

Besides, they were at her resort and she wanted them to have fun. The mysterious man was her responsibility and, by default, Dexter's. But he wasn't on his honeymoon, so Mari didn't feel it should bother him too much.

She watched the men finishing up their game, playing furiously to see who would win the last match. Finally, Dexter lobbed it over his brother's head and it landed once inside the lines and jetted away from Brian's racket, shooting across to the other side of the court.

"Ah!" Brian raged. He lifted his racket and his other fist, and shook them both at the sky, roaring like a lion. When he was done, he completely relaxed and walked toward the net to shake hands with his brother.

"Well, you beat me again, Dex. I just hate you for that."

Dexter laughed. "Don't worry, next time I'll let you win."

"You will not!" Brian said, sternly. They parted at the gate as they came out, with Dexter staying with his equipment, and Brian coming through to meet Laura on the other side. He nodded at Mari and gave her a wink as she passed him. She smiled at him.

Dexter looked at her closely as she approached. Her smile grew wide when he asked, "I'm gonna go clean up. You wanna come and watch after my balls for me?"

She laughed. "What did you say?"

He held up his sleeve of tennis balls and shook them. "You can watch my balls for me. Make sure no one steals them. Fifteen bucks for three. Don't wanna waste money."

The more he spoke, the more Mari laughed. She was going to enjoy being in love.

Chapter 21

Dexter pulled out the chair and smiled at Mari. She smiled back, sliding into the chair as he pushed it in, and settling herself comfortably. He circled the table, his eyes on her face. She was looking radiant. He couldn't believe his luck. A good woman on his arm to make up for his painful past.

While he got ready for their date, he thought about what had made him come to the decision that he never wanted to get married. He had never told Mari what happened to make him stop looking forward to marriage and a family. He had never told anyone. For an hour, he wrestled with himself. Did he want to tell her? Should he tell her?

By the time he'd left, he decided it was the night to have a heart-to-heart. He'd decided he wanted to be with her for the rest of his life, and intended to ask her to marry him. But he wasn't going to tonight. He had no ring and he wanted to see her reaction to his past before he got on one knee, which he fully intended to do.

He gazed at her over the tabletop. He was glad they'd decided to go out to eat. There were a lot of fine restaurants in Queen Anne that catered to the elite class that the location brought in. He'd spent the last few weeks scouting them out. He wanted to take Mari to all of them. She deserved to see the finer things in life. She'd been denied all those things with her meager but comfortable upbringing.

He had never felt more relaxed in his life. He always felt that way when Mari was around, despite the mysterious and difficult challenges they were facing.

Tonight, he planned to ask Mari what she was thinking about Brittany. He wasn't sure how or when to approach the topic, so they talked about normal things for a solid half hour. He asked about the business, when they would be holding another wedding, if they planned any extensions or renovations.

She didn't question his motives about wanting to know the

ins and outs of the business, and he wouldn't have had a good answer if she'd asked. He was just trying to make conversation, while he gathered the courage to ask her about it.

The first half hour went by quickly for Dexter. He enjoyed talking with her, and listening to her stories of adventure with her sisters. They were childhood adventures, and she had a humorous way of recounting the stories. He smiled as he listened and laughed often. She made him feel on top of the world.

At one point, she stopped and looked closely at him. "You've been awfully quiet so far, Dex. Are you feeling all right?"

The look of concern on her face touched him. He looked at her through soft eyes, smiling gently. "I'm fine, Mari. I just have a lot on my mind."

She returned his loving look. "We both do. So, let's talk about it."

His chest tightened with that anxious feeling he'd been getting lately. He'd never felt such intensity with a woman before. "Yes," he said in a low voice. "Let's."

She grinned. "Where should we start?"

Dexter thought about it for a second before replying, "Let's talk about my ex."

He was surprised to see a humorous look on her face. "Okay, let's. You go first."

He loved the way she put a positive spin on their discussion from the beginning. She didn't look stressed, and when he brought up Brittany, her face didn't change at all. "Are you concerned about what she's saying?"

Mari looked thoughtful. She moved her eyes around the room casually as she spoke. "I'm concerned, of course. But she's an ex-girlfriend, and I can see why. I can see why you broke up with her and I can see why you might not believe her when she says she's pregnant." She gave him a close look. "*Do* you think she's lying about it?"

Dexter nodded, immediately. "Yes. If she is pregnant, it

isn't mine, I can tell you that. It's been almost five months since the last time I was… with her. Like that." He blushed, embarrassed that he had to talk about the love life he had with Brittany, with the only woman he really cared about.

She gazed at him softly, a look he adored and was happy to see, considering their topic of conversation. "Don't be embarrassed, Dex. I have exes, too."

Dexter shook his head, sitting back in his chair and staring at his menu. "I will never understand what makes a woman think she can lie about something like that, and expect a man to just… give in to what she wants. We aren't right together, and I don't even like her anymore, as a person. You know what I'm saying?"

"I know exactly what you're saying."

They both looked up when a server approached the table. "Good evening," he said. "My name's Josh. I'll be your server tonight. Would you like to hear about our specials?"

Mari looked over the table at him. "I've never been here before, Dex. I'm going to let you order for me, if you would?"

Dexter raised one eyebrow. He searched the back of his mind to see if she'd ever told him what kind of food she liked the most.

"Do you have any allergies?" He asked.

The look of delight that crossed Mari's face confused him. "I don't. But thank you for asking!"

Dexter chuckled and looked at the server. He lifted the menu and pointed at the dish he wanted. "We'll have two of these, a bottle of your best wine, and rolls." He looked at Mari. "Do you want an appetizer?"

She nodded. Her eyes were intently watching his face. He could feel them as if they were bright beacons of light shining on him. He ordered salads and soups for them both. Josh nodded, took the menus, thanked them, and left the table.

"So…" Mari drew out the word slowly. "What did you get for me?"

Dexter grinned. "You'll have to wait and see. I don't know any woman who doesn't like that particular dish. You're not vegetarian, are you?"

Mari laughed, a soft sound that melted Dexter's heart. He leaned forward, stretching one arm out on the table and resting his hand close to her water glass. She immediately reached out and placed her hand over his, which was exactly what he wanted her to do. "If I was a vegetarian, Babe, I would have told you."

He nodded. "Good. So, where were we?"

"Discussing your lying girlfriend. I think…"

"Ex," Dexter cut in.

She pressed her lips together. "Yes. Ex-girlfriend. Sorry."

He chuckled. "Continue, Honey."

"We need to prove she's lying about that. I don't know how we could ever get away from her if we don't. She'll be pressing you for a paternity test."

"I'd happily take a paternity test," Dexter said quickly. His medical past gave him some confidence in the matter, as well as the fact that Brittany did not look as pregnant as she would have to be, for the child to be his.

"Do you think she's been with anyone else since you broke up with her?"

Dexter looked across the restaurant, crossing his arms over his chest. "You know, I really can't say. I never thought of her as a slutty woman. She wasn't obsessed with sex. I never thought she was cheating. So…" he shrugged. "I just don't know. If she is pregnant, all I know is that it isn't mine."

Mari looked thoughtful. She was gazing down at their hands. He turned his hand over and folded his fingers around hers. She looked up at him with the most loving look he'd ever seen.

"Tell me your idea, Mari." She made talking about this difficult situation so much easier. Her calm, sweet demeanor eased the pain he was feeling, from Brittany's lies and his past.

"Do you happen to know who her OB/GYN is?"

Dexter's eyebrows shot up. He blinked a few times, trying to remember if she'd ever mentioned that to him. A name came to his mind, and he realized why he would remember something like that.

He nodded, looking directly at Mari. "Actually, I do."

She looked surprised. "You do? Like, off the top of your head?"

He laughed. "Yeah, and there's a reason why. You'll understand when you hear his name."

"Well, don't keep me in suspense!" Mari's voice was anxious. "What is it?"

"His name is Dr. Jeffrey Harms. Dr. Harms."

Mari laughed. "No. Oh, no. I don't think I could do it. Is he an OB/GYN or just her gyno?"

"I think that's her gynecologist. Will that help?"

"I don't know. I'll check it out."

Dexter sat forward, squeezing her hand. "What are you planning?"

"I'm going to make an appointment with the doctor," she replied, looking in his eyes. "To see if I'm pregnant." She giggled.

Dexter's grin spread across his face. "Uh oh. Am I going to have two pregnant women on my hands?"

Mari's laugh was delightful to his ears. "Not unless God made me the new Mary. And I don't think there's a possibility of that. So…"

They both laughed.

"What will you do once you have the appointment? You can't just ask about her."

Mari's smile was devious. "I can't? Why not?"

"Isn't there a doctor/patient privilege somewhere there?"

Mari winked at him. "I'll find a way. Don't worry about that."

"Well, well. I didn't know you had a mischievous side. Who's going to keep me in line if you are just as bad as me?"

"Oh, you'll do fine," she replied. "I'm not mischievous all the time. We'll balance each other out."

Dexter wanted, at that very moment, to tell her he loved her.

But not yet.

Chapter 22

Mari was feeling a little nervous, but was unsure of why, as she stepped out of the car. She was at the clinic, and would be getting a pregnancy test done, that she already knew the answer to. It was exciting, as well as nerve-wracking. She wasn't a liar, though she did her fair share of acting when she was in high school.

She'd made an appointment under a false name and could only hope no one recognized her. She hadn't gone to the clinic since coming to the resort, but her picture had been in the paper when she and her sisters took ownership of the place.

Thoughts ran through her mind like a whirlwind as she went toward the large hospital. The clinic was in an adjacent building, connected by a long hallway to the main facility. The building itself was 12 stories tall, stretching up into the sky, looking like it was touching the clouds. It dwarfed the clinic, which was only one story high.

Every time Mari passed the hospital, she thought the clinic looked like a small foot sticking out. She wished they would add a similar building to the other side of the hospital. It would look just like a building with two feet. What a meme she could make out of that!

She caught herself laughing at her thoughts as she crossed the parking lot, looking both ways and hurrying past a car that had slowed to let her cross. She waved at the woman in the car, who lifted the fingers of her hand on the steering wheel in return.

She pulled open the door and went inside the building, feeling a sweep of cool air brush over her. She had only been in the clinic once before. It was smaller than she was used to, but Queen Anne wasn't a big town, either. It was still considered a village. Most of the people who lived there were just glad to have a hospital. The nearest was much too far away, and the town council had petitioned the elite who came to Queen Anne and the Emerald Resort to invest in the Queen Anne Hospital and Clinic.

The council had the money they needed in less than a month. That was the power of the Emerald Resort. Nathan had made sure of that.

She checked in at the front desk, and sat down until her "name" was called. She knew she would have to fill out paperwork, if she decided to stay for the unnecessary cost of just seeing the doctor. What information would she put on there? It made her nervous to put false information down. She felt like she was in too deep to get out, though.

She looked to her side, at the small table that connected the row of chairs she sat in to the next row of chairs. There were several magazines spread across the surface. She picked one up and began to flip through it. She didn't see any of the words, or even the pictures. She was inside her mind, thinking about how she was going to find out what she needed.

She heard her name and looked up at the woman behind the desk. She set the magazine aside and went to greet her.

"Ms. Greer. We have these papers for you to fill out so we can get your history from your other place of residence."

"Okay, thanks." She took the forms from the woman and an idea popped in her head. She leaned forward and spoke in the friendliest tone she could. "I was referred here by my sister. Well, she's not really my sister, I'm going out with her brother and we've gotten close." Mari waved her hand in the air dismissively. "She said Dr. Harms is her obstetrician. Her name is Brittany. Brittany Langley."

She was actually surprised by how easily she got exactly what she'd come for. The receptionist's eyebrows shot up. She swiveled in her chair, and looked at another woman behind the glass that kept the staff from being exposed to the germs floating around in the lobby.

"Claire. You hear anything about Brittany Langley being pregnant?"

Claire shook her head, making her long curly black hair shake back and forth. "No, ma'am. She's due in for a checkup any day now, though."

Mari dropped her eyes to the woman's nametag and read it. She looked back up when the woman swiveled back to her. "No, she's just a regular patient here. I don't think she's pregnant."

Mari raised her eyebrows, trying to imitate being haughty like some of the women she'd seen at the resort. "Oh, dear, I must be thinking about someone else. She said she's about five months along already."

Sophia shook her head. "No, Brittany would have come here, I'm sure."

"Hmmm. I would have sworn it was Britt." She looked up at the ceiling as if pondering it. "Well, Sophia, thank you. Let me fill these out and I'll get them back to you as soon as I can."

"Thank you, Ms. Greer." The woman smiled and closed the small window they'd been speaking through. She turned to Claire again and Mari heard, clear as day, "What do you think of that? Brittany Langley, pregnant. You think she'd go to another doctor?"

Mari dropped one of the papers and bent over to pick it up as slowly as she could, so she could hear the answer.

"Nope," Claire said promptly. "She's got an appointment this afternoon. She should be here any minute. Besides, five months? There's no way. She's always in here demanding something or another. I swear, the woman is intolerable sometimes."

Mari already felt that way about Brittany, and didn't feel the need to eavesdrop any more than she had to, so she swiped up the paper and hurried toward the bathrooms located on one side of the clinic. She slipped into the women's restroom and looked around. It was empty.

Her heart was pounding.

She wouldn't say she was exactly afraid of Brittany, but the thought of a sure confrontation made her nervous. She wasn't the fighting type at all. She hadn't had to fight growing up. She didn't have a lot to live on, but she never wanted for anything, either.

She had no doubt Brittany would likely come to blows with her if she saw her. The woman had very little class, for having so much wealth. Money didn't buy manners, apparently.

She looked up at the ceiling, praying for some guidance; and if not guidance, then at least courage. She felt like the cowardly lion. She went to the mirror, folding the papers up and sliding them in her purse. She looked in the mirror, into her own eyes.

"All right, Mari," she said to herself. "You can do this. It's just a little embarrassing. Well, not really. These ladies don't know what's going on. And one of them didn't seem to like Brittany, anyway. Maybe neither of them did." She shrugged. "Could be, right?"

She didn't expect her reflection to answer, so when it didn't, she scrunched up her face and pressed her pinky gently into her lower lid, to satisfy a small itch. She wiped away what looked like a stray eyelash.

She breathed slowly, trying to calm herself down. She obviously couldn't stay. How could she possibly have made an appointment at the very same time as Brittany? How crazy was that?

She shook her head, staring at herself for another moment. "You can do it," she whispered softly.

Mari turned from the mirror, after pinching a stray curl back from her forehead. She straightened her shoulders, looked at the door, and pulled in a deep breath.

She marched to the door and swung it open.

She immediately swung it shut again. At that very moment, Brittany was coming through the entrance doors.

Her heart raced and she pressed her back against the door. What could she do? Would the receptionists say something to Brittany immediately? She clutched her purse to her chest and jogged to the first stall. She went in and closed the door behind her.

A few seconds later, the door to the bathroom opened and someone came in. There had been a few other patients waiting to be called back. It could be one of them. She heard the woman go to the mirrors and stand in silence, which usually meant they were on their phone or staring in the mirror, as she had done.

"Hello?" the woman's voice echoed through the bathroom.

It was Brittany.

Mari dropped her head back in exasperation. Of course! It was like God wanted her to get caught for her misdeeds.

"Yeah, I'm here. I just signed in. No one was at the reception desk, which I thought was weird, but I only had to sign my name. My appointment isn't for, like, twenty minutes." She was silent, as she listened to the person on the other side.

Mari pushed her palms against her forehead. She desperately wanted to get up on the toilet seat, but if it made any noise, she would be given away. She didn't want Brittany to realize there was someone else in the bathroom. She could only pray the doors were low enough to hide her feet.

She was frozen in place from fear, anyway, even if she wanted to risk it. For all she knew, Brittany had a gun in that little purse of hers.

"Yeah, I know. But I don't care." Silence. "I said no, I do *not* care! She can tag along like a little doggie anywhere she wants to, but Dex is mine. He was before, and he will be again. I'm gonna get that little tramp away from him somehow." Silence. "Well, I told him I was pregnant, with his baby."

This time the pause was extensive. Mari wished Brittany would just go in a stall or leave the bathroom. She would prefer the stall because she would be out the door as quickly and quietly as she could be. She prayed it wouldn't be the stall directly to her left or right, or she'd be making a mad dash to the door.

She would probably be making a mad dash to it, regardless. She wanted out. Now.

She felt relief flood through her when she heard Brittany

moving toward one of the far stalls.

"Of course, I'm not," Brittany said. "But he doesn't have to know that. I'll tell him I miscarried or something."

Mari heard the click of the door as Brittany locked herself in.

She felt another sweep of relief when she realized she hadn't pushed the lock on her stall door. It was just pushed closed. She pressed her fingertips around the edge as quietly as possible, and squeezed her eyes shut, willing the door not to squeak.

It was stunningly silent as it swung open, allowing her to hightail it on her tip toes to the door. She went through, and was grateful there was someone at both the check in and check out desks, drawing the staff's attention away from her.

Mari crossed the room at lightning speed, not looking around. She didn't care if the other patients were giving her strange looks. She had to get out of there.

She pushed through the entrance doors and stepped out into the sunlight, feeling an immense weight lift off her shoulders. She wasn't quite home free yet, so she speed-walked across the parking lot to her car, fumbling in her purse for her keys. At the same time, she pulled out her cell phone and stopped it from recording.

Chapter 23

Her heart calmed after she left the parking lot, and she almost immediately pulled into the lot of the fast food restaurant across the street. She sat in her car, which she'd backed into a spot facing the building. She lifted her elbow to rest on the windowsill and covered her mouth with her hand. She stared toward the clinic across the street.

She lifted her phone with the other hand and looked down at the screen. A few taps from her thumb brought up the recording she'd just made. She looked down at the screen until it started, and then raised her eyes to stare blankly at the front of the restaurant.

She listened to the entire conversation between herself and the receptionist. If there was one thing Mari was sure of, it was that the ladies would mention her to Brittany. They probably already had. Right at that moment, Brittany was seething.

Mari figured that Brittany had only told Dexter, who in turn would tell Mari. Even if she'd let a few friends in on the scheme, like the one on the phone, it wouldn't have been any of them trying to find proof she was lying. It could only be her inquiring about it, and Brittany knew that.

She ran her hand through her hair, nervous again, but confident that she had done what was needed to prove that Brittany was a liar. Once she gave the recording to Dexter, he would have the proof he needed to get out from under her thumb, and could threaten to expose her to everyone by releasing a recording of her phone conversation on the Internet. Everyone would see what she really was.

Nervousness slid through Mari, thinking about the impact of something being revealed like that. It made her all the more thankful she'd been a good girl most of her life. She didn't set out to hurt anyone else, and had a live-and-let-live attitude.

She was suddenly drawn from her thoughts when she spotted someone coming out of the restaurant. Chills covered her body. It was the assistant. The mystery man she'd been looking for. She sat up straight in her car, and then ducked down in the seat. He had to walk at an angle past her car, but there was no reason for him to look in her direction.

She raised up just enough to look over the dashboard. He was walking away from her, toward a row of cars to her right. She pushed up a little further, her breathing shallow, as if he might hear her and turn around.

Her heart thumped in her chest. She was feeling more and more like a private investigator. It was invigorating. She turned off the recording on her phone by tapping the back button, and turned her car back on.

Wherever he was going, she was following.

The man got in a small blue Chevy and pulled out a few moments later. She crept along behind him, paying close attention to which direction he was going. She went to a different exit of the parking lot and waited until he pulled out, so she could pull out behind him.

She stayed in the other lane, watching for his turn signal. She'd slipped on her sunglasses, so if he saw her, he wouldn't recognize her. At least, that was what she was hoping. She turned when he did, and was able to stay a safe distance behind him.

Eventually, he pulled into a dark alley. Mari was instantly terrified to follow him into the alley. If he knew he was being followed and lured her in there, she was in a great deal of danger. She would be trapped in there, between two tall apartment buildings.

She drove past slowly, her eyes peering down the alley, while still trying to look innocent.

The man got out of his vehicle not far into the alley, and was heading away from the entrance. From the brief moment she saw him, he was walking fast, and was looking down at what appeared to be his keys.

Mari blinked rapidly, her heart beating fast. She looked down the street, trying to come up with a good plan. What could she do now?

She turned the car around and went back toward the alley. On impulse, she pulled over on the side of the street and parked the car. She got out, looked both ways, and crossed to the other side of the street. There were a few people walking up and down the populated street. Small shops lined the side across from the apartment buildings. Most of the customers were probably residents who just walked across the street.

She got to the alley and stopped. It felt like ice was pumping through her veins. She was terrified. She peeked around the corner quickly. She didn't care if she looked like an idiot. The man could be dangerous if she actually confronted him.

She took a step back and looked at the sign hanging above her. It said, "Ridgewood Apartments". She went to the front door, but it was locked tight. A box next to the front door had a speaker with a button, but she didn't dare push it. She had no excuse for going in.

She went back to the alley and looked around. She inhaled sharply when she saw the man was returning to his car. Panic swept through her. The small parking lot between the two buildings was hidden from the street. It made it look like it was another one-way alley. But the road was merely an entrance to a large lot between the buildings for residents to park.

If he pulled out, he might see her.

Mari wasn't leaving yet. She would get his license plate number. Maybe Dexter knew someone on the police force who could help them out.

She didn't hear a car start, and dared to look around the corner again. The man was halfway in his car on the passenger side, obviously digging for something he'd lost. He pulled out and stood up straight, slamming the car door in frustration. He stomped back toward the door he'd already entered.

Mari's heart jumped into her throat. Now was the time.

She ran as quietly as possible to the door and, inhaling deep and holding her breath, pulled it open. The man was at the end of a long hallway, and turned to the right, disappearing from her sight.

150

She went in and closed the door quietly behind her. She walked softly across the carpeted floor, somewhat surprised by the clean and pleasant state of the interior, despite the rough exterior. The walls were a pure bright white, and every few feet, sconces held brilliant bulbs in elaborate light fixtures.

She got to the end of the hall and looked around, just in time to see the man go into one of the apartments.

She turned back and pressed herself against the wall, willing her heart to calm down. Now, all she had to do was casually walk past the door and note the number. An address was better than anything else.

Taking a deep breath, Mari turned the corner. As she walked, she repeated the phrase "Don't come out, don't come out", over and over. He would recognize her if he did. She got to the door, glanced at the number 6 and continued walking, just a little faster.

She got to the end of the hallway and turned to the right, seeing a glass door at the end of the hallway with a bright red EXIT sign hanging above it. Releasing some nervous energy, she took off in a dead run.

She was out of breath by the time she got to the door, but not because it was a long way. She could barely breathe because of her fear that he would know who she was.

She was just about to go out the door when she had another idea. She turned back around and looked toward the hallway she had just left. There was another hallway in the distance, running parallel to it, and two double doors at the end, like the one she was standing in front of now.

She reoriented herself, and realized she was about to exit the back of the building. If she went in the other direction to the double doors, they would let her out into the front lobby.

Where the mailboxes were.

Mailboxes with names on them.

She decided she would never have another chance like this.

She jogged softly on the carpet, her slip-on shoes making absolutely no sound, whatsoever. She passed the hallway where the man lived and glanced down it. There was no one there. She jogged a little faster to the double doors, and felt immense relief when she opened one of them easily and slipped through.

She tried to catch her breath when she reached the other side, but she wasn't done yet. Her spying was still in full swing.

She put one hand on her chest, over her slamming heart, and tried to take in a deep breath. She searched the row of mail slots for each apartment. Her eyes zeroed in on number six. At the bottom was a small, rectangular, metal label holder. A name was written on a piece of paper and shoved inside.

She made a beeline for the mail box and leaned over to look at the paper. Disappointment flooded her when she only saw the initials NAW.

She felt confusion slide through her when she stood up straight. She frowned, staring at the initials. They were very similar to her uncle's.

A chill ran up her spine, when she briefly considered whether her uncle might have faked his own death.

It wasn't a possibility, though. He would have had to be a magician.

The second thought Mari had was that someone was using her uncle's identity.

That, again, was not a possibility, since everyone in Queen Anne knew who Uncle Nathan was. He was a regular on the social scene, and was beloved by many.

She backed up and turned away from the boxes. Her phone buzzed in her back pocket, vibrating against her skin. She whipped it out and saw it was Dexter calling her. What timing he had.

She was glad she had put the phone on silent before she came in. In actuality, she hadn't done it consciously. She'd just forgotten to take it *off* silent, and it had worked to her benefit that time. She didn't want to draw any extra attention to herself.

She stepped out of the building through the front door and crossed the street, in a hurry to get to her car. As she went across, she pulled her phone out and answered it.

Chapter 24

"Mari?"

She was relieved to hear his voice.

"Hey, Dex." She was suddenly overcome with emotions. Her hands started to shake, and her breathing was rapid, as she hurried to her car.

"What are you doing? Sounds like you're running a marathon. Where are you?"

"I'm getting back in my car. I have so much to tell you, Dexter. So much. We have to meet. Are you busy?"

"I have a business meeting in ten minutes, and that's going to be at least an hour long. I don't have to stay till the end, though. Is it really important? Can't you tell me now?"

Mari thought about it for a moment. She really wanted to show Dexter the recording and let him hear everything himself, instead of giving him a summary.

"Let's just say I have all the evidence you need to prove Brittany is lying about her pregnancy. But there's something else. I saw the assistant. The mystery man."

"Oh?" Mari heard trepidation in Dexter's voice. "Where?"

Everything that led up to seeing the man flooded through her mind. She couldn't possibly go over all of it on the phone in less than ten minutes. She got to her car and slid in the driver's seat.

She closed the door and locked it, sitting for a moment to relax and breathe. "I wish you didn't have to go to that meeting. It's a long story, and I want to be with you when I tell you about it. I don't want to do it over the phone."

Dexter's response sent a wave of affection through Mari. "I'm sorry, Honey, I have to go to this meeting. But I'll cut it short and come straight there. The resort?"

"Yes, please." Mari nodded, even though he couldn't see

her. She lowered her head and rubbed her forehead with her fingers. She felt a headache coming on, from the adrenaline that had pumped through her body for the last hour.

"Okay, I'll come to the study. I'll be there. I promise."

"Thank you, Dexter. I…" Mari stopped herself. She had been about to say, "I love you". That wasn't something they'd said yet. Nervousness filled her and she hurried to finish her sentence. "I can't wait to see you. I really want to tell you what I just went through."

"I'm anxious to hear about it, Mari. Trust me. I'll see you soon, okay?" She heard the affection in his voice. It filled her heart and made her feel warm inside.

"Okay. Bye."

"Bye."

The simplistic ending made Mari feel lonely when she hung up. She wanted to say so much more to him. She was on the edge of her seat, and wanted to spring forward and tell him everything, from what had happened to her, to how much she adored him. Just the sound of his voice made her feel better inside.

She started the car and pulled out, turning to the left to go in the direction of the resort.

By the time Mari was pulling into the long entrance driveway to the resort, she was feeling better. She didn't have a headache, and was feeling comfortable and confident. She glanced over the landscape, examining the tennis courts for needed repairs, and surveying the cleanliness of everything around her. From the moment she'd pulled up to the resort, she'd started training herself to look for anything that might need to be done.

She was concerned for the safety of the customers and her employees. She drove fairly slow, allowing herself time to look around. Everything looked fine. It was clean and inviting. That would keep the elites coming back and spending their money.

She turned the car into the private garage and drove to her spot.

Mari stayed in her car for a moment, making sure everything was back in her purse before getting out. When she did step out, she noticed someone lurking near the entrance to the lobby of the resort.

Whoever it was stood with their back to her, on front side of the building. She could see through the glass. It was a woman. Mari took a few steps closer. It had to be Brittany. It was definitely a woman.

Mari dropped her eyes to the woman's feet and recognized the shoes. It was Brittany.

She pulled in a deep breath, a bit of panic sliding through her. She could call her sisters. She pulled out her phone and dialed Sue's number.

"Sue?" she said as soon as her sister said "Hello". "I need you to come down to the parking lot. That woman is here and I'm gonna end up in a fight."

"What?" Sue said, confused. "You don't fight. What are you talking about?"

"It's Dexter's ex-girlfriend, Brittany," Mari hissed into the phone, not wanting to be heard. "She's gonna start a fight with me."

"Look," Sue said in a stern voice. "We are not in high school. What makes you think she's going to start a fight with you? Just be an adult and handle her, Mari."

"Sue!" Mari barked as softly as she could. "Just come down. We may not be in high school, but this woman's behavior suggests her mind never left there. I can't handle her, but I know you can. Come down here!"

"I'll send someone down," Sue said. "I'm not anywhere near the main building. I'm out at the swimming pools. It will take me twenty minutes to get to you and…"

"Okay, okay," Mari said. "Just send someone down. I'm not going to hide from her, but when she sees me, I know she will pick a fight."

"How do you know that?"

Mari rolled her eyes. "It's a long story. Just send someone. Please."

"Okay."

Mari pulled the phone away from her ear and clicked the end button.

She looked up in time to see that Brittany had turned around. She was staring at her through the two sets of glass between them. Mari pulled in a deep breath and began to walk to the entrance. Her heartbeat sped up when Brittany came around the corner. She had an angry look on her face, but Mari expected that.

"Mari Wright!" Brittany exclaimed, as if surprised to see her.

Mari raised her eyebrows, attempting to look more confident than she felt. "Brittany Langley. May I ask what you're doing here?"

"May I ask why you pried information out of receptionists at my doctor's office?"

Mari let out a short laugh. "Brittany, if you don't know the answer to that, you must be dumber than a box of rocks."

Brittany's face turned white. Her eyes widened in shock. Mari wondered if the woman had ever been insulted before. And in Mari's opinion, what she said was an extremely mild insult.

"How dare you?"

Mari snorted. "Look, Brittany, you are not a southern belle. You've been lying to Dexter about being pregnant. Since Dex and I are dating, I wanted to find out if it was true. I'm not going to let you get away with forcing him into some kind of relationship with you. How did you plan to skirt the paternity test?"

Brittany's eyes narrowed in anger. "You won't have him, Mari. I will get him back. One way or another, I will get him back."

Mari's eyebrows shot up. "Is that a threat? Are you

threatening us?"

Brittany looked a bit confused.

"Exactly what does 'one way or another' mean?" Mari snapped at her. She wouldn't put up with being threatened by someone, just because they had a lot of money and social status to throw around. Mari's reputation was solid with the people that mattered. Brittany's, not so much.

"I'll get him back," Brittany repeated. "He loves me. I know he does."

Suddenly Mari felt sorry for the woman in front of her. She must have terribly low self-esteem to try stunts like that, just to have a man who clearly doesn't want her.

"Can I ask you a question?" Mari kept her voice as level as possible. Brittany stared at her for a moment. She suspected she'd confused the woman with her calm demeanor.

"What could you possibly have to ask me?" Brittany snapped.

"What has Dexter done that makes you think he still wants you?" Mari intentionally left the question open. If Brittany wanted to make up a lie, now would be the time to do it. Mari's only real intention was to keep Brittany from any fighting or drama, until someone came to get her out of this situation.

Brittany appeared to be thinking about the question. "I know he does," she finally said. "Because he's always telling me so in texts and on the phone. Even these last few days... he's... he's been..."

She stopped when Mari started shaking her head. "You have some texts to show to me as proof?" Mari asked.

Brittany looked aghast, her face going pale again.

"I think you have a circulatory problem, Brittany," Mari said. "You keep losing all the blood in your face. Better watch that blood pressure. We might be young, but you never know."

Brittany looked enraged. Her eyebrows drew together, and

suddenly she looked very unattractive. Mari took a step back. Her sarcasm had not helped the situation. She regretted it, but it was too late.

"Don't patronize me, Mari Wright!" Brittany shrieked. "You think he's yours, but you'll find out that his heart belongs to me. I was destined to be his wife. It can't be any other way."

Mari was feeling a bit disheartened. If Brittany was this adamant about it, it seemed almost impossible to get rid of her.

"It just isn't going to happen, Brittany," Mari said calmly, glancing at the elevator doors inside the lobby when they slid open. She saw a security guard step off and head in their direction. Breathing a sigh of relief, she looked back at Brittany.

Brittany spun around to see what Mari had been looking at. She turned back abruptly. Now her face was red with rage. "Are you having me thrown off this property, Ms. Wright? Do you know what I will do to your reputation, if you have the gall to force me from this resort? I have a lot of friends. I suggest you take that into account before you make any rash decisions."

Mari thought about it for a moment. She experienced a slight sense of fear, before she remembered that Dexter was on her side one-hundred percent. He would rebut anything Brittany had to say about her or him, and he would be believed. The people of the resort and Queen Anne might not know Mari that well, but they knew Dexter.

The door swung open and the big, burly security guard approached. His eyes were set on Mari as he stomped up to them.

"Ms. Wright? Are you all right, ma'am?"

Mari kept her eyes on Brittany, who was staring right back at her.

"I'm fine, Grady," she said in a firm voice. "I just need this young woman escorted off the property, please. She is causing an unnecessary nuisance."

Brittany's jaw dropped, and she made a squeaking sound of outrage in the back of her throat. Grady took hold of her shoulder and roughly turned her toward the front gate.

"Don't touch me!" Brittany screamed, slapping at him. He lifted both hands in the air.

"I just need to make sure you leave the property, ma'am. I won't touch you unless I have to."

"You don't ever have to touch me!" she shrieked, glaring at Mari over her shoulder. "This isn't the last time you'll see me, Mari Wright. We are going to have this out, once and for all. You will see that Dexter is meant to be with me! You will see!"

"Yes, yes, let's go, Ms. Langley."

Mari thought it funny the guard knew Brittany's name. They must have met a few times in the past. Probably under the same circumstances.

Chapter 25

Checking her watch, Mari noticed nearly twenty minutes had passed. She calculated in her mind how long it should take for Dexter to get there. She wanted to talk to him as soon as possible. She wished he was already there.

As she went inside and hurried to her office, she had the sudden urge to go to one of the kitchens and see if any lunch snacks were left over. It was a good way for her to check on the staff, and make sure they were happy and didn't need anything.

It was also an extra opportunity to grill them on the presence of the mysterious assistant.

Mari passed through the swinging doors into the kitchen. She looked to see who the head chef for the day was, and was pleased to see Connie at the helm. She raised one hand in greeting. It was immediately returned.

"Mari! Are you hungry?" Connie tilted her head to the side, and asked the question as if she were speaking to a little girl.

Mari laughed. "I am, actually. How did you know?"

Connie laughed with her. "You only come in here when you're hungry. At least at this time of day. I've noticed it's almost like a pattern for you."

Mari was surprised. She hadn't noticed she was doing it.

"And you probably want to ask me some questions about the resort and the secret passages and the assistant, too, right?"

Mari's eyebrows shot up. "How could you possibly know that?"

Connie continued her laughter. "Because I watch and observe. I hear things. I know you're curious. I know you found the passage in the cloak room. And you've been asking about that assistant since you heard about him."

Mari stayed calm. "Are you going to tell me anything I don't already know?"

Connie moved to the refrigerator and pulled out a plate with plastic wrap covering it. "I saved this for you. We made a special chicken lunch today and I know you like these things, so I put it in the fridge for you."

Mari was pleasantly surprised. She smiled wide. "Well, thank you, Connie. That was really thoughtful of you."

"I'll heat it up and you can take it to your study, if you want."

"Wow, that's really sweet of you. I'd like that." Mari was feeling more and more upbeat, the longer she spent in the presence of her friend and head chef.

"Will Mr. Scofield be joining you? There are a few other plates."

Mari was impressed. She looked at Connie through admiring eyes. "Why do you keep the food like that? Just for us?"

"I keep them for anyone who might be going without. Queen Anne is small, but it has its fair share of the poorer side of life. I, myself, make a good living here. I live in a nice house with my husband and kids. But there are a lot of people around here, and in other places, that don't. I give them these plates."

Mari looked down at it. Through the plastic, she could see a healthy serving each of green beans, corn, bread rolls, slices of chicken breast on top of some leafy greens, with little sauce cups to the side, held in place by the plastic wrap.

"Well, this is a full meal. I'll take one for him, and if he doesn't eat it, I'll eat it later. I have a microwave in my study. I'll heat them up there. Thank you again, Connie."

Connie nodded. "I love to help out whenever I can, and this is the only way I really know how." She gave Mari a friendly smile. "And don't worry, the food that is sent to people in the village or over in St. Simons, is all put on plates that I purchase myself. I'm not stealing them from the resort."

Mari lifted her eyebrows. "I wasn't even thinking that, but I thank you for your thoughtfulness to others, and for being honest with me."

Connie set the second plate on top of the first. "Enjoy, Mari. And have a good time with your man. He certainly is a handsome one."

"He certainly is. I will, and thanks again. See you later."

"Yes, we will." Connie smiled until Mari had left the room and couldn't see it anymore. Mari had left feeling better. She pulled her phone out and looked down at the screen. She estimated another ten minutes before Dexter would arrive.

She hurried down the hallway. She didn't want Dexter to get there early, and find out he'd left his business meeting for someone who wasn't even there.

Especially not her. What would he think?

If he left, it would devastate her. She didn't want to be apart from him anymore. The thought of being his wife, and being by his side forever, made her feel giddy and a little hot.

She passed through the door into her study and sighed with relief. He wasn't there yet. She went to the small refrigerator in the "kitchen" area of the study, equipped with a small sink, a soap dispenser and paper towels, a refrigerator, a microwave, and even a small dishwasher.

All Nathan's choice. Mari approved. She wondered what her late uncle knew about the secret passages through the building. It was apparent the assistant knew.

Mari placed the two plates in the refrigerator and went to her desk. She got cold chills when she thought that maybe the assistant was using the secret passages to spy on her uncle, or steal from him in some way.

Her dislike for the stranger grew, day by day.

And now she knew where he lived. At least she thought she did.

She placed her bag on the desk and opened it, pulling out her notebook and pen. She sat in the chair and began to write down

163

what she'd seen of the mysterious man. The initials on the mailbox that made no sense to her. Only the middle one was different from her uncle's.

She noted how strange it had been, seeing both Brittany and the mysterious man in such a short period of time.

She sat back and tapped her pen against her lips, staring out into space as she thought. Could there be a connection between them? Was he now spying on her and Dexter, as he had on her uncle? If so, what was he planning?

Mari sat forward and wrote down her questions. She sat back and continued to ponder, wishing Dexter would hurry up. Brittany had said she would have Dexter "one way or another". Was she dangerous? Was she plotting with the assistant to somehow hurt Mari or her sisters? Or Dexter?

Mari shook her head. She was being paranoid. Brittany couldn't possibly be that way.

Or could she?

Mari wrote the question down with the intention of asking Dexter. He would know if she was dangerous or not.

It wasn't long before a knock on the door drew her out of her thoughts. Her heart raced for a moment in anticipation. She called out "Come in", and felt a wave of pleasure sweep through her when Dexter popped his head in.

"Safe to come in?" he asked.

Mari lifted her eyebrows, sitting up in her chair. "Of course, Dex. What are you talking about?"

"I saw Grady out front. He said he had to escort Brittany from the premises."

Mari smiled, feeling relieved. "Yes, he did."

"Well, I guess you have a few things to tell me then, don't you?" Dexter crossed the room and went around the desk, drawing Mari into a hug. She straightened so she could wrap her arms around him. He smelled good. She took in a deep breath, vowing to remember that smell forever.

"I'm so glad you're here, Dexter. I really am." She said in a low voice. She brought one arm around and tugged on the jacket he was wearing. She looked up into his eyes with a smile, and was overwhelmed with emotion when he lowered his head and pressed his lips against hers.

She felt a tingling sensation all through her body, and put her arms around his neck, kissing him back with as much passion as she felt in her heart.

He pulled away and smiled at her. "That was nice." His voice was deep and smooth. "I hope to have a bunch more of those before all this is over."

"All this will never be over," she said. "One of us would have to give up, and I don't think that's going to happen. Do you?"

He gazed into her eyes. She was sure she could see how much he loved her in the deep swirls of his blue eyes.

"You're such a handsome man," she murmured. "I don't know how you keep the women away from you."

"Forcefully," Dexter joked. "And with restraining orders."

They both laughed.

"No, I'm not as social as you might think," Dexter continued. "I have… things from my past I don't discuss with many people, but everyone knows the gist of it."

"I don't," Mari replied in a simple tone. She gazed at him through wide eyes, hoping he could tell there was no judgment there. "But you don't have to tell me until you decide you're ready to, Dex. And if that takes the rest of our lives, or until we're seventy or something, that's fine, too. It's your life. I'm patient."

Dexter's face turned slightly red. The look in his eyes melted Mari's heart. "Thank you, Mari. Trust me, I'll be telling you all about it soon enough. Right now, we have so much other stuff to discuss. Come on, let's sit down and talk. I want to hear all about your day."

"Are you hungry? Connie made us a couple of plates from lunch. Chicken, green beans, corn, and some rolls. You want me to heat a plate up for you?"

"I'd love that." Dexter put his hand on his stomach and growled under his breath. "You hear that? That's my stomach saying, "Feed me!"."

Mari burst out in laughter, going to the refrigerator to take out the plates. She heated each of them in the microwave, turning around and leaning back against the counter while it ran.

Dexter sat at the two-person table used for quick dining. He pushed her chair out a bit with his foot and smiled at her. "Sit."

"I'm going to wait until these are done." She replied, gesturing with her head at the cooking food.

"Okay, then." Dexter leaned forward on his elbows and clasped his hands together on top of the table. "So, you saw the mystery man today."

"Yeah, the assistant. But there's something else I want to show you, Dexter. And I think it's really going to surprise you."

Dexter lifted his eyebrows. "Oh? What is it?"

Mari walked to the little table and laid her phone down.

"Press play."

Chapter 26

Dexter sat in silence while he listened to the recording. He couldn't believe Mari had the courage to do what she'd done, just to prove he wasn't the father. It only saved him a ton of hassle and money, but she acted like his life was on the line.

He'd never met another woman in his life that genuinely cared that much. She'd risked getting hurt, either by Brittany or by this mystery man.

He reached out and picked the phone up when the recording was over. She was watching him as he scanned the screen for the time it was recorded. He brought up the information on it and read through it.

"That was only a couple of hours ago." He shook his head. "You're not still shaken up, are you?"

Mari shook her head. She'd cut in while the recording was playing, telling Dexter where she was at that moment. Dexter was astounded when she told him what had been going on when she went into the bathroom. He ended up laughing a few times, because Mari exaggerated her fear, trying to be overly dramatic.

She was taking everything in such a positive way. Dexter felt his chest tighten. He suddenly felt very hot, as if he'd stepped into a sauna. He cleared his throat.

"Here you go." Mari set the plate down in front of him, and sat down across from him with her own. "I hope you like it. It's one of my favorite meals."

Dexter stabbed some of the green beans with his fork. "I love green beans. Glad to see them on this plate."

"I love them, too." Mari said in an affectionate tone. He rewarded her with a brilliant smile, before shoving the forkful in his mouth and chewing with his mouth closed.

He closed his eyes and shook his head vehemently. "Mmm mmm mmm, these are the best I've ever had. I'm stealing your chef away."

Mari raised her eyebrows. "Just because she makes good green beans?"

"These green beans are from heaven, Mari. Taste them and tell me different."

Mari laughed.

"So, after you left the clinic, where did you go?" Dexter asked in an inquiring voice. "You said you saw the assistant?"

"Yes, it was the strangest thing." Mari got up and walked over to her desk, retrieving the notebook with her questions written in it. She returned to her seat and set the notebook down, spinning it so Dexter could read the questions. "I just went across the street to listen to the recording and see how it sounded. I'm so glad it came out so clear."

Dexter nodded, looking at her before dropping his eyes back to the notebook. "Me too. I can easily understood every word."

Mari nodded at him. "So, I went to that parking lot across the street from the restaurant and saw the man coming out with a bag of food."

Dexter looked pleasantly surprised. "Well isn't that a coincidence?"

"I thought it was pretty strange," Mari admitted. "I had almost been caught by Brittany, and then see this mystery man. Hard to believe. I watched him get in his car. I don't think he saw me."

She stopped talking for a moment and Dexter gazed at her face. He could tell there was more to this story. He hoped she didn't take any unnecessary risks. The assistant had not posed a threat so far. He wasn't sure what drove Mari to pursue the assistant so hard.

"I went after him in my car."

Dexter was stunned. He felt the blood drain from his face. "You went after him with your car?" He asked in a panicky voice. She stared at him for a moment, and then shook her head.

"No, I didn't go after him with my car. I went after him in my car. I followed him."

Dexter rolled his eyes and shook his head, relaxing his tense muscles. "Oh, thank God. I thought you tried to run him down."

A quick laugh came from Mari. Dexter scanned her face. She looked cute with that surprised expression. It made him want to kiss her again. He picked up his coffee cup and took a sip of the hot, swirling liquid. He held it up toward Mari. "Thanks for making a coffee for me."

Mari shook her head. "It's nothing anymore. A quick cup in the machine, and a few seconds later you have coffee. Simple, really."

Dexter nodded. "Thanks for the thought." He took a sip. "So, you followed him, did you? You're one brave lady." He smiled at her. "I like that about you. But I do wish you'd be a little more cautious. You're gonna get yourself killed someday, if you keep trying to solve mysteries left and right."

Mari furrowed her brows, looking at him through amused eyes. "What in heaven's name are you talking about?" she asked. "I've never been embroiled in a mystery before."

"Oh really? Well, I guess we're witnessing history right now." Dexter meant it as a compliment, but Mari looked like she wasn't taking it as one. He had no way of knowing what she was thinking, so he went further with it. "We'll have to put it down as a holiday. These are the days of many first adventures. We can make it three or four days long."

Mari was staring at him over her plate. She was holding her fork, but it was resting loosely on top of a piece of chicken. "Dexter, are you all right? You're not on anything weird, are you?"

Dexter laughed. "Oh, no. I'm just running my mouth. Probably too much caffeine. So, is that all to your story?

Mari told him about the apartment buildings and what she'd done. He felt an overwhelming desire to strangle her and smother her in kisses at the same time. He was annoyed with her for risking her life that way.

"Do you know what could have happened to you, Mari?" he asked in a gruff voice. He couldn't help it. The thought of the mystery man, or any other man, hurting Mari was more than he could bear to think about. "I wish you had called me. You could have called me while you were following him. You could have read me the plate numbers and you wouldn't have had to go through all that."

"I don't know if I was ever really in danger, though," she replied, finishing her plate and taking it to the sink. "I was afraid, for sure, but I was cautious. I don't think he even noticed me."

"I'm sure he wouldn't expect to see you around there," Dexter said, contemplatively. "But that's no excuse for not calling me while you were on the road."

Mari shook her head. "Thinking back now, I agree. I should have called you. But I didn't. And I probably didn't because I was trying so hard to not losing sight of him. I mean, I was so focused on that, I didn't even memorize the license plate number while I had a chance. But I did get the make and model, and the last three digits I can't forget. My birthday, 724. Those are the last three digits, and I think the first part had two letters in it, but I can't be sure."

"I'll contact someone who might be able to tell us," Dexter said. "Go on. So, you got to the apartment buildings and saw where he lived?"

"Yeah," Mari had already told him that. "He lives in number six at Ridgewood apartments."

Dexter raised his eyebrows at her. He was going to ask the question, and he hoped he got the answer he wanted.

"So… did you knock on his door?"

Mari looked utterly surprised, and then amused. "Uh. No." She spoke to him as if he'd just stated something that made him look ridiculous. "I'm not stupid."

Dexter shook his head. He hated it when he blurted things

out, and then felt guilty for it.

"Sorry about that, Honey. I didn't mean any offense."

Mari gave him a sweet grin, causing a strong desire to pass through him. He wanted her lips again. He wanted to grab her up and hold her against him.

He restrained himself. "What did you do, then?"

"I went past, and then down this long hallway to the front of the building," Mari finally continued, wrapping her arms around herself. "I looked at his mailbox. It had his name... well, his initials, there. NAW."

"NAW." Dexter repeated. "What does that mean to you?"

"It means he has the same initials as my Uncle Nathan," Mari said in a matter-of-fact tone. Dexter turned his eyes in her direction, widening them.

"I beg your pardon?"

Mari nodded at him. He felt confused, which frustrated him. "Well, what does that mean?" he asked in an exasperated tone. "I don't get it. We all saw the... the body. We saw him after. We know he died."

"And you never saw him after that?" Dexter asked. He hoped not. He would have to make those phone calls soon.

"No, I never saw him after that. He went into his apartment and stayed there."

"I think we need to find out who this man is." Dexter sat forward in the chair, standing to put the plate in the sink. Before he knew it, Mari had snatched it from him and was placing it in the sink next to the stove. She gave him a big smile.

"You don't have to do that for me. Don't put yourself out."

Mari giggled. "Oh, it's my pleasure. How do you propose we find out? Do you know someone on the police force?"

"No, but I know the governor."

It was Mari's turn to be surprised. "You do? Well, how do

you think he can help us?"

"I'm gonna call him in a little bit and talk to him. I want to know what other information you have to give me about this assistant."

"What about Brittany?" Mari's voice sounded nervous.

Dexter wasn't nervous. Mari had supplied him with exactly what he needed to make sure Brittany never bothered him again. He wasn't about to reach out to her. She would have to approach him this time. He wasn't going to let Brittany think she controlled him. She was just another temporary love that came and went.

He'd never wanted to keep any of them by his side, until Mari came along. He saw his soulmate in her. He was afraid to tell her how he felt, but it was true. He held back from saying he loved her, and for some reason, she hadn't said it either.

He wanted to concentrate on the assistant for now. He would deal with Brittany later. He leaned forward and pulled out his phone, while staring down at Mari's phone. "So, we have the address and initials. That's not bad. One step behind snagging a social security number, and you're home free."

Mari looked at him solemnly. "I don't want to know his social. I just want to find out who he is and why he's stalking me."

Dexter's smile left his face and he became somber. "We're gonna get through this, Honey, because we're meant to be. You don't want anyone else, and I don't want anyone else, right? We should just see how far we can take this, whatever we have here, and run with it."

Chapter 27

Mari was overjoyed to hear the words from Dexter. She smiled brightly and nodded. "I'd like that a lot," she replied.

"So, here's the first thing we should do," Dexter said, leaning forward. "Let's see what you think of this plan."

Mari scooted her chair closer to him. She couldn't help gazing at him with loving eyes. That new-love feeling was bursting inside her, making her heart thump and her blood race.

"Let's go to that apartment. The two of us."

Mari sat up straight, staring at him, now confused. "Just confront him?"

Dexter nodded. "I'll be with you. You don't have to worry. I'm bigger than him, aren't I?"

Mari thought of the man in her mind. He was not as big as Dexter, that was true. She nodded. "You are. But what if he has a weapon?"

Dexter shook his head. "I feel like if he was going to hurt you, he would have already. He wouldn't have run every time you saw him. You said he knows about the secret passages, so he's had plenty of opportunity. I don't think we have to worry about a weapon, but I'm much more comfortable knowing you didn't go alone."

"I'm glad I didn't. I'm not good at self-defense."

Dexter reached over and ran two fingers down her cheek. She blushed. The feel of his skin on hers made her shiver with pleasure. She smiled at him. She wished he would tell her he loved her, so she could say it back.

"You want to go now?" He asked.

She nodded, "Unless you have an appointment or something."

He shook his head. "Nope. My day is free to spend with you. The rest of it, anyway."

173

She grinned. "I'm glad. And we've eaten a good meal, too. That's a bonus for us."

He laughed, getting up from the chair and stretching his arms above his head, taking in a deep breath. He let it out, patting his stomach. "And what a fine meal it was, too. Thanks, Mari. I know Connie made it, but you got one for me, and I'm not one to turn down good food."

"You're welcome, Dexter. To be honest with you, it's hard for me not to think about you."

He gazed down at her, closing the distance between them with two steps. He took her face in his hands and leaned over to kiss her soft lips. "I think you're an amazing woman," he whispered, leaving his lips close enough that his breath whispered softly over her skin. She shivered with pleasure. He kissed her again, and then he let go.

The moment he moved away, she felt cold. She wanted him to come back.

But he was already heading toward the door, unaware of the weak state he'd left her in. She gathered herself and went after him quickly, grabbing her sweater from the back of the chair she'd been sitting in, and snatched her purse from the table.

She caught up with him in the lobby, breathing hard. He looked down at her. "Oh, I'm sorry, Mari. I thought you were right behind me. I'll slow down."

He shortened his stride and she was grateful. It was hard to keep up with him when he was in a hurry. He had longer legs, by far.

"Let's take my car," he suggested, holding the glass door open for her to pass through. He came out behind her and lifted one hand to point. "I'm parked over there."

The car was fairly close to the entrance. The two of them were there in no time, both sliding into the car at the same time. Mari had never been in Dexter's car before. It was nicer than anything she'd ever been in. He leaned forward and pressed a button. The engine roared to life.

Mari blinked, scanning the elegant dashboard, with a built-in screen, and the unique swerves and curves that made it a luxury car.

She breathed in a pleasant musky scent. "This is a really nice car, Dexter. I'm impressed."

Dexter was sliding his seatbelt over his shoulder. He gave her a curious look. "You know, you're the first person who's ever told me that."

Mari couldn't help looking at him in surprise. "What? No way. Why?"

Dexter shrugged, looking at the rearview screen on the dashboard as he backed out. "I don't know. I guess because it's nothing fancier than any of my friends or exes had. I've had this car for a couple of years now, and my friends keep telling me to get an updated version. But I like this one. It still runs excellent."

"You don't want to sell it?" Mari understood. She'd only had a few cars in her life, because she kept them until the repairs cost more than the car itself. That's when she'd purchase a new one. It sounded like, despite his wealth, Dexter felt the same way.

"Nope." Dexter reached forward and gently patted the dash. "I love this baby. It gets me where I need to go, hardly ever breaks down, and still looks as good, inside and out, as it did the day it came off the factory floor."

Mari looked in the backseat as they drove. "It does look like it's brand new. Most people's cars wouldn't get so bad if they just took proper care of it. I can see that you do."

When Mari turned her head to the front again, she glanced at Dexter's face, and noticed he was giving her a strange look. She raised her eyes to meet his, lifting her eyebrows.

"What?"

Dexter shook his head. "I just don't hear very many females talk with common sense about car maintenance, that's all." He lifted one hand in the air, as if he was swearing on the Bible. "And I'm not saying women don't know about it, or can't do it, or any of that other stuff. I'm just saying, it's something I haven't *personally* seen before."

"I understand. I wasn't offended." Mari chuckled, to reiterate her point.

"Okay, I don't know where I'm going here."

Mari gave him directions to Ridgewood apartments.

"Are we just going to knock on the door and introduce ourselves?" Mari asked, watching the scenery pass outside the car. She felt Dexter's eyes on her, before she turned toward him.

"I don't think we'll need to introduce ourselves, but yeah. Just knock on the door. Once he sees who it is, he won't have anywhere to run, except back in his apartment. I'm going to make him give us some answers."

"I don't like him, Dex. He's creepy."

"You don't know him, yet," was Dexter's response. "Don't go in there with that in your mind, or you'll make it harder to get the truth out of him."

Mari thought about that for a moment. "Won't the fact that you're there intimidate him?"

"I'm hoping so," Dexter replied. "But I don't want him to think we're dangerous, either."

Mari shifted in her seat, trying to get comfortable. "I know I'm not dangerous, and he was even running from me."

"Exactly. So, are we close?"

"Yes, it's right up there, to the left, by that little garden school and the coffee shop."

"Okay. I know where that is."

They were quiet as Dexter drove the last two blocks. He pulled into the same parking lot the man had pulled into, and parked in a visitor's spot. He looked at Mari, taking her wrist before they got out.

"You promise me you'll be careful. Don't go all 'riot act'

176

on me, okay?"

Mari laughed. "I'm not that kind of woman, Dex. You have nothing to worry about."

"Good." He leaned close to her, tilting his head to the side slightly. She was delighted that he wanted to kiss her so much, even if they weren't all deep and passionate. The little pecks, even on her cheek, were like little gold nuggets to her.

They got out of the car together. As they walked away from it, Mari heard the alarm set. She glanced over her shoulder at it, and then took Dexter's arm when he held it out for her. She looked up at him with amused eyes.

"I hear that car alarm a lot. You must be around the resort more often than I thought."

"Well, I do play tennis there regularly," Dexter said, matching her humorous tone. "I also take advantage of the golf courses, on occasion. And the pools; you know, those things." He smiled down at her, sending a wave of love through her body. "Plus, there's this really good-looking woman there that I admire."

Mari raised her eyebrows at him. "Is that so? Is this someone I know?"

Dexter grinned mischievously. "She is. You know her very well, I must say."

They were almost to the door. She had her arm wrapped around his waist and pinched his side lightly. "I think I know who you're talking about," she said sweetly.

His grin remained steadfast. "I bet you do."

She let her smile fade slowly, and said in a serious tone, "It's Lynn, isn't it? You're there to see Lynn. I should have known." She couldn't maintain the seriousness anymore, and broke out in a giggling grin.

He touched the end of her nose and said softly. "No, Honey. It's you. I won't even pretend like it's someone else."

Mari was overwhelmed with passion and desire. Her

affection for Dexter grew exponentially, with just his words. And he was proving himself to be just the kind of compassionate protector she desired. She wanted a man she could love forever, that would return those feelings and make her happy, while she was doing the same for him.

They stopped in front of the door. Dexter reached up and knocked on it. Mari pushed down the desire to press her thumb over the peephole. He might look through and not answer, seeing it was them.

They waited a few minutes, but there was nothing but silence from the other side of the door. They looked at each other.

"Do you think he's out? He's not home?" Mari asked, pondering.

"Too bad we couldn't call ahead," Dexter mumbled. Mari giggled softly.

Dexter grabbed the handle, and before she could protest, he rattled it back and forth. He looked at Mari. "It's locked. I expected that. Look, we drove all the way out here. What do you say we wait till he comes back, and confront him out here in the hallway?"

"It's kind of narrow," Mari remarked, looking around them.

Dexter did the same. "Well, we have to do something. How about we see if any of his neighbors can tell us anything about him."

Mari's spirits lifted. "Yes, I think we should do that."

They turned to the apartment directly across the hall. The woman who answered was wearing a long red robe, and had her hair up in a shower cap. A bit of dark red dye had dripped down her forehead. She squinted her eyes from the bright glare. Mari noticed the apartment behind her was dark in almost every room she could see.

"Can I help you?" she asked.

"I'm sorry to bother you, miss," Dexter said in his friendliest voice. "Do you know the young man who lives across from you?"

"Nathan? Yes, I know him. Of course, I do. Come on in. He isn't home. You can wait for him here."

Dexter and Mari stared at each other, but didn't turn down the older woman's kind offer.

Chapter 28

"So, do you know where he is right now, Miss?"

The woman laughed, walking to a window and pushing it up. In the sunlight, Mari could see her face a little better. She looked like she was in her fifties, old enough to be Mari's mother.

Or Nathan's.

She went to the other window in her small living room and opened it, as well. She responded to Dexter as she spoke. "I'm Mrs. Rugby. You can call me Dolores. I hope you don't mind, but I'm going to smoke a cigarette. I hate them, but I smoke them anyway. I have to have the windows open because I don't like the smell."

Dexter nodded. Mari decided to let him do the talking. He's the one who knew everybody in town. "I'm Dexter," he said, putting one hand on his chest, then he swept it in Mari's direction. "This is Mari."

"It's nice to meet you."

When Mrs. Rugby said the mystery man's name was Nathan, Mari had nearly fainted. He was using Nathan's name. How could he get away with it? How could he not be recognized as a fraud, when so many people knew what Nathan looked like.

"Is he friendly to you?" she asked. The older woman turned to her with a look of surprise on her face.

"Why, of course he is. Isn't he a friend of yours?" She looked back and forth between the two of them. Mari sensed that Mrs. Rugby was reevaluating whether she should have let them into her apartment. She hurried to put the woman's mind at ease.

"I don't know him personally, but I know some people who do, and I'm curious about him."

To her surprise, Mrs. Rugby nodded and dropped in the seat nearest the first window she had raised. She waved her hand at the couch. "Please, sit."

Dexter and Mari sat close to each other on the couch.

"I was curious about Nathan, too, when he first came here. Some were suspicious of him, but with time, he... he just grew on everyone. He's a good boy. He's had it rough."

"I don't know a lot about his past," Mari said in a kind voice. "Will you fill me in?"

Mrs. Rugby nodded as she lit a cigarette. She took just one puff before holding it out the window and flicking it with her thumb nail repeatedly. Mari would have thought the woman was nervous, if she didn't have such a relaxed look on her face.

"Nathan's got it rough. When he first came here, he was searching for his father. His father, you see, was Nathan Wright."

Mari felt goose bumps cover her arms. "Are you sure?" she asked.

Mrs. Rugby nodded, taking another puff. Then out the window and flick, flick, flick, repeatedly.

"Oh, there were plenty in this part of Queen Anne who didn't believe him. But, like I said, he convinced us all. He was devastated when his father died."

"But how could Nathan have been his father when he was never married, and laid no claim to any children?" Mari asked, completely confused. She glanced at Dexter, who looked as confused as she did.

"He was illegitimate," Mrs. Rugby said. "And Nathan's dear mother never told his father he had a child. So, Nathan grew up not knowing he was heir to that fortune up there."

Mari was once again covered in chills. She and her sisters weren't the rightful owners of Emerald Resort. Fear sliced through her, as she thought about having to go back to her old life. She glanced again at Dexter, wondering what he would think of her if she was living her old life again.

She didn't want to leave him. She didn't want to lose the resort. She had come to love the place as her own. Running the place was almost a dream come true for her and her sisters. She felt a heavy sadness weigh on her chest.

"Oh dear. I didn't know that," she murmured.

Mrs. Rugby chuckled. "Well, why would you, dear?"

"If he should be the owner of Emerald Resort, why doesn't he say something?" She asked. *Instead of creeping around scaring people,* she added in her mind.

Mrs. Rugby sighed. "I don't know, really. The ladies running the resort seem very nice, he says, and very capable of running the place. He may feel he is too young for those responsibilities."

"Why doesn't he say something to the owners, and explain how he feels?" Dexter said in a calm, collected tone. "There are ways around this predicament. He should come out and tell them."

"I can't speak for him," Mrs. Rugby said. "But I can tell you what I know of him. He's a kind person, with a gentle soul. He's a lot like the Nathan I used to know. Very generous and so smart. But he's a mess of emotions." The older woman shook her head. "Such a mess. You never know what kind of depressing thoughts that boy will have next."

Mari's opinion of young Nathan was changing rapidly during their conversation.

"He's really all those things?" she asked breathlessly. Confusion had taken over her mind. This did not sound like the man she repeatedly saw in the resort, trespassing in the walls, and through secret passages. "I'm so confused."

Mrs. Rugby settled her green eyes on Mari's face. "Why are you confused, my dear?"

Mari was staring at the floor. She shook her head and raised her eyes to meet the woman's. "Because I'm Mari Wright. I'm one of the sisters that took over the resort. I am Nathan's niece."

"So that makes you a relative, then," Mrs. Rugby said, her eyebrows shooting up, creating wrinkles in her forehead. "You are one of the sisters who run the resort right now."

Mari nodded. She saw no change for the better or worse on the woman's face. She looked like she had no real opinion about what she'd just found out.

"You don't know why he's so afraid to come and speak to us?"

Mrs. Rugby shook her head. "No. I think it may be just a case of immaturity and insecurity. He's young. You have to keep that in mind. He's only twenty-one."

"Oh my, that is young," Mari said, looking at Dexter with a smile. She herself was only thirty, but she knew it was a fact that men mature later than women. And there was no telling what kind of upbringing Nathan may have had with his single mother.

"Do you know a lot about his childhood?" Dexter asked, picking up on Mari's thoughts. She turned to gaze lovingly at him. He caught the look and winked, a motion that made Mari's body light up in delighted chills.

"You mean how his momma treated him?" The woman asked, pushing up on her shower cap a little. Mari imagined the dye was probably burning her scalp.

"Yes, ma'am." Dexter replied respectfully.

"Oh, he had everything he needed, and went without some things he didn't. He was raised away from all that luxury up there, because of his mother's decision to treat him like his father didn't exist. Nathan would have helped that boy with money. He might have even married his mother, if she'd told him."

"Maybe someone should ask her why she kept Nathan away from his father." Dexter suggested.

Mrs. Rugby shook her head solemnly. "She died a few years ago. That's why Nathan moved here. He was searching for his father. He told me when he was packing his mother's things sorting out mementos and donations, he found a lot of papers, and even a paternity test his mother had done."

"How'd she do that?"

"Got a hair from one of Nathan Wright's hairbrushes. She

183

sent it in for analysis when young Nathan was born. Or it may have been through a pre-birth procedure. I don't know many things like that. He decided to come to Queen Anne, and the resort, to visit. He came once and met the older Nathan, but didn't have the nerve to say anything. Then he read about Nathan's death, and put two and two together."

"She named him after his father," Mari said softly.

Mrs. Rugby nodded. "She loved Nathan, by all accounts. The love letters, the few I got to read, were beautiful and sweet. But something happened and he had to split up with her. Then she was afraid to tell him about his son, and raised young Nathan without telling him who his father was. He did everything he could to find his father, and he finally did." She had a note of pride in her voice that surprised Mari.

"I really can't thank you enough for all this information, Mrs. Rugby," Dexter said. "Can you tell us anything more about him that would help us understand him a little better?"

"I don't know if there's much more to tell, really. He is a good man. I hope I haven't said anything that will hurt his chances of progressing in the future."

Mari shook her head. "Not at all. I would love to meet him, and hear what he has to say for himself, though. The only way to negotiate matters is face to face, unless such meetings aren't convenient. We have to talk, in other words, at the first opportunity."

Mrs. Rugby had a satisfied look on her face as she nodded. "I don't want that boy getting in any trouble. He needs support and encouragement. He seems so… well, *lost* to me." The woman's breathy voice sounded a bit melancholy for a moment.

"To be honest with you, Mrs. Rugby," Mari said in an announcer's voice. "I believe every word you told us. There's no reason for me to doubt you. I would like to meet him and discuss this like reasonable adults."

Mrs. Rugby smiled. "I'm sure you would, Ms. Wright."

"Mari, please."

"Mari, it is. You may call me Alice."

Mari gave her a friendly smile.

"I'm sure he will be home soon. I always hear him coming down the hallway. The walls make his footsteps echo. They make everyone's footsteps echo. I've come to recognize footsteps, and know who is behind the door, even if they don't stop in front of my apartment."

"That's quite a unique talent."

"I've been honing it for years!" Alice said, grinning at her.

They all chuckled softly. Alice's eyes darted toward the door. "Speak of the devil. I do believe I hear him coming now. I'll open my door and see if it's him." She shot to her feet and crossed the room quickly. Mari leaned toward Dexter, suddenly nervous about meeting her newfound relative.

He put his arm around her shoulders and squeezed. "It's gonna be all right, Mari. Come on, let's stand up. We are going to want to talk to Nathan in private, aren't we? Not here, in Mrs. Alice Rugby's apartment."

She glanced up at him. "Sounds like a mom and pop café," she whispered, making him chuckle under his breath.

They walked to the door and watched Alice's body bounce with excitement as she spoke. Mari couldn't help smiling at the woman's energy.

"Nathan!" Alice called out. "Come over here and meet some friends."

Chapter 29

Alice took a step back and Nathan stared into the room at the two of them. His eyes widened, and he immediately looked like he was ready to run back out of the building. Mari took several steps toward him, speaking quickly. "Don't go, Nathan. I need to talk to you."

She used a friendly, understanding tone. She hoped he could see the look on her face wasn't hostile. This close to him, she could see Nathan didn't really look like she thought he would. She'd pictured him as being much older, even though she'd seen him. He looked older from far away.

It did explain how he traversed the vent and went through the secret passageways with ease, though.

He was hesitant, but he finally took a step into the apartment. Mari looked at Alice and said, "Do you think we could go over to Nathan's? I'd like to talk to him privately, if we could. Just the three of us."

Alice chuckled, taking a draw off her cigarette, while holding one eyelid closed. "You go right ahead, dear. I don't mind."

She waved them toward the door, the way a teacher waves at children to exit the class room. She had just as bright a smile as any good elementary teacher, as well.

"Thank you, Alice," Mari said, reaching out to take the older woman's hand in both of hers. "This means a lot to me. It's a huge weight off my shoulders, to know this is the man I've been seeing around the property." She turned her eyes to Nathan. "And that I don't have to be afraid of him."

Nathan still looked terribly confused. He watched Dexter approach and took a big step backwards, toward his door. He was clearly afraid of Dexter.

"Dexter," Mari said, before he could continue. Nathan looked like a frightened rabbit, about to dash away as quickly as possible. Dexter turned to look at her. She lifted her finger.

"Wait a minute. Let me go in first. Nathan, this is okay with you, isn't it? I'm really not trying to cause you any trouble. Please trust me."

Nathan still looked doubtful, but he nodded. He moved his eyes from one to the other, and had yet to say a word to either of them.

He turned his back to them long enough to unlock his door. He wasn't doing it well, because his hands were shaking.

Mari came up behind him but didn't get too close. She'd never seen a young man who was so skittish. "It's okay, Nathan. You don't have anything to worry about. I'm... we're not going to hurt you, okay?"

Nathan looked over his shoulder at her. She could see the resemblance to her uncle. Young Nathan's hair was the same dark brown, curly and down to his shoulders, while his father had kept his short. His eyes were the same dark chocolate pools, with gold specks scattered here and there. He was a handsome young man.

But he was thin and wiry, and didn't look like he got much sun. Mari was surprised at how different he looked from a distance. He must have been wearing several layers of clothes. He'd apparently hidden the long hair under a hat when she'd seen him before.

Nathan opened the door, finally getting the key in the hole. He swung the door open and stepped in. He kept his head down as Mari and Dexter came through. He closed the door and Mari was almost surprised when he finally spoke up.

"You can sit wherever you want. I like to keep things neat, but if you make a mess, it's okay. I'll clean it up later or get a new one. I like this chair. It's the one I sit in whenever I come home. Sometimes I like to eat here too. It lines up perfectly with the TV. See?"

Nathan sat in his favorite chair and waved at the TV.

Mari felt an emotion she hadn't felt in a long time. There was something different about the young man's behavior.

"Nathan, how have you been taking care of yourself?" Mari asked, compassionately. She saw Dexter glance at her in alarm. She shook her head, and leaned forward to get Nathan's attention, which was on the TV he'd flipped on.

"Can we talk without the TV on, Nathan?"

Nathan looked at her, rolled his eyes and lifted the remote to turn the TV back off. "You want me to get my things and go home, don't you?" he said in a defeated tone. His shoulders slumped and he looked terribly sad.

Mari shook her head, leaping up and getting closer to Nathan. "No. Not at all, Nathan. I see no reason why you should do that. You can come out to the resort. Is what Alice told us true? You are the true heir of the place?"

Nathan moved his eyes slowly between Mari and Dexter. Finally, he nodded. "But I don't want it," he said vehemently. "I can't run it, and dad knew it. He told me what he was gonna do, but he forgot to say something about me when he left his will. Somebody told me I could contest it and take the resort, but I don't want it. You and your sisters would do a much better job than me."

Mari was surprised by the level of logic in his reasoning.

"Why did you keep hiding from me? Why were you stalking me?"

Nathan's eyes dropped back to his hands, which were twisting around each other in his lap. He sighed. "I didn't mean to do that."

"You didn't mean to stalk me?" Mari asked, trying to understand. Dexter hadn't caught on, apparently, because he spoke with a harsh tone.

"You can't accidentally stalk someone," he barked. "You either are or you aren't. No in-between."

Mari saw the way Nathan jumped when Dexter spoke loudly. She turned pleading eyes to him and shook her head. His face turned to confusion, but he pulled back a little.

She turned back to Nathan. "Please, Nathan, tell me why I

kept seeing you."

"I... I was trying to tell you. Every time I saw you, it was because I went there to tell you, but then I would see you, and I was afraid you would reject me."

Mari's heart ached for the young man.

"People don't always understand the way I am and... I've gotten hurt by people's words a lot. And I don't think I could... I wouldn't want to hear something like that from you or your sisters. Dad was always nice to me. He let me have a couple rooms in the basement for some of my collections and things."

Realization dawned on Mari. That's why she kept seeing him at the resort. He had rooms there and he wanted to visit them.

"I wish you had come to see me and introduced yourself," she said softly. "You didn't have to run around hiding. Her heart had warmed while listening to him. She got down on one knee in front of the young man, and looked up at him. "Hey, I'm really not gonna hurt you. My sisters would welcome you with open arms. I know we can find a job for you on the resort grounds, and you can stay there with us. If you want us to run the place, we will; but we're going to have to draw up some papers showing that you own some of it, too. That way you'll always have a home. How does that sound?"

She smiled up at him, hoping to see a smile in return. It took a few moments. She could see him thinking it over. He lifted his eyes to meet hers and grinned. Feeling elated, she leaned forward, propelling herself upwards and pulled him into a hug.

She could tell she surprised him because, for a moment, he didn't hug her back. But he finally did, and they embraced for a few moments. She pulled away from him and looked into his eyes.

"Pack a bag and stay with us tonight. We'll take care of whatever you want in your apartment, I mean packing and all that. We'll hire someone. If there's anything you need, let me know. Okay, cousin?"

Nathan blinked at her, a slow smile spreading across his face. "You're not rejecting me?"

Mari frowned. "Of course not. Why would I?"

He shook his head, a look of bewilderment on his face.

"That woman told me to get off the property once when I came there. I saw her a couple times before I got away. She's not a very nice girl. She's a thief and a problem-maker."

"Who are you talking about?" Mari stood up and returned to her seat. She and Dexter shared an inquisitive look.

Nathan seemed to relax a little, but he still had a nervous tick that Mari soon became accustomed to, and then no longer noticed at all. She sensed a good soul in the boy, and regretted her earlier dislike for him. He was just scared and had been trying to get to her. He meant no harm.

It was a tremendous relief.

"I don't know her name. I didn't see her there before dad… passed on. She's got blond hair and has a very nice shape."

Mari giggled. "Nathan!" she scolded, with amusement in her voice.

He looked back at her. "What?" he asked, his tone matching hers. "I'm different, not dead."

Mari and Dexter both burst out laughing. Nathan smiled for the first time, and dazzled Mari with it. He had straight, white teeth that he obviously took very good care of. He pushed himself up from the chair and went to one of the doors in the apartment. He opened it to expose a very large bed made up perfectly, as if it had never been slept in, but was a display in a department store instead.

Mari swore she could bounce a quarter on it. She didn't follow him into the bedroom, but she could hear him muttering to himself as he packed his things. She saw him drop an open piece of luggage on his bed. Back and forth he went, from the dresser to the luggage trunk. She got up and went to the door, hoping it wouldn't bother him if she watched.

As she approached, she could actually hear what he was saying.

"Three pairs of socks, with a backup pair just in case. Three shirts, in case one gets dirty and I don't get back. Two pairs of boxers..." He counted methodically, and put the clothes he was retrieving in very specific places in the trunk.

Mari didn't say anything to him. She watched in fascination, as he packed the perfect overnight bag, suitable for possibly two nights, if all went well on the first one.

She could clearly see her uncle in him, even though he was not as socially adept as Uncle Nathan had been. Her heart had warmed for the young man. She wanted to do whatever she could to welcome him to her family, and make sure he knew he was loved and wanted.

No more hiding and running. He was a part of her family now, and a part of her heart.

Chapter 30

Bright and early the next morning, Dexter met his brother, Laura, and Mari on the tennis court for a few matches.

The summer sun warmed the air quickly.

His first thought when he stepped out onto the court was that he was ready for a drink of water already. He laughed at the thought, looking over at the gazebo. Laura and Mari were sitting there. They were leaning in toward each other. Laura's eyes kept flipping to the phone she was holding sideways. Mari's eyes were focused on the phone, obviously watching some kind of video.

Dexter stopped walking for a second, observing a shocked reaction on Mari's face. Mari lifted one hand and clapped it over her open mouth. Her eyes were wide when they turned to Laura. She said something Dexter couldn't hear, and Laura nodded her head in response.

Dexter heard the next words out of her mouth. "I cannot believe that. No! No way!"

Now he had to know what was going on. He hurried across the court and hopped over the fence, crossing the sidewalk and going up the steps to the gazebo to meet the ladies.

"Hey there," he said, getting the girls' attention. He shook his head, looking intentionally melancholy. "I never thought there would be a time when I could sneak up on two beautiful women. I always give myself away."

"Dexter! You have to see this!" Mari exclaimed. "You have to! I know you haven't seen it yet."

Dexter saw that Laura had pulled her phone back and was restarting the screen. She lifted it up and stood up, so she had her back to Dexter, and they could both look at her phone at the same time. Mari moved to stand by his other side, looking around his arm at the video.

Laura turned the volume up to max, just as the video started playing.

Shock engulfed Dexter, the kind of feeling his fiancée had felt just the day before. Dexter knew what he was watching immediately. It was the local TV news station. They were making an arrest outside of Brittany's home, where she lived with her parents in their mansion on the hill.

Brittany and her father were being led out in handcuffs, as well as two other men Dexter didn't recognize. The headline, and the announcer, were blasting the Langleys from top to bottom. Nearly three-quarters of the business deals they were involved with ended in bankruptcy. All the while, they were embezzling millions of dollars, and bleeding the other companies dry.

Dexter found the words caught in his throat. He wasn't able to get out more than a grunt. Thinking him bored, Laura lowered her phone.

"No, I'd like to see that, if that's okay," Dexter prompted her. Laura looked up and smiled at him. She pressed play again and it resumed from where it had been stopped.

"I think it's safe to say you don't have to worry about her anymore," Mari said. He could feel her studying his face, to see what his reaction would be to seeing Brittany and her father being arrested. He didn't know how he felt. Elated? Sad for them? Whatever Mari thought he might be feeling was probably not it, though.

He tried to resist it, but a smile lifted the corners of his lips. He covered his mouth with one hand and let his eyes move to Mari's face. Her face lit up with delight. He was embarrassed that he was petty enough to laugh at Brittany's misfortune. On the other hand, it looked like she was actually a greedy, rotten liar, just like her father.

He had dodged a bullet on that one.

It was because of Mari, too.

His brother was calling out to them from a distance, waving his racket above his head. Laura jumped up. "I'm going to go with Brian and give you two some privacy." She used a coy tone of voice that made Mari giggle. Dexter liked the sound of it. It made him want to tickle her.

Once Laura was far enough away, Dexter leaned in and gave Mari a soft kiss on the lips. Her touch always sent tingles through his skin. It was a pleasant feeling he wanted to experience as often as possible.

"I want to tell you something before we play today," he said.

Mari raised her eyebrows. "You do?"

"Yes."

Dexter had planned it ahead of time, telling Laura and Brian to hold off on coming to the gazebo, until they saw him do what he wanted to do. Laura would be taking pictures from a distance. She would do so under the pretense of showing her husband a video, and just happening to have the phone facing the gazebo.

Dexter chuckled inside, thinking now they really did have a video to watch. At least, after she was finished with the pictures.

He glanced over at them and saw that Laura was in the perfect position. He looked back at Mari. He took one of her hands in his and slid off the chair. He bent on one knee in front of Mari and smiled up at her.

"I would be so honored if you would be my wife, Mari. I love you with all my heart, and I can't deny it anymore. I can't not say it to you. I keep getting the urge to say I love you, and I don't say it because I'm so nervous. I hope you feel the same way about me." He chuckled. "I'm counting on it, actually."

Mari gazed softly into his eyes. The corners of her lips lifted, and she tilted her head to the side. "I won't make you wait for an answer. I will marry you, Dex. I would love to be your wife."

She threw her arms around his neck and he picked her up. She wrapped her legs around his waist, and Dexter hopped up and down, holding onto her tightly.

"What is that?"

Dexter stopped jumping when they heard cheering from the distance. He set Mari down and they both looked at Laura and Brian, who were cheering and doing their own little funny dances. Laura was laughing, and screaming "Congratulations", pointing at her phone to indicate she caught the whole thing on tape.

"That's goin' online, brother!" Brian yelled out, pointing at Dexter.

Dexter laughed, looking down at Mari. His cheeks were hot. They were probably as red as Mari's.

"I love your brother and sister-in-law," she said in a lighthearted voice.

"Good thing," Dexter's voice was smooth and low. "Now they're your relatives, too."

"They sure are, aren't they?"

Dexter had never felt this happy in his life. He couldn't remember a time that compared to it.

"I really didn't think you wanted to get married, Dex," Mari said affectionately, pushing her body up against his, and holding on to him with her hands pressed against his back. She looked up in his eyes, admiring them.

Dexter thought about what had brought him to the decisions he'd made, and he decided to explain what had made him unwilling to have a family.

"I'm thirty years old. When I was twenty, I was in love with my college sweetheart. We were planning to get married. We fooled around before..." He knew he was rushing through the story, and it wouldn't have the impact on her that it should, but he didn't want to recount it. For years it played through his mind.

"Before we got married, she told me she was pregnant. I was going to marry her."

Dexter wanted to rush through what happened, but make Mari understood how traumatic it was.

"I was driving one night, and the car slid on some ice on

the road. We hit a tree. She wasn't securely fastened in her seat belt. It had come loose or something. She was... she was killed in that accident."

Mari's heart sank. She pressed her cheek against his chest and pulled him to her. "Oh, Dexter."

"I had very few injuries, and there were no charges filed because it was a legitimate accident. Her parents tried to sue me, but my attorneys weren't having it. Then I found out... later... I found out that she... she had lied about the pregnancy. She'd been forging checks in my name. She was taking money from our business and using it frivolously. She was sleeping with other men."

He shook his head. "You name something that destroys relationships, and she was doing it. I wasn't an angel, mind you, but what I was doing wasn't any of those things."

"Of course not," Mari said comfortingly.

"So, I harbored a lot of guilt at first, thinking she was someone that she was not, and mourned the loss of a child that didn't even exist. When the truth came crashing down on me... well, I was young. I didn't know how to take it. I decided, then and there, that I wouldn't get serious about any of the women I dated. I didn't treat them badly. I gave them all a chance, and I had some fun in the meantime. But I was never able to get serous with any of them. None of them make me feel the way you do."

"I'm so glad to hear that, Dex."

He leaned down to kiss her lips.

"I want to have a family again." He didn't want to tell Mari about his medical history, so he'd already left papers for her to find that explained everything so much better than he ever could. "And it's all because of you."

"Oh, I'm so happy, Dex. I'm so happy I'm going to be your wife!" Dexter had to give her a few more kisses, this time longer and more meaningful.

"Where is Nathan?" Dexter asked, searching the areas of

the resort that he could see. "I thought he wanted to come out and watch us play today."

"He might be out later. I think he's quite preoccupied with his rooms. Now that he has free access to them again, he'll probably always be down there."

"He needs to get some sun and breath some fresh air."

Mari smiled. "I'm just going to let him live how he wants to live. Do you know that our staff members would have given up their jobs, if they thought I was ruthless enough to deny him what's his? They care so much about that boy, they vowed they wouldn't say anything when he asked them not to."

"It seems like such a smart move to make," Dexter said. "But he really doesn't take very good care of himself. Like I said, without getting out, and getting exercise, fresh air and sun, you waste away like a raisin."

Mari tilted her head to the side, giving him an odd look. "Did you say, 'like a raisin'?"

Dexter nodded. She turned away from him, sweeping her gaze over the landscape in front of her. "How strange. I've never heard that before."

"It's an old saying I just made up," Dexter replied, casually. Before Mari could respond, he lifted his hand in the air and called to his brother. "Come on! Let's play some tennis!"

Mari laughed, throwing her head back. She couldn't believe how happy she finally was.

Epilogue

Mari and Dexter planned their wedding for the first week in September, which was in between their birthdays.

Mari stared in the mirror, barely able to believe the day had finally arrived. Laura was humming a tune behind her, as she fastened Mari into the gorgeous white wedding dress she had chosen.

"My goodness," Laura said, coming around to look at Mari from the front. She looked up at her friend with happy eyes. "This makes you look like an angel, Mari. You and your sisters have good taste."

Mari scanned the dress. It was elegant but simple. No big bows, but plenty of lace. It was fitted to her curves perfectly. She pulled in a breath and sighed. "I would never have dreamed I would have a wedding like this. I really am… so grateful…" She sighed again.

Laura gazed at her. "Now don't you start crying, Mari, or I will, too. I am so happy for you and Dex. Remember when I told you I thought you would be perfect for him? And look where we are."

She pulled Mari into a hug. Mari's heart warmed for the woman, and she hugged her back. She and Laura had planned the wedding together. The Wright sisters' mother and father were coming for the wedding, and she couldn't wait to see them again.,

"I'm your sister now, too," Laura said, as she stepped back and admired Mari. "And that's just so wonderful. I've never had a sister!"

Mari chuckled softly. "It's not all it's cracked up to be."

Laura laughed. "Nonsense. There are good times and bad times in every relationship. I hope we never argue, but if we do, just remember, I do love you. With all my heart. Sincerely. You and Dexter… oh!" She exclaimed, rolling her eyes. She waved her hand in front of herself. "I am such a fan of you and Dexter."

Mari's chuckle turned into a laugh and her tears slipped away. She didn't want to cry and mess up the perfect makeup job Laura's beautician had done for her.

"It's almost time to walk down the aisle to your husband," Laura said, standing with a grin. "Are you nervous?" She moved around Mari one more time, circling to scan for anything she had missed, any flaw in the dress.

"Of course, I'm nervous. Everyone will be looking at me."

"We're gonna have fun at the reception, though, so just remember that, and you'll get through the first part of it easily. I was nervous, too. But you look absolutely stunning. You should be proud of yourself. And happy. Just stay happy. Be happy!"

The more she spoke, the higher pitch her voice took.

"Brian and I will be right up there with you guys. Moral support. I got your back, Honey. You'll do fine."

"Thank you for doing this for me, Laura. I'm glad my sisters let you be my matron of honor. After all, I didn't want to choose between them."

"I'm glad they understood. I love you, girl. Let's get you out there. We don't want to be late."

***

Laura was right about one thing. The reception was turning out to be a huge success. There was laughter all around the room, lots of people up and dancing, and the best food Mari had ever tasted.

She sat at the main table next to Dexter, watching everyone have fun. Dexter got her attention by taking her hand. When she looked at him, she saw the love in his eyes and didn't ever want to look away. She turned her body so she was facing him, her knees pressing up against his thigh.

"Do you know how much I love you, Mari?" he asked, his

199

tone resonating with passion for her.

"Deeply?" she supplied, nearly whispering the word.

"Deeply, yes, from the very bottom of my heart. I... I'm not sure I could survive a single day without you by my side now."

Mari's heart swelled and sped up. Tingles spread through her body. "Oh, Dex. I feel the same way. I don't ever want to be away from you."

"Except for work and stuff like that," he joked. "I mean, we can't spend 24/7 with each other. We'll go crazy."

Mari was a little surprised by his words. She didn't think she would ever be tired of him. She wanted to shrink up and hop in his pocket, so she could be with him always.

She laughed at her own thoughts, and noticed when his smile grew at the sound of her laughter.

"I love you, Mari. I'm so glad we're married. I'm going to try to be the best husband I can be. I'll love you forever, I promise."

"I hope so, Dexter," she responded, leaning forward and giving him a peck on the lips. "Because I plan to be the best wife you could ever have. I adore everything about you."

His eyebrows shot up into the loose blond hair that fell over his forehead. "Everything?"

Mari laughed. "Everything. Even if your feet are stinky or you have bad breath, I still love you."

He scrunched his face up and shook his head. "Nobody loves stinky breath, Mari. If it's like that, I expect to be told. Understood?"

Mari's laughter continued. "Okay, Dex. I promise."

"Good deal."

He leaned toward her and they met with another kiss. "Do you want to dance?" he asked, squeezing her hand in excitement.

"I think our first dance together is coming up soon."

"I guess you've been keeping an eye on the clock this whole time, haven't you?" he asked, joyfully. "You planned your own wedding, and you're still making sure everything is timed just right."

Mari nodded. "Of course. Everyone I know is here. I want our reputation to stay solid, don't I?"

Dexter pulled her into a hug. "I love you, my little businesswoman."

Mari lifted her hands and wrapped them around his shoulders. She could smell his cologne, and remembered when she'd promised herself that she would always remember that smell. She closed her eyes and took a deep breath.

"Mari?"

She and Dexter parted so she could look across the table to Nathan, who was smiling wide.

"Nathan! Are you having a good time, cousin?" Mari pulled away from Dexter and stood up. She went around the table and gave Nathan a hug, which he returned, and squeezed her so hard, all her breath practically left her lungs.

She laughed when he picked her up slightly off the floor and shook her gently.

"Oh, Nathan. You are having a good time, aren't you?"

"Oh yes, very much so!" Nathan answered in an excited voice. He swept his dark eyes around the room. "There are a lot of people here I don't know. But I know a lot of people, too. It's kind of strange."

"Did a lot of people know who you were?" She asked.

He shook his head. "No, mostly just the staff here, and a few special friends of Dad's."

"Well, I'm glad there were still people looking out for you. I really am."

Nathan smiled at her. "I know you are. You're a good friend."

"We're cousins. Don't forget that."

"Yes, cousins." Nathan nodded.

"Are you going to dance later?"

"I will if you will!" Nathan responded enthusiastically.

"I have to." Mari laughed, delightedly. "I have my first dance with my husband coming up soon."

"I'll be here for that, and then maybe we can dance after that."

Mari's heart warmed for the young man. He looked so much happier than he had been in the past. He was like a skinny teddy bear that you wanted to cuddle and take care of.

She heard her name being called and squeezed Nathan's arm. "I think that's it!" She looked over at Dexter and waved at him. He was already coming around the table. "It's time for our dance, Dex!" she said, grabbing his hand with one of hers, and pulling up the skirt of her dress with the other.

"See you later, Nathan!" she called out happily. He waved to her, laughing, as she dashed to the dance floor, practically dragging the tall man behind her. Dexter was laughing though, allowing himself to be pulled along, exaggerating it a little to play to the audience. Everyone laughed, cheered and clapped.

Once they were facing each other, their bodies close together, their hands entwined in each other's, and gazing into each other's eyes, Mari knew she had made the right choice from the very beginning. Despite the obstacles and challenges, she knew there was something different about Dexter.

He leaned down and pressed his lips to hers, causing cheers to rise up around the room. The music started and they began to sway in time to it. Dexter pulled back and they gazed at each other.

"You're gonna love me forever, aren't you?" Mari whispered.

Dexter nodded, never taking his eyes from hers. "You're damn right, I am. I love you, Mari Wright Scofield."

When he spoke those words, Mari believed every one of them. She had broken down his walls, and he had opened her eyes to a different life. Laura was right. They were about as right for each other as two people could get.

Her life at that moment was perfect. She hoped it would stay that way for the rest of her life.

Book 2: Sue

Prologue

Sue could barely hear her sisters as they chatted back and forth. Their voices mixed in with every other voice in the bar. She reached for her cocktail as her eyes ran over the crowd. Queen Anne was a popular place for the 30 to 50 age range, which was good, because she and her sisters were steadily approaching the 30-year mark in their lives. Mari had one year left, she had two and Lynn had four.

She liked the atmosphere of the Badlands, one of the two successful bars in Queen Anne, which was one of the smallest coastal towns in Georgia, situated close to St. Simon's Island. It had a family-run atmosphere, had interesting and unique décor and incredibly comfortable seats surrounding small round tables.

Sue didn't want to know how much the owner of the bar spent on just the seats. She was in charge of the accounts for Emerald Resort, a huge money-generating machine their uncle left them in his will. Already the prime spot for wealthy vacationers, Sue and her two sisters hadn't had to do anything more than update and bring new ideas to the organization. It was already thriving.

"What do you think, Sue?" Mari suddenly turned to her, leaning forward and speaking loudly. Sue was brought out of her thoughts, her eyes turning to her sister.

"I think we're gonna have to call Hank to get a ride back to the resort. I'm not driving, that's for sure."

Mari and Lynn both laughed.

"You're probably right," Mari said, her voice distinct over the others around Sue, when she was facing her directly. "But that's not what I was talking about. Didn't you hear any of that?"

Sue raised her eyebrows and took a sip from her Roadhouse Red, some kind of pineapple concoction that tasted like magic in her mouth. "I'm pretty sure the last thing you two were talking about was additions to the tennis courts or the pool or something. I'm just not into talking about the resort tonight. I thought we were going to have a good night out, not bring business into it."

Her head was a little fuzzy from the alcohol in the drink, but it was a comfortable feeling. The one thing she knew was that she did not want to talk about business.

Mari and Lynn looked at each other sheepishly. Sue moved her eyes away from them slowly.

They stopped on a man emerging from a back room. He was so tall he had to duck into the room, as the door was too short.

Sue's breath caught in her throat. He was the best-looking man she'd ever seen. He had dark brown, wavy hair, down to his shoulders, a wicked grin revealing straight, white teeth, and dark eyes that flashed when he looked around the room. He was carrying a guitar case.

He stopped and spoke with the bartender. Sue was instantly jealous. She could see the close relationship the two of them had.

She was surprised at herself. She couldn't remember the last time she'd felt a streak of jealousy. She wasn't sure she ever had. The man broke away from the bartender, a curvy blond with perfect makeup and large breasts, to walk out into the dining area of the bar. He crossed the room, dodging tables as he went.

Sue saw him coming. Her heartbeat sped up. She held her breath and smiled shakily at him as he passed.

He smiled back.

Sue pressed her lips together as he passed behind her chair. She turned around and watched him step up on the stage.

"Oh, wow, I didn't know there was entertainment tonight," Mari said in a softer voice, now that the bar had quieted some.

Sue looked back at her. "How do we find out who he is?"

Mari laughed softly. "I'm sure he'll tell us all his name. Musicians don't want you to forget that, do they?"

Sue agreed, giving a nod before turning back to watch the

man take an electric guitar from his case and plug it in.

"Is he going to play by himself?" she heard Lynn ask from behind her.

"That's what it looks like," Mari answered.

Sue reached around to get her drink. She had a feeling she was going to enjoy this show. She put the straw in her mouth and took a sip, not taking her eyes off of him.

He strummed to make sure the strings were in key, and rested his hand against them, settling on the bar stool in front of the microphone. He reached up and turned the microphone slightly, adjusting it so it was directly in front of his mouth.

"Good evening, folks," he said, smiling at the audience. His voice boomed out through the speakers set up all around the room.

"Good evening!" Many voices called back to him, including Sue's.

"I want to welcome you here to Badlands Bar and Grill. I'm glad you've decided to come here tonight, you know. You're the reason I can pay my bills, so thanks for coming!"

The room lit up with cheers and claps.

Sue had come to the Badlands only once before, and hadn't stayed for long. She'd only left because she was pressed for time. She could tell by the reaction of the customers that the man on stage was very popular already.

The man lifted one hand and waved it up and down. "Thank you. Thank you, guys. Okay, tonight I've got some pretty good songs picked out for you, I think. I don't know how many of you were here last week for the charity benefit. You? Yeah, some of you out there were here. That's cool. Thanks for coming. But…"

The man continued to talk, relating to the entire crowd, as if he was talking to a group of friends. Sue quickly realized that he was, as she heard several people calling out "You tell 'em, Mike!" and "That's right, Mike!"

She turned her attention back to what he was saying.

"So, these songs are picked out by the people who dropped their requests in that box and, I gotta say, they're some of my favorites. This week, I'm taking names for duets. That's right, ladies. I'm open for a duet partner for my show next week, and if you think you've got the voice to take me on, drop your name in that box and I'll give you a call. All right, let's get this show on the road."

His voice was so energetic, bouncing through the room, Sue enjoyed every minute of it. It made her feel excited and happy. She looked down and noticed her drink was almost gone. She didn't feel drunk. She felt a little silly, actually, because she had a huge crush on the man who'd taken the stage.

She turned back and looked at her sisters, her cheeks aflame. She knew one look at her and they would know what was going on. Or maybe they wouldn't. She'd never felt like this before. It was almost more than she could stand at one time.

As she thought, Mari tilted her head to the side with a knowing look on her face. "Oh, Lynn," she said in a teasing voice. "I think Sue's got a thing for the musician."

Sue felt her cheeks get hotter, as she slid her eyes from one sister to the other. Their teasing smiles didn't hide the love they had for her. She was glad she had them to keep her sensible. She'd always tried to take the hard road with the two of them. Mari was so indecisive as a young girl, never knowing what she wanted in her future, even if it was the next day.

Lynn was a flighty girl, and was now a flighty woman. She wore flowing shirts and skirts, or dressed like a dancer, with small slip on shoes and leggings, her long blond hair left to fly behind her wherever she went. She had a contagious laugh and sparkling blue eyes that many men had fallen in love with, but none had captured her heart. She was young and willing to bide her time.

"Well, I have to say it's about time," Lynn said, teasing her sister softly. "We didn't think the day would come."

"All right, you two. Keep up with the teasing."

207

Her sisters laughed and Sue joined them. She turned back around and watched the show, pondering if she wanted to put her name in that box and audition to duet with him. She'd been in choir at school. It was one of her favorite classes. She hadn't pursued much more singing than in the shower until right at that moment.

It might be fun.

She smiled wide, making her decision. It had been a long time since she'd done something fun, just for herself, without her sisters.

Chapter 1

Sue hadn't thought about that Saturday night, since the banging headache she'd had on Sunday finally went away. Monday and Tuesday rolled around with no hiccups.

It wasn't until Wednesday that Sue even remembered what she'd done. Her cell phone rang. She pulled it out her pocket and looked at the screen. The number was foreign to her, but it was a local area code.

If it was her business cell, she would have answered regardless. She often got calls from people all around the world, asking about Emerald Resort. But this was her personal cell, a number only a select few in Queen Anne knew.

She pushed the talk button skeptically and put the phone to her ear. "Hello?"

"Hey, is this Susanne Wright?"

She instantly recognized the voice. It was Mike, from Saturday night. Memories from that night flooded her mind. She had to stop walking, nearly losing the pile of papers in her hand, in her shock.

"H… hello." She stammered, feeling like a fool.

"You know who this is?"

Sue had a moment of doubt. Apparently, she hesitated too long because the man continued almost immediately.

"This is Mike Nelson from the Badlands. I got your name out of my suggestion box. You want to come sing with me?"

He asked the question so casually, it was as if he'd known her for years. She couldn't help smiling, adjusting the papers in her hands so they were straight again. She squeezed the phone to her ear with her shoulder. "I… I would like that. I haven't sung in years, but I used to love it. I think it would be fun."

"How long have you been in Queen Anne, Susanne?"

She heard the lilt in his voice, and knew he'd said her name that way on purpose, so it would rhyme. Her grin widened. She took the phone back into her hand and looked up at the sky, her smile stretching wide.

"You can call me Sue. All my friends do. I've been here about, oh, nine months now."

"I'm glad I can call you a friend, Sue. I'm Mike. To everyone. What do you do, if you don't mind me asking?"

"I'm part owner of the Emerald Resort," she said bluntly. Most people in the small town of roughly 10,000 residents knew who she and her sisters were by name, and not by sight. She was a little surprised he didn't recognize her the same way.

There was a pause on the other end. Sue could picture him trying to sort that information through his mind.

"You're *that* Sue Wright?" Mike asked incredulously.

She smiled again, hoping it would come through her voice when she spoke. "That's me. In the flesh."

"Are you busy right now?"

The urgency in his voice made Sue go into alarm mode. She pulled the phone from her face and peered at the time. "I have a few minutes before my meeting. What's up?"

"I have been hoping to find a way to get in touch with one of you three directly. It's... well, I'm hoping to get some bookings set up there at the resort, for weddings and other things like that. I've got a friend who does photography, and we had it in our heads that if we could get a contract with whoever plans the weddings you ladies host, we can showcase our talent to the local community a lot better. And at the same time, we'd be reaching a bigger crowd, maybe with some people who can help us in our careers. Am I rambling? I'm sorry."

Sue listened to the pitch with great interest. She didn't consider it rambling. As soon as Mike mentioned bookings, Sue's mind went into business mode.

"I heard you play last Saturday, Mike, and I think that sounds like a good idea. Let me talk to my sisters about it, and we'll have you come in and show us what you've got. How does that sound?"

Mike was extremely grateful. She could hear it in his voice. "Oh, man, thank you, Sue. That… that's a really great opportunity for us."

Sue laughed. "You're welcome, Mike. Just remember, this isn't saying yes, yet, I mean, I have to talk to them, and we all have to talk to you. You'd better have a good selling story for us. We're hard to convince."

She made it sound as ridiculous as possible, so he would know she was not serious. She enjoyed the chuckle he let out.

"Got any tips for me?"

"As a matter of fact, I do." Aware of the time, Sue began walking again, her eyes focused on the door at the end of the hallway. She'd seen her sisters go in with their new client moments ago, but was listening to Mike and not really paying attention to them.

They were waiting for her.

"I have to go, but one thing I'll tell you is that you might want to familiarize yourself with the modern songs people like to have played at their weddings. Pick out the ones you think we'd hear the most."

"The most?"

"Yes. Don't try anything unique at first. It's the best way to get my sisters on board."

"You got it. Thanks! Oh, and can you come by the bar after work tonight? I'd like to see about the duet competition, too."

"Yeah, what time?"

"Whenever is good for you."

Sue thought quickly. "All right, I'll be there at 6:30. Sound good?"

She heard the smile in his voice when he replied. It sent a chill of pleasure through her. "Sounds good. See you then, Sue."

"Okay, Mike. Bye."

Sue pushed through the door, pressing the button on her phone and moving quickly to her chair at the table. Her sisters didn't look up from the papers they were studying, but the client stood up and held out his hand to her.

"Hello, you must be Sue," he said, politely. She smiled and shook his hand.

"That's me. Sorry I'm late, I was on the phone."

He waved his hand dismissively, shaking his head. "Not a problem at all. We've only been in here a few minutes. I have some papers my fiancé wanted me to give you, about her preferences." He sat back down. "I'm Nathan Hawke, by the way. Sorry." He grinned.

Sue chuckled softly. "I know who you are, Mr. Hawke. I did the booking."

He laughed with her, handing her two sheets of paper stapled together. Her eyes immediately dropped down to "music". The woman had listed several songs she wanted, and specifically requested a local musician. She didn't care which, she just wanted someone local.

Sue raised her eyebrows at the irony of the situation. She knew exactly who to recommend.

She was overcome by the same sense of urgency she heard in Mike's voice, when he found out who she was. She giggled, thinking his excitement had invaded her spirit. She couldn't wait to get off work and sing with him.

More than that, she wanted the meeting to be over so she could tell her sisters.

Their client was very accommodating. He didn't stay long, looked over their color schemes and themes, and left them with a number to call his fiancé. Once he was out of the room, the ladies gathered their papers together. Sue did so anxiously, noticing with a giggle that her hands were shaking.

Mari noticed, too, which Sue expected. Her observant sister

didn't miss a thing. Sue felt Mari's eyes when they settled on her. A slow smile spread across her lips.

"All right, Sue. Tell us what's on your mind."

Sue tried to look innocent, knowing it wouldn't fool either of them. She pursed her lips and pretended to be very busy with her papers.

"Come on, Sue," Lynn prompted her. "I'm curious, too. What do you have going on?"

Sue felt like she was going to burst with excitement. When she spoke, it was obvious in her tone. "Do you girls remember that bar we went to? The Badlands? And the man who went onstage, Mike?"

Both of her sisters nodded. They shared a look of excited anticipation. Sue grinned wide, biting her bottom lip. "I put my name in the box to sing duets with him."

Lynn gasped and slapped a hand over her mouth. "You didn't!" she said with a laugh. "That's so... so wonderful! But... so odd for you. Are you sure you want to do that?"

Sue nodded, shrugging. "I was in choir in high school, remember? I was really good, according to my teacher. I had a couple solos. I guess you don't remember. You were too busy being a social butterfly."

"Oh, stop. I do remember. But you're not as... outgoing as you used to be." Lynn sounded hesitant. Sue just gave her a smile.

"I know. That's true. But... well, I'm excited this time. I think this is going to be a lot of fun."

"So, he called you up then?" Mari asked, shoving her stack of papers in a leather binder and zipping it closed.

Sue stood up when she did. "He called me before I got in here. That's why I was a little late. But I do want to talk to both of you about something. When he found out who I was, he got really excited and said he's been trying to get in touch with one of us for months. He offered his services as a wedding singer. I'm assuming he has a band. I told him he could come in and interview with the two of you."

Sue noticed the look on Mari's face change slightly. She recognized the suspicious look her sister got when something didn't quite sit right with her.

"He asked you for a job?" she asked.

"No, he offered his services. He's been trying to get in touch with us because the resort would bring him a lot of money. Especially now that we've started booking and hosting wedding parties."

Mari looked skeptical. "I kind of assumed you liked this guy for personal reasons. Do you?"

Sue drew her eyebrows together, picking up her papers and holding them against her chest. "I do."

"Well, make sure you guard your heart. Men can be deceiving. It sounds like he might just be interested in what you can do for him."

Sue shook her head. "No, I don't think it's that. But I'll be careful, Mari. When he called, he only knew my name. He didn't know I was one of the owners here. So, he called to see if I would sing with him."

"Did he pick names randomly out of a hat or is he calling everyone?" Mari asked.

Sue raised her eyebrows. "I... How would I know that?"

Mari propped her glasses up on her head. "Just be careful, Sue. He might just be out for your money."

Sue was irritated, frowning. Mari came around from her side of the table and put her hand on her sister's arm. "Don't look like that, Sue. I'm not saying you don't have redeeming factors and qualities that a man could love. I'm saying, when you see someone once and they call you for a totally unrelated reason, you can't go jumping through hoops for a relationship. It's a little too soon to be thinking about that, don't you think?"

Sue couldn't help breathing out a sigh. Her sister was right.

But she was still going to have a blast singing with Mike.

Chapter 2

Mike sat behind the desk in his office, looking down at the mess of papers on his desk. He'd sorted through each of them, so he knew exactly which receipts went with each stack. He picked through them, lifting up different stacks and stapling them together.

The door opened and he looked up, grateful for the break. Mandy stuck her head in, a bright smile on her pretty face. His general manager, and a good friend, Mandy had been working in Mike's bar for almost four years. She knew a lot about the business, and was one of the best bartenders Mike had ever seen. She'd been on television in the past as a bartending expert.

She came in, her straight blond hair swinging forward and settling gently against her ample bosom. Mike suspected she wore tighter shirts to show off, and possibly to get more tips. He'd stopped noticing them long ago.

Most of the time.

He ran his eyes over her body, admiring her shape. He dropped them down to the papers in his hand, careful not to staple his thumb.

"Hey, Mandy, how are you today?"

"Better now," she replied in a cheerful voice, dropping into the chair on the other side of his desk. "What are you up to? Busy work?"

"Yeah, papers, receipts. Tax season is coming up."

"Yep. I'd offer to help, but that's not my part of the company."

Mike chuckled, shaking his head. "I'll take care of it, thanks."

"So, I hear you called one of the names you picked out of the box. You gonna do it that way, or give all of them a chance?"

Mike set the papers down and rested his elbows on the

desk, leaning forward slightly. He looked directly at Mandy as he spoke. "I picked one out," he said, his voice smooth. "And it was the only one I ended up calling. It was my intention to get at least three or four girls down here to sing, and I would choose which one was the best. But… I only called the one."

Mandy raised her eyebrows, her blue eyes sparkling behind thick dark lashes, that Mike was certain were fake. "Why just one?"

Mike hesitated before answering, forming the words in his mind so they wouldn't sound ridiculous. "I… I liked the sound of her voice."

Mandy blinked at him. "Did she sing for you on the phone?" she asked incredulously.

Mike shook his head, laughing softly. "No. It wasn't… I didn't need to hear her sing. I could tell she's got a great voice just from listening to her talk. Plus, there's an extra benefit."

Mandy narrowed her eyes impatiently when he stopped speaking. "Don't make me guess, Mike. Tell me."

"It's Sue Wright." He slapped his hand down on the desktop triumphantly, beaming at her.

Mandy raised her eyebrows, giving him a blank look.

"You don't know who that is?" Mike asked excitedly.

Mandy shook her head. "No. Sue Wright, you say?" A look of realization crossed her face and she lifted her chin up. "Oh, you're talking about those women that took over Emerald Resort when Nathan died. Is that her?"

Mike nodded, his grin returning full blast. Mandy looked impressed. "So, they came in last Saturday. I didn't think I'd seen them before."

Mike nodded. "I was thinking the same thing when I saw them. I was going to greet them, but they left before my set was over. I'm gonna have to ask Sue about that when she gets here. It's rude to leave in the middle of someone's set."

216

Mandy laughed. "Not if they're playing after midnight in a bar. I'm sure those ladies had work to do the next day."

"I'm just glad she agreed to come. She'll be here any minute, I expect. She was coming right after work. How are things looking out there?"

Mandy turned her head to glance over her shoulder at the closed door behind her, as if she could see through it into the seating area. "Oh, there's a few of the regulars in there. I don't think we'll see anyone till at least 7 or 8."

Mike nodded. "Nice weather."

"Exactly," Mandy agreed with him. "That means people will be out doing stuff until the sun goes down. They're not likely to come in the bar till then."

"Glad we agree on that."

"I don't think we'll have a busy night tonight. There's a game on. I think it's basketball. I'm not really sure." Mandy shifted in the seat, crossing her legs so her ankles were also intertwined. She stretched them out behind her and tapped one of her black boots on the leg of the chair she sat in. "When's your new little girlfriend showing up?"

Mike heard the teasing in her voice, but thought for the first time, that Mandy might not be happy about him singing with a woman. He knew she considered him her property, though they weren't dating and never had. He didn't look at her like that and had told her so repeatedly.

That didn't mean she wasn't quite a looker. She was, in fact, one of the most beautiful women Mike had ever seen. He was more than pleased to hire her on as his main bartender and give her control of the floor in that area. She did it best. He wouldn't interfere.

"First of all, she's not my girlfriend, and second, I'd say in about a half hour. It's coming up on seven, and she said 6:30 or so."

Mandy's eyebrows shot up. "She said she'd be here at 6:30,

and she's running late? Sounds like she's not too interested."

Mike snorted, shaking his head. "Cut it out, Mandy. She just got off work, she can take her time. She's only coming to audition to sing with me, anyway."

"Well, I hope she does a great job, and it's a big successful thing for you. You could use the promotion. I'm sure she's got a lot of ties to rich people who could jump start your music career."

Mike felt a tingle of excitement run through him. He grinned. "I asked her if she needed a music planner for the weddings. We're going to talk about that tonight, too."

"Well, you just have it all planned out, don't you?"

Mike detected that bit of jealousy he'd expected as soon as she found out about the duet situation. He brushed it off as typical Mandy behavior.

"Yeah, it's gonna be a lot of fun."

Mandy stood up, placing her hands on her hips. It was the way she usually stood, showing off her fine features. She smiled, her red lips stretching up into her cheeks in a gentle slope. "I'll let you know if I see her coming through. Let me guess. She looks like a ball-busting librarian, right?"

Mike laughed. "I don't think any of those three women looked ball-busting, but I don't know which one it is until she gets here. You go on out there and let me know something. I don't want her feeling confused."

Mandy went to the door, looking over her shoulder to say, "You should have directed her to the back entrance. Then she'd just walk in on you. I'm sure you wouldn't mind that."

Mike grinned and rolled his eyes as Mandy threw back her head and laughed, disappearing when the door closed behind her as she left.

He tried to remember what the three women in the bar looked like that Saturday night, but the lights were dim on purpose. He didn't remember any of them being particularly ugly, nor were they gorgeous like Mandy.

But he couldn't be certain. And what difference did that make anyway?

He grinned. He'd done many charities and events with women of all degrees of beauty. One thing he'd noticed was that the beauty they carried inside came out when they were treated with respect and dignity, no matter what their outer appearance displayed.

He looked down at the papers on his desk. He didn't want to go through them anymore. Thinking about Sue getting there at any moment had him distracted. He didn't do money work when he wasn't focused.

He gathered them all in a stack and put them in his to-do box, along with the receipt papers. He'd deal with them later.

He swiveled in his chair, glancing down at his cell phone. He pressed the power button. He hadn't missed any calls. Hopefully that meant she was still coming. It was eight minutes till 7:00, and he was starting to get a little worried she wouldn't come.

He stepped away from his desk and crossed the room to get his guitar. He'd set his office up with a practice space, for himself and two other people, if he decided to use drums or keyboards in his set. He'd purchased a second microphone and stand just a month ago, when he decided on the duet challenge for the bar.

He went through his busy work as much as he could, setting everything up the way he wanted it, looking through the book of songs he had programmed into the computer for karaoke. He'd written a quick list of wedding songs and planned to go over them with Sue when she arrived.

He felt his impatience growing and hit the power button on his cell again to see how late Sue really was.

Four minutes had passed.

He stared at the phone, astounded. It still wasn't seven o'clock.

Sighing, Mike wandered to the door of his office and swung it open. He moved out just enough to lean against the doorjamb, his hands pushed into the pockets of his jeans, and his black boots crossed over one another.

His bar wasn't full, but it wasn't empty either. They offered only the basics when it came to food, and had a few signature dishes the locals liked a lot. He could smell the food cooking for early dinner customers.

There were four men lined up along the bar. They all seemed to be talking to Mandy at the same time. She responded as she always did, with a smile and swing of her hair, as she prepared some sort of cocktail. He watched her move gracefully, wondering why he had never developed feelings for her. He had nothing bad to say about her. It had just never come to that for him, despite her constant flirting.

She caught his eye and smiled at him. He smiled back. The men at the bar all turned to look at him and raised their hands in greeting.

"Mike! Come on and have a drink with us!" One of them called out.

Mike chuckled loudly. "Now, you know I don't drink my profits, Dan," he replied. "That's the best way to go under in business."

Dan made a sound of loud appreciation. "Yeah, you're probably right, there, Mike. Wise decision, my friend. Wise decision."

Mike turned his eyes to Mandy. He could tell she knew what he was thinking. It appeared Dan was drinking before he came in the Badlands. Mandy knew when to cut him off, and how to handle the situation. He was lucky to have someone like her.

A tingle of pleasure slid through him when the door to the bar opened and a stranger came through. A woman with long blond hair and a nice figure, dressed in pretty, casual clothes.

Mike grinned. If that was Sue, she didn't look like the millionaire he knew she was.

That was to her credit, as far as he was concerned.

Chapter 3

Sue tapped her foot repeatedly on the floorboard of her car, watching the train pass. It was the only train in Queen Anne, and it had to go through right during rush hour traffic.

Not that rush hour traffic was anything like the city she and her sisters had come from. The population was smaller, even on-season.

But for the life of her, she didn't know why the only time she had ever been in a rush to get somewhere, she had to catch this one train?

She sighed in frustration, and reacted swiftly when she saw the end of the train approaching. She pressed the brake, gripped the steering wheel with one hand and wrapped the other around the gear shift. It had already added to her tardiness. She didn't want Mike to think she'd changed her mind, and call someone else to fill her position.

The gates slowly rose and she urged the people in front of her to hurry, with a few words under her breath.

"Come on, come on, slow pokes. That's what shocks are for. Just go over the tracks already." She continued murmuring similar phrases, until she was over the tracks and almost free of the congestion the train had caused.

Her heartbeat sped up the closer she got to the bar. By the time she was pulling in the driveway, she thought it might come straight out of her chest.

She put one hand over it and pulled in a slow breath. She let it out just as slowly and tried to calm herself. It had been a long time since she'd felt an attraction like this. She wasn't quite sure how to handle it.

"All right, get yourself under control for goodness sake," she murmured. She grabbed her purse from the passenger seat, her cell phone from the holder on the dashboard and pushed open the door.

The air was crisp, as the evening settled in. It would be dark in an hour. Not that she cared. She enjoyed the weather in Georgia, no matter what time of year it was. At times it could get sticky with humidity, but she just stayed inside if it was a day like that.

She walked across the parking lot, scanning the front door of the bar. It was well-lit, with bright, attractive colors and neon signs that looked welcoming. She liked the atmosphere from the outside so much the last time, she'd mentioned it to her sisters as they went in.

She appreciated it just as much the second time.

She grinned, reaching out to pull the door open. A man was inside, pushing out at the same time. He swung the door open wide and stepped back so she could enter.

"Here you go, miss," he said pleasantly.

She turned her smile to him. "Thank you." She used her friendliest voice.

They nodded at each other as she passed him. She grasped the strap of her purse with one hand and looked around the bar.

She remembered it from the Saturday night out, but they had come when it was bustling. It was calmer now, more peaceful. The men at the bar were staring at the television set, which displayed some kind of sports game. Sue didn't pay enough attention to figure out which one.

A handful of families and couples had taken tables, and were eating food with satisfied looks on their faces. It was a nice bar. And it was nice for the owner to let Mike play there. She hoped he was allowed to freelance. She didn't want him to get in trouble.

Her eyes fell on the pretty blond bartender, who was eyeing her up and down.

"Hey there, miss!" the woman called out to her, making her the center of attention, when every head in the room swiveled to look at her. She grinned sheepishly, feeling her cheeks burning red.

"You lookin' for Mike?"

Sue hurried across the room to the bar and spoke in a quiet voice.

"Yes, is he here?"

The bartender studied her for a moment, letting out an abrupt laugh. "Of course, he's here. He's been waiting for you. Just go right around there, missy, through that door. He's standing right there. That's Mike."

Sue moved her eyes to take in Mike's majestic form, leaning against the doorjamb comfortably, a handsome smile on his face. He was looking straight at her. She was once again taken aback by how good-looking he was and what a strong effect he had on her.

She swallowed her nervousness and ignored the constant scrutiny of the bartender, walking behind the men at the bar lined up on their stools. She turned to the left and approached Mike, looking into his eyes as she came closer.

"You are Mike?"

His grin widened. "I am. And you must be Sue. I remember you from Saturday night. I didn't get to see you well, and didn't know which one of you was you, but here you are. It's you."

Sue swallowed the instant giggle that came to her throat. She didn't want to look like a fool in front of the man.

"I'm excited to talk to you about your proposal," she began. "And to sing with you, too. I'm so sorry I'm late. I had to take care of some things at the office and I caught a train and..."

Mike chuckled, stepping back to let her into his office. "Don't mention it," he interrupted her. "I'm just glad you came. I was beginning to think you'd changed your mind."

Sue's eyes widened. That was exactly what she was afraid of. She stopped a few steps into the office and looked back at him. "I hope you didn't call someone else to do the duets with you."

Mike gave her a look of surprise, which confused her. He

223

shook his head, coming up behind her and holding his hand out toward the practice area.

"No, you're the only one I called. I... I'd like to see what we can do, before I try getting anyone else involved. I mean... trying out other people, you know."

Sue had to swallow the giggling she felt inside, when his hand brushed against her back. He was directing her toward the practice area. She could feel his warmth behind her. It sent a chill up her spine. A pleasant chill.

She allowed herself to be pushed gently to the microphone stand in front of the small drum set.

"Do you play drums, too?" she asked, curiously, looking over her shoulder at him. He shook his head.

"No, I've got a buddy who comes over and jams with me sometimes. We like to do those old rock songs no one likes anymore."

Sue chuckled. "You can't go wrong with some of the old classics. It just depends on which one it is. I mean, some of them are done to death. Who wants to hear more Free Bird?"

Mike's eyebrows shot up to mix in with the dark strands of hair that had fallen over his forehead. "Free Bird? Where are you from again?"

Sue laughed. "Virginia."

Mike nodded. "Oh, I see. Yeah, I don't have that requested a lot down here. But I know it's a popular one."

"I mean no disrespect," Sue continued in a laughing voice. He shook his head.

"None taken. Did you have a chance to talk to your sisters about allowing me to do some of the music planning?"

Sue set her bag down on a nearby chair and stood behind the microphone, adjusting it to her height like a pro. She was proud of herself and hoped she'd impressed him with the quick maneuver. "Well," she said casually. "I did. And first of all, if you take over music planning, you will be in charge of it all. Not just some of it. You know? You'd be the expert. Our go-to man."

He flashed a handsome grin at her. "Do I detect a positive thing here?"

Sue grinned. "I think you will easily charm my sisters when you meet with them. I said a few nice things about you and they are willing to consider it. After all, it will be one extra thing we don't have to take care of. And you'd be paid well for your services."

Mike nodded. "I appreciate that. When do they want to meet with me?"

Sue liked the way he was down to business, wanting to get things done. It impressed on her that he was fired up for the endeavor. That was always a good way to make money. She was also pleased that he hadn't asked about the payment and was not behaving in an overtly flirtatious way, as if he was more interested in money than anything else.

If he was hiding his greed, he was doing it well.

"As soon as you like, I guess. I can fit you in tomorrow, if you'd like."

"That sounds great. Do you want to sit and have a drink before we start? I think we should try to get to know each other a little, if we're going to be singing together, and be business partners, too."

Sue grinned at him. She hadn't been so comfortable and happy for a long time.

"I think, technically, you'll be an employee of the Resort."

His eyebrows shot up. "So, you'll be my boss?"

Sue laughed. "I suppose so. Don't worry. I'll go easy on you."

He dropped a wink and said in a low voice. "No need to go that far."

They both laughed. He strolled back to the door and opened

225

it, holding his hand out for her to go first.

"Just take any seat at the bar or in the dining area, Sue. I'll grab us some drinks. Anything you like in particular?"

"What kind of drink are we talking about?" she asked.

He gave her a closed-mouth grin. "It's whatever you want, my dear. You can have a Coke or a cocktail or a beer. It's up to you."

"I'll take a Blue Motorcycle."

He nodded once, following her out and crossing over to the bar, while she found a table for them to sit at.

She went all the way to the other side of the bar, as far away from the bar as she could get. She didn't want to be stared at by the bartender the entire time she chatted with Mike. The woman had daggers in her eyes. Sue foresaw trouble with that woman, but hoped she was just being paranoid.

If she was curious enough, she'd ask Mike about her. His responses would determine whether she needed to be concerned or not.

She hoped not. She didn't like drama any more than anyone else. But some women thrived on it. The woman behind the bar looked like she might be one of those kinds of women.

Chapter 4

Sue dropped down in the chair again, feeling refreshed and invigorated. She'd stayed at the bar through the whole night, spending much of it in the office, pretending she could play the drums, laughing at Mike's ridiculous antics and stories of his wild band days, and generally having the best time of her life.

It was past midnight, but she didn't care. She wasn't drunk enough to worry about making a fool of herself, and was prepared for at least one more drink before she sobered up to drive home. Or get a ride. She hadn't seen Mike take an alcoholic drink since she'd first arrived.

"I hope you've had a good time tonight," Mike said, smiling at her as he slid into the chair opposite her. She nodded energetically.

"I really have, Mike. I think we sound good together, don't you?"

"Oh, yeah." She could hear he was impressed by the tone of his voice. "I can't believe you've never done anything with that talent. Not even karaoke?"

Sue shook her head. "I'm not the kind of woman who goes to bars and does that scene, to be really honest with you. I just like to be in my house, doing the things I like to do. I sing when I'm by myself and that satisfies me."

"So, you've never wanted to make a career out of it?" Mike set the drinks he'd gotten from the bar on the table, sliding hers closer. She smiled at him, wrapping one hand around the glass and leaning toward him.

"No, not really. I'm sure at some point in my teenage years, I was like, someday I'll be a famous singer!" She giggled, shaking her head. "No, that's just not my thing. I'd rather crunch some numbers or organize something beautiful. I'm really blessed to have been left the resort by my Uncle Nathan. I really didn't have a direction yet in my life. In between my sisters, I guess I didn't have the best excuses for not getting things done."

Mike raised one eyebrow. "I think all of you have your own special traits. You should be proud of what you've done with the resort."

She nodded. "Oh, I am, believe me." She took a sip of the drink, and twirled the straw around as she swallowed, staring into the colorful liquid. "I am. I know my sisters are. I really think it was what we all needed. My sister, Mari, found her husband. They've been married for a year."

"That's wonderful. I remember the wedding. Well, reading about it in the paper. I, uh…" he grinned. "I don't think I received an invitation."

One side of Sue's lips lifted in a half-grin. "It was an open invitation to anyone in Queen Anne. I think you might have just been busy doing your daily stuff, not thinking about those rich ladies on the hill."

Mike's grin faded and he gave her a contemplative look. "You don't think I asked you here just because of who you are, do you?"

Sue studied his face. She didn't want to believe that. Mari's words of warning rang in her ears. But the way he'd treated her throughout the night didn't speak to that kind of behavior. He was a gentleman and she'd had a great time with him. She hadn't felt unsafe even once. She didn't even think he'd lied to her about any of his outlandishly wild stories of his band days.

He just seemed like an honest, fun person to be around.

"I don't," she replied softly, lifting one shoulder and tilting her head to meet it halfway. "I really don't, Mike. You're… you seem genuine to me. Does that make sense?"

His responsive grin said it all. "It does. That's a nice word. It's flattering to be described that way. I like it."

"I'm glad to hear it. I'm just being honest. I've had a great time tonight." Sue looked at him, enjoying his handsome face, embedding it in her memory. She would be dreaming about him. She was certain of that.

"And how are you two doing tonight?"

Their moment was interrupted by the bartender's voice, cutting into Sue's thoughts like a razor blade. She reluctantly turned her eyes away from Mike, dragging them to the bartender's radiant smile. It wasn't directed at her, though. The woman was looking directly at Mike.

Sue returned her eyes to Mike, noticing the awkward look on his face. He held his hand out to the woman. "Sue, this is Mandy. Mandy is my general manager, and the head bartender here. You want a delicious drink made by the best, she's the one you call."

"Aww, thanks, Mike." Mandy moved closer to him and draped her arm over his shoulder, running her finger along his cheek.

Sue felt an instant pang of jealousy. She swallowed it as quickly as it came on her, not willing to let the woman get to her. It was obvious what she was trying to do.

"It's almost time for closing, Mikey. Don't you think we better be wrapping things up?"

Mike's eyebrows shot up, making his forehead wrinkle. Sue had to bite back a laugh at the look of shock on his face when he looked at Mandy. "What? It's a little after one. We have plenty of time."

"I know," Mandy said in a sulky voice, dropping her eyes seductively at him. "But there are closing things that have to be done, and the sooner we get started on them, the better. Isn't that what you always say? I know you like to get out of here as quick as you can at night."

Mike turned his eyes to Sue, looking uncomfortable by how much Mandy was touching him.

"I'm sorry, Sue. She usually doesn't act like this in front of customers."

Mandy looked hurt and pulled away from him, her cheeks darkening slightly. She still refused to look at Sue, who was just fine with that.

"Act like what, Mikey?"

"Stop calling me Mikey," Mike barked the words, but managed to keep it at a level tone so no one else left in the bar would hear him. He looked at Sue again. "She never calls me Mikey. No one does. Please, don't do it."

Sue grinned at him. "No one calls you that? I think I've found your weakness. Finally, something I can use against you."

Sue delighted in the look that crossed Mike's face. That handsome smile she loved so much was back, and he laughed a genuine laugh. "Oh, Sue! You better not. I haven't found your weakness yet. What are you afraid of? Come on, you gotta give me something."

Sue tilted her head to the side and grinned at him. "Not in public."

Mandy's jaw dropped. She stared at Sue as if she'd said she would strip naked for Mike right there in the bar. Sue giggled inside. It had taken an off-hand comment to get the bartender to finally acknowledge her presence and all she could do was gawk at her.

Mike, however, laughed heartily, throwing his head back. He raised his glass and she did the same, so he could clink his against hers. "That was a good one, Sue. You've got a wicked sense of humor. I'm glad you came by tonight."

"I'm glad you called me, Mike. I haven't had such a good time like this since... I can't even remember."

Mike turned his eyes purposefully to Mandy, whose face had taken on a dark look. The corners of her pretty lips were turned down, and she was staring rather hatefully at Sue. Sue tried not to let it make her uncomfortable, but it wasn't until later that she would admit to her sisters how awful it made her feel. Her stomach churned with nervousness, expecting the bartender to swing at her at any moment.

If Mike hadn't been so charming, handsome, and fun to be

around, she might have decided it wasn't the atmosphere she wanted to be in.

But he was all of those things and more. She wanted to spend all her time at the bar, just talking to him, listening to him, just to be in his presence.

"Mike, don't you think it's time we…"

Mike cut Mandy's words off with a simple raised hand. "No. You go do your things and get out of here early if you want. I'll get done with what I have to do when I'm done. Don't worry about my chores. Worry about your own. Look, there are still people in here who want to be served until two am, am I right?"

Mandy's jaw clenched visibly. She didn't say anything, despite Mike's insistent stare.

"Am I right?" he repeated more forcefully, making Mandy flinch.

Sue almost felt sorry for the woman, but not enough to sympathize or say anything.

"Yes, I suppose you're right. I just thought…"

"You thought wrong. What you need to get done isn't dependent on me getting my stuff done. So, go on back behind that bar and do your job, all right?"

Mandy cleared her throat. When it looked like she was going to say something, Mike shook his head slowly. She closed her mouth and stomped away from him, fuming silently.

Sue stared at Mike, who looked angry. His face didn't change until he rested his eyes on her face. She saw him relax and was internally pleased that she'd made that happen, just by being there.

"I'm so sorry she was rude to you," he said in a low voice. "I never would have expected that from her, but I guess I should have. I haven't had a girlfriend since she's known me."

Sue froze, blinking at him. "Do you have one now?" she asked in a breathless voice. If he meant her, he was jumping way

231

ahead in the relationship area. She immediately felt the urge to put up a roadblock to stop that from happening, no matter how attractive she found him. That was way too soon, and a big red flag.

Mike laughed. "No. I didn't mean you're my girlfriend. I meant, with no girlfriend, and never dating anyone, she expects me to be a bachelor for life. She's never even seen me laugh or spend time with a woman like I have with you tonight."

"I hope you enjoyed my company," Sue said softly, gazing into his dark eyes. She loved the flash of his smile when he nodded.

"I did, Sue. I hope we can do it again sometime. I'll try to make it on a night when Mandy isn't here."

"I hope that me coming around doesn't cause friction between the two of you," Sue said, seeing an opening to find out a little more. "It looks like you're pretty close."

Mike moved his eyes away from her for a moment, letting them trail across the room to the bar in the distance. "I guess we are close. We're really good friends. I guess she has some feelings for me that aren't returned. But overall, she's been a great bartender, a good friend, and someone I trust, you know?"

"You aren't going to trust her, about going out with me?"

Mike gave her a sober look and then grinned wide. "If you're willing to take that chance, so am I."

Sue's smile matched his.

Chapter 5

Sue pushed open the door to the Badlands and exited, stepping out in the cool breeze, and lifting her chin up to smile at the moon. She closed her eyes briefly and took in a deep breath.

"Nice night, isn't it?"

Her head snapped to the side. She was staring at Mandy, who was immersed in shadows, only the glow of her cigarette indicating where she was. Sue watched her take in a draw from the cigarette, the embers burning bright orange in the pitch darkness.

"What are you doing, standing in the shadows like that?" Sue asked, aggravated. "You nearly gave me a heart attack."

Mandy stepped forward, the dim light from the street lamp barely casting any light on her. Sue frowned.

"I'm sorry about that," Mandy said in an apologetic voice, surprising Sue. "I wasn't thinking about it. I come out here whenever I need a cigarette, no matter what time of day or night it is. I don't even think twice. What time is it anyway? It's gotta be pushing 3:00."

"I left the table when the clock said 2:00. I don't want to keep either of you here all night," Sue replied, cautiously. Mandy's voice didn't reflect any of the spite she'd seen on the woman's face before.

"I'll walk you to your car, if you like," Mandy said, amiably. "It's pretty safe here in Queen Anne. The locals don't put up with riff-raff. Even on-season, when we get the city people here, it's just not tolerated."

"I've noticed the crime rate is really low here."

Mandy nodded. "For the most part."

The woman continued for a moment, gabbing about the effectiveness of the small but efficient police force of Queen Anne, but Sue was barely listening to her. She was thinking about how different Mandy seemed out here, as opposed to earlier, in the bar.

Was it just the presence of Mike that caused Mandy to act so rudely?

Sue brought her focus back to Mandy when they reached her car. "I'm glad you feel safe here," she said, reaching in her purse for the keys to unlock the door. "It makes me feel more comfortable coming and going."

"I guess you'll be around a lot more, now that you're gonna sing with Mike, huh?" Sue listened for the spite in Mandy's voice, but didn't hear a trace of it. She dug through her purse, looking down into its black depths, trying to hide the second wave of surprise that swept over her.

"I guess so." She finally found her keys and pulled them out, pressing the unlock button on the key fob.

She reached to open her door, when Mandy reached out, with the hand clutching the cigarette between her fingers, and snagged Sue's shirt, pulling on it gently.

"Can we talk?"

Sue was immediately suspicious, narrowing her eyes at the taller woman. Mandy lifted the cigarette to her lips again, and took a deep draw on it. The smoke curled from her mouth as she spoke, making Sue feel slightly sick to her stomach.

"I don't want to start any drama. I just want to give you my insight because… well, I know Mike really well, and I don't want anyone getting hurt."

Sue contemplated the woman's words for a moment. She was sure Mandy had a thing for Mike, but didn't believe it was reciprocated. However, she didn't know Mike. Anything Mandy might say would be from her experience with him. She couldn't exactly trust Mandy, since she didn't know her. But she didn't know Mike, either.

Torn between her curiosity and good sense, Sue finally nodded, gesturing with her head toward her car. "Get in the passenger side. We'll talk, but you can't smoke that in my car."

Sue felt another pang of disgust when Mandy nodded and

flicked the cigarette off into the nearby bushes. She fought the urge to go get the butt or at least put it all the way out. She turned away from the bushes and opened her door, pulling in a heavy sigh.

Mandy went around the car and got in the passenger side, bringing with her the scent of cigarettes, and a perfume Sue wouldn't have minded, if it wasn't invaded by the fouler stench of smoke.

Sue didn't feel completely uncomfortable, but she didn't want the conversation to be long. She wasn't sure how blunt she could be with the woman without making an enemy out of her. She turned to look at Mandy, her eyebrows raised.

"It's really late and I've had alcohol, so I'm pretty tired. What did you want to say to me?"

"I just want you to know that Mike is a great guy and… well, he and I used to have something, but there's nothing there now. You don't have to worry about that."

Sue licked her lips. "I don't know if Mike and I are actually what you'd call dating exclusively, Mandy. I just met him tonight."

Mandy nodded. "Oh, I understand that. But, well, I saw the way you were looking at him. I just thought it would be a good idea for me to… well, warn you, I guess."

The word 'warn' sent a chill through Sue. She bristled, narrowing her eyes at Mandy. "What do you mean?"

Mandy used a gentle voice when she responded. Sue wasn't sure if that was meant to keep her calm, or to make Mandy's words more believable.

"I really did like Mike a lot. He's a great businessman and all that. But… he's a heartbreaker. A lady's man. He's always got some new girl on his arm. I just want you to know that it's a good idea for you to be careful, you know. With your heart."

Sue didn't know how to feel about Mandy's warning. It sounded like something a concerned friend might say to another but Mandy was not a friend of Sue's and Sue wasn't sure about her true intentions.

It sounded to her like Mandy was trying to get Sue to back off. Thereby leaving the door open for her to continue her pursuit of the gentle musician.

Sue tilted her head back, thinking about what Mandy said.

"I don't want you to be upset with me for telling you this," Mandy continued. "But I think, since I've been with Mike for so long now, it's always a good idea to warn ladies before he gets a chance to hurt them."

Sue couldn't picture Mike doing anything to hurt her. But then again, it was the best cheaters that didn't get caught until someone was hurt. He wasn't a violent man, but that didn't make him loyal. How could she possibly judge his loyalty, when she'd only met him that day?

She shook her head to clear the confused thoughts.

"I don't know what I'm thinking right now, Mandy," she said in a tired voice. "It's late. I'm not even dating Mike, and I don't really know you either, so... you'll forgive me, but all I really want to do is go home."

Mandy nodded, turning her body halfway in the seat so she was facing Sue. Sue sighed internally, noticing Mandy was not reaching for the door, like she wanted her to.

Get out of my car, she thought miserably.

"I just think you should be careful, Sue. I know he will play with your heart and your emotions. I can tell you really like him a lot already, don't you?"

Sue sighed. Mandy took the sound to mean a yes, and nodded vigorously.

"I thought so. I'm not surprised. I feel... felt like that about him, too. He's very handsome, and yes, he can come off at first as the gentleman of the century. But he's not, Sue. He's just a snake in the grass. He'll hurt you if you let him."

Sue rolled her head to the side and stared at Mandy, picturing herself drop kicking the woman out the passenger side door.

"Why should I trust you? I don't know you."

Mandy's eyes widened and she pulled back a little. "I'm just trying to do you a favor," she replied in a haughty tone.

Sue grunted. "If you want to do me a favor, Mandy, you'll let me go home. You can lecture me about Mike's flaws and faults another night. Right now, I just need to get home. I have to be up in less than five hours to get to work. My sisters will be mad if I take the morning off. Please, I'm asking you nicely to get out of my car and let me go home."

Mandy frowned, but put her hand on the door handle. "I don't want anyone else to hurt like I did, that's all."

"If he hurt you so bad, why are you still working for him? He told me he owns this bar. You don't have to work for him, if he hurts you every time he looks at you."

Mandy covered her mouth with her hand, making Sue regret she'd continued the conversation. If she'd kept her mouth shut, maybe Mandy would just get out of the car. Then she could go home and slip into the bed that was calling out to her across the air waves.

"Did he say that?" Her voice was light and airy.

Sue rolled her eyes, straightening her head so she was looking up at the ceiling of her car. "No, Mandy. I said that. If you don't like being around him because he hurts you, find another job. I'm sure there are other jobs for you out there somewhere."

"Mandy!"

Both women's eyes snapped to the back drivers-side door to see Mike approaching the car.

"You in there?"

Mike came around the driver's side door and looked in, his eyes focusing on Mandy on the other side.

"Are you harassing our customers?" he asked, trying to use a calm tone. Sue instantly admired him for that. If he had a problem with his general manager and bartender, he wasn't going

237

to bring it outside the bar, and certainly not in a customer's car. "Come on in. We've got work to do. Isn't that what you were telling me earlier?"

Mandy gave him a brilliant, beautiful smile. Sue felt sick to her stomach. The other woman opened the door, giving Sue a direct look. "I'm glad we talked, Sue. Keep what I said in mind. And have a good time singing with Mike. He really is one of the best I've ever heard."

Mike chuckled. Sue turned her eyes to study his face. He was looking at Mandy and moved his gaze to meet hers.

"I'll see you soon, right?" he said in a soft voice, as Mandy got out of Sue's SUV.

Sue nodded. "If you want to, Mike. I guess… just give me a call whenever you want to."

"I will. But we are meeting here in two days for the first practice, right? You'll make time during the day?"

Sue gave him another nod, trying to avoid making eye contact with him. If she did, she might not be able to resist leaning over to kiss him. She pictured what it would be like to kiss him. A pleasant, warm tingle spread through her body.

Not tonight, she thought. *Not tonight, but soon.*

Chapter 6

"So, what was that all about?" Mike asked. He was perturbed to find Mandy in Sue's car. There was no telling what the woman might have said about him.

Fortunately, Sue didn't treat him any differently. Whatever she'd said, it must not have had much of an impact. He saw the same flirty look in her eye that he saw when she was inside his bar.

His mind went over the evening as he walked into Badlands behind Mandy. Her hips swayed from side to side, but for the first time in a long time, the sight had no impact on him. He passed by her without saying anything, and went behind the bar to count bottles and money.

"What was what about?" Mandy asked innocently.

He frowned at her. "Don't act stupid with me, Mandy. I know you went out there just to talk to Sue."

Mandy shook her head, frowning. She leaned over and took a towel from behind the counter and began to wipe down the ice bin, removing chunks of ice into a bucket behind her. She wiped the inside of the bin as she talked. "I didn't. I went out to smoke a cigarette and she came out before I was done. We got to talking, that's all. I walked her to her car for safety reasons. It's always good for two women to walk together, even if neither can fight."

Mike grunted, running his fingers over the small POS system monitor next to the rows of liquor bottles lining the back wall. "You didn't have to get in her car. You could have talked to her outside."

Mandy gave him a sardonic look. "Exactly what are you saying, Mike? I'm not allowed to talk to her? Is she somehow your possession, now that you're singing with her? Nice pick, by the way. Did you even audition anyone else?"

Mike frowned, his eyes on the POS monitor in front of him. His fingers flicked across the screen, closing the bar for the night. "I don't need to hear anyone else. She's got a great voice."

Mandy snorted lightly. "Oh, Mike. I think you're making decisions with the wrong brain."

Mike's frown deepened and his eyes moved to her face. "Oh, yeah? What's wrong with her voice?"

"Mike…" Mandy left his name hanging, as if he knew what she was going to say next, tilting her head to the side. She made it sound as if Sue had a terrible singing voice, which was far from the truth. Mike stopped moving his fingers on the screen and stared at her.

She raised her eyebrows, continuing to wipe down bar glasses and set them in the dishwasher bin. "Don't give me that look. You're out of your mind if you think she's got what it takes to be a star."

Mike curled his lip and shook his head. "She's not looking for fame, and neither am I. I just want to do what I love for a living, that's all. I want to sing and play my music, and be able to pay my bills that way. I don't need mansions and big cars and all that."

Mike tried to concentrate on counting out the open cash drawer, but Mandy's words bothered him. It didn't seem she was going to be forthcoming about what she said to Sue. He had to guess. He hated guessing. He bristled at the thought she might have threatened Sue.

His mind reverted to Sue's face when he said goodbye to her. The strong urge to kiss her had passed over him, but he let it go. It was too soon for that, no matter how strong the feeling had been. He liked her too much, and didn't want to disrespect her. Moving too fast might push her away.

"I didn't say anything bad to her," Mandy protested in a soft voice, coming back from the kitchen where she'd taken the leftover glasses. "I just talked to her about what a great guy you are and how I'm glad she'll be singing with you. I didn't mention that she can't really sing. And you have to admit, Mike, she's kind of mediocre."

Mike thought back to his mini-audition with Sue. Mandy

was right about one thing. He'd decided to do the duet with her before she'd even arrived, as long as she could somewhat carry a tune. But he'd been pleasantly surprised to hear she had a wide range of vocal talent and her voice merged with his as if they were both on autotune.

He felt a tingle run through him and grinned. "She's not mediocre, Mandy," he said. "You're just jealous." He slapped the drawer of the register so it would close and waited with his hand over the small receipt printer, as it began spitting out long lines of numbers. He gathered the papers together as they printed out.

"I'm not jealous," Mandy said in an unconvincing voice. She was actually smiling softly, and he noticed her eyes twinkling when she looked at him. He recognized the seductive look and dropped his eyes to the printer.

"You are definitely jealous. If you wanted to do the duets with me, why didn't you just say so?" Mike regretted the words as soon as they came out of his mouth. He knew what her next question would be, as well as how he would answer it. And it was a mean thing for him to do to her.

As predicted, Mandy's eyebrows shot up and she asked, "Would you have let me sing duets with you?"

Mike sighed. "No. You know our voices don't go well together."

In truth, Mandy was a terrible singer. She didn't realize that just because you can belt something out and you have a lot of passion, doesn't mean you sound good doing it. Mike felt sorry for her, but not sorry enough to sing on stage with her. He wouldn't even play guitar with her.

Mandy's shoulders dropped and she looked discouraged. She leaned over the counter, gathering up the ash trays and dumping them in a sink of soapy water. Mike wished he could give her some words of encouragement, but there were none he could say.

"I hope you have a good time with her," he heard her mumble. Rolling his eyes, he turned away from the POS monitor and strolled toward his office door.

"Mike!" He turned when Mandy called his name. She was leaning on the counter, staring at him. "I… I just want to ask you… are you serious about this girl?"

Mike looked surprised. He couldn't help it. What kind of question was that at closing time, 3:00 in the morning, when both of them needed to finish their work and go home to bed? "Mandy, this isn't the time or the place to talk about all this. I barely know the woman. Right now, I'm interested in doing business with her and possibly singing a few songs with her. It's as simple as that. Do I find her attractive? Hell, yeah, of course I do. But that doesn't mean I'm jumping in bed with her, or putting a wedding ring on her finger."

He turned away from her, not wanting to see the desperate look on her face. It seemed like any time she looked at him lately, that's all he saw. Her desperation. Her desire. It was almost too much for him, sometimes.

"Mike." When he heard her say his name again, he pulled in a deep breath and held it for a moment. He had to keep his temper. Losing it would do no one any good. He turned around again, looking at her.

"What is it, Mandy?"

"Why couldn't you feel like that about me?"

Fire ran through Mike. He didn't want to talk to a drunk bartender about her deep, inconsolable feelings. He had to uncurl his fingers from around the receipts he was crushing. "Mandy, not now."

"But…"

"Not now!" he barked, making her flinch. She backed off the counter and gave him a weepy look. "You need to go home, Mandy. You've obviously tossed a couple back after hours. Like three, four shots, maybe? You shouldn't even drive. Maybe you should stay here on the cot in the back."

Mandy pulled herself to the edge of the counter with both

hands, wobbling on her feet. "I am a little tired," she said. She held out her arms to him. "Help me to the cot, Mike. Please."

Mike hesitated. Mandy hadn't appeared that drunk only ten minutes ago. Now she was playing it up for all it was worth.

Mandy tilted her head to the side, giving him a pleading look. "Please, Mike. Pleeeaasse." She drew the word out, sounding like a small child. Mike closed his eyes in frustration, opened them and walked to take hold of her around her waist.

She rested her head against him, sighing comfortably. He frowned and helped her walk to the back room where the cot was set up. The small room was perfect for people who needed to sleep it off, and it wasn't used often by anyone who didn't work at the bar.

She wasn't making it easy on him. He hadn't expected her to. She wanted to hang all over him, making body contact as much as possible. At one point, she lifted her head to him, smiling and closed her eyes, pursing her lips, as if he was going in for a kiss. He ignored her and dragged her toward the back room. She reacted with surprise, a little bit hurt, and then she giggled.

Mike reached out to grab the doorknob, but she put her hand out and covered his with it.

"Wait a minute, Mike. I mean, that cot in there, it's sturdy. It's really sturdy, isn't it? You could join me. We could have a lot of fun."

Mike scowled, studying his friend's drunken face, her eyes half closed, her smile crooked. When she was slam drunk, she wasn't as pretty as when she was sober. In fact, she bordered on ugly when she was very drunk. He didn't like to see it.

"I don't know how you managed to get this drunk in less than ten minutes, Mandy. Come on, let me open the door. I don't want to hurt you. I don't want to…"

Mandy laughed, slapping his hand away from the door and getting in his way so he couldn't turn the knob. She continued slapping out at him, even after he told her to stop, and let him open the door, because she needed to lay down.

"Mandy, stop it!" he roared in her face, making her eyes widen and her jaw drop. "I am not in the mood to play games with you! I'm tired, I've had a long day, and I don't want to be here anymore! You need to lay down and sleep this off. And the next time you decide to have a couple shots on me, you'll see that coming out of your paycheck. Do you understand me?"

Mandy blinked a few times, giving him a hurt look. She stopped messing with his hand and let him turn the knob to open the door.

He helped her inside, and to the cot in the corner by the window. He lowered her to it gently, pulling the small but comfortable quilt down so she could slide under it.

"Now, you just get some sleep. I'll be here in the morning to check on you, okay?"

Mandy nodded, giving him one last pleading look, which he ignored, clicking off the light as he left the room.

Chapter 7

Sue found herself singing the tunes she and Mike had practiced, for the next several days. She couldn't wait to go back to the bar, but was forcing herself to be patient. She hadn't texted Mike or called him, or checked social media.

"You've got some sick desire to torture yourself," Lynn said at one point, after asking if Sue had contacted Mike yet.

Sue just laughed. "What is that supposed to mean?" she asked.

Lynn shook her head. "There's no way I would be able to keep myself from texting him and calling him, if I was in love with him."

"Wait a minute. I just had one date with him, and I don't really think he considered that a date. I'm not in love with him."

Lynn had given her a skeptical look. "You are. You already are. Just admit it."

The memory of her night with Mike at the bar ran through her mind, as she walked behind Mari and the financier they had invited to survey the grounds for possible improvements.

Lynn was walking beside her, her head down as she scanned the tablet in her hand. She ran her finger over the screen, moving objects around. Sue glanced at the screen, wondering how Lynn could even see it.

"What are you working on?" she asked, curiously. Lynn looked up at her.

"I want to make some improvements to the snack bar on the east side, near the outdoor swimming pools. I showed this to Mari earlier, but I'm not really finished with it, so I haven't shown it to you both. I was just giving her an idea of what I envisioned, to see what she thought."

Sue nodded. She was the numbers girl. When Mari approved of the changes, Lynn would bring her the plans, so she could crunch the numbers and see if it was in the budget.

Very few improvements weren't in the Emerald Resort budget. Uncle Nathan had done an excellent job of making it a profitable, popular place, that turned money hand over fist for the sisters.

She noticed when Lynn continued looking at her. "You look like your mind is somewhere else," she said quietly.

Sue looked at Mari's profile, as her older sister conversed with the financier. It was usually her who consulted with the man, but the business they had today was in Mari's hands. She'd only come along in case her services were needed.

She turned her eyes back to Lynn. "Let's go see that snack bar arrangement you want to change," she suggested. "I could use a bite to eat, too. I'm hungry. What about you?"

Lynn looked a bit surprised by Sue's invitation. She glanced at Mari, and then back to Sue. "Well, I suppose Mari doesn't really need us, does she?"

Sue shook her head, smiling. "Nah, she really doesn't."

"Mari, we're going for a bite to eat," Lynn called out, interrupting the conversation Mari was engaged in. Their sister just glanced at them nodding, her eyes immediately reverting back to the man in front of her. He'd paused briefly, so Mari could acknowledge them, and went right back into his sentence, where he'd left off.

Lynn looked at her. "Let's go."

Sue followed Lynn across the wide lawn to the front of the east wing. Her mind drifted to Mike's handsome face. She got an uncomfortable feeling every time Mandy invaded her thoughts, and she couldn't seem to make it stop. One minute, she was thinking about Mike, the next, Mandy would be seated next to her, in her own car, contaminating it with her sweet perfume and rancid cigarette smoke.

Her face alternated between frowning and smiling. She wouldn't have noticed at all, if Lynn hadn't pointed it out as soon as they reached the East wing snack area.

246

"You have got to tell me what's on your mind, Sue." Lynn gestured to the nearest table, and slid into one of the seats, laying her papers down in front of her. She placed both hands on them protectively, as if a wind might gust and blow them away.

"What makes you think something is on my mind?" Sue asked, feeling exposed. She knew her cheeks were already flushing.

"Because you can't keep the same emotion on your face for longer than a few minutes," Sue replied. Her tone was gentle and caring. She tilted her head to the side. "Are you thinking about that musician? What's his name again?"

"Mike."

"Yes. Mike. The one that owns the Badlands."

Sue raised her eyebrows, gazing at her younger sister. "I didn't know he owned the Badlands until I went to see him Wednesday. How did you know?"

Lynn grinned and giggled softly. "You know how you like to look up people on the Internet? Well, I know how to do that, too. He's really handsome, Sue. Do you think he likes you? Like, really likes you?"

Sue felt suddenly transported back to high school, remembering how she and her sisters had conversations just like this one, every Saturday night for years. She felt comfortable and safe talking to Lynn about her feelings.

She sighed. "I guess I'm worried I might be falling too fast, Lynn," she confessed. "I think about him all the time. I worry about him and his bartender. You know they used to be a couple. And she came out and warned me the other night, too. Wednesday, before I left the bar."

"She warned you?" Lynn frowned, her voice deepening. "Like threatened you?"

Sue shook her head. "No, not threatening. Just warning me. She said Mike has a way of breaking girl's hearts. And well, he is a musician. They have a reputation for doing that, don't they?"

Lynn nodded. "Yeah, they do. But if you want my opinion on it, they have that reputation because that's the kind of career that draws a lot of attention from girls. If construction workers had the same opportunities, I bet there would be just as much heartbreak for their stereotype."

Sue raised her eyebrows, glancing up at the server when he came to take their orders. Once he was gone, she replied, "That's really deep, Lynn. But right now, I have to think of a way to find out if he is who he says he is."

Lynn pulled her eyebrows together, giving her sister a crude look. "You gotta be kidding me," she said softly. Sue was confused.

"What did I say?"

Sue felt more and more stupid, as her sister explained why she looked at her that way. "Sue, whenever we date someone, we're finding out about them. That's the risk of it all. You won't know what kind of man he is if you never spend time with him. Dating him is finding out if he is who he says he is. The only real question is, do you think a broken heart is worth the time you'll spend finding out? You have just as much of a chance of being happy, and having some kind of happily ever after."

Sue didn't think she'd heard Lynn speak so much at one time in years. She processed everything her sister said, and came to a quick conclusion. She did want to risk being hurt. She didn't want to believe Mandy. In fact, she was determined to prove the woman wrong.

"His bartender says he goes through a lot of women," she mumbled, more to herself than to her sister.

"Some men make poor choices when they are looking for a woman. They choose based on the wrong things. It's a good thing Mike has the ability and willingness to break it off, instead of hanging on just so he won't be alone."

Sue was feeling better and better about her choice to give Mike a chance, despite what Mandy said. There was a good chance she was only speaking out of jealousy.

"I like the way you think, Lynn," she said appreciatively. "I'm really glad I talked to you about this."

Lynn smiled wide. "Anytime, Sue. You know I'm always here with good advice."

Sue laughed. Her younger sister, the youngest of the three, was not known for her good advice. She was the flighty sister, thinking more with her heart than her brain 99% of the time.

The server brought Lynn's burger and Sue's milkshake. She sipped on the delicious drink, thinking about how anxious she was for Mike to come to the resort and meet her sisters. His appointment was the next day, and she didn't think it could come fast enough.

"Have you talked to Mari about this at all?" Lynn asked, after consuming half her burger. She was sitting back, her hand on her full belly, looking at Sue, with satisfaction written on her face. Sue smiled at her.

"I think your eyes were bigger than your stomach."

Lynn acknowledge the half burger still on her tray. "Yeah, happens every time. But that will make a nice lunch for Collie. That dog eats anything, but especially liked the burgers from the kitchen here."

"Isn't that nice?" Sue said, teasingly. "You're feeding our profits to your dog."

Lynn's eyebrows shot up and she gave Sue a testy look, which was replaced by a grin moments later. "I don't know who you think you're talking to, but I own a third of this place. That extends to my family and my Collie is my family."

Sue chuckled, shaking her head. She didn't really care about the dog eating the hamburgers. She was fond of Collie, but thought Lynn could have been a little more creative when picking out names. After all, it was a Collie, and Lynn named it Collie. It was like calling your cat, "Cat" or your dog, simply "Dog".

It made little sense to Sue.

"I guess I could talk to her," Sue said reverting back to

Lynn's unanswered question. "Do you think she'd have some good advice for me?"

Lynn shrugged, dipping the last of her fries in ketchup. She ate them and began to gather the paper and trash together on her tray. "I think that, of all of us, she would know what to tell you. She's the only one who's married. You know?"

Sue had to agree with that. Mari had been married for a while now, and she dated her husband for almost a year before marrying him. She would know the ins and outs of courting better than her sisters.

Sue laughed at herself for thinking the word courting. Was Mike going to court her like some lady in regency England? She inadvertently laughed out loud. Lynn looked at her like she'd lost her mind.

"Are you all right? You're not losing it, are you? If so, I want your portion of the resort." Lynn grinned wide. "Ahh, the things I could do with all the power!" she rubbed her hands together, and set a delighted, plotting look on her face, like a comical evil villain.

Sue shook her head, laughing. "You are always good for a laugh, Lynn. Thanks for bringing me here and listening to me jabber on about this. I guess I'm not sure what I want to do."

"I understand. But I think, deep in your heart, you know what you have to do. If he's right for you, you'll know it. And you're smart. You'll know it fast."

Chapter 8

Mike popped open a can of beer and set it down in front of his customer on a blue square napkin.

"Here ya go, Johnny. Enjoy."

"Thanks, Mike. Tell me, how's business around here? I hear you got a new server."

Mike nodded. "Yeah, we've been through several in the last few months, actually. People come and go in Queen Anne. It's not easy to live in a village that seems like it's stuck in the past."

Johnny nodded, taking a sip from the beer and setting it back down. He lifted it once more and took a longer swallow. This time, when he set it down, he wiped his mouth with the back of his sleeve and let out a soft snort.

"Yeah, it does seem like that sometimes. But, you know, I've been doing maintenance around this town for the past thirty years, and I've noticed the changes. I know a lot of folks don't, but I do." He nodded, as if agreeing with himself. "Yeah, a lot of changes."

"Change is inevitable," Mike said. Sue crossed his mind, giving him a warm feeling. "Like that place up there, you know, the Emerald Resort. Time had to come for some change."

"That's death for ya," Johnny mumbled. Mike could see the older man was lost in his memories. He was only in his mid-fifties but he was born and raised in Queen Anne. He'd never left. It was his home.

Queen Anne would not be the same place when Johnny finally kicked the bucket. He instantly missed his friend, even though Johnny was sitting right in front of him. He put a hand over the bar and grasped Johnny's shoulder.

"I'm glad you're here, Johnny. I'm glad you consider me a friend and come in my bar as much as you do."

Johnny snorted. "You want me in your bar so I can give you my hard-earned money. That's what you want."

Both men laughed.

"No, I sincerely like your company," Mike said earnestly. "I want you to know that."

Johnny nodded at him, lifting his beer in the air. "Thanks for that, Mike. Always nice to be appreciated."

Mike nodded back. "You bet, my friend. You bet." He was quiet for a moment, leaning back to rest his back against the tall counter behind him. He crossed his arms over his chest. "So, what do you know about the women up at Emerald Resort?"

Johnny gave him a stern onceover. "You talking about the Wright sisters? Those girls? Mighty fine girls. I'd give them the time of day."

"Have you met them?"

"I have a weekly golf game with the mayor, so yeah, I have met them several times. Have you not gone up there? Don't you ever visit?"

Mike lowered his head, giving Johnny an apologetic look. No doubt the man was offended that Mike could live in Queen Anne, own a business, and make profit, without visiting the number one attraction of the area.

"I just became interested in it," Mike said hurriedly. "Actually, I've been interested for a while now, but never could figure out how to get to the Wright sisters. Finally, the ladies came into the bar last week and I got to meet Sue. I think she's the middle sister, isn't she?"

Mike moved away from Johnny for a moment, to send a bottle of beer down to the end of the counter for a customer whose hand was out waiting. He looked back at Johnny. "Sorry about that. What were you saying?"

"You said you were interested in Sue?" Johnny repeated, giving Mike a hard look that the younger man didn't understand.

He nodded. "Yeah. Sue. The middle one."

"Huh." Mike couldn't tell if the sound was one of approval

or disbelief. He blinked a few times, contemplating how to ask Johnny what he meant by his grunt. As it turned out, he didn't have to wait long for his explanation. "That's kind of surprising," Johnny finally said.

"It is? Why?"

Johnny tapped a single cigarette on the counter in front of him, filter side down. He seemed to be doing it mindlessly. "That girl is no social butterfly. I don't think I ever saw her smile while we were at that wedding we attended. And when I go for my golf game, or take the missus up there for dinner, if we see her at all, she looks sour and unhappy. Frankly, we thought she'd be the first to go."

Mike was surprised to hear that. He pictured Sue's smiling, laughing face. He couldn't fathom seeing her dark and sullen. "That's pretty strange," he said. "I don't see her like that at all. She's always laughing, and full of fun and spark. I like that in a woman."

Johnny moved his eyes to the younger man. "You sure you ain't talking about Lynn? Lynn is the youngest of the three. Now there's a free spirit, right there. She's probably got the voice of an angel. She sure looks enough like one."

"Strong words of praise. You don't think Sue is like that?" Mike could easily think of Sue as an angel. She was beautiful inside and out, as far as he was concerned.

Johnny shrugged. "No, that's not the kind of woman Sue is at all. Maybe you just thought you were talking to Sue. Maybe they played a joke on you."

Mike thought that possibility was highly unlikely. He pushed himself off the counter he was leaning on and saluted Johnny, as he walked to the other side of the bar.

As he served the people their drinks, Mike couldn't get his mind off Sue. When he thought about it, she *had* looked nervous when she first got to the Badlands. His phone call preceding the meeting probably loosened her up some.

He wasn't foolish enough to think his looks didn't have

253

something to do with it. He was naturally handsome and knew it, but was humble about it. He'd only used it to his advantage a few times, but it made him feel guilty, so he tried to downplay it as much as he could. He just wanted to be a decent human being, and surround himself with other people who wanted to be decent human beings.

After an hour of serving drinks, the second bartender arrived and Mike was able to go to the back room to rest for a minute. He went around his desk and sat in the big comfortable chair, telling himself he was not going to fall asleep. He hadn't done enough physical work to warrant a nap.

He grinned at his thoughts.

He pushed the button on the side of the monitor of his laptop. It lit up, and he put in the password to show the surveillance cameras that were placed in four sections around the bar. Every now and then he checked the cameras, but he trusted his workers and his profits hadn't declined, nor had anything come up missing.

He considered himself lucky to have employees who were trustworthy.

He let his eyes drift over the customers instead, watching to see if anyone got rowdy. That was another rare thing to happen in his classy bar. He found his mind wandering back to Sue. His appointment with her sisters was the next day. He'd spent the whole week working on songs to play for them, or at least suggest, as Sue had told him to do.

He wouldn't admit to anyone that he was nervous about it. Sue could hook him up to a lie detector machine and he'd pass, before he'd admit to being nervous.

He chuckled.

He was *incredibly* nervous.

For some reason, it felt like he was auditioning to play Carnegie Hall, or to play back-up guitar for his favorite band, or to sing as a replacement for someone famous.

But it was just the remaining two Wright sisters. Why was he close to freaking out?

He knew the answer, but didn't want to admit it. He'd never fallen for a woman so fast in his life. It scared him to death. There was something about Sue that grabbed him the moment he saw her enter his bar. Not the night she'd visited with her sisters, but when she came alone, looking so elegant, so classy, so beautiful.

She spoke with intelligence and again, more class. He was impressed with everything about her. That kind of feeling was something he wanted to get used to. He wanted to wake up next to her every morning and give her a kiss, make her breakfast, take out her trash and do her laundry.

Mike shook his head to clear his thoughts. He was letting his emotions take over. If he planned to work for the Wright sisters, he had to keep that desire in check. He could date her, but he would have to tone it down and move slow.

He was not comfortable with the prospect of mixing business and pleasure. It had just happened that way. There was nothing he could do to change it.

Her laughter rang in his mind, his eyes still focused on the four videos playing on the monitor in front of him. She was the quiet one, according to Johnny, the serious one. No one had fun with Sue around.

He didn't understand that. An idea came to his mind, and he all but dismissed it immediately. The more he thought about it, though, the more he wanted to do it. Finally, he hit the 'x' button on the videos he was watching and pulled up a folder on his screen. He looked for the videos from the night Sue had come to the bar.

Trying not to feel like he was spying on Sue, he brought up the videos from the two of them singing. He smiled as he replayed it, turning up the sound so he could get a better idea of her talent. The audio was somewhat muffled, but her voice came through loud and clear, melding with his perfectly.

Mandy didn't know what she was talking about. Sue had a

wonderful voice. Mike couldn't wait to showcase her at one of the big shows. He planned to do it all along, but now, with Mandy's apparent jealousy shining like a beacon in the night, he was going to delight in doing it. Maybe he would have several showcases.

He grunted softly, fast forwarding and rewinding his favorite parts. He focused mostly on her laughter. He laughed himself, remembering her joy. She looked like she was having fun to him.

Tomorrow he would meet the sisters. He was going extra early. He wanted plenty of time to look around, and maybe talk to Sue.

He reached forward and clicked the button on the mouse to close out the videos from Wednesday. He brought up the current videos and left them running on the screen. He hadn't told anyone they'd been installed. He was the only one who knew about them. The only one the employees knew about was above the front POS monitor and register. The other two POS systems were unregistered, so the camera only needed to be where the money was.

His chest tightened when his eyes slid over to the practice area. He'd left everything the way it was from when Sue visited. He was unconsciously waiting for her to return, so they could do that night all over again.

Chapter 9

Sue was up early the next morning. She showered and got ready for the day, but her excitement had her on edge. She was anxious for Mike's arrival. The appointment was set for 11:30. She'd set it up for that time so he could stay for lunch after, if he wanted. Or perhaps the two of them could go get something to eat. If he wanted to.

But it was 7am when her eyes popped open, and her brain told her to get up and go. She followed her brain's suggestion and was out at the tennis courts by 8:30.

She walked down the slight slope to the courts, bouncing her racket on one hand. She hadn't played in a long time. She always intended to take it up again, but never seemed to have the energy.

Until now. Since she'd met Mike, she had more energy than she ever thought she could have. She wanted to get up in the morning, and didn't want to sleep at night, except to possibly dream of the handsome man in the bar.

It was a beautiful spring day, a little chilly for the early morning, but her light sweater kept her warm when she was standing still. She wore a short skirt and stockings to keep her legs warm. Her new shoes put a spring in her step that wasn't there before.

"Brandon!" she called out, waving her racket in the air. The young man was bent over, adjusting the settings on the automatic tennis ball pitcher. He stood up straight, his head snapping in her direction. When he saw who was calling him, a bright smile covered his face. He lifted one hand and waved back.

"Sue! How are you this morning? And what the heck are you doing out here? You look like you want to play some tennis." His voice was pleasant.

Sue laughed. She lowered her voice as she closed in on him. "You're right. I usually don't come out this time of the morning, not out here anyway. Indoor heated pool for me, right?"

Brandon laughed, tossing his head back. He ran one hand through his short brown hair and placed the other on his hip. "So, what's up?"

"I wonder if you'll play against me this morning? Show me a few tips? I need to get back to exercising. I used to play all the time. If I'm going to exercise, I want to be doing something I enjoy, you know?"

Brandon nodded. "I would love to play a few rounds with you this morning, Sue. As it happens, I don't have any lessons until the afternoon."

"I'll be long gone by then. I have an appointment at 11:30."

"Well, that works out perfectly, doesn't it."

Brandon reached to the side of the ball pitcher and picked up a sleeve of balls. "I'll serve first, if you don't care. You go on out there."

He gestured with his head, expertly popping the top off the sleeve with one finger, and carrying the balls to his side of the net.

"Are you ready?" he called out.

"Yeah. Serve already!" Sue joked back. She noticed the amusement on Brandon's face. He tossed the ball up and whacked it toward her.

Sue was pleasantly surprised to learn she had not lost her talent in the sport of tennis. It was another one of her high school favorite pastimes.

She ran back and forth across the court, hitting the ball back so frequently, the two had several ten-minute long matches.

She raised her racket when it was closing in on 9 o'clock, signaling it was time for her to take a break.

Brandon caught the ball in mid-air and walked toward the net. "You ready for something to drink? You've been going at this for a lot longer than I thought you would."

Sue was breathing hard, her heart pounding in her chest. "I don't... think I've... moved that much in a long time... not that fast anyway."

She walked on one side of the net, while Brandon was on the other, toward the bleachers beyond the gate.

"Who you meeting today, if you don't mind me asking?"

Sue looked at Brandon curiously. She had only spoken to the tennis coach three times. None of those chats established them as friends. But her curiosity won out, and she responded to him. "Mike Nelson, from the Badlands bar in Queen Anne. Why would you ask?"

Brandon nodded. "I kind of thought that's who you'd say. I've been waiting to see his face around here."

Sue blinked in confusion. "What do you mean?"

Brandon shrugged. "I don't know. He's a good musician. I've always thought he could add something to the place. He'd be a good wedding singer. I know he wants more than that, but he'd enjoy it, you know? I think that might mean more to him than any amount of money or prestige."

Sue was sorely tempted to ask Brandon if Mike was the kind of man who treated women like tissues, to be used and thrown away. The question seemed so personal to her, though, she couldn't bring herself to vocalize it.

"I have been thinking about that," Sue said. "He and I connected when my sisters and I visited his bar. He called me up, and when he found out I own part of the resort, he mentioned to me that he'd like to do music planning. So that's why he's coming here."

"I think he'd be a great music planner," Brandon repeated. "He really knows what he's doing."

Sue gazed at the tennis instructor, amusement on her face. She wondered if he might possibly be related to Mike. It was rare to find someone who automatically acted as cheerleader for someone else.

"I didn't know you knew him," she said, dropping to the lowest seat on the bleacher and lifting one leg to rest her ankle on her other knee. She pulled her tennis shoe from her foot and rubbed the white sock underneath, relishing the pleasure that slid up through her tired muscles as she massaged them.

Brandon went around her and sat nearby, pulling an energy drink from the bag he'd grabbed from near the fence as he passed. He cracked open the top and looked at her over the rim, as he took a couple swallows.

"I used to go see his band when they played at St. Simons Island during the Spring Break season. A lot of the rich kids go there, you know. That's a good place to find rich kids."

Sue raised her eyebrows, thinking how strange it was to hear Brandon say rich kids. She knew very little of his background, since Mari did most of the hiring and firing, and Brandon had been there before the girls took over anyway.

"Is that a good thing?"

Brandon laughed. "It is when your only real talent is playing tennis, and the only real way to make money at that is to teach rich kids."

Sue laughed.

"And bored rich wives," Brandon added affectionately. "God love 'em. I don't know where I'd be without them. I've had my experiences with some real idiots over the past ten years, and there's some wickedly spoiled rich kids out there. But tennis is one of those sports where you're either good or you're not. I didn't pander to those kids. If they didn't like the sport or weren't any good at it, I'd let their parents know they were wasting their money. That way neither me nor the kid had to stress about it."

Sue listened with interest. She liked learning more about the people who worked for Emerald Resort. It gave her good insight into the kind of man her uncle was. He never seemed to go wrong with his choice in hiring. It was one of the things Sue realized, posthumously, that made her miss him more.

"That's a good policy to have. You don't want to stress yourself, or the kid, out over a game that's supposed to be fun."

Brandon nodded vehemently. "Exactly. That's exactly right. I wouldn't want to get rid of my clients and rich customers. I love them all, even if they're a pain in the butt."

"I like your attitude. I guess that's why Uncle Nathan hired you, huh?"

Brandon chuckled. "Yeah, I guess so. He was a nice guy. I'm sorry he's gone. I wish you ladies had come and taken over while he was still alive, or worked with him. It's too bad it took him dying to get you here."

Sue nodded. "I wish he had invited us. We didn't even know about this place, and we certainly didn't know that he would leave the entire business to us."

Brandon stood up. "You want to play some more? Get some more exercise before your meeting with Mike?"

Sue pushed herself to her feet, giving him a smile. "I suppose so. I don't want to be exhausted though, so maybe just a few more rounds."

As they walked back to the court, Brandon raised his racket, scanning it closely. "What did Mike do with Mandy?"

Sue halted in place, glaring at Brandon. "Excuse me?"

Brandon looked back at her, a sheepish look crossing his face. "Mandy. His general manager. Is she still bartending there?"

"She was as of a few days ago," Sue said curtly, narrowing her eyes. "Why?"

Brandon pressed his lips together and sighed. "I shouldn't have brought her up. I just figured if he was gonna have another woman around, he'd have to get rid of Mandy. That woman's got claws, Sue. If she's still hanging around Mike, you gotta watch yourself."

Anger split through her. Since Brandon had brought it up, she decided to ask her personal question.

"So, if any other woman is around, Mike isn't really free? He's with Mandy?"

Brandon stopped walking, turned and came back, closing the distance so they didn't have to call out loudly to one another.

"Mike is a free man, Sue," Brandon said reassuringly. "If that's the kind of relationship you want with him, and he wants it too, he's free to do what he wants. But if Mandy is still around, I'm just saying, you have to watch out. She is possessive and territorial and jealous. I mean bad."

Sue felt a chill run up her spine. "Is she dangerous?"

Brandon looked doubtful. "I mean, I don't think she'd really hurt you or Mike, or herself. I think she's just the kind of drama queen that will keep starting problems with you, and harassing you or something like that. The last woman Mike had a business deal with, and I'm talking straight business deal, no relationship or sex or any of that stuff, just straight business..." he shook his head. "Mandy was seriously off her rocker then. She practically hired a PI to follow the woman, to make sure she wasn't meeting Mike behind Mandy's back. And Mike wasn't even dating her. I don't think he ever has."

Sue frowned. "Why doesn't Mike do something about that?"

"He does. But she's his friend and he's never taken it very seriously." Brandon gave her a close look. "Maybe the right woman will make him change that."

Chapter 10

Mike strolled across the grounds, surveying everything around him. He contemplated taking the tour they offered, but didn't want to bother any of the sisters with it. Plus, he was more interested in exploring on his own.

He was glad he did when he saw Sue from a distance, as he walked past the tennis courts. She was dressed in a cute mini-skirt with tight white athletic shorts underneath it, a matching athletic top and a band to hold back her long hair.

His heart skipped a beat. A smile came to his face. She looked exhausted and a little angry. He almost regretted having come early. He was willing to bet she was not going to be happy he saw her in that state.

He turned toward the courts, and went over the grass to the sidewalk that ran along the fence. He faced the fence, putting both hands up on top of it, watching her bat the ball back and forth with a young man. He squinted and recognized the tennis coach as Brandon Walker, a friend of his from his band days.

Brandon acknowledged him, causing Sue to turn abruptly. When she saw who it was, she twisted unnaturally and fell to the side, catching herself with her hands. Both Mike and Brandon ran to her side, with Mike slinging the gate open and pounding the pavement to reach her. Brandon leapt over the net between them.

They both reached her at the same time.

"Oh, my God, are you okay?" They both said the same thing at the same time. Glancing at each other to acknowledge that fact, they both reached down to help Sue up. She gave Brandon one arm and Mike the other. They lifted her to her feet.

She stood gently, testing both ankles before letting go of their arms.

"Okay, I don't think I broke anything." She gave Mike a hard stare. "What are you doing, sneaking up on someone when they're doing something athletic, that makes them hot and sweaty and tired looking?"

Mike and Brandon both laughed. Mike held out his hand to his young friend.

"Good to see you, Brandon. How've you been?"

Brandon shook his hand, nodding. "I've been good, Mike. Thanks for asking. Hope the bar scene is going well for you."

"It is. I can't ask for more, to be honest. I'm happy with it."

"That's great. That's great. I'm gonna go… over there…" Brandon jabbed a thumb over his shoulder toward the gazebo on the other side of the courts. "I gotta… do something…" He turned and walked away purposefully, giving Mike a pleasant grin before going.

Mike looked down at Sue, an amused feeling passing through him. "I think you two might have been talking about me. Am I right about that?"

Sue raised one eyebrow. "You might be."

Mike laughed. "Okay, what did he say? Did he tell you about that time at my birthday party? Listen, that wasn't my fault. They were all drinking, and I didn't think anything of it. It's not my fault."

Sue gave him a shocked look. He could tell she was trying not to burst out laughing. He could also tell she hadn't been told about his birthday faux pau. He grinned, feeling the need to rewind and take back his words.

"Ah," he said. "I see no one told you about that birthday fiasco. Well, I'm afraid you'll have to wait on that one. Maybe I'll tell you someday, when I feel like revealing something embarrassing about myself. If you ever do something embarrassing, I'll tell you about it, so we'll both have something on the other one."

Sue laughed, giving Mike a thrill of delight. "That's so funny, Mike. Okay. That's a deal. So why did you come early? Look how you caught me."

Mike shrugged, giving her a once over. He liked the way she looked. He thought a woman who kept herself in good physical

264

shape was sexy. "I have no problem with the way you look, Sue. You'd look pretty no matter what you were doing."

"Oh, you think so, huh?" Sue's appreciative grin made Mike feel good inside.

"I don't think so, I know so. After all, right now you're a disheveled sweaty mess, and I still think you look beautiful."

Mike could tell he'd said the right thing. Her cheeks flushed a soft pink. He felt his attraction to her explode in his chest. He resisted the urge to grab her into a kiss. It was too soon, he said to himself. He needed more time and so did she. A second meeting did not merit the kind of passionate kiss he was ready to give her.

"I... I think that's a compliment," Sue said softly.

He nodded. "It's definitely a compliment. Do you want me to walk back to the hotel with you? I'll wait in the snack area or the lounge, or anywhere you want me to wait, while you get ready; unless you're you not done with your tennis?"

Sue turned her head, looking across to the gazebo. Brandon's head was down. She looked back at him, meeting his eyes. He felt a twitch in his chest, and was once again fighting the urge to grab her to him and cover her face with kisses.

"No, I'm done with the tennis game. I only need to fall once to know it's time to take a break. I've been out here for almost two hours, anyway. I've gotten some good exercise."

Mike nodded. He put his hand up against her back and gently pushed her toward the fence gate. He enjoyed the feel of the soft fabric of her shirt against the skin of his palm. He held the gate open and followed her through.

"I'll get that," he said and hurried around her to pick up her tennis bag. He took the towel from on top and handed it to her, tapping the sides of her face first with it. "Just had a little sweat there. I got it."

Sue laughed, snatching the towel from him. "You're being silly. I can dry myself off, thank you."

"It's a good thing you didn't stay out after noon," Mike said, as they walked across the lawn toward the main hotel.

"Why is that?"

"It gets hot in the afternoon. If you're sweating this much from the cool morning, you'd probably melt in the afternoon."

Sue nodded. "That's a good point. I'll have to keep it in mind. I'm glad I came out in the morning then, huh."

"I was wondering, do you think your sisters will be all right with me coming out here early? They won't think I'm overstepping, will they?"

Sue seemed to ponder that for a moment. She shook her head, looking up to meet his eyes. He enjoyed it when she looked directly at him. He could look in her eyes for hours and never look away.

"No, I don't think so. They are looking forward to meeting you. Plus, it shows incentive. If you want to work here, in any capacity, you should probably visit first and get to know what kind of people we hire. I... I guess you could say you really are a stranger to us. But I have to tell you, Mike. You seem so familiar to me. I feel like I've known you for a long time. You seem really trustworthy to me."

Mike was delighted to hear Sue say those words. He smiled wide, a genuine feeling of appreciation filling him.

"I think that's the nicest thing I've ever heard, Sue. Thank you. I am trustworthy, I promise you that. I won't let you or your sisters down. I know every part of a wedding has to be perfect, or it reflects back on the person who planned it, and the hosts, and in both those cases, that's you. I wouldn't want to do anything to mess up your reputation."

Sue sighed audibly. He could see satisfaction on her face.

"I'm glad to hear that, Mike. I've talked you up to my sisters. I don't think you'll have any trouble convincing them you're the one for the job. Besides, they like to hire locally. It gives residents of Queen Anne a reason to visit Emerald Resort.

And who wouldn't want that?"

Mike laughed. "Of course!"

They kept walking, eventually reaching the steps to go into the building where the offices were kept. Mike couldn't resist putting his hand on her back to "help" her up the stairs. The light touch of the fabric of her shirt against his skin made his breath catch in his throat. Just being around her made him feel jumpy inside. He felt like a teenager again.

She was the only woman who'd ever had that kind of effect on him. And she wasn't a model, nor did she try to claim a place as one. She was beautiful to Mike, but she wouldn't grace any magazine covers. It wasn't her looks that drew him to her. It was everything else. The entire package. The whole combination.

Mike walked into the large foyer of the office building behind Sue, shaking his head to clear his thoughts. He pulled his guitar around and set in on the ground standing up, so he was holding the neck of the case with both hands. He gazed at Sue.

"So, where do we go from here?"

He looked around the inside of the office building. It wasn't as grand as he expected the rest of the resort to be. He knew for a fact that some of the best suites had gold faucets, and gold knobs on the toilets and sinks. Not gold-plated, but actual gold. Mike couldn't imagine spending the kind of money that had to take, on something as simple as sink knobs.

The office looked much like any other office building Mike had ever been in. The doors were plain, and the floor was tiled white. There was a receptionist desk not far from where he stood, with rows of chairs, for visitors who were asked to wait.

Their eyes again when Sue said, "My sisters are anxious to meet you. I've told them all about you and our meeting the other night. My... audition." She grinned wide. He was overcome by the pleasant sight and smiled back.

"I hope they only heard good things," he said with a soft chuckle.

She glanced over her shoulder. "Of course. I have nothing bad to say about you."

Mike followed her past the receptionist, who gave him an admiring smile and a nod. He nodded back. Sue was walking quickly, but Mike had no trouble keeping up with her. He was glad she'd said nothing negative about him, but had she mentioned Mandy?

Mike didn't know if he even wanted to question Sue about Mandy. He wanted to know what she'd said to Sue in the car, but really, was it important enough to ask? Should he even bring her up? After all, who really wanted to talk about Mandy?

Chapter 11

Sue watched Mike talking to her sisters with a completely confident, friendly look on his face. His smiles were genuine, and when he cracked a joke, it left the three of them laughing without hesitation. He won them over only a few minutes after entering. He had a natural charm and was a keen businessman. Sue listened to him rattle off names of famous people he'd played with, as well as financial numbers, having to do with his bar, that astounded Mike. To look at him, she wouldn't have guessed he was an all-out business genius.

They were only halfway through the meeting, just getting down to brass tax, when Mike's cell phone began to buzz, moving itself slowly across the table in front of him. He snatched it up and looked at the screen. He looked at Sue and turned the phone to face her.

Sue glanced at the screen and saw the word "Mandy" on the front, indicating it was Mandy who was calling. She felt a thick knife of jealousy slide through her, and she hoped to God it didn't show on her face. She forced a smile and nodded.

"Go ahead. There's a separate conference room right there." She pointed to a door behind Mike. He turned to see where it was, looked back at Sue apologetically, and put the phone to his ear after pressing the call button.

"What do you want?" Sue heard him say as he went toward the door. It gave her a sense of satisfaction that he answered Mandy's call that way. He would never answer her calls that way. She was positive of that. She wasn't a crazy psycho stalker.

Mike was at the door with his hand on the knob, just standing there, listening. He didn't go into the conference room. He turned back, his eyes settling on Sue. She shot to her feet, alarmed by the look on his face.

His entire face had turned red. His brows were knitted together and his eyes flashed with emotion. He looked down at the floor, plunging one hand through his wavy, brown hair. He hadn't spoken a word since his initial question.

"Mike?" Sue dared to ask the question. She was concerned.

Mike's eyes darted up to her face. He lifted one finger in the air and dropped his eyes to the floor again.

"When?" he asked. He waited for the answer and then said, "Did you check the office?"

Sue could hear the high pitch of Mandy's voice on the other end of the line. She must have been hysterical for Sue to hear her. Curiosity and worry spread through her like a thick salve. She could barely contain herself, and had to keep herself from questioning Mike again. She chided herself silently and told herself to be patient, for goodness sake.

Finally, after a few more chopped sentences, Mike said, "I'm leaving now. I'll be right there. Don't leave." He paused, listening to Mandy. "Yes, of course you need to call the police. You should have called them first, not me. What's wrong with... Oh, just hang up the phone and call the police now. I'll be right there."

Mike pulled the phone away and pressed the red end button. His hand was clutching the phone so tight his knuckles were white. Sue approached him from around the desk. Her sisters had both stood up. Lynn had her arms crossed over her chest, a worried expression on her face, and Mari had her fingers splayed out on the surface of the table, leaning over, her eyes on Mike.

"What's happened, Mike?" Sue asked urgently.

He crossed back to the table in a few long strides. "I'm sorry, ladies, it looks like I'll have to finish this meeting with you later. I hope you will still consider me for this proposal."

Sue moved closer to him, looking up into his worried eyes.

"Don't you be concerned about that, Mike," Mari said in a businesslike tone. "Obviously, something's happened at your bar that you need to attend to. We can pick this back up when you're ready."

"Thank you, Mari," Mike said, his voice stern. Sue pressed

270

her lips together, trying not to look desperate. He dropped his eyes and studied her face. "My bar was broken into last night," he said. "I closed it today, so I could make this meeting and not bother Mandy. She didn't go in until just now." He lifted his arm and looked at his wristwatch.

"Oh, no!" Sue exclaimed, her hands covering her mouth in shock. "You have to go! You have to see what damage has been done!"

Mike nodded, but the look in his eyes told Sue he had something else on his mind. She blinked at him, wondering what it could be.

"You, uh... you think you'd like to come with me? I figure, if anybody would be a help to me right now, it would be you."

Sue lifted her eyebrows. Mike didn't know how much that invitation meant to her. She would have beamed at him, if the situation wasn't so serious. "I... I would love to come with you. But don't you think I'd kind of be in the way?"

Mike gave her a solemn look. "Why? Because you don't know anything about crime scenes?"

She couldn't resist when the corners of her lips lifted. "Well... yeah..."

"I don't know anything about crime scenes either," was his reply. "So, let's check it out together. I promise, our second date won't be so serious."

A pleasant tingle spread through Sue's body. Her eyes flipped to Lynn's smiling face and she scrunched her nose at her sister. Lynn just shook her head.

"Go on," Lynn said. "Go on. Let us know all the details later."

To her utter pleasure and surprise, Mike grabbed Sue's hand and made a dash for the door. Sue looked over her shoulder at her sisters, waving at them.

The two hurried to the front door, and Sue's voice wobbled as she spoke, "I don't have my purse or my cell phone or my keys…" She hated to sound like she was complaining, but those were things she didn't leave the house without. He looked over his shoulder at her, nodding.

"I'm going to get my car. I'll pull it around front, and you can hop in. Go ahead and get your stuff."

Sue nodded and reluctantly pulled her hand from his. He gripped it tight before she could take it completely away. He gently moved closer to her until their chests were almost touching. His gaze on her face was so intense, it made Sue's heart hammer in her chest.

The next moment was bliss to Sue. Mike leaned down and placed two quick, soft kisses on her lips. He stood up and moved away so quickly, she wondered if he'd been embarrassed by doing that. She only paused a moment, her fingers covering her lips, as she watched him hurry to the front door.

Sue turned and dashed to the door of her personal office. She'd left her things there the day before. Her purse and cell phone sat together on her desk. She picked up the cell phone and pressed the power button to see how much charge it had. It was supposed to be full, since it had sat on the flat charging pad all night long, with Sue's tablet next to it, charging at the same time.

To her relief, it had a full charge.

She slipped it into her purse and turned back to the door.

At the last minute, she decided she had time to make a quick change. She kept a second outfit in her office, just in case the one she was wearing got dirty during the day.

In a flash, she stripped off her casual clothes and threw on the capri pants, silk top and slipper shoes she liked to wear. She had a classy style of fashion, and what she chose to wear gave off a hint of her personality. She wanted to be stylish, without being garish.

She snatched up her purse and dashed to the door.

She was out on the porch, shading her eyes from the sun with one hand, searching for Mike's car in the parking lot. She didn't know what it looked like, but she was sure she'd know it when she saw it. He was the only one who would be driving up to the offices.

She frowned when she didn't see the car. Surely, he hadn't left without her.

Was he the kind of man who would do that?

She was beginning to feel a little sick to her stomach, when she saw a little green topless Jaguar pull through the parking lot at breakneck speed.

"Where the heck did you park?" she mumbled, going quickly down the steps to meet him at the bottom.

He swung the car around the circle and came to a stop abruptly, his wheels causing a huge dust cloud to form in front of his car, a few rocks spraying over the ground.

Sue grabbed the car door, yanked it open and practically threw herself in the passenger seat. She quickly settled in, closing the door. The seat belt automatically wrapped around her, something that surprised her so much she cried out softly.

She gave him a short, embarrassed laugh, before settling her hands in her lap on top of her purse. Mike didn't hesitate, before tearing back out of the parking lot.

He whizzed through the back roads, taking the drive from the resort to Queen Anne in less time than Sue had seen since she'd arrived. Her heart was pounding. She was anxious for him, but she dared not speak a word. He was obviously troubled by the whole thing, and all she could do was hope she didn't get in the way.

The police were there when Mike and Sue pulled up. They both got out, and Sue hurried behind long-legged Mike as he crossed quickly to the door. He yanked it open and waited impatiently for Sue to get to him. She jogged, passing through the door, mumbling "thank you" as she went.

He came in behind her, and though the look on his face was sour and he hadn't said a word to her the entire trip, Sue was grateful to feel his hand firmly on her back, as they crossed to the office behind the bar.

There were police officers scattered around the interior of the bar, taking notes and snapping pictures, recording what they saw. Sue scanned the room, noticing several chairs had been overturned, and one of the big mirrors on one wall was busted into pieces. It was a pretty piece before it was destroyed, an eclectic mix of bright, vibrant colors placed on mirror glass. It was a shame to see it in ruins.

Sue turned back to see Mike disappear into the office, the door slamming behind him. She didn't know what to do. Should she go to the door and knock? Just go in? Stay out here?

She pondered the thought, but seconds after the door closed, it was yanked open and Mike stuck his head out. His eyes met hers and he gestured with his head.

"Come on," he said, in a gentler voice than his facial expression implied.

Chapter 12

The rage tumbling through Mike, as he listened to Mandy talk to the police officers, was almost too much for him to bear. As soon as he entered the office, his eyes settled on his general manager, sitting in his chair behind his desk, looking up at two police officers in front of her. Both the officers turned to stare at Mike, when he went busting in. He didn't care. It was his bar and he could bust in if he wanted to. Let them shoot him.

"What's going on here?" he asked, slamming the door behind him, casting his eyes directly on Mandy. She looked apologetic and shot to her feet.

"Mike! I was just… explaining to the police officers what happened here."

Mike suddenly remembered Sue had come with him. Guilt and regret flooded him, and he turned, pulling the door back open. When he saw her looking alone and uncertain, her arms crossed in front of her, he called to her.

"Come on." He was grateful to see her practically run to him. When he turned back and saw the look on Mandy's face when Sue came in, he was immediately suspicious that something was wrong with this whole scene.

He'd noticed a few overturned chairs in the dining room. There was no purpose for the chairs to be overturned. He didn't see anything other than the chairs and a few broken glasses on the floor behind the bar.

He narrowed his eyes, putting one hand back to pull Sue closer to him. His eyes moved to the police officers. "What has she told you?"

"We'll just go ahead and let her tell you, Sir," said one, whose nametag identified him as K. Durham. He turned back to Mandy and gave her an inquisitive look. "Would you mind repeating what you said to us for your boss, Miss?"

Mike could tell the officer already didn't think much of Mandy. He wondered why. Mandy gave him an apologetic look, spreading her hands out wide in front of her as she spoke. "I just told them how... we'd been getting a few unsavory types in here lately and... this must be a result of that."

Mike frowned deep. "Unsavory types?" he repeated incredulously. "What are you talking about?"

Officer Durham turned skeptical eyes to Mike. "That's what I was wondering, Mr. Nelson. This bar isn't known for that kind of atmosphere. I can't imagine you letting it happen now."

Mike shook his head. "No more than I would have five years ago, Kevin. You know me. We don't get that type in here. And this is Queen Anne, for pity's sake, not Chicago. You're out of your mind, Mandy." He turned his ire to his bartender, who was still giving him innocent eyes, though when she happened to see Sue, he saw the snakelike snarl cross her face, only for an instant.

She shook her head, spreading her hands out again. "Well, somebody had to do it."

"Where are the surveillance cameras?"

Mandy's face took on a look Mike recognized, from incidents when she'd done something she shouldn't have done. The look was unmistakable, but Mike knew he was the only one who saw it. He'd known her for a very long time and seen her every single day for years.

He knew that look. So, when she responded with an absurd answer, he expected it.

"I... I guess they were turned off last night. Or one of us forgot to turn them on."

Rage filled Mike. He clenched his hands into fists. He might have blown his stack, if Sue hadn't put one small hand on his arm. He looked over at her, the words ready to explode from his chest. He wanted to lay Mandy out. There was no way the surveillance cameras were turned off. As far as he knew, no one but him knew about the three extras. That meant someone had gone into his laptop and turned them off.

He realized Mandy couldn't be talking about the cameras

276

he'd personally installed. She was talking about the one above the register. She was able to access that footage from her cell phone and had probably deleted it or turned the cameras off before she staged the scene.

Mike was all but certain she'd committed the crime, when Sue spoke up.

"Well, what was stolen?" she asked softly, directing the question at Mandy, as if they were close friends. "I'm glad you weren't here when it happened. You could have been hurt."

Surprise ran through Mike. Sue sounded genuine when she said that to Mandy. He couldn't imagine why Sue would be at all concerned about what happened to Mandy. Mike was beginning to wonder why *he* cared so much.

He was disappointed in Mandy, more than anything else. She'd just turned 29, and told him old age was approaching, even though he was two years older than her. She'd mentioned her life as a 'youngster' was over. If she was feeling her clock ticking, maybe that's why she was acting out like this.

Whatever the excuse was, Mike just wished he could have his old friend back. The one who wasn't completely insane.

"Nothing was taken," Mandy said.

A heavy silence fell over the occupants of the small room. Mike noticed that, while he and Sue were giving Mandy stunned looks, both officers were looking at him. He moved his eyes from one to the other, taking in both faces.

He could practically see their thoughts written on both of their faces. False report.

The words resonated through Mike's mind. Mandy could have just opened herself up for some major trouble with the law. They didn't take kindly to wasting law enforcement time, and there were men in the outer part of the bar, *taking fingerprints*.

Mike found himself speechless for once in his life. He opened his mouth and searched for words, but closed it when they didn't come. He was completely flabbergasted. He glanced down at Sue, whose face perfectly matched how he was feeling inside.

"So…" Mike said slowly. "Let me get this straight. You came in today and saw that the bar was broken into. Nothing was taken and nothing was damaged, except the mirror out front. But you were so panicked, you called me and then called the police afterward?"

"You told me to call them," Mandy said in an accusatory voice. Mike looked aghast.

He exhaled sharply and said, "That's because you told me the place was a shambles, and you were scared. You didn't know if the vandals were still here, remember? You said you might be in danger, and that I needed to get here immediately. There are two or three overturned chairs out there. The nice mirror I bought in Australia is smashed to bits. Do you realize what you just did?"

Mandy sat back, looking haughtily at him. "I did what I was told. You told me to call the police, so I did."

Mike was stunned. It didn't matter what he said or how much he tried to talk sense to her, she wasn't going to budge from her position. She'd laid the blame squarely on his shoulders for wasting the officers' time. He looked at each of them apologetically.

"I… I am so sorry. I don't think there's any real need for me to file a report. If nothing was stolen and one old mirror destroyed, that's just not enough for all of us to go through some big investigation or anything." Mike looked at his friend, Officer Durham. "Kevin, you know me. I wouldn't do something like this on purpose."

Kevin shook his head, taking a few steps toward him, both hands propped on his waist; one on his gun holster, the other on his flashlight. He reached forward and patted Mike firmly on the shoulder.

"You're right, Mike. I do know you. I wouldn't think you did this on purpose if I was paid to think it."

Mike gave him a humorless smile. "Thanks, Kev."

Kevin shook his head. He gestured to the other officer, who moved toward the door. "We're gonna let you sort this out, Mike," Officer Durham said. "You give us a call anytime you need us, you hear?" He turned his eyes to Mandy. "If Mike says it's necessary, you give us a call. If not, let him handle it. All right?"

Mandy nodded, giving Kevin and the other officer such a sickeningly sweet grin, Mike's stomach did a flip.

The door closed behind the officers and Mike turned back to Mandy, doing his best to keep his temper. He didn't want to lose it in front of Sue. That was the last thing he wanted Sue to see.

He was still clenching his hands into hard fists, but it was the only way he could keep himself from launching over the desk and strangling the woman on the other side.

"Mandy..." He drew out her name, using a warning tone. "What did you do?"

Mandy stood up, giving him a sultry look. "Whatever do you mean?"

Mike's anger brewed inside him. "Mandy, I know you did this. I know you staged this whole thing, and called me because you didn't want me at the resort with Sue. Admit it!"

Mandy leaned forward, placing her hands on Mike's desk, her fingers spread out. "You didn't need to bring her here! This is bar business! I'm still your general manager, right? Why is she here at all?"

Mike was surprised at first. He wasn't used to Mandy being forceful, in an angry way. She was usually trying to seduce him, but only when they were alone. Her claws came out when another woman was present, and Sue was right next to him.

He turned to her. "I think I might need a few moments alone with Mandy. I hope you don't mind."

"No, I understand. Of course."

He studied her face as she answered, trying to see whether she really didn't mind, or was just saying so. She turned away from him and hurried to the door. He didn't want her feelings hurt.

He took three steps, and was able to intercept her before she got to the door. He gazed down into her eyes.

"Wait a minute," he said, in the softest voice she'd ever heard him use.

She blinked at him slowly. "What is it, Mike?" she asked in a voice equally soft.

He waited a moment, taking the time to really look into her eyes. It filled him with emotions he couldn't recall ever having before; not just by looking in a woman's eyes. He felt contentment, love, warmth, happiness… everything a man could ever want in a woman.

Unable to resist any longer, he put his arms around her and pulled her to him. He lowered his head and pressed his lips against hers in a passionate kiss. She returned it immediately, lifting one hand to put behind his neck. He could feel her fingers massaging his muscles. It sent a tingle of pleasure through his whole body.

He didn't want to break away from the kiss when he did, but he had to. It was becoming too intense for the office at his bar, with Mandy watching.

He looked into her eyes and whispered, "You're precious to me. Don't go anywhere. Just wait for me, okay? Have a beer or something."

Sue giggled, nodding. "Okay, Mike. I'll wait."

Chapter 13

Sue didn't mean to eavesdrop. In fact, she was pretty sure that no one in the bar at that time meant to eavesdrop, but they were all doing it. It was unavoidable. The volume of Mike and Mandy's voices was so high, it could probably be heard outside.

She took a seat at the bar but faced away from it instead of toward it.

"You want something, Miss? I'll get you a drink, on the house. I saw you came in with Mike."

Sue looked over her shoulder at the second bartender. He was the assistant to either Mike or Mandy, whichever one was head bartender for the night. He was a shorter guy, with tight, curly brown hair, a faint mustache and the olive skin of a pure Italian boy. He was as American as they came, but proud of his Italian ancestors.

He was pushing a towel into a glass and twisting it, before placing the clean glass upside down in a row of similar ones. The look on his face was pleasant and sympathetic at the same time.

She shook her head.

"No, thanks, Francesco," she said. "I don't drink during the day."

Francesco gestured at the door to the office, where the two were yelling at each other. "You might want to, if you're gonna deal with all that stuff."

Sue's eyes trailed over to the door, but she wasn't nervous. Mike would take care of everything. She tried not to listen, but Mandy's words drifted across through the air, as if she was speaking from right next to the two of them.

"I didn't want to tell them, or your girlfriend," Mandy said the word condescendingly. "But there is stuff missing, Mike, and it's the kind of stuff you have to have to run a bar."

"What are you talking about?" Mike yelled back. "The police were just here! Why didn't you say anything then?"

Sue heard the spontaneous sound of Mandy's words. She could tell the woman was making it up as she went along, saying whatever came to her mind first. "Because! I... I don't want them to think... that you... would go out of business! I don't want them spreading rumors about you! We're having a hard enough time keeping the doors open as it is."

Sue heard a roar of exasperation from Mike. "Mandy, what are you talking about? There's nothing wrong with our books! We've been in the black all year so far! And you still haven't said what equipment was stolen!"

"The big bins in the back that we do the frying in, the new ones that we bought to replace the old ones, they were taken, those two big freezers in the back, my God, they were filled with frozen meats and ice creams and stuff like that! I mean even a freezer was in that truck."

There was silence on the other side of the door. Sue pictured Mike staring blankly at his Mandy. She couldn't make out what his response was, because he'd lowered his voice, but she could tell by the tone that he was enraged.

She imagined he was asking what truck she could possibly be talking about. Sue sorted through it in her mind, and concluded there was a supply truck in the back, holding some of the bigger pieces of equipment that didn't fit in the building. She guessed the truck was the only thing really taken, and it had a lot of valuable things in it.

She felt bad for Mike. She'd never run a bar, but she knew it was impossible to run any restaurant or business without the proper equipment. She wondered what kind of insurance Mike had. The thought crossed her mind, that he might not even have insurance.

She shook her head. It was a silly notion. Of course, Mike had insurance. He'd been in business too long not to. He knew what he was doing. Just that morning, she'd been thinking about how smart he was, how well-thought-out his plans were, when he presented them to the Wright sisters.

He was an amazing man in her eyes, and she shrugged off

the notion that she just had new love jitters. The feeling of happiness he sent through her body, especially when he touched her or kissed her, made her want to feel that way all the time. She didn't ever want to frown or cry or yell. She wanted to smile, and look into his eyes for the rest of her life.

Sue cleared her throat, surprised by the heavy emotions sweeping through her when she thought of him. She couldn't help but giggle at herself, lowering her head to hide it from Francesco. She was afraid he would think she was laughing at Mike. She didn't want something like that getting back to him. She cleared her throat again, and gave a cough to mask the giggling.

She wasn't sixteen years old. She'd had her high school crushes, boyfriends every few months, that she never did more than make out with. She was a good girl, until college. After college, she'd matured quickly and decided that no man would get in her way. She wanted a certain future, and she was going to have it, whether she had to work for it all her life or not. She didn't need a man.

And then her Uncle Nathan had died, and left his beautiful Georgian resort in the hands of her and her sisters. Her life was completely upended, and everything was different now.

She'd adapted. She was living a good life and wouldn't ask for different. Her goals had changed. And now, Mike was a part of her future. She wanted a future with him.

It was all right to be a giddy schoolgirl for a couple weeks at least, she thought. Maybe longer.

She grinned, turning her head so Francesco couldn't see it. She glanced back to see that he'd moved off into another part of the bar anyway, and was disbursing salt and pepper shakers for the patrons. The doors weren't open yet, and all the cops were gone, leaving her, Francesco and two servers, who sat at one of the tables folding napkins over utensils.

And they were all listening to Mike and Mandy scream at each other. She'd said something personal and he'd exploded, returning a few choice insults that made the servers glance up at each other, without stopping the task they were doing.

Sue swallowed hard. She hoped she never angered Mike that way.

But whatever he thought Mandy had done, he wasn't backing down.

Sue's heart pounded as she waited for her name to be brought up. They'd covered every other base, every other topic Sue could think of, at least, except her. She had to be next.

It didn't take long. They were mumbling now, and the low murmur of voices was all that could be heard. The two servers picked up their trays of napkin-covered utensils and left the room, going back into the kitchen. Neither said a word, to each other or to Sue, as they passed. It was two females, and one, a petite girl who looked like she might be related to Francesco, a long nearly-black braid hanging almost to her rear end, glanced at her as she went by. She shook her head and rolled her eyes.

Sue shrugged. The girl went past with her coworker and disappeared through the swinging door to the kitchen. Sue turned her eyes just in time to see Francesco heading toward the front door. She wondered if he was about to open the bar. Surely, he wouldn't let customers in when it was so easy to hear Mike and Mandy.

No bar owner would want their customers to hear a fight like that one.

She stood up and hurried toward the front door, intending to warn Francesco not to open quite yet, when she heard her name. She halted in place, her eyes peering through the glass door partitions at Francesco. He was going through, but locking the doors behind him. He turned and headed into the parking lot.

Sue couldn't help stepping a little closer to the office door. If she was being discussed, she wanted to know what was being said.

"You have no right to bring her here," Mandy hissed.

Sue heard Mike scoff at her. "What are you talking about? You don't own this bar. You don't even own part of it. This is my bar. You work here. Don't you get that?"

"She doesn't know anything about our business. Nothing. You would be better off with someone who knows more about the bar industry than she does. She'll be useless to you here!"

Sue felt the hair on the back of her neck stand on end. Mandy didn't know anything about her. She silently wondered how long she would be able to listen to Mandy talk about her, without going in that room and standing up for herself.

"She doesn't need to know anything about the bar industry!" Mike roared back. Sue took a step back, her breath catching in her throat. "I'm not going to employ her! She's not going to work here!"

"If you keep offering her chances to be around you, she'll try to be. It's inevitable."

Sue's confusion as to Mandy's line of thinking came across in Mike's tone of voice, when he replied, "You have got to be kidding me, Mandy. Is there nothing you won't say to keep me away from other women? How many times do I have to tell you. I'm. Not. Interested. In. You. If you want to keep your job, you'll come to accept that. I'm willing to employ you, but you have to keep it business and you have to stay away from Sue."

"Or any woman you date?"

Sue listened closely, turning her head to the side and down so she was staring at the floor.

"Of course. But I don't plan on... I'm not thinking about other women... don't you start with me, Mandy. I like Sue a lot. I don't want you ruining it for me, filling her head with stories. You know I don't date a lot, and haven't all these years. You made sure of that, I guess. You mess with Sue, and you'll be sorry."

"What are you gonna do?" Mandy asked in a mocking tone. "Hurt me? You gonna be a bully to little ol' me? You gonna hit me, Mike?"

Mike's answer was spoken with seething rage. Sue felt it for him, too. "I did not say that. I would never do that. Don't accuse me of being that kind of man. You know that's not me."

"Well, then what can you do?"

Mike hesitated. Sue waited for his answer with bated breath.

"I'll fire you first," Mike said, his voice low but audible to Sue. "And then, if I have to, I'll make sure everyone in Queen Anne knows all about your schemes over the years. The way you've done me dirty behind my back. You're lucky you've still got a job, after all the sneaky things you've done."

Sue curled her lip in disgust. How could Mike let himself be a patsy to this woman? He was a strong, intelligent man. Was his heart that soft? Or was it just Mandy?

Sue recoiled at the sound of Mandy's harsh laughter. "I'm lucky? You're gonna be lucky to keep this bar without all that equipment. You're gonna need at least 50 grand to get it all back. I know you don't have that. And the banks aren't gonna give you a loan, either. You've already got two out, don't you?"

Mike fell quiet. It angered Sue, that Mandy surely felt she got the better of the man. Her heart ached for Mike.

But she had a solution.

Chapter 14

Without knocking, Sue burst in the room, making Mike and Mandy jump in surprise. Mike's eyes were wide, his face red, his hands clenched into fists. He was seething.

Sue lifted both hands, looking directly at him. "Mike. I heard what she said. I'm sorry, but everyone outside this room can hear everything the two of you have been shouting at each other." She looked pointedly at Mandy. "So, don't accuse me of eavesdropping."

She turned her eyes back to Mike. "You don't have to worry about the equipment you lost, Mike. I'll help you buy it back."

As she expected, the first thing Mike did was start shaking his head. "I can't take money from you."

"No, it won't be a gift. It won't be charity. I…"

"He said he doesn't want your money, lady," Mandy said in a snide voice. "Just turn around and walk back out of here, and let us discuss our business. You aren't wanted here."

"Mandy!" Mike barked. Mandy's eyes darted to his face. "You will not talk to Sue like that. She deserves respect. She's done nothing to you!"

Mandy snarled and dropped herself back in the desk chair.

"And get your butt out of my chair!" Mike roared, slamming one fist down on the desktop. Mandy hopped out of the chair immediately, and moved around the desk, standing between it and the wall on her other side. She crossed her arms in front of her chest and blinked at Mike, a hurt look on her face.

Sue didn't believe Mandy was hurt. She was too self-centered to be hurt.

Mike looked at Sue with apologetic eyes. Sue could drown in those chocolate eyes. Her heartbeat sped up and her lips twitched, as she forced away a smile. "I'm sorry, Sue. I can't take your money or let you loan it to me. That would ruin our relationship before it even starts."

Sue shook her head.

"Look, Mike, I did a lot of research about the bar before I came here, because you wanted to bring your music to the resort. I wanted to see if you are a trustworthy businessman. From what I saw, you are and..." Sue stopped talking, her eyes swiveling to Mandy. "Do you own stock in Mike's bar?" she asked in a smooth voice.

Mandy blinked at her. "Wh... what do you mean? Stock?"

Sue nodded. She turned her eyes to Mike. "Does she own any of your business? Stocks or a percentage of anything? Anything at all?"

Mike shook his head, his eyes moving between the two women. He seemed to be struggling to grasp Sue's point, which surprised her. "Has she purchased any equipment for the bar or made any changes that required her to put in her own money?" Sue continued.

He shook his head again. "No. I pay for everything."

"So, she just earns a salary here."

"No, she's paid hourly and tips."

Sue lowered her eyelids and gave Mike a narrow look. "Do you think she should be involved in this business meeting?"

She thoroughly enjoyed the look of relief and light that crossed over Mike's sullen face. He straightened up and leaned over to speak to Mandy. He used slow words, as if he was speaking to a child.

"Go ahead and clean up anything that needs to be cleaned up, Mandy. Tell Francesco and the girls we aren't opening today. Tell them I'll call them with their next shifts, and we'll consider these to be paid holidays."

Mandy's jaw dropped. "But you can't afford to pay them if the bar is closed!" she protested. "You have to have the bar open!"

"I know you don't want to go several days without getting

your tips," Mike said, condescendingly. "But this is a problem. Without my equipment, my bar so severely damaged by thieves and vandals, the surveillance camera not working. Mmm mm." He shook his head. "Just go, Mandy. I'll call you later. Tell the others what I said and lock up as you leave."

"But, Mike..." Mandy cut herself off when she saw the look on his face. He was glaring at her with white hot anger, and Sue would have had the same reaction the other woman did.

She moved quickly between the two of them, and headed for the door. She went through, and did not turn around when she closed it behind her.

Sue looked up at Mike.

"I... I don't know how you do it, Mike," she said quietly, knowing her words could be heard on the other side of the door. He gazed at her. As if he knew what she was thinking, he put one finger to his lips and shook his head.

He moved silently to the door, reached out and turned the knob, yanking it open. Mandy was standing nearby. To her credit, she wasn't directly in front of the door, pressing her ear against it. That would have been classic.

Sue watched Mike glare at Mandy with more daggers in his eyes. The woman moved out of Sue's vision. Mike watched her with a look of disgust on his face.

He turned to Sue and closed the door. She assumed he'd watched her leave, or go in the kitchen to tell the servers and Francesco, if he'd returned.

"Let me talk to you about this, Mike. Please hear me out." Sue didn't want to talk about Mandy, or even think about Mandy any more. She was excited to present her impromptu plan to Mike. She enjoyed seeing the excitement in his eyes. She was contagious.

The thought made her giggle.

He went around the desk and plopped in his chair, swiveling it to face the desk. He gestured to the big comfortable chair on the other side. "Please sit, but I have to tell you, Sue, I don't know what you're driving at."

Sue laughed. "You should. I know what an astute businessman you are. I want to invest in your bar." She hurried to continue, when she saw the skeptical look on his face. "Oh, Mike. I shouldn't be the one trying to convince you to take my money. I don't want a lot of your bar, and when you've made a solid profit at the Resort, we'll just call it even. I'll invest in your bar and you can invest in our resort."

Mike's eyes widened. "I don't have the money to buy stocks in your resort," he said in a guilty tone.

Sue shook her head vigorously. "No, no. You'd be investing in the Resort with your time and talents. Of course, you'd be getting paid. But you would be an asset to the company and bring our reputation up. That, in itself is a good business deal, because it brings us more clients. More profit for us, more profit for you... it's a good deal."

"How much of a percentage would you want to take, and how much are you offering?"

Sue felt a little giddy at their negotiating process. She was debating with the man she'd given her heart to, on a serious business matter. It made her feel warm and fuzzy inside. And it turned her on.

She cleared her throat, getting back to business. "I don't have to take much, but I don't want to be insulted by the deal. Plus, my sisters would skin me alive if I don't do this right. They won't want me making decisions – financial decisions, especially – because of the emotions I feel."

Mike nodded. "But you did say you did your research on me." He didn't say the words like he was insulted by what she'd done. She nodded. "Then you know I am a solid businessman. I pay my taxes, I don't skim off the books, what I make is what I make. I just like running my bar. I wouldn't want to do anything else."

Sue agreed with him. "You are good at it, Mike. You don't drink your profits, you've got sound taste in décor and you keep good books. You don't have too high a turnover rate, but what you do have should be expected for a coastal town like this one. It's more tourists than anything else."

Mike nodded. "Sounds like you know what you're talking about. You really did your research, didn't you?"

Sue grinned. "It was one of the best classes I took in college. I mean, I was really good in that class. Never got less than an A on a research paper."

Mike looked impressed, which made Sue suddenly embarrassed that she was boasting. She blushed and looked down at her hands.

"Hey, now," Mike said, in a voice that made her quickly look up. "Don't you go getting embarrassed. Though, when your cheeks get pink and red like that, it makes you even prettier. But you're already pretty. It makes me want to kiss you."

Sue giggled, a tingle of delight passing through her. "We're supposed to be discussing business."

Mike raised one eyebrow, spreading one arm out over the desk and leaning back with his desk chair facing sideways. "There's nothing in the rule book that says two people discussing business can't flirt with each other. Is there?"

Sue raised both her eyebrows and blinked. "Is there even a rule book?"

This made Mike laugh heartily, to Sue's utmost delight. She couldn't help the wide smile that spread across her lips.

"As a matter of fact, there is *no* rule book!" Mike continued to laugh as he spoke. "So, I guess we can do any darn thing we wanna do! Come on around this desk and give your man a kiss."

Sue's breath caught in her throat. From the moment he arrived at the resort that morning, Mike had given her the impression he was very interested in her, for much more than the music planning and the duet singing.

Now he was *her man*.

She pressed her lips together to keep from giggling.

Chapter 15

Mike sat back, debating whether he really wanted Sue to be a part of the bar business. It could be stressful, keeping up with the industry, but he'd found what he believed were the right tools to help him remain successful.

What if she wanted to come in and make changes?

He almost wished he hadn't started flirting with her that day, two days ago. He couldn't help himself. She was so darn pretty and when she blushed like that...

Mike shook his head. Even now, two days later, he felt that urge pass through his body. She wasn't even there and he wanted to kiss her.

He chuckled, shaking his head to clear it. He was trying to decide if he would take her on as an investor, something he'd never done before. He had never considered getting a partner or any kind of investor. He'd worked for, and purchased, everything with his own hard-earned money.

That, and the two loans he'd taken out in the last five years. Both were down to less than a couple thousand each, which was quite an accomplishment.

It meant that Mike could live comfortably, but would never be a rich man. His bar would never make the kind of profits a Main Street Chicago pub might bring in. But he was willing to sacrifice being wealthy for the small town atmosphere he loved, and the friends he'd made since coming to Queen Anne.

Plus, the wealthy visitors paid higher prices, and left generous tips for his servers and bartenders. His establishment drew the elite crowd, that liked to drink in a safe and comfortable environment. The Badlands provided that. Mike was proud of it.

He turned to his desk, after swiveling precariously back and forth in the chair, and opened his laptop. He plugged it in to charge it, and started it up. As he waited for the screen to load and typed in his password, he wondered about his cameras. He'd looked and, somehow, the time period when the "robbery" happened was erased. It was as if losing the battery charge in his laptop had shut the cameras off.

Mike didn't believe that was how it worked. He had the sneaking suspicion he'd been hacked. He could only imagine who would have done that. His eyes darted to the door. He couldn't see Mandy, but he was thinking her name with a vengeance. If he found out she hacked his laptop, there would be hell to pay.

He clicked on the camera option and watched what was on the screen. Mandy was behind the bar, tending to the customers as she always did. Mike watched her precision and motion, her friendly attitude toward the customers, and the speediness with which she moved. She never left anyone waiting longer than she absolutely had to. Her skills ensured that rarely happened to her.

In the past, Mike was always impressed with the way she worked. The work ethic was strong in her. But the past few weeks had been rough. He'd just begun to realize how obsessed she was with him. She considered him hers, and there was no changing her mind.

He didn't want to fire her. She wouldn't be able to stay in Queen Anne, and get another job that made her the kind of money she made at the Badlands. A good night in tips probably garnered her about $600 to $1000. That was a fortune in a small town like Queen Anne, even if the prices were a little higher, because of the tourist crowd it drew. Where else would $500 be considered a bad night in tips?

But her behavior was quickly becoming intolerable. He wanted to pursue a relationship with Sue. He didn't see how he could do that with Mandy hovering over him like she did.

And if she staged the robbery, that meant she'd done something with his equipment. That made her a legitimate criminal. He couldn't employ a criminal just because she was his friend for so long, or because he felt sorry for her.

She needed to pay for her crime.

But without evidence that she'd done it, there was nothing to accuse her of, nothing she could be prosecuted with. He couldn't file charges against her with just his gut feeling.

He sighed, his eyes still on her as she moved behind the bar.

"Why did you have to turn out to be a lunatic?" he mumbled.

His eyes flicked up to the door when there was a knock. "Come in," he called out, going through his mind, trying to remember if he had any appointments.

The door opened and his friend, the very same tennis instructor from the resort, came in.

"Hey, Mike," he said. "How's it going?"

"Brandon. Things are good." Mike stood up and leaned across his desk, holding his hand out. Brandon shook it and dropped into the chair opposite Mike as if he was exhausted.

"That's good to hear."

"What's up?" Mike asked curiously, sitting back down. He hadn't seen Brandon since that day at the resort, and they'd barely spoken that day. Thinking back, Mike hadn't recognized Brandon. Or he was too focused on Sue to realize he knew the young man.

"I was just curious about how things were going," Brandon said in a neutral voice. "I don't know a lot about what goes on at the Resort, but I do know they're bringing you in for some work. I've heard that. I haven't talked to ya in a while. I just thought I'd stop by."

Mike got the clear impression that Brandon had a reason for being there. He wasn't there just to chat. But if Brandon wanted to prolong it, Mike had the time. He wasn't doing anything and Brandon was a friend. He could wait.

"Yeah, I hear they are seriously considering bringing me on as music planner."

Brandon grinned shaking his head. "They're not considering it. They've already hired you. You just don't know it yet."

Mike chuckled. "Well, why are you here ruining the surprise for me?"

Brandon's grin widened. "I guess I should have left that to Sue, huh?"

Mike felt a twitch in his chest. He studied Brandon's face to see if he was being sarcastic. Brandon's smile didn't waver.

"You got a crush on her, do ya?" His friend kept his voice casual.

Mike nodded. "Yeah, we're dating."

Brandon sat forward abruptly, looking directly at Mike. "Good for you, man. Good for you."

His voice was so serious, Mike couldn't help frowning in confusion. "You're acting weird. Why are you acting like that? What's up with you, man?"

Brandon chuckled, shaking his head as he relaxed into the chair. "I'm just relieved, is all. That girl... When they got here last year, I really thought she hated it here. She was always unhappy and sour-faced. After Mari got married, she got bossy. I mean, for a couple months, no one could do anything to her satisfaction."

Mike was beginning to feel uncomfortable, as if Brandon was gossiping and he was contributing to it. Brandon must have caught the look on his face, because he said, "No offense to the lady. That's why I'm so glad you're in her life. I figured the two of you were dating, because she's been walkin' on cloud nine lately."

A streak of pleasure zipped through Mike. He reached forward and took a handful of peanuts from the bowl on his desk. He sat back, popping them in his mouth, a look of satisfaction on his face.

"Yeah, you should look like that," Brandon laughed. "I'm telling you, she was one unhappy camper when they first came. She got better, but since you've been in her life..." His young friend shook his head again. "I'm glad for her, Mike. If I'd known you two would hit it off, I would have insisted on a meeting long ago."

Mike shook his head, thinking over the last year's events. It had been a struggle for him. He'd leaned on Mandy a lot. In hindsight, having Sue there would have been better. But not both at once. His problems were big enough, without doubling the female factor.

He didn't want it doubled now, either. He just wanted one. He wanted Sue.

"Everything happens when it's supposed to," Mike murmured, his eyes dropping to his laptop screen. He wasn't watching the action there. He was thinking about being with Sue; just hearing her laugh, and saying his name, calling him "babe". He loved it.

She told him she appreciated the way he texted back so quickly.

It always made him laugh, remembering that.

"We talked about you, that morning we were playing tennis when you got there," Brandon said in an innocent tone. When Mike gave him a curious look, he continued quickly. "Not, like, talking about you. Nothing bad. I just asked her who she was meeting and she said you."

"She told you she was meeting with me?" he asked. It seemed strange that Sue would disclose resort business to the tennis instructor.

"Yeah, I kind of pulled it out of her, because I figured it was you coming. I'd heard your name mentioned a lot, and every time Sue was around, which was only once or twice in *my* presence, her face would just light up like a Christmas tree!"

A pleasant tingle slipped through Mike. His heartbeat sped up. "What… what did she say about me when you two talked?"

"Just that you were coming for the music planning position, the one they created for you."

Mike was a little disappointed. "That's it?"

Brandon laughed. "Well, she's not going into depth with *me*, Mike. She doesn't know me. In fact, at this point, she knows you better than she knows me, and I've been working there for years now. But that's neither here nor there. I'm an employee. It's not the same as a boyfriend."

Mike chuckled softly. He enjoyed being referred to as Sue's boyfriend.

"But I gotta tell you something, Mike, man-to-man, friend-to-friend."

Mike's eyebrows shot up into his brown wavy hair. "Oh yeah?" He sat forward, grabbing more peanuts, and gave Brandon an intense, unblinking look, tossing them one by one in his mouth.

Brandon nodded, with a serious look on his face. "I'm not joking around here, Mike, and I'm only saying this as a friend. Remember that, okay? I, uh, I see you've still got Mandy here." He dropped the volume of his voice as though he expected Mandy to be listening in. "Why do you still have her here, man? You know she's no good for you."

Mike pulled in a deep breath. Brandon was privy to some of what Mike had gone through over the last year. He knew enough to know that, though Mandy had been of some help to Mike, she ended up acting more like a crazy stalker. Like her talks with him, and her times of comforting him with a hug, or an hour spent on the phone, somehow qualified her to be possessive, territorial, and jealous of every other female in his life.

That Mandy could not be trusted, was becoming more and more apparent. Mike didn't understand his inability to get rid of her. He wanted to help her. He wanted to give her another chance.

He looked up at Brandon and the young man seemed to read his mind. He let out an exasperated gasp and shook his head.

"Mike. You gotta get rid of her, man. You can't keep her here if you want Sue to come around. And especially if you two go into business together."

Mike blinked and narrowed his eyes. "How did you know she wants to invest in my bar?" he asked testily. No one knew about their plan. Why would Sue tell the tennis instructor such personal business?

Brandon's eyebrows shot up. He looked completely taken aback, making Mike rethink his question. He knew he had inadvertently told Brandon about the plan.

"I meant, you coming to work as a music planner at the resort," Brandon said, innocently. "Is she really going to invest in the bar? That's fantastic!" His face went from pleased to concerned in half a second. "But, Mike, that just means you have to get rid of Mandy, now. Or at least soon. She won't tolerate having another female around like that. I bet you haven't told her yet, have you?"

Mike shook his head, looking Brandon squarely in the eye. "She hasn't been told because it's none of her business, and it doesn't matter what she will and will not tolerate. This isn't her bar, and it never will be. She has no say here."

Chapter 16

Sue sat in front of her computer, staring at it, trying to concentrate. She understood completely when Mike asked for a couple days to think about her offer, but she was anxious, and had already drawn up the paperwork and consulted her attorney about making it legal.

She didn't tell her sisters about the plan. She was a little nervous that Mari might get upset at the notion Sue was venturing into something unknown, without her sisters. But she was 25 years old, and it was about time she did something on her own.

Her mind was completely occupied with daydreams about dates with Mike, kissing him, telling him all her heartfelt feelings. His face flashed through her mind, a smile on his lips, his white teeth like a beacon in the dark.

Her heart pounded. His laughter…

She sighed.

She wouldn't admit she was waiting for that phone call. They'd kept in touch for two days by text, but Sue didn't want to put pressure on him, so she never asked him about the business investment. Their texts had been simple check-ins, as they went about their regular work days.

If she'd thought about it, she might have realized how much of her brain was occupied by the man and his bar.

She pulled in a deep breath, turning in her chair to a stack of papers on the desk, to her right. Her desk was shaped like a wide U, giving her a lot of space to fill with everything under the sun. The more space there was to occupy, the more she would occupy it with papers, books, and miscellaneous office items. Sticky notes, pushpins, replacement staples, paper clips, two mini-staplers, stamps, ink stamps; you name it, she had one somewhere on her desk.

She turned once more so her back was to her desk and stood up to stretch her legs. She'd come in early to get some extra work done. She was hoping the afternoon would be spent on a long lunch with Mike. She planned to surprise him at the bar sometime before noon, and stay for a few hours.

She could only hope Mandy was taking the day off, and that Mike wouldn't have to work through lunch. If he did, she'd just have a drink and come back to the resort. No big deal. That's how it was when you surprise someone at their place of business. You took your chances.

Sue just wanted to see Mike anyway; listen to his voice, look into his eyes. Just five minutes would fill her up for the rest of the day.

She chuckled, lifting her arms above her head and reaching for the ceiling, lifting up on her tip toes to stretch her entire body. She tilted her head back and looked at the ceiling.

Five minutes definitely wasn't long enough. She wanted to shrink up and jump in his pocket, staying with him all day, every day...

Again, she chuckled, relaxing her muscles. She rotated her wrists and her neck at the same time, enjoying the releasing sensation she got as she stretched.

If she wasn't careful, she would end up just another Mike Nelson stalker. And she wouldn't be his employee. She'd be his *business partner*. Oh, what havoc a scorned woman could wreak on a man and his business.

"What a horrible thought, Sue Wright," Sue said aloud, to herself. "You're a horrible person. Shame on you."

Sue had read about, and seen episodes on, true crime shows that suggested there were a lot of women who'd do some pretty awful things to a man after they are scorned. She shuddered just thinking about it.

When her cell phone on the desk buzzed and rattled on the hard wood, Sue spun around and snatched it up. She looked at the screen and smiled. Pleasure ran through her when she pressed the call button.

"Hello, Mike," she said, holding it up to her ear. She turned around again and lowered herself to her chair, hanging on the edge as if she just might slip off for the fun of it. "How's everything in your world?"

"Better, now that I'm talking to you," Mike said.

Sue grinned wide, rolling her eyes and chuckling softly. "Oh, that's such an old cliché!" she exclaimed. "I'm happy to hear from you. What have you got going on today?"

She listened to Mike rattle off some bar stuff, enjoying the sound of his voice in her ear. She'd been hearing it for the last two days in her dreams and her memories. Listening to him now, Sue couldn't help the adrenaline that rushed through her body.

She felt like she could run a marathon.

"That sounds like a full day's work in just one morning," Sue said finally, when it seemed like he was done venting. "Does it sound like you might want to take a break this afternoon? Maybe a long lunch with me? I came in early. I was going to surprise you, but if you have the rest of the day packed with business, I'll make it another day."

"You were going to surprise me, huh?" Sue heard the delight in Mike's voice. Her smile was unwavering.

"Yeah."

The sound of Mike chuckling on the other end of the line was a new memory she would have forever. It sounded satisfied… proud… she couldn't quite place the emotion attached to it. But the sound made her bite her bottom lip and look around the room as if she'd never seen any of her possessions before.

But she wasn't really looking at them. She could only see Mike in the forefront of her mind, interfering with her actual vision. She hoped Mike didn't have a full schedule the rest of the day.

"I'd love to see you and have a long lunch. There's a restaurant I want to take you to. They've got the best steaks and seafood. You'll love it."

"That sounds fantastic!" Sue enthused. "I can't wait."

She lost her smile when she heard the sound of Mandy's voice coming through Mike's phone. She had obviously stepped into the room.

"Mike, we need you out here."

Sue didn't hear Mike's response, which must have been visual. Whatever he did, didn't sit well with Mandy.

"I don't care if you're on the phone with her or not. We need you out here."

"No, you don't," Mike said. "I can see on the camera that we aren't really busy. What do you need me for?"

Sue frowned. She wished Mandy would get out of there, so she could finish talking to her man. She couldn't hear Mandy's response. The woman probably lowered her voice so she couldn't be heard. She pictured Mike listening. She wished she was there with him. She'd throw that woman out the door and slam it in her face.

"I'll be there in a minute. You can handle it until then."

Sue heard Mike direct his voice back into his phone. "I've got to go, Sue. I'll pick you up for lunch. When should I be there?"

Sue wanted to tell him to come immediately, but she still had a few hours of work to do.

"Pick me up at eleven?"

"You bet. I'll be there. Nothing will stop me."

Sue smiled. "Okay, Mike. See you then."

She was surprised when the urge to say "I love you" came to her lips. She bit it back. It was much, much too soon for that. She'd known him for going on three weeks, and was ready to marry the man.

"See you then, babe."

His term of endearment made a tingle run through her body. She pressed the end button and held her phone against her chest, feeling her heart beat through her skin. She couldn't help it. He was almost like a drug she couldn't live without.

Puppy love, she thought. I haven't felt like this since I was fifteen years old.

She turned back to her desk and looked at the mess. With all her nervous energy, she spent the next twenty minutes cleaning up, putting away odd items that didn't need to be out, sorting through papers and filing them away where they needed to go.

She didn't want to do any more work. She wanted to find a game on her phone and occupy her mind with entertainment until eleven.

But she did her best to concentrate and finished up three accounts by eleven o'clock, which was good. Not good enough for Mari, maybe, but good enough for Sue. Mari concentrated too much on business. She even brought her baby with her to her office, which was perfectly fine, since the child slept more than anything else. She was a quiet little girl. The sisters celebrated when the child was born as a single child and not three. They'd joked a lot about that during Mari's pregnancy.

Finally, she looked up at the clock and saw she had ten minutes left. She closed her laptop and pushed herself away from the desk.

Turning around, she leaned over to put on her boots. She would just freshen up a little before he got there. She wanted to look pretty for Mike.

The weather didn't warrant her boots, but it had been chilly that morning when she dressed. She knew she was going to heat up outside, but the restaurant would probably be cool. She'd probably be thankful she dressed that way.

She hurried out of her office, snatching up her purse, and went to the bathroom just outside her office. She touched up her makeup and stared at herself in the mirror. Her heart was beating nervously. She smiled wide, baring her teeth. She checked them and was satisfied they were clean of debris or lipstick.

She pulled in a deep breath, pushing her fingers through her hair.

"Calm down. It's not like he's going to propose or

303

something." Just the thought covered her in chills. She shook her head. "It's too soon for all this, Sue. Get your mind together. Keep your wits about you."

She tried to think of a few more clichés her father would have told her, if he was there to council her. She grinned. He would like Mike, when they met. Mr. Wright was an old metal head himself, having played in a few bands when he was a young man. Sue remembered the pictures and cassette tapes he played for her and her sisters when they were growing up.

Maybe that was why she was so attracted to Mike. He was a musician, like her father.

Whatever the reason, she was very attracted to him. She saw a bright future with him.

Chapter 17

The phone was ringing as Mike went toward the door to his office. He glanced at his wristwatch and back at the phone. He was leaving early, anxious to pick up Sue, so he'd left himself plenty of time to answer it.

But what if it was a lengthy, drawn-out conversation? What if it was his mom calling?

The thought made Mike snicker. He crossed the room to his desk and picked up the phone.

"Badlands Bar and Grill. This is Mike. How can I help you?"

"Mike?" a female voice said his name on the other end.

"That's me," he replied in a friendly tone. He didn't recognize the voice but it sounded familiar.

"Hey, Mike, it's me, Mari. Wright. From Emerald Resort. You know my sister, Sue."

Mike chuckled. He knew Sue. He planned to know everything about Sue very soon, from her favorite color, to what kind of ice cream she preferred. "I do know Sue. I met with the three of you, so I know you, too. What's up?"

Mari laughed. "Of course, you did. How dumb of me. Yes, I want to offer you the position we've created for you as a music planner for any events we hold here. We all liked your music and your presentation very much, and you seem to be an excellent entertainer and businessman."

Mike lifted his eyebrows. "That's a lot of compliments. Thank you so much, I appreciate it."

He could hear Mari's smile through the phone. "Next time you come to the resort, can you bring your accountant and any business advisors you use so I can go over the documents with them?"

"You already have everything drawn up?"

"Yes, I did it this morning. Sue had already gone over all the numbers and had everything ready for me to make a decision. I'm glad she found you, Mike. I think you'll be a real asset to our business."

"Thanks again, Mari. Actually, I'm picking Sue up in about 45 minutes. Do you have time this afternoon?"

Mari hesitated. Mike pictured her going through her schedule book. He didn't know what it looked like, but he pictured it anyway, a grin spreading on his face. This was very good news. He had just doubled his income, if not more. He would have to hire another bartender. He would need an assistant manager for Mandy... if he kept her on.

He suddenly felt energized and ready to move. There were so many things he needed to do to make this a successful business launch. He wouldn't need to do much. He knew that. There were a lot of things on his agenda that needed taken care of now.

"I do have time this afternoon, but only if your people will do a business lunch. If I don't eat at noon, I'll simply keel over dead."

Mike chuckled. "I'm supposed to pick her up at 11. I have only one person who helps me out, my accountant, Gordon Kramer. I'll call him now and see if he'll come with me, or meet you at the same time. Do you think an hour is enough?"

"Sure. It's just going over the papers and signing some documents. When you come back from your lunch with Sue, I'll have some papers for you to sign, too. Lynn is a notary so we won't have to worry about that."

"That's great. Okay, let me call him. Do you want me to call you back?"

"I'd appreciate it. Otherwise, I won't know if he's coming for sure, will I?" Mari laughed softly.

"True, true. Okay, I'll call you back."

"Actually, I'm coming up on a meeting with the pool supervisor. Just text it to me, would you?"

"Did you call from your cell?"

"I did, yeah."

Mike nodded, looking down at his business phone, where the number of the person calling was displayed on a small screen at the top of the square box. "I've got it. I'll text you after I talk to him."

"Awesome. See you soon."

"Will do. Oh, and Mari. Thanks again. I really appreciate this opportunity."

"You're welcome, Mike. Welcome to the Emerald Resort team."

Mike hung up the phone and immediately picked it back up. He pushed speed dial 3 and waited for Gordon to answer. His accountant was also a lawyer and a good friend, a trustworthy man who Mike had known before he bought the bar. He'd never had any trouble with his books, which he reviewed every two months, like clockwork. He'd stopped practicing law because there were so few cases in Queen Anne, and plenty of need for a good accountant.

"Yello?" Gordon answered the line.

"Hey, Gordie, it's Mike."

"Hey, Mikey, how many times do I gotta tell you, don't call me Gordie."

"But it's so fashionable and smart!" Mike laughed along with his friend.

"What's up?" Gordon asked.

"I've got a new business venture, Gordon." Mike proceeded to give Gordon all the information he could about the music planner position at Emerald Resort, explaining that he needed Gordon to go review the contract and any financial papers they might have.

"Make it good for me, man. I'm also taking on an investor for the bar."

Gordon was quiet for a moment. Mike was sure he'd taken the man by surprise. "An investor? Why would you want to do that?"

"Because somebody broke into my bar and stole a bunch of equipment. I don't have the funds to replace that stuff. It's almost 50k, and I still have bills to pay, too. She's going to become an investor, and I'll need your help drawing up that contract, too."

"You got it, Mike. When do you want me at Emerald Resort?"

"I'm going up there now. I've got a lunch date at eleven with one of the sisters."

"Do you really now?" Mike heard the tone Gordon was using. He was probably thinking "sly dog".

Mike grinned wide. "Yeah, the middle sister, Sue. She came to audition to sing duets with me, and we really hit it off. We're dating now."

"That's great, Mike!" Mike enjoyed the enthusiasm in his friend's voice. "I'm really happy for you. But you want me there at eleven? Isn't that when you're going on your lunch date?"

Mike explained the situation to him, and was relieved when Gordon agreed to meet him there.

"It's kind of a long drive from the bar," Gordon said. "I hope you're already on your way, or you're gonna be late."

Mike glanced down at his wristwatch. His chest tightened with anxiety. "Oh, my God. I gotta go. I'm on the office phone. I'll see you there."

"See ya."

The phone disconnected. Mike ran to the office door and crossed the bar to the front door without looking around him. He didn't see Mandy glaring at him, completely forgetting she'd asked for his help more than an hour ago.

Mike crossed the parking lot to the front of the resort office building. He regretted not telling Gordon where to go. He glanced around the parking lot and caught sight of Gordon's car. He must have done business with the Wright sisters before. Or, more likely, their Uncle Nathan.

He took the steps up two at a time, stopping halfway when he heard his name being called behind him.

"Hey! Mike!"

He turned to see Gordon just stepping out of his car. He, was waving.

Mike waved back. "Didn't see you there, Gordon. Sorry!"

He went back down a few steps to meet his friend and then turned to ascend beside him. "You having a good day so far?" Gordon asked, looking him up and down, as if assessing his choice of clothing for his date. "You look like it's been fairly stress free."

Mike chuckled, shrugging. "I'm not sure about that. But I can tell you that getting this new job, new equipment for my bar, an investor and a girlfriend, in a span of about two weeks, is a first for me."

Gordon snorted humorously. "Getting a girlfriend is the one that surprises me, Mike. You're really talented musically, and smart in business. But I have to say, I haven't seen you with many ladies. That's kind of surprising, since you've got those damn good looks." Gordon shook his head, acting exasperated and rolling his eyes.

Mike shook his head, too, grinning. "Whatever, man. You're going to meet Mari Wright. She's the oldest sister, and the majority stockholder in the business, so she makes most of the decisions."

Gordon raised his eyebrows. "Does that sit well with the other two?"

Mike shrugged. "They don't seem to mind. I don't think either of them want all those responsibilities. Mari is friendly. They all are. Have you worked with them before?"

Gordon shook his head. "Nope. I did some work for their

uncle, but not for them.

Mike nodded. That's what he'd expected.

"You'll like Mari. You'll like them all."

They crossed the room while they talked, walking toward the receptionist desk.

"Mike!"

He spun to the left when he heard Sue's voice, a wide smile on his face. Sue was emerging from the hallway to his left, looking as pretty as a new penny. He liked the green blouse she was wearing. It looked light and airy, covering her like a soft, shiny blanket.

"Look at you, looking all pretty," he said in a smooth voice, leaning to kiss her cheek, with one hand on her arm.

She lifted her head to receive the kiss and touched his hand with hers. "Hello, Mike. You look great."

"Okay, okay, you two." Gordon pretended to look at a wristwatch that wasn't there. He tapped his wrist. "Times a'tickin'."

Sue gave Gordon a smile, but turned her confused eyes to Mike. He laughed. "Sue, this is my good friend, accountant and lawyer, Gordon Kramer. He's come to look over the contract to be music planner, and he's also going to take care of the investment deal you and I are hatching."

He delighted in the beautiful smile that covered her face, reaching into her eyes and making them shine. "You've decided to do it!" she said happily. "I'm so happy, Mike. I don't want you to lose that bar!"

He shook his head. "Me neither, my dear." He couldn't resist pulling her into a hug. She was so warm. He got chills when she wrapped her small arms around him and squeezed back. He wanted to say "I just love you" but was afraid of her reaction.

He looked back at Gordon. "Come on. We'll take you to Mari."

"How did all this happen?" Sue asked in a curious voice, as the three of them went down the short hallway to the ladies' offices.

"Mari called me right as I was leaving to come out here. I arranged for Gordon to come and talk to her, and go over the papers and all."

Sue leaned back to look around Mike at the other man. "You drove yourself? If not, we can have a limo take you back."

Gordon snickered, moving his eyes to Mike. "I should have gotten a ride with you."

Sue grinned wide. "You can always go for a ride in it and come back. Go do some grocery shopping or something."

Gordon laughed heartily, throwing his head back. He slapped Mike hard on the shoulder twice. "You've got a lady with a sense of humor, Mike. Good for you."

Pleasure and pride swam through Mike. He gave Sue a warm smile. He really couldn't have asked for a woman more perfect for him.

Chapter 18

Mike pulled the chair out for Sue. She sat in it, and helped him push it toward the table.

"Thank you," she said softly, gazing up at him. She hadn't gotten rid of her nervousness. She felt like she was meeting the President of the United States. "I'm... I'm glad we're doing this somewhere away from the bar."

Mike sighed. "I know. You don't like Mandy."

Sue shook her head, setting her purse on the floor between her feet. She folded her hands on the table. "It's not that I don't like her," she responded. "She doesn't like me. And I know why."

The server stopped by the table and asked what they wanted to drink. They gave their orders and the girl walked away.

Sue looked down at her menu. She didn't want to talk about Mandy through their whole date. It wasn't her intention to bring the woman up to begin with. She knew Mike had responded the way he did because of the tone of her voice. She made the bar sound like a bad place to be.

"I love your bar," she said, her thoughts prompting her words. "I really do. And I'm happy to invest in it, seeing as how you make a lot of profit there, and you've got a head for the bar business. I just don't feel comfortable with her staring daggers at me every time I'm there."

"That's unfortunate." Mike shook his head. "I've been told by more than one person that if I want to date you, I have to make her leave the bar. If I want to date at all, I have to make her leave. But she's a real asset, a great manager, and all the other employees love her. I'm afraid I'll have a mutiny on my hands."

"That's such a shame." Sue kept her eyes down on the menu, scanning the items. In her old life, the prices would have been on the menu, and if they weren't, she would have said something. She wasn't going to buy something she didn't know the price of. But there were no prices on this menu. The customer had to assume the cost and be willing to pay whatever it was.

She looked up at Mike. He wasn't a wealthy man. What was he doing bringing her to a place like this? Did he want her to pay her half?

She cleared her throat, unsure what to say. "Uh, I've never been here before. What kind of price range is it?"

A slow smile spread across Mike's face when he looked up at her from the menu. "This is Queen Anne Township, the first restaurant built in Queen Anne. It dates back at least 150 years. There are no prices because people pay what they can afford to pay."

Sue's eyebrows shot up and she looked around the room, noticing the fancy décor, the tuxedos and black and white dresses the servers were wearing, the luxury all around her. "I… I've never heard of such a thing."

"It's a family owned restaurant. The family has more money than God. They also have big hearts and generous natures. They also know how to run their other businesses, where they can take any losses they may have here. It helps with tourists who don't have the kind of money that the elite you see at Emerald Resort might have."

His words brought Brandon to mind, when he'd talked about the "rich kids", while they were on the tennis court the other day. He'd said there was more in Queen Anne than Emerald Resort. She wondered if he offered his services to the less wealthy.

He probably did. He was a nice guy that way.

"Well, all right then, I guess I'll have exactly what I want then, since you're going to decide how much we pay for it all."

Mike grinned. "I brought a hundred-dollar bill. That's what I usually give them, even when I'm alone; which I usually am. I think that's more than enough, don't you?"

Sue nodded in agreement. "Yes, I think you're right. Okay, let's see…"

She scanned the menu until her eyes landed on one of her favorite meals, steak and potatoes. She had to try it. Mike had mentioned it, too. She wanted to make him feel good.

"So, steak and shrimp, then?" Mike asked. "Red potatoes and broccoli on the side?"

Sue grinned. "Are you telling me what I can have here tonight?" she teased him.

He assumed a stern look and leaned forward. "It is my ultimate goal, to crush your will and make you grant all my wishes without question."

He leaned back, as they both laughed. "You actually read my mind, Mike. I want the steak and potatoes, and shrimp sounds wonderful, and I do like broccoli."

Mike's grin beamed from his face. "I did hit the nail on the head, didn't I?"

"You did," Sue nodded. She was feeling bubbly inside, as if she was filled with carbonation. Her skin tingled with excitement and anticipation. She was glad they were off the troublesome topic of Mandy and her jealous ways. The subject would come up again, she was sure, but in the meantime, she planned to enjoy herself.

"I've been thinking about our duets," Mike said.

Sue raised her eyebrows. "With all that you've been going through? I figured you'd put that on the back burner."

He shook his head. It was a relief to her. She didn't want to give up that opportunity. It was not only a way to see Mike more often, but also a way to share something they both loved.

"There is no way that's going on the back burner. I want to do it. I don't announce things in my bar, and then have it fall through."

"I understand."

Sue waited to continue, until after Mike ordered for both of them. When the server took the menus and walked away, she leaned forward slightly.

"What have you been thinking about? Do you want to do some heavy metal? Maybe some screaming, mosh-pit goth horror music?"

Mike let out an abrupt laugh, and gave her an amused look that she immediately fell in love with. She would have to make him laugh more often. "I don't even know what kind of music that is," he replied, chuckling. "Or if it even is a kind of music."

"I think it is, from some of the stuff I've been hearing."

Mike shook his head. "You've been listening to the wrong stations, then. That's not the kind of music I listen to, and certainly not the kind I play. But you know that? I know you're teasing me. I think you'll like the songs I've picked for us. I think I've got…" He leaned to the side and reached into his back pocket, pulling out a folded piece of paper. It was folded into four squares. He opened it, nodded and handed it over the table to her.

"Here. Take a look and see what you think."

Sue looked down at the list, impressed by the song choices. She nodded. "I like it. I can sing all of these. They're all in my range."

"Yeah, that's what I figured." Mike held out his hand, and she gave him the list back. "I'll make a copy for you, and make a CD of the guitar part, so you know how to sing along with it. We can also do it to karaoke background music, if you don't want just the guitar. I have the place set up for that, too."

"You don't have karaoke nights, though, do you?"

Mike shook his head. "Not right now. Too much other stuff going on. I don't really have a KJ to work the machine or run a karaoke night." He narrowed his eyes. "Unless you want to do it. You want a twice a week nightly job in my bar?"

"Well, we're just gonna end up with both of us as each other's bosses, aren't we?"

They both laughed at that.

They talked casually for twenty minutes, until their food came out. It had to be one of the biggest, best-tasting meals Sue had ever had. She was astounded by the quality of the food.

"They must really rake in the dough in this place," she said. "This is really high-quality food. The steak is cooked perfectly. Everything is perfect."

She was halfway through her lunch, forcing herself to finish. She didn't want to take a doggie bag with her, but if she had to, she would. She wasn't giving up even a little bit of this food.

"I'll definitely be back," she said, continuing to eat.

She looked up to see Mike giving her an amused smile. "I'm glad you like this place, Sue. I've been coming here since the family took it over, and made it into the donation restaurant of the East Coast. Sometimes, if you work it right, you can spot a celebrity or two in here. I've seen a couple myself."

Sue grinned. "That's cool."

Mike nodded. "I know. It really is. I see you've got more stomach space than you thought you did."

Sue looked down at her plate and shook her head. "I think I just gained ten pounds, and you might have to carry me out of the restaurant."

Mike laughed. "Over ten pounds? No way. You'll be fine. Go home and take a laxative."

Sue gasped, laughing at the same time and covering her mouth with one hand. She was glad she didn't have a mouth full of food. She squeezed her eyes together until she was done laughing.

"Mike!" she said exasperatedly, shaking her head. "You almost made me choke."

He shook his head back at her. "No way. Not gonna let that happen either. I know CPR. It's just another excuse to kiss you, I say."

"I hope you don't wait for me to pass out before you stop me from choking!" Sue cried out softly.

The rest of their lunch went by without the topic of Mandy coming up. Sue was relieved. She hadn't laughed so much, or had such a good time, in years. She thought maybe back in her teenage years, she might have been as happy.

Her smile beamed at him, as he picked up the plates and stacked them one on top of the other, aligning all the utensils up on the top plate. Then, he stacked the napkins on top of that, and any ramekins that came with their meal, on top of the napkins.

He caught her gazing at him and lifted his eyebrows.

"What?"

"It's obvious you work in the restaurant industry. Not everyone stacks the stuff for the servers."

"It makes it easier for them," Mike said casually, shrugging.

"Yes, it does. It's really respectful of you to do that. I like it."

"I'm glad I impressed you," Mike said genuinely. "I'm glad you like it here. We'll come here again."

"You got that right." Sue glanced around the room. She didn't see an unhappy face in the room.

She sighed. She wished she could always be this content, not worried about anything, and no evil, jealous women corroding her happiness.

Chapter 19

Mike told Sue he was going to hire a new bartender, and make sure they were familiar with karaoke machines and the work of a karaoke jockey. He needed a new bartender anyway, because his time would be taken up with the new music planning business.

He didn't mind taking a step back from the bar. He knew Mandy was capable of running things. She had keys to everything, and knew the bar like the back of her hand. He tried not to worry that he would come back and find the place bare, everything removed or burned down. He refused to believe Mandy could be that kind of woman.

In hindsight, it would have been a good idea to get another manager on board and teach them the ropes, in case something ever happened to Mandy. There was always a chance she might die in a car accident or something like that.

Mike tried not to think like that, but other than himself, she really was the only one who knew the ins and outs of Badlands Bar and Grill. He was disappointed with himself. He couldn't give someone a crash course in running the bar, and then fire Mandy. The bar was too important to be run by an amateur.

"I don't think I thought this through very well," he said, sitting back in his office chair, lifting one hand to cup his chin with his fingers. He stared at the ceiling, lost in thought.

It was a Thursday, three days since he had his lunch date with Sue. They'd kept in contact by phone, text and social media, but hadn't found any time to see each other in person. He wasn't too concerned. Tonight was the night they planned to do their duet practicing. She would be at the bar in a few hours, anyway.

Whenever he thought about her, his heart filled with peace. He was so happy when he was with her, so content with his life. It was like he didn't have any worries or cares in the world.

When he was away from her, reality hit him like a ton of bricks. He had a lot of work to do in a very short amount of time. Mari wanted to start the event music planning in two weeks, when they had a wedding planning appointment with a wealthy stockbroker from New York. Those were the worst kind, she said, not because of the man's money or position, but because they tended to choose bullying women who pushed "servants" around.

"But it's money," Mari had said. "And lots of guests, with lots of money themselves. So, I guess that's what the business is all about."

"In a way," Mike had responded in their phone conversation the day before. "But I know you ladies put your heart and soul into that place, just like your Uncle Nathan did. It just happens to be a real money maker."

"That it is."

"You ladies have contributed a lot to the community. I'm glad he gave it to you. Everyone is."

"Aww, thanks, Mike. That means a lot. I'll talk to you in about a week, to let you know how things are going."

"I'll have a couple of set lists and questionnaires ready for the clients."

They'd ended their conversation warmly. Mike liked Mari and Lynn. He was still astounded that Sue had been described as being cold and stern. He didn't see that in her at all.

He saw a warm, loving, intelligent, vibrant woman. A woman he wanted by his side from now on.

The hours passed slowly for Mike, but soon enough, Mandy was leaving the property and Sue would soon be there.

Mike watched as Mandy got in her car and pulled out of the parking lot. She hadn't spoken to him the entire day, not even to ask him a question about business. She'd come in for her lunch shift, bartended, and left without a word.

He wasn't sure how he felt about that. She was his friend. She knew she'd done something wrong, and he couldn't prove it. She knew that he knew she'd done it. But to ignore him, shun him, as if he was the one doing the wrong, was unacceptable.

He narrowed his eyes as she pulled out without looking back. He didn't want her to look back. She'd see how mad he was, and probably come back and want to fight it out in front of the customers.

"Brandy," he nodded as his new bartender came through the door.

"Hi, Mr. Mike. I thought I'd come in and get a head start on the evening shift."

"If you need any help, you ask me, okay? Francesco will be here, too but not until later on. He knows a lot about the bar. I'm sure he can answer any questions you have. You're familiar with the regular POS systems?"

Brandy nodded. "Oh, yeah. I worked at bars in the big city. I'm sure I can handle it here."

"Good to hear. I'm going to be in my office with my singing partner, and I don't want to be disturbed unless it's an emergency. And that means, the place is burning down around us. Okay?"

Brandy blinked at him. "I understand."

He heard the intimidated tone of her voice, and softened his own to ease her discomfort. "I don't mean to sound harsh," he said apologetically. "I sometimes have trouble getting Mandy to leave me alone. Especially…" He stopped. There was no need to add "when I'm with a woman" because it was none of Brandy's business.

She was a new hire, 23 years old, with the brightest blue hair Mike had ever seen. For some reason, the color and style fit her light use of makeup, her hazel eyes and her slim figure, without making her look like a freak. He'd liked her attitude the moment she walked in the bar for her interview. Ten minutes later, she was behind the bar, whipping up cocktails faster than Mike had seen anyone but Mandy do in years.

He immediately hired her. He liked her quick wit and ready

smile. It seemed the girl never stopped smiling.

She turned away when he didn't continue, but just nodded at her.

"Okay. Thanks, Mr. Mike."

"Just call me Mike," he called after her. She smiled over her shoulder at him.

Mike turned his eyes back to the parking lot, watching for Sue. He was anxious for her to get there. He'd planned something special for her. He'd been working on it during every free moment he had.

He'd written her a song, lyrics and guitar, and planned to play it for her that night.

He thought back on his practicing. The last time he'd picked up his guitar and strummed it out, singing softly under his breath, Mandy had come bursting in, telling him how beautiful it was.

"I wish you'd write something like that for me," she said cheerfully. "That would be so wonderful."

Mike's first thought had been to wonder why he would want to write a song for her. He wasn't in love with her. He wished she'd understand that. He was beginning to think she never would.

"It's for Sue," he'd said. He didn't care if it hurt her feelings. She had to know that, if he wrote a love song, it would be about Sue. He was glad she hadn't assumed it was for her. She might have come in and attacked him with her lips and groping hands. He didn't want to have to smack some sense into her.

He noted the look of disappointment on her face. She said, "I know it is. I didn't think it was for anyone else. I just think it would be nice if you wrote a song for me. We've been friends for a long time. I've been working here for you for a long time. I took care of you this last year, when you got sick, and when we were having trouble here."

Mike felt a guilty streak pass through him. It was true, Mandy had been by his side through his troubled year. But did that entitle her to more?

He didn't think so. He wasn't giving his heart to a woman he didn't love, no matter how grateful he was to her.

It wasn't like she'd brought him back to life or something.

It was Sue that had done that. She had brought him to life. He knew it was true when he saw her car pulling into the lot, and his heart began to pound. A quick smile lit up his face and he stepped out into the late afternoon sun.

He crossed the parking lot as soon as she pulled into a spot, and greeted her at the door of her car.

She grinned at him. "My goodness. A little anxious, are we?"

He chuckled. "I hope *we* are. You're looking really good, Sue. You always do, though."

Sue blushed prettily. He leaned down and kissed her cheek softly, and then her lips.

"It's good to be here," she said softly. She was only inches away from him, gazing up into his brown eyes with deep affection. He could feel the warm love emanating from her pores. He hoped she knew he felt the same way.

He kept having to keep himself from expressing his love for her. He didn't know how much longer he could keep resisting. He wanted to tell her every single time he saw her.

But it was so soon. They'd known each other not even a month. What if it scared her off, knowing that his feelings were so strong, so soon?

He took her through the bar and back into his office. She immediately went to the practice area, grabbed a phone and began thrashing around, singing a metal song with great energy and vibrance. She collapsed on the couch, dropping the mic in front of her on the floor, giving him a hard stare.

He burst out laughing, shaking his head. "What was that?"

"That was my version of the next song we do. I call it Metal Islands in the Stream."

Mike was struck with amusement, throwing his head back and laughing. "That's the funniest thing I've seen in a long time!" He crossed the room and dropped onto the couch next to her, stretching his arm out behind her. She gave him a sad look, sticking out her lower lip.

"You don't like my rendition?"

Mike widened his eyes and gave her a solemn look. "I think maybe we can work it in somehow."

They both laughed at that. Mike noticed when she placed her small hand on his knee. It sent a chill up his thigh.

A knock on the door made Mike frown. "What is it?" he called out. He looked at Sue. "I told them not to disrupt us unless it was an emergency."

The door opened and Francesco stuck his head through. "I've got your drinks, Mr. Mike."

Suddenly, Mike knew where Brandy had gotten that term from. He'd never even noticed Francesco calling him that.

"Drinks?"

"Yes, sir. I found the bottle in the cooler with two glasses beside it. I thought they must be for you."

Mike didn't remember putting a glass of wine in the cooler. He waved his hand at the young man. It must have been Francesco's gift to them. The young man was generous. He would have to thank him later.

"Bring it in, Francesco. Thanks. But make sure no one disturbs us for the rest of the night, okay? We've got to work on our singing, if we're going to be ready to showcase in a couple weeks."

Sue gasped, turning her eyes up to him. "In a couple weeks? We're going to sing in a couple weeks?"

Mike chuckled. "Yep. That's the plan."

Chapter 20

Pain throughout her body woke Sue in the early hours of the next morning. She rolled over in bed and vomited on the floor beside it. Tears streaking down her face, Sue reached for her cell phone beside the bed.

Weakly, she pushed herself up enough to see the numbers on the phone. She pressed the picture of Mari's face and dropped back on the bed, holding the phone to her ear with one hand, the other one on her burning forehead.

"Sue?" Mari's confused, sleepy voice answered.

"Mari," Sue breathed out. "I'm sick. Please come help me."

"What? I'll be right there. You're in bed?"

"Yes."

The phone was disconnected. Sue rested it on her chest, trying to breathe. Her stomach was turning over and cramping terribly. She could feel the heat burning through her body. Her entire body ached.

But it wasn't a head cold. It wasn't the stomach flu. This was new. It was different from anything she'd ever felt before.

She let the tears slip from her eyes, rolling over her cheeks and pooling in her ears. Irritated by the water, she slapped angrily at her ears, lifting the sheet to press it against her face.

Mari was in her room moments later. She left the door wide open so the hall light would come in and she could see without turning on the overhead.

"Sue, don't you have a small lamp in here, too?"

"Yeah," Sue replied breathlessly. "It's over here."

She moved her hand to gesture to the left side of her bed. Mari went around the bed to that side and flipped it on. Sue kept a dim bulb in it, so there wasn't a lot of light on her face when she was reading in bed.

"Oh, Sue. What's wrong? How did you get sick so quickly?"

"I... I need a hospital, Mari. I'm burning up. I'm in pain. I don't know what..." She stopped when a flash of pain slid through her stomach. She groaned and put her hand over it, bending forward in the bed and drawing up into the fetal position.

"Oh my God, oh my God," Mari's worrisome words repeated over and over as she pulled out her phone and dialed 911.

An hour later, Sue was in a hospital room, writhing in pain. The doctor had just come to examine her. She practically begged him for pain medicine.

"I can't... it hurts... I can't take it..." Sue felt like a whining child, but couldn't help it. The pain was so strong. It made her want to curl up into a ball or crawl into a hole and die.

The doctor was extremely sympathetic. He looked concerned as he went through some tests and ordered some blood work.

It was the blood work they were waiting for now. He'd prescribed a medicine, but so far, it wasn't working for her. The pain ebbed and flowed through her body, rippling through her veins, making her muscles tense.

She wanted to call Mike, but she was in and out of consciousness from the pain and the medication.

During her time in mid-consciousness, she heard Mari and Lynn talking.

"I think we should call him," Lynn said, the words catching Sue's attention. Sue tried to turn her head, but it remained where it was, her eyes closed.

"I don't. She was with him last night. He's probably responsible for this. I mean, how could he not know if there's something wrong with his food or the drinks out there? What if he has one of those disgusting, greasy kitchens, with rats crawling around on the food and in the equipment."

"Oh, Mari!" Lynn said in a worrisome voice. "Of course, he doesn't. You've met him. You've talked to him several times. You know he's not like that. He runs a good place. You know that."

"Do I?" Mari was very upset. "Do I know that? How? Because he decided to be interested in my sister, and has a good voice and can play the guitar? Our sister is sick because of him!"

"You don't know that," Lynn replied in an insistent voice. "He might be sick himself! He might not even realize Sue is sick!"

"He doesn't need to be called. I'm not calling him."

"Well, you can't stop me. I'm going to call him. He cares about her. He'd want to know if she was sick. Besides, I want to see if he's sick, too. If he is, we know it's got something to do with his bar."

Before Sue could pull her phone from her bag, a nurse came through the door, knocking twice before pushing it open and entering. She was pushing a cart with a tray on top. A flat tablet sat on top of the tray.

"Ms. Wright. Ms. Wright. Ms. Wright." The nurse grinned at the three of them. They were acquainted with her, as she'd done volunteer blood drives at the resort on several occasions since the women had taken it over.

"Good to see you, Heather," Mari said, standing up. "Did the results come back yet?"

"Yes. They did." Heather was suddenly serious, picking her tablet up from the tray and stepping to the side of Sue's bed. She looked down at Sue, who had managed to turn her head when she came in. "Are you awake enough, Sue? Can you understand me?"

Sue nodded.

"Your blood work came back, and it shows that you've been poisoned."

Mari and Lynn both gasped, covering their mouths with their hands, both sporting a look of horror on their pretty faces. They both rushed over to the bed. Lynn reached over and put one hand on the blanket over Sue's foot. She squeezed her sister's toes, comfortingly.

"How did that happen?" Mari raged at the nurse, who looked distraught.

"Please, Ms. Wright. Stay calm. It's not going to kill her. She got to the hospital in time." Heather looked down at Sue again. "The chemicals in your system are consistent with the chemicals used in rat poison."

"Someone put rat poison in Sue's food?"

Heather looked up at Mari, nodding. "Or her drink. It could be either." She turned back to Sue. "Where were you last night, Ms. Wright? Do you know how you got this in your system?"

In her hazy, drugged mind, Sue could only think of one way she'd been poisoned. The bottle Francesco had brought to them. The food they'd had was delicious. Nothing tasted out of the ordinary. Other than the first bottle the young bartender had brought them, Sue drank nothing but Coke and a bottle of water. She wasn't a heavy drinker by nature, and preferred to stay away from the stuff.

But why would Francesco want to poison her? And Mike?

Panic slipped through her, invading her pain. She forced herself to roll over and looked directly at Lynn's concerned face.

"Lynn," she breathed through a scratchy throat, from being unable to keep any food down. "Call Mike. Find out if he's okay."

Lynn nodded, and moved away from the bed toward her purse. The room was quiet while the nurse did a quick check of Sue's vitals. Heather left the room before Lynn's call was connected.

"He's not answering. Why isn't he ans… Hello? Mike? It's Lynn. How are you feeling today?"

She was quiet for a moment. Sue watched her face. If anything, she looked more confused.

"So, you're feeling all right?... Yes… well, Sue is in the

hospital... yes, Queen Anne hospital, it's the only one here, isn't it?" Lynn sounded irked. "She wants you to... the doctor said she's been poisoned."

Even from her place on the bed, Sue could hear Mike shout, "What?"

Lynn briefly pulled the phone away from her ear, gazing over at Sue with bemusement. She placed the phone back to her ear. "Mike. You need to get down here, right now, so you can be tested, too. You need to come now."

She was quiet, and then pulled the phone away from her ear and pushed the end button. She looked up at her sister. "He's coming, Sue. He'll be here quick. He says he only lives five minutes away."

Sue nodded. Her heart beat anxiously for him to come, but it was hard to concentrate with the poison running through her body. She had never felt so weak in her entire life. Her mind was in a fog.

She glanced at Mari's angry, brooding face. Her sister's arms were crossed over her chest, and she was staring out into space, deep in thought.

"Mari," she said quietly, through a raw throat. Her sister looked down at her, the look on her face changing from angry to loving and concerned. Mari bent at the waist, putting one hand on Sue's.

"What is it, Sue? You need anything? Water? Another pillow?"

Sue shook her head. "I don't want you blaming Mike for this. He didn't do it. He doesn't have... a mean bone in his body. He wouldn't do this to me."

Mari shook her head. "I don't see how you can be sure of that, Sue. You were at his bar. He was the one serving you drinks and food, right?"

"He's not the one who made the food or brought the drinks to us," Sue said, trying to reason with her stubborn sister. "You know him, too, Mari. Stop acting like he's the devil. He's not. He's a good man. I... I love him."

Mari blinked at Sue, her face becoming frighteningly blank. Sue swallowed, wondering what her sister was thinking.

"You love him?" Mari asked softly.

Sue nodded, a single tear falling from her eye, crossing her cheek and soaking into her hair, which was spread out on the hospital pillow.

Mari stood up straight and glanced at Lynn. "You were right, Lynn. She does love him." She looked back down at Sue, sighing heavily. "Alright, Sue. I'll give him a chance to explain."

Sue shook her head. "You don't have to. I can explain. At least I can tell you what I think."

As she spoke, Sue began to feel the effects of the heavy drugs wearing off, but at the same time, her pain was easing away. She hoped it was more than a temporary relief. Whatever they had given her to kill the pain was finally working.

Sue proceeded to fill her sisters in on what she'd been going through with Mandy. She told them about the confrontation, or what she thought of as a confrontation, in her car that night at the bar. She told them about the supposed break in, and that Mandy was most likely responsible for the missing equipment.

When she was done telling them about the drama in her life, both her sisters were shaking their heads.

"Do you think Mandy might have done this to you?" Mari asked.

Sue gave her a hard stare. "I'm going to ask Mike. I didn't think she was working. That's why I went last night. She was supposed to be off."

"Did you see her at all?" Mari asked.

Sue shook her head. "No, not the whole night."

"Sue!" Her head whipped to the door when she heard Mike's voice. He came barreling in and dropped himself on the side of the bed.

Chapter 21

Sue looked at her sisters. "Girls, can you let me talk to Mike alone, please."

Mari frowned. "Are you sure?" Mike cast a look over his shoulder. Sue could tell he was confused by Mari's response. "Of course. Go on. I'll be fine."

Lynn already had the door open and was waiting expectantly for Mari to go through it. Sue could tell by the look on her younger sister's face, that she didn't think Mari should hold Mike responsible. Lynn lifted her eyebrows and gave Mari a direct look. Her eyes darted to the open door. Mari turned and walked out, giving Sue a reluctant but accepting look.

Mike turned back to Sue, reaching out to take her hand. "What happened, Sue? You've been poisoned? How did this happen?"

Sue swallowed hard, trying to keep her eyes from filling up with tears. She was overwhelmed with a warm feeling the moment she saw his face. His hand was warm in hers, covering it completely.

"Mike, I think Mandy's behind this." Sue's throat was still sore, from when they pumped her stomach earlier that morning. Sue had thought about how she would approach it with Mike, since her sisters told her he was coming. She was nervous about how he would react, but the direct approach had always been her way.

He pulled back slightly, blinking at her. His face was a whirlwind of emotions. She tried to figure out what he was thinking. She could only hope he wasn't mad at her, for suggesting his longtime friend, employee and bar manager would go so far as to poison her. He didn't say anything for a good while.

His jaw was working. She could feel how angry he was getting by the tightness of his grip on her hand.

"Mike," she said softly. "Please don't be mad at me for saying that. I don't want to lie to you about how I feel and I'm... really suspicious of her. I'm not sure she's in her right mind, to be honest with you."

Mike pulled in a deep breath and held it for a moment. His eyes glanced around the room. Sue got the impression he didn't really want to look at her. Her heart ached.

"I'm sorry." She dropped her gaze to her lap and gently pulled her hand from his.

His eyes snapped to her face and he grabbed her hand again. "I won't hear you apologizing to me, Sue Wright," he said in a stern voice, as though he was speaking to a child. "You didn't do anything here. And I hate to think of it, I hate it, but Mandy might be behind this. I just don't know how. She wasn't scheduled last night, I watched her drive off... She didn't even speak to me most of the day."

Sue blinked back tears. His words meant so much to her. Relief swept through her.

"It couldn't have happened any other way. When I got home last night, I went straight to bed. I talked to Mari and Lynn separately, and only for a few minutes. I went to bed and was asleep quickly. My head was... spinning. I had such a good time with you, Mike."

He gave her a warm smile, squeezing her hand. He covered it with his other hand and leaned forward to place a soft kiss on her lips.

"I did, too," he murmured when he drew back. "You don't even know how bad I feel about this happening to you. I'm so sorry, Sue. I can't let you apologize to me for suggesting Mandy did it. She... she's responsible for my missing equipment. I..." He shook his head. "I wish I didn't think it was possible. But... I think it might be."

They were quiet for a moment, gazing into each other's eyes. Sue's heartbeat sped up, indicated by the beeping monitor to her left. They both looked at it at the same time.

Chuckling, their eyes met again.

"I see I have an effect on you." Mike's voice was teasing.

331

"Let's see what this does."

He leaned over and pressed his lips on hers. Her body erupted in tingles, as he drew out the kiss until they were both out of breath. When he pulled back, she lifted up with him, not wanting him to stop.

She fell back against her pillow, grunting and sulking. He laughed, his eyes lifting up to the heart rate monitor. "Well, would you look at that. It does go up when you kiss. I read that it did in a science magazine one time." He dropped his eyes back to her face, his lips stretched in a smile that reached his eyes. "I'm kidding. I've never read a science magazine. I think I read it on Facebook or something. It might have even been a video."

Sue shook her head, laughing. "Modern technology. That's what you get."

Mike sighed heavily, his face suddenly becoming concerned again. "Sue, how are you feeling, really? Are you in a lot of pain? Will you tell me what happened?"

Sue pushed herself up into a half-sitting position. When she leaned forward to scoot back, Mike reached around her and grabbed the two pillows, propping them up behind her. She glanced at him with a warm expression and he smiled again.

"I want you to be comfortable. I know you must be in pain."

"The medicine they gave me is working," she said. "And I'm not as groggy as I was before, thank God. I was loopy there for a bit. When I woke up this morning, I was throwing up and in a lot of pain. My whole body felt like it was on fire and being stabbed with needles at the same time. I... can't really describe it."

"I guess they pumped your stomach when you got here?"

Sue wished she didn't have to talk about these things with Mike. It was embarrassing. She nodded.

"So, they got it all, right? You're going to be okay?"

His voice was so concerned. It touched Sue's heart. "I guess that's a question for the doctor."

Mike looked over his shoulder at the door. "Well, where is the doctor? He needs to get in here and answer my questions."

It's a little soon for you to interrogate, Mike. Am I supposed to expect this kind of behavior from you every time I get hurt?"

He raised his eyebrows. "You better not be going around getting hurt all the time. I don't really like hospitals, and I really don't like seeing you in that bed."

"I won't be here long, Mike. The nurse said earlier that I was flushed out good, and should be able to go home this evening. Will you give me a ride?"

Mike nodded, turning back to face her again. "Of course, Sue. Listen…" He hesitated, dropping his eyes. "I'd like to keep an eye on you. You're welcome to come stay at my place, if you want. Just… to let me take care of you. This wouldn't have happened to you if you, if it weren't for me. We both know that. Plus, it will give us time to figure this out. Maybe we can make a plan to catch her doing something illegal… I don't know."

Sue licked her bottom lip. Mike was asking her to stay with him overnight. The implications of that struck her deeply. She blinked and pressed her lips together, her heart hammering in her chest, once again indicated by the monitor at her side.

Mike was staring directly at her, waiting for an answer.

"I'm not pressuring you," he said, softly. "And it's okay if you don't want to. I just thought it would be nice if you let me make you a nice dinner. We can sit in front of the fireplace and talk for a while. I have a spare room you can use. It would be nice to have someone there to take care of, besides my old rotten self."

Sue let out an amused laugh. "I like the sound of that, Mike. I really do. Who would turn down being waited on hand and foot?"

"Now wait a minute, I didn't say…"

They were laughing softly when the door behind Mike opened and a nurse stuck her head through. She looked solemn.

Sue stopped laughing and tilted her head to the side, smiling.

"Hello. Come on in."

The nurse pushed the door in further, revealing two police officers behind her. She had a nervous look on her face, as her eyes darted from the officers to Mike and Sue.

"These officers need to speak with you, if you're up for it, Ms. Wright."

Sue raised her eyebrows. She could see Mari and Lynn behind the officers, as they came into the room. They were both hovering just outside, their arms crossed, their faces worried.

"What? Why?"

Sue turned confused eyes to the nurse, who looked afraid. "I didn't call anyone, Ms. Wright," she said, scurrying around the officers and closing the door. Sue frowned. It was the strangest experience she'd ever had with a nurse.

She turned to look up at Mike, who had stood up from the bed and let go of her hand. He was facing the police officers, who both had serious looks on their faces. After a moment, one of them stepped forward and squared off with Mike, chest to chest.

"Mr. Nelson. It seems we keep running into each other."

Sue turned wide eyes to Mike, fear running like ice through her veins.

"Yeah, I guess we do," Mike replied in an equally serious voice. A second later, the big police officer threw his arms out and wrapped them around Mike in a bear hug.

"How you been, man. It's been ages. How can it be ages when we live in Queen Anne?"

Mike returned the hug, slapping his friend's back. His chuckle didn't last long. His eyes dropped down to Sue, who was stunned into silence, watching their embrace with confusion.

"We're gonna have to talk to Sue, you know. There's not much crime here to keep us busy. When we hear that one of our prominent citizens has been poisoned, we have to investigate."

"You're the one whose equipment was stolen, right?" the other officer said, pointing a finger at Mike, who nodded. "Yeah, crime is just following you around, ain't it?" He was smiling without humor.

Mike nodded again. "I guess." He looked down at Sue. She wondered if he was thinking the same thing as her. It wasn't crime that was following Mike around. It was Mandy.

"You can have him in here if you want," the first officer said. "But we'd rather be able to speak to you alone."

Sue nodded. "I'm sure Mike won't mind, will you, Mike?"

Mike shook his head. "No, of course not. I'll be just outside with your sisters."

Sue responded when he leaned down and kissed her softly. She watched him go past the officers, shaking both their hands and patting them on the shoulder as he went by. She wondered what kind of reception he would get from her sisters. If they weren't nice to him, she would give them a piece of her mind.

"I'm Officer Wilkins. This is Officer Danes. Are you all right to answer a few questions?"

Sue nodded. "I can. Do you know Mike well?"

Officer Wilkins glanced at the door. "Yeah, he's an old friend. He's a good guy."

Chapter 22

Mike stepped out into the hallway, noting how sparkling clean and white it was. He could smell disinfectant in the air. He wasn't lying when he told Sue he didn't like hospitals. The only good thing to ever come out of a hospital was a newborn baby. Other than that, it was hallway after hallway of sick, injured, and dying people.

Not his idea of a good time.

Mari and Lynn greeted him with nods as he walked to where they were seated.

"Mind if I sit with you? The police want to talk to Sue. I'd like to find out who her doctor is and ask him some questions."

Without waiting for their response, Mike sat down next to Lynn, leaning forward and holding himself up with his elbows on his knees. He clasped his hands together under his chin, and turned his head to look at the women.

He studied their faces. Lynn was looking at him, but Mari wasn't. She had her arms folded over her chest, and was staring through the window on the opposite side of the room. He kept his eyes on her face for a moment before speaking.

"Mari, it looks like you're blaming me for what happened here."

Mari snapped her head around to look at him. "Well, you aren't sick, are you? You weren't poisoned."

Mike felt like he'd been slapped. He respected and cared about both Mari and Lynn. He was hurt to think they would suspect him of being behind this terrible event. He shook his head. When he spoke, it was in a firm voice.

"Mari, I had nothing to do with this. I'm as baffled as you are. I want to find out how this happened, just as much as you."

Mari's shoulders relaxed slightly, and she moved her worried eyes to his face. "How can you be so calm?" she asked. "My sister almost died. She really cares about you, Mike, but it seems like it's one thing after another, now that she's with you. And now she almost died? I don't know if it's a good idea for her to keep seeing you."

Mike's breath caught in his throat. He didn't like being reprimanded by his friend, and he wasn't a child to be told what to do. Thoughts whipped through his mind. He tried to remain calm and not let his temper take over. While he was gathering himself together, Lynn stepped in and spoke up for him.

"Wait a minute, Mari. First of all, we don't get to tell Sue who she can and can't see." Lynn's voice was stern and motherly. "Second, just because Mike isn't sick doesn't mean he's behind it. No man is going to poison a woman, and then show up immediately like he did."

Lynn turned to Mike. "You must know something, though, Mike. Something you've forgotten. You and Sue had a good time last night, didn't you? She seemed happy when she came home."

"We did have a good time. I think we did. No, we did." Mike tried to clear his thoughts. He was still in shock that Mari would blame him for Sue's condition. "The first thing we had was a glass of wine. It was left in the fridge for us by my bar assistant, Francesco. He brought them to us. If it had been on the glasses or in the wine, I'd be sick, too. I don't know of anything we didn't share last night."

"Plus, you were probably kissing her, weren't you?" Lynn asked the question in a serious tone.

He nodded. "Yes, there was some kissing going on."

Mari turned her head back to him. "I'm sorry, Mike. There must be something that's being missed. She was fine until this morning. The only thing she did, between leaving your bar and waking up this morning, was sleep."

"I can't explain it, Mari," Mike said. A determined feeling filled him and he pulled in a deep breath. "I'm going to find out, though. I have to put a stop to all of this, without losing Sue."

Lynn gave him the first smile he'd seen since he'd left Sue's room. "You really care about her, don't you?"

Mike nodded. "I do. I think it could be something pretty wonderful."

"Do you love her?"

Mike swallowed, gazing directly at Lynn. "I... I do love her."

Lynn smiled, turning satisfied eyes to Mari. "See? I told you."

Amusement slid through Mike, when he caught the look Mari gave back to her sister. He pressed his lips together to keep from smiling.

"Ms. Wrights?"

The three of them looked up when a doctor spoke to them. He was looking back and forth between the women. Mike was amused to see what a short man he was, with thick, black-rimmed glasses and the thickest eyebrows Mike had ever seen. The look on his face was very serious.

Mari and Lynn both stood up. When they did, they were both taller than the doctor and had to look down at him.

"What is it, Dr. Lambert? Is Sue all right?"

"She's going to be all right," the doctor confirmed. "But she is going to be weak for a few days. She shouldn't be moving too much. All that walking up at the resort is going to have to be put on hold. I hope you don't have any big important plans for her until next week."

"Next week?"

Mike watched Mari glance around the room. He could tell that she was going over her schedule in her mind. She nodded after a few seconds.

"Our next wedding isn't for two weeks. Hopefully she'll be fully recovered by then."

"And if she's not," Lynn hurried to say. "We'll just let her take it easy with the stuff she does have to do." She looked at Mike appreciatively. "She was in charge of music before, and now she's not, so that's one less thing for her to stress about."

The doctor nodded. "Stress will kill her. She needs to stay calm. The poison wreaked havoc inside her, and she needs time to heal."

"Did you figure out how she got it in her system?" Mike asked, hurriedly.

The doctor looked up at him, almost dwarfed by Mike's tall stature.

"It was found in great quantity in her stomach contents. It was food or drink. I suspect food, because of the way it was diluted, but quite a bit of it was used. It may have been in a midnight chocolate bar."

Mari frowned. "Are you saying the source of that food poisoning could have come from our very own house?" Her voice rose in pitch, as fear crossed her slender face.

The doctor gave her a direct look. "Anything is possible, Ms. Wright."

Mari shook her head. "No. That's not possible. No one at the resort would have any reason at all to hurt Sue, or any of us. It couldn't have happened that way."

The first thought that ran through Mike's mind was, that if it was someone on resort property, he didn't have to suspect Mandy. He still held out some hope that the bartender wasn't actually behind it.

"Can you think of anyone at all that would want to do harm to you three?" he asked, looking at Mari. The woman shook her head.

"No. No one. We treat everyone with kindness and consideration, no matter how high up they are in the business, or what they do. Pool cleaners are as important as the chairman of the board."

Mike nodded. It was something he'd noticed about the women, and their style of running the resort. He'd never seen a one of them disrespect any of the staff. He'd also never heard any former employees complaining.

Not that there were many of those. Emerald Resort was like a vortex. Once you started working there, you would always return. It was inevitable.

Mike didn't mind that vortex. It was what would keep him close to the woman he loved.

"I'll keep you updated on her condition," Dr. Lambert said, flipping the tablet under his arm and tucking his stylus in the breast pocket of his white coat. "She'll be released this evening, unless something changes with her condition. But be aware that she will need to be cared for. I suggest hiring a nurse for at least three days, to monitor her while she's home."

Lynn lifted one hand and covered her mouth with it. Mike didn't like to see the look of horror on the woman's face. "Oh dear, was it that bad?"

The doctor lifted his shaggy eyebrows and nodded. "Yes, she ingested quite a lot of that poison. It must not have tasted bad, whatever she ate or drank."

Mike looked at the sisters as the doctor walked away.

"Something she ate. It had to be something she ate. Like a breath mint or something. Maybe something in her toothpaste?"

Ideas passed through his mind quickly. He wanted badly to deflect the blame from Mandy. But in each scenario, no matter how Sue was poisoned, he always came back to her as the only suspect.

"You know," Mari said, as if a thought had just popped up in her mind. "I think you should tell the police about your bartender and all the trouble she's been giving Sue."

A chill ran over Mike. He stared at the two women for a moment. "Are you talking about Mandy?" he asked after a moment. Mari nodded, glancing at Lynn, who also nodded.

"Yes, that's the one. She's been harassing Sue. You should tell the police about it."

Dismay slid through Mike. How bad was it? Sue had never told him Mandy was harassing her.

"What has Mandy been doing?" Mike asked, his voice distressed. Both women's faces changed when he asked the question. He wondered if they could hear the agony he felt in the tone of his voice.

He frowned so deep it made his forehead hurt.

"Please, tell me. I have to have something to confront Mandy with, not just accusations."

"Do you mean you don't know what Mandy's been doing?" Mari asked, skepticism in her voice. Mike shook his head vigorously.

"I had no idea she was doing anything to Sue. I knew she didn't even treat her with common decency when they crossed paths at the bar. But other than that, no, I don't know anything. I do wish you'd tell me, though."

The sisters looked at each other. Mike found himself once again struggling with his temper. He wasn't mad at either of the sisters. He was mad that he hadn't done something about it sooner, hadn't seen through Mandy's façade.

"We'll tell you what Sue told us," Mari said. "But you're not going to like what we have to say about it. As far as I'm concerned, anything that woman does to Sue is on your shoulders."

"That's not fair, Mari," Lynn said in a scolding voice. "He isn't responsible for the actions of someone else." She turned her eyes back to Mike. "Come and sit down with me, Mike. I'll tell you what Sue told us."

Chapter 23

Sue looked up when Mari came in the room. Her sister appeared demure, but Sue could tell she had something on her mind. She was holding her elbows with her hands and gazing at Sue with a forlorn look.

"What's the look for, Mari?" Sue asked. She had a suspicion her sister was going to say something about Mike again.

Mari didn't say anything at first. She went to a nearby chair and dragged it closer to the bed. Sue watched her, curious to know what was on her sister's mind.

Mari sat in the chair and leaned forward, placing one hand on the edge of Sue's bed. She played with the fabric of the sheet while she spoke, keeping her eyes down.

"I'm really worried about you, Sue," she finally said. "I waited for the cops to leave before I came in here, because I... I knew you didn't want me to tell them what I think."

Sue shook her head, an ache already filling her heart. "Mari, I know you think Mike is bad for me but..."

She stopped when Mari looked up at her, shaking her head. "No, Sue. It's not that I think Mike is bad for you. It's just that, since we've come here, things have been really peaceful, for the most part. And now, there's just... so much drama." She said the word with disgust. "I just don't like to see you get mixed up with people like that. This Mandy person..."

"She's not Mike's responsibility. She's an employee who has a crush on her boss. Nothing more."

"But it is something more!" Mari exclaimed, in a louder voice than she probably intended. Sue's eyes flipped to the door and back to her sister's red face. "I'm sorry, Sue." Mari dropped the volume of her voice. "It becomes something more when you end up in the hospital. I just don't think getting involved with someone who can employ a crazy person is a good idea for you."

"It's not a good idea for anyone," Sue retorted. "But I'm

telling you again, Mike is not responsible for what Mandy does. And you never know, she might not even be the one who did this. It could have been a mistake, or an accident."

Mari raised her eyebrows. "An accident? In the kitchen of Mike's bar? You're telling me they're so unprofessional that somehow, rat poison was spilled into their food or in your drink? Just your drink? Not Mike's?"

Sue sighed. She had a feeling she wasn't going to get through to Mari. It was depressing. She had always counted on her sisters to be on her side. This time, it seemed Mari just didn't want to listen.

"No, no. Not an accident like that. There's nothing wrong with Mike's kitchen."

"Have you been back there?"

Sue looked directly at her sister, who pursed her lips and raised her eyebrows.

"Well, have you?"

Sue shook her head. "No, but I'm sure it's as clean as a whistle. You can't pin this on Mike. He didn't poison me. He's just as confused as we are, and he's going to help me get to the bottom of this. Look, you can either work with me on this, or against me, but I'm not going to judge Mike because of something Mandy's doing. She's crazy. That's not his fault."

"He employs her. He gives her access to all his business and…"

"Mari!" Sue barked her sister's name. Mari's eyes opened wide and she pulled away from Sue. "Stop it! If this is all you came in here to talk about, you can leave now. I'm not holding Mike responsible. You know how I feel about him. I think you need to back off."

"Is everything okay in here?"

Their eyes turned to the door. Mike was peering in at them, from behind the curtain in front of the door.

"I guess you heard what we were talking about, didn't you?" Mari said in a sheepish voice.

Mike raised his eyebrows. "I could. But the door was partially open, so pretty much everyone in the hall heard you two arguing. Mari, if you want to come to my bar and investigate, to make sure it's clean, you can. You can do that right now, if you want. I'm planning on taking Sue there when she gets out, so we can do a little looking around of our own. Do you want to come?"

An overwhelming sense of gratitude swept over Sue. Even though he was being accused, Mike was willing to work with Mari to assure her. His gentle treatment of her sister made Sue fall even deeper in love with him. She didn't care that it had been such a short amount of time. She knew he was the one for her. She'd fight tooth and nail to keep him by her side.

Sue could tell Mari wasn't expecting the invitation. It was odd, since she'd had nothing negative to say about him until today. She hesitated for a moment before giving Mike a contemplative look.

"All right. That might help. I'm just worried about Sue. I hope you understand that. I won't tolerate something bad happening to her."

"You weren't able to control this," Sue pointed out. "And you won't be able to keep bad things from happening to me. You've got to give up that need for control sometime, Mari. I love you for wanting to protect me, but you can't. I have to live my life."

Mike kept quiet through Sue's short speech, but his eyes were soft as he gazed at her, listening. Her heart thumped in her chest. She wanted him to come back and sit next to her, hold her hand, kiss her.

Mari looked behind her, and then back to Sue. She stood up and took one step, so she was next to the bed. She leaned over and gave Sue a kiss on the forehead. As she stood back up, she ran her fingers through the light-colored bangs on Sue's forehead.

"I'm sorry. I can't stop being your older sister, honey. I'm used to watching out for you."

Sue laughed. "I'm nearly 25 years old. There is no need for that anymore. Besides, you have your beautiful baby to raise, and there will probably be more. Concentrate on them. I can take care of myself."

The sisters smiled at each other. Sue felt much better. She pulled in a content sigh and turned her eyes to Mike.

"I'm gonna let you two have some time together," Mari said. She looked at her sister. "I hate to see you like this. I really do. I'll be back later. Lynn and I really need to get back to the resort and catch up on some business."

"I'll be right as rain tomorrow, Sis," Sue said. "I'll catch up on my work then."

Mari set one hand on Sue's. "You just rest up and don't worry about anything right now. Mike is here… to take care of you." She gave the man a faltering smile.

Sue felt sorry for her sister. Mari was used to taking care of her and Lynn. She'd been doing it for 27 years. She couldn't be blamed for having a hard time letting go.

"If you feel up to coming to work, you can," Mari said, looking back at her sister. "But you can take a few days off if you want to. Keep that in mind."

She stood up and turned to Mike, looking up at his handsome face. Sue moved her eyes between the two, hoping not to see an unhappy look on either of their faces.

"Take care of her, Mike. I'm worried about her."

Mike nodded. "You know I will, Mari. I love her. If I can stop it, I won't let anything happen to her."

Mari gave him a close look, scanning his face. She turned back to Sue before she went out the door.

"I'll see you at home."

"Mari," Sue kept her from leaving the room. "I'm going to stay with Mike tonight. He has a spare room and wants to make me dinner."

Mari's look of disapproval made Sue's stomach ache. She nodded, however, and said, "All right. Be careful. I'll see you back here when you're discharged, anyway. I'm coming back."

"You don't have to. Mike will be here for me. But if you would come, I'd like that." She smiled, adding the last part, remembering how much Mari missed taking care of her.

Mari smiled back at her, her face relaxing into a sad look. She closed the door softly behind her.

Mike moved closer to the bed, his eyes moving over her body. Sue could almost feel the warmth of his loving gaze.

"Sue, let me say something, and I don't want you to say anything until I'm done, okay?"

He sat on the edge of the bed, taking her hand again. Sue felt a nervous tingle run through her. She nodded.

"Go ahead. I'm listening."

"I've fallen in love with you. I think you know that. And I hate what's happened. I want to apologize to you, and I don't want you to tell me not to, okay? This is partially my fault, because I trusted Mandy and kept her on, even after I knew she'd stolen that equipment. She's trying to destroy my life because I don't love her. I'm gonna ask you now... do you think Mari is right? Maybe I should do something about Mandy before we go any further together."

Sue's heart squeezed in her chest. "No, Mike. She's not right. I'm an adult. I'm a grown woman and I can handle myself. Mandy's jealousy has gone too far, but it's not just you who needs to take care of it. It's me, too. I don't need someone else fighting my battles for me, but I appreciate that you want to."

"It's not really just my battle or yours," Mike said in a reasonable tone. "It's ours, because we want to be together. You do want to be with me, don't you?"

Sue giggled. "Of course, I do."

He smiled.

She glanced at the clock on the wall, next to the mounted TV. "It's almost five hours till they said I could be released. You don't have to stay here that whole time. I know you have work to do."

Mike nodded. "I'm going back to the bar. I have a few things to take care of there. I am going to find out what's happening with Mandy. She's there. It's her shift today."

Sue licked her lips. "What are you going to do? Are you going to confront her?"

Mike looked around the room. "I don't know yet. I... there's a few other things I want to check first. If I can find something to confront her with, I will. But not if I don't. I need to be sure, you know?"

Sue nodded. "I understand. You do what you have to do. I've got my cell phone. Keep in touch with me." She frowned, the sudden thought that, if Mandy was willing to take her life, she might be equally willing to take Mike's. The "if I can't have you, no one can" attitude.

"You'd better be careful, Mike," she said abruptly, sitting up a little further in the bed. "I just found you. I don't want to lose you to some crazy woman."

Mike's voice was deep and serious when he responded, "You won't."

Chapter 24

Mike left the room, his mind riddled with anger and confusion. He'd never had such a thing happen to him in his life. It was hard for him to believe Mandy could be responsible for putting Sue in such danger. She had never seemed that over-the-top to him before.

He jumped into his SUV and left the parking lot in a hurry. He had the rest of the afternoon to do some exploring. When he pulled into the lot of the Badlands, he immediately spotted Mandy's vehicle. His stomach churned and anger spilled through him like a tidal wave.

It was at that moment, he realized he already knew Mandy was guilty, and was in denial. She was not the woman he thought she was. If she had been, she would have accepted his refusal of her advances and moved on. Even changing jobs, if that's what was necessary. Leaving Queen Anne. He didn't care. She'd taken this obsession much too far.

He pulled into a parking space and got out, slamming the door behind him. He regretted that action, and tried his best to pull his anger inside, so it wouldn't show when he walked in. He wasn't a good liar, and had never tried his hand at acting. He struggled to put on a neutral face when he went in the bar.

Mandy was behind the counter, serving drinks to several customers. Her face was lit up with a smile as she served, chatting with the customers, laughing as usual. She looked gorgeous. Mike's heart thumped when he thought about the evil she'd committed against the woman he loved. He did his best not to give her an angry look.

He passed the bar without looking at her, but he could feel her eyes on him. He went through to his office and closed the door behind him. He stood in the room, looking around, unsure of his next move. He wanted to explore the kitchen, to see if he could find the remnants of last night's festivities, a glass or the bottle of wine that was left for them.

He turned and opened the door, looking out into the bar. He didn't see Francesco, not that the man would be out in the bar at that time. He would be in the kitchen, preparing and making food. He sighed, leaving the office, and skirting around the bar to go through the door to the kitchen, ignoring Mandy.

He pushed the door open and went through, immediately hit with the heavy heat and smell of food cooking. Delicious scents filled the air around him and made him hungry, bringing a smile to his face. He was proud of Francesco and the work his chefs did for him.

He lifted his chin in acknowledgement when one of the employees, Darren, greeted him.

"Have you seen Francesco?" he asked.

Darren raised his eyebrows. Mike got the impression the young man expected he should know that kind of information already. "He doesn't come in till four. Can I help you?"

Mike shook his head. "I don't know. You might. Last night, I had a friend here and we had a bottle of wine together. You don't happen to know if that bottle is still around or not, do you? Or the glasses?"

Darren looked even more confused. "No, sir. The glasses have been washed, I'm sure. Everything has been washed from last night. As far as a wine bottle, I really couldn't tell you. I don't know."

Mike nodded. "I didn't think so. I just thought I'd ask. I have to find Francesco. He's the one who brought us the drinks."

Darren nodded, giving him a look like he expected more.

"I'll give him a call. Thanks."

Darren nodded, and with one last questioning look, he turned and went back to his duties.

Mike looked around the kitchen in frustration, his eyes searching for a stray wine bottle. The idea that it might have been thrown away crossed his mind. He walked through the kitchen, still looking around him for anything suspicious, to the back door. The trash bags from the night before would be stacked in or near the dumpster out back.

The thought of going through the trash in the dumpster turned Mike's stomach. But he would do anything he had to for Sue. He needed to figure this out. Rat poison had made its way into Sue's system somehow and he knew the only way to prove it would be to find that bottle.

He pushed open the door, the latch clanking loudly, as if it hadn't been used in years. It was probably just the force with which he pushed it, he figured, because the whole door, though loaded on a pressure spring, slammed back against its barrier, and almost hit him as it closed. He held out one hand, ignoring the searing pain that split through him when the metal hit his palm. It didn't hit his face, and that's all that mattered at that moment.

He glanced to the right to see a stack of three big black bags. His heart jumped nervously, as he hoped going through those bags would bring him the results he wanted. If the bottle wasn't in there, he would check the security cameras on his laptop. That would give him answers, too. But the bottle was crucial. It would probably have fingerprints, as well as traces of the poison.

But if the bottle had been poisoned, wouldn't he have been sick, too?

The question haunted his brain as he ripped open the first bag. It had to have been put in Sue's glass alone. Francesco wouldn't do that and Mandy wasn't on the property.

Mike looked up, staring out into space as thoughts filled his mind. What if she *had* been on the property? What if she'd snuck in somehow, and managed to poison just Sue's drink? Or was it something she'd eaten?

He looked down at the bag in front of him. It was filled with empty boxes, cigarette ashes, chocolate bar wrappers, everything anyone would expect from a bar's trash bin. He shuffled through the bag a little, but saw no wine bottles. He moved on to the second bag, and instead of ripping it open, he felt around the edges for bottles. He frowned when he felt none. It was a bar. Where were the bottles?

The third bag proved to be the one he was looking for, as far as bottles were concerned. It was filled with nothing *but* bottles.

He ripped the top open and looked down. It had to be the bottles from the last week. Some were wine, but most of them were liquor bottles. He carefully picked through them, pushing some aside and avoiding the sharp, jagged pieces of the ones that were broken. Most of them were solid. He'd noticed liquor bottles were incredibly hard to break. It took a great bit of force to shatter them.

There were a half dozen wine bottles in the bag. It wasn't a big seller at Badlands. Mostly beer and mixed drinks were served. For such a wealthy, elite crowd, Mike was always surprised by how few drank wine. He'd always assumed they were drinking that at home, and came out for a mixed drink.

That suited him just fine.

He scanned the bottles he pulled out, and noted that none of them appeared to be the wine he'd been given. After many years in the bar business, he not only knew his liquor, he knew wine and beer, as well. He could differentiate between the tastes.

He sighed heavily and turned to go back inside, when he spotted something to his right. He turned his head and saw that it was a broken bottle, in the corner of the lot near the building. He narrowed his eyes, going toward it. Judging by the small bit of paper on a portion that wasn't too broken, he knew it was the same kind of wine he'd been drinking with Sue the night before.

He stooped and peered at the broken glass, not wanting to pick it up and smear any fingerprints that might still be on it. Pondering what he should do, to pick it up without smearing the prints, he glanced over his shoulder at the Badlands back door. Maybe a bag? He had watched enough Law and Order to know how to get a broken bottle off the ground, didn't he?

The thought brought a satisfied grin to his face. At least he had the bottle. Or what appeared to be the bottle. It only took one piece to have a print on it and some traces of poison in it.

He felt in his pockets but had nothing he could pick up the bottle pieces with. Reluctantly, he slipped back into the kitchen, went to the pantry and searched for plastic bags. He was hoping to have a bunch from the local grocery store, like he had in his pantry at home, but the smallest bag he saw was a trash can bag for the bathroom. It was bigger than he needed, but he grabbed one anyway and headed back out to the alley behind the bar.

He could only hope no one was watching him. At least, not Mandy. No one else would have told her, but he didn't want to take any chances. He carefully picked up the pieces using the plastic bag to touch them, doing his best not to smear them in any way.

Folding the bag to keep the contents safe, he went back into the bar, going directly to his office. He didn't care if Mandy saw the bag at that point, but he did glance over to see what she was doing when he passed through. It was just a quick glance, but he saw her eyes move to the bag in his hand, and then to the glass she was filling.

He went to the security camera DVD recorder and pushed the button to release the current DVD in the slot. It was empty. His skin crawled in anger. He should have known she would do something like that.

He crossed the room quickly to his desk and opened his laptop.

"Come on, come on, come on," he murmured anxiously, as the laptop loaded up.

He moved the curser to the security footage he had installed. He clicked on it and waited as it loaded up.

It was only a few seconds, but he shook as he waited, his anger spilling over into rage, his memory seeing only Sue in his mind, laying in the hospital bed in agony.

He tapped in the night before and waited for the footage to rewind.

He started the tape at 4 pm, when Mandy had left the building. He fast-forwarded in the parking lot, watching for her car. At 7 pm, just a few minutes after Sue pulled in, he saw Mandy's car pull into the lot.

Chapter 25

Two hours after Mike left, Sue was sitting up in bed, a laptop open in front of her. She scanned through the workload Mari sent to her email every morning. The Nathan Hawke wedding was approaching quickly, and there was still more work to be done in preparation.

Sue had already taken care of her part of the wedding, but there were other things in the works that she needed to concentrate on. She had people to contact and numbers to crunch.

The workload felt a little overwhelming right then, as Sue's pain was just ebbing away. The doctor told her it would take at least a week to feel up to par again. Sue didn't want to wait that long. She had always been considered a strong spirit. She needed that strength back.

She sighed and closed the laptop. It was too much for her addled brain at that moment.

She set the laptop aside, grateful it was brought to her, but unable to do anything with it.

She pushed herself down in the bed and stared up at the ceiling. Mike's agitation was on her mind. He was so angry about what had happened to her. She wondered if she knew him well enough to know what he would do in a situation like this.

She had just closed her eyes when she heard the door open. She peeked through one eye to see if it was a nurse or one of her sisters. If it was anyone but Mike, she would pretend to be asleep.

She hurriedly closed her eye when she saw it was Mandy who entered. She hoped her heart rate wouldn't give away the fact that she was awake. She made a conscious effort to keep her heart beating steadily, as usual. She breathed heavy, as if she was deep asleep.

If Mandy tried to finish the job, she would defend herself. There would be no pillows on the face today.

She waited patiently, steadily breathing, clearing her

353

thoughts of all anxiety, so her heart rate wouldn't speed up in her anxiety.

Sue was proud of herself for the remarkable job she did staying calm.

She felt the woman approach her bed, and could hear her breathing over her. When she began to speak, Sue did her best to remain passive, as if she was truly asleep.

"I know you think you've got him," Mandy murmured in a low voice. "But you don't. He's a man with certain needs, and I know you don't have what it takes to make him happy. Only I know what to do. Only I know what truly makes him happy."

Sue fought the urge to open her eyes and ask Mandy exactly what she thought Mike needed to be happy, other than love, affection, attention, all the things she was completely willing to give him. She felt the woman lean down toward her, when Mandy's breath blew hot on her face.

"He loves me," she whispered. "Not you. Only I can make him happy."

Unable to resist any longer, Sue opened her eyes and stared at Mandy. The woman pulled back, her eyes wide, giving Sue a shocked look.

"Exactly what are you doing here, Mandy?" she asked in a cold voice.

Mandy snarled, making her pretty face ugly. "I just wanted to let you in on some cold, hard facts, Sue Wright."

Suddenly feeling energetic, Sue placed her hands on the side of the bed and shot up into a sitting position, nearly knocking heads with the woman standing over her.

"First of all, you need to get the hell out of my room," she said. "Second, there is nothing you can tell me about Mike, my relationship with him, or anything else. I know what you are. I know what you've done, and I'll find a way to prove it."

Mandy laughed without humor. "Oh? I'd like to see you try."

Sue grinned. "So, you admit it? Nice. Too bad the police aren't here like they were earlier."

She enjoyed the look of fear that crossed the woman's face.

"Yeah, they were here. Did you expect them not to be? The very fact that you knew I was here shows that you knew exactly what happened." She lifted one hand and put it in Mandy's face, when it looked like the woman was about to protest. "Don't. I know Mike didn't tell you what happened to me. It's doubtful he would ever tell you anything at all about me or our relationship. Don't even bother."

The look of fury on Mandy's face sent a jolt of satisfaction through Sue. She had no doubt it was Mandy who had poisoned her. Somehow, she had done it without anyone noticing.

"He *did* tell me. He tells me a lot more than you think he does."

Mandy sounded confident, but Sue had trouble believing her. She narrowed her eyes, anger sliding through her.

"I don't believe a word that comes out of your mouth. Mike knows you're responsible for putting me in here. He's not going to put up with it."

Mandy's chuckle made Sue's anger rise. She struggled to control it. She didn't want the woman rattling her.

"He's not gonna do anything to me," Mandy snarled, leaning forward again.

Sue pulled in a deep breath, grateful that her monitors didn't reflect how aggravated she was.

"Why are you even here? Haven't you done enough? Get out of my room!"

Mandy raised her eyebrows. "You think you've got him, don't you? You think he loves you." The woman's sarcastic laughter rang through the room. "You don't know anything about him. I've known him for years. There's nothing about him I don't know."

New relationship insecurities crept into Sue's mind. She pushed them back as hard as she could, but the question was still there. Mandy was right that she knew Mike a lot longer, but Sue had trouble believing he'd shared as much with the bartender as he had with her. He told her he didn't have the feelings for Mandy, that she had for him.

"I don't care what you think," she said, keeping her cool, narrowing her eyes and glaring at Mandy. "Get out of my room, before I call security and tell them the person who poisoned me is in my room trying to finish the job. You know what? I'm not going to wait."

She reached to the side and grabbed up the receiver of the phone. Mandy snatched it from her hand and shook it in her face.

"You're not calling anyone! Leave Mike alone, or else!"

Sue's anger took over, giving her the energy and adrenaline she needed to yank the phone from Mandy's hand. She made a sweeping motion and clocked the woman in the side of the head with the receiver.

Mandy moved back, holding the side of her head, screaming out in pain. Sue's strength was sapped, so she knew she hadn't done any deadly damage. She fell back against the pillows, grabbing up the button to call a nurse, and pressing it several times.

She didn't need to, as the door was thrown open shortly after Mandy's scream. Two nurses and a doctor ran in, their eyes alert.

"Get her out of here!" Sue cried out. Mandy turned to the caretakers, feigning innocence.

"I don't know what happened," she said in a whining voice, still holding the side of her head. A long red mark from the phone receiver enflamed that side of her face, going from her cheekbone up into her hairline. "She just attacked me with the phone. I was only going to hand it to her and…"

Sue could tell, from the looks she was getting from the doctor and nurses, that they didn't believe a word Mandy was saying.

"Please," she said quietly. "Get her out of my room. She's the one who poisoned me. Please make her leave."

Sue was a little shocked by how quickly the doctor reacted. He grabbed Mandy by the arms and pulled her toward the door.

"It's time for you to leave. I'll call security and let them know you'll be at the front exit, so they can talk to you about Ms. Wright's accusation."

Mandy cried out in surprise and fear, as the doctor shoved her to the door. "I didn't do anything! I didn't poison her! I just came to visit her! I don't know why she's..."

"You'll have to leave, miss," one of the nurses spoke up, taking the arm the doctor had let go of firmly, and pushing Mandy through the door.

Sue could hear the woman protesting all the way down the hallway, proclaiming her innocence. Her heart rate monitor was finally beeping, indicating the speed had gone up dramatically.

The nurse still in the room approached her bed quickly, scanning the monitors and looking at her with great concern. "Oh, my God, are you all right? Did she hurt you?"

Sue pursed her lips. "Last night she did. She did this to me. I just don't have any proof. Not yet."

The nurse shook her head, reaching behind her and pulling a portable status check machine over to the bed.

"I'm going to take your vitals to make sure your blood pressure isn't too high. Try to calm down, Sue. You're in a safe place. She won't get to you in here. I'm sorry she managed to get in your room at all. She won't be back."

I'm leaving in a few hours, Sue thought, but didn't speak it aloud. It wasn't the nurse's fault she didn't know what was going on.

"Thank you," she said quietly, trying to calm down. She waited while the woman did her thing, relaxing her muscles consciously.

The doctor poked his head back in and looked at Sue. "She's gone. Do you need security in here, or outside your door, to make sure she doesn't come back?"

Sue shook her head. "I'll be leaving in a few hours," she replied. "She won't be back. Thank you for getting her out of my room."

The doctor looked disgruntled, shaking his head and stepping into the room. "She shouldn't have been allowed in here in the first place."

"I didn't really think she'd be that brave, or I would have said something," Sue said. "There's no way any of us could have known she would come here. I don't blame anyone here."

She noticed the grateful, kind look the nurse gave her. She lowered her eyes to the nametag on the woman's scrubs and smiled. Her name was Lynnette.

"You have my sister's name," she said, looking up at the nurse with a smile.

It was returned when the nurse said, "Oh? How cool." She took the blood pressure cuff off Sue's arm. "You're going to be okay. Just keep trying to stay calm. You're going to need a good night's sleep tonight. I hope you have a peaceful place to stay."

Sue nodded, thinking about her upcoming dinner, and a night spent with the man she loved.

"Oh, I will be. Don't worry about that."

Chapter 26

What Mike saw sent chills through him. He stared at the screen, watching as Mandy slipped in through the back door. She looked all around her for anyone else who might be in the room before going to the cooler.

When she emerged, she was holding a wine bottle that looked very much like the one in pieces he'd picked up behind the bar. She took two glasses from the rack and set them on the silver tray Francesco had used to bring the drinks to them.

He felt like a fool, thinking Francesco had provided the special drinks for them. He should have known.

What he saw next gave him chills. Mandy went to the pantry and disappeared for a few minutes. When she came out, she was holding a box in one hand and something clutched in the other, her fingers closed around it so it couldn't be seen.

She walked back to the counter where the tray was and dropped what was in her hand on it. He was stunned, watching her take a small needle from her pocket. She filled it halfway with water. She spooned a bit of the rat poison into the vial, closed the top and shook it to mix it up.

Next, she picked up one of the pistachios she'd had clutched in her hand and injected it with the poison. She did it with all four of the pistachios.

Rage filled Mike. Mandy knew he was allergic to pistachios. He hadn't even noticed them on the tray. Thinking back, he couldn't remember seeing Sue pick them up and eat them. But she must have, because Mandy didn't touch the wine or the glasses, other than to set them on the tray.

When she was done, she wiped the pistachios with a napkin. She reached over and took out a notepad from a nearby drawer. She took out a pen and wrote something on the paper.

She tucked it under the tray and stepped back to study her work.

Mike could barely contain his anger. He balled up one fist and slammed it on his desk. Sue's pained face ran through his mind. Thinking about what had happened to her that morning, he felt like picking up his laptop and throwing it against the wall.

He leaned to the side and pulled open a drawer, looking for a zip drive. He shuffled through the items. He looked up at the laptop screen when a popup flashed.

A chill of rage lifted every hair on his neck and arms.

"No!"

The video files were deleting. Mandy must have downloaded the security app, and was deleting it from somewhere else.

Mike grabbed both sides of the screen and shook it, as if he could keep it from deleting. He screamed in anger when the video disappeared.

He slammed the cover shut and grabbed the laptop in both hands. It took everything he had not to throw it across the room. He shoved the chair back with his legs and crossed the room in a few strides, throwing open the door.

He stomped out of the office, glaring at Becky, who was behind the counter.

"Where's Mandy?" he asked.

Becky's eyes widened. "She left a little after you came in, Mike."

He clenched his jaw, struggling not to take his anger out on Becky. "If you see her, tell her I want to talk to her immediately." He looked out at the customers and walked to the counter, so he was closer to Becky. He leaned forward and said in a low voice, "Call me on my cell immediately, if you see her. Don't let her do anything behind the bar. If she tries to, call the police. Do you understand?"

Becky blinked, staring at him. "Okay," she responded in a weak voice.

Mike nodded curtly and moved away from the counter. He forced himself to smile at a few of the customers as he passed. He didn't want to give them a bad impression. Most of them were tourists. He could only hope they hadn't heard him yelling in the office. Chances were, they did.

He was shaking when he got in his SUV, his only thought was to go to Sue and tell her what he'd seen. He hoped one of the sisters knew how to retrieve the footage. He hoped it wasn't permanently deleted.

Either way, he was firing Mandy. His hopes that the prints on the bottle would help weren't going to work. There wouldn't be any traces of poison on it and she worked at the bar, so her prints would likely be on a lot more than just that one bottle. He was sure she'd taken the needle she'd used with her, so that the evidence was irretrievable.

His frustration continued to mount as he drove toward the hospital. Without evidence, how could they prove it was Mandy who'd poisoned Sue?

When he got to the hospital, he jumped out of the car, forgetting his laptop on the passenger seat, in his rush to get to Sue.

He crossed the busy parking lot, barely looking around him, to make sure he wouldn't get run over. It wasn't a big hospital, as there weren't very many people in Queen Anne on a regular basis.

He was passing through the front doors, when he spotted Mandy in one of the waiting rooms. She was standing near a window, her eyes down on her phone.

Rage filled him. He clenched his hands into fists and held them at his sides. He had to resist the urge to beat the woman to a pulp. He crossed the room as calmly as he could, and stood behind her, glancing around. There were two other people in the room, a young miserable-looking couple, whose faces were also buried in their phones.

The man turned his head, apparently sensing Mike's eyes

on him. His eyes rested on Mike for a second, before they moved to Mandy. He looked at the woman who was with him, and jostled her lightly with his arm. She looked at him.

He gestured with his head toward the door, and then toward Mike. The woman looked over at Mike. Her eyes widened. She grabbed her purse, nodded at the man and stood up.

The man put his hand on the woman's back, giving Mike a knowing look as the two walked out the door.

Mike turned back to Mandy, once they were on the other side of the door. He lifted one hand and held it up over her shoulder, struggling to stay calm. He laid it firmly down and spun her around. She looked at him, a shocked expression painted on her face.

"Mike." She said his name breathlessly, her skin taking on an ashen look.

"Mandy," Mike growled. "I know what you did. I know you poisoned Sue, I know how you did it, and I know you deleted my security footage. But that's not good enough, Mandy. I already saw it. And since I'm your boss, you just lost everything in your life you cared about, unless you have a pet I don't know about."

Mandy's eyes widened. "No, no, Mike. Wait a minute. I just... I just want you to be... happy."

Mike did everything he could not to yell in her face. He wanted to be an adult about it, but he kept seeing Sue's face in his mind, Mari's anger toward him for letting it happen and the footage on the video. "You don't know anything about making someone else happy. You expect everything to be the way you want it, because you want it that way. I've been telling you for years there will never be anything between us. Now, there definitely won't."

Mandy's eyes filled with tears. She pressed her phone against her chest and gave him a pleading look. "No, Mike, please. I just want... you to be happy... with me. We're meant to be, Mike, don't you know that?"

"I know that's what you want to believe," Mike replied,

362

still controlling the volume of his voice. "You're fired. Don't go back to my bar. I'll have your things cleared out and at your apartment later tonight."

"Just talk to me, Mike. You don't have to do that. We can still work together." Her desperate tone made Mike even angrier.

He clenched his jaw, biting back the words he wanted to say.

"No. You are banned from my bar."

Mandy let a few tears slide down her cheeks. "Mike. Mike, please."

"Don't bother. I know what you're like now."

He suddenly realized he was in the hospital. He frowned. The tension in his chest maximized to the point that he felt like he could barely breathe.

"Why are you here?" he asked in alarm. "What are you doing here?"

"I… I just came to…"

He grabbed her shoulders and shook her. "You went to see Sue, didn't you!" he yelled. "What did you do? What did you say to her? I swear if you did anything more to hurt my relationship with her, you're going to pay."

Mandy's eyes narrowed. "Are you threatening me? How dare you threaten me."

Mike felt like he was about to lose control. He released her shoulders and took a step back, putting both hands up to the sides of his head. He pressed in, keeping himself under control.

"You're not going to make me lose it," he mumbled. "I'm not going to jail because of you. I've told the staff to call the police, if you go back to the bar. I'll make sure the police are there before you even get there. I'll call them now." He glared at Mandy, lowering his hands. "I should have known you were like this. I should have known you're nuts. You tried to kill the woman I love. You're out of your mind."

He turned sideways and backed out of the room, keeping his eye on her. She followed him, the pleading look returning to her face.

"Mike, I love you. I really do. That's the only reason I did what I've done. I never meant to hurt you."

"You meant to hurt Sue. I love her, not you, and you couldn't handle the rejection. You'll pay for this, one way or another. But I'm not going to get in trouble because of you. I'm not losing everything because of you. I know what you are now. You need to stay away from me and away from my bar. This is a small town. You might want to leave."

He didn't listen to her pleas, as he went out the door into the hallway. He stopped a few feet away from the waiting room, trying to catch his breath and calm down. He could hear Mandy crying in the waiting room. He was glad she hadn't come screaming after him, like some kind of crazy banshee. He didn't want any more attention drawn to himself than there already was.

He went down the hall quickly, avoiding the eyes of anyone who might be watching him. People walked around him; patients, caregivers, no one cared about him. He took the elevator to the third floor, staring at the digital numbers as he went up, thinking it was taking way too long to get there.

When the doors finally opened, he shot out from the elevator and jogged down the hall to Sue's room. It would be a relief to see her face. He hoped she wasn't angry at him because Mandy came to the hospital. Just before he went into her room, he remembered he'd left his laptop in the front seat of his car.

Chapter 27

When Mike stepped into the room, Sue felt an immense wave of relief. She had three pillows behind her, propping her up, but pushed herself to sit up even more. He looked so worried and distressed.

She threw her arms up to him and he crossed the room to her.

"Sue! Are you all right?"

Her heart thumped with joy. She could hear the emotion and concern in his voice. She hugged him tight to her, relishing in the warmth of his body against hers.

"Oh, Mike, I'm so glad you're here! Mandy came by and…"

He pulled away from her, holding her at arm's length, dropping to sit on the edge of the bed. "Did she hurt you? More, I mean? What did she do?"

Sue blinked back tears. "She didn't hurt me, but she has to be the one who did this to me. She has to be. How else would she have known to come here?"

"I wish you'd texted me when she got here. I would have been here in a heartbeat. I don't care how many traffic laws I'd be breaking."

Sue smiled gently. "I know you would, honey. I wasn't expecting her, and didn't have my phone near me. It's still over there in my purse." She waved her hand at the bag sitting on the window sill. "I can handle myself, and I was prepared, in case she tried to do something."

Mike nodded. "I saw her downstairs in a waiting room. But listen, when I left earlier, I went to the bar and looked through the security footage. She did administer the poison, but not in the wine bottle."

Sue was confused. She pulled her eyebrows together, giving him a questioning look.

365

"It was in the pistachios." His voice was gentle, as if he thought a louder tone might hurt her. She sat back against the bed, still staring at him, stunned. She remembered eating two of the pistachios. They tasted rotten so she didn't eat the other two. She didn't tell Mike not to eat them, because he'd mentioned before that he was allergic to them.

She pulled in a deep breath, realizing what had happened. Realizing how Mandy had gotten to her, knowing Mike wouldn't be poisoned at the same time. There was literally no chance he would have eaten any of those pistachios.

"I'm so sorry, Mike..." She was on the verge of tears again. He frowned.

"You're sorry? For what? You haven't done anything wrong here. Don't apologize."

Sue let her tears out, covering her face with one hand. She felt Mike reach out to her, grabbing her other hand and squeezing it.

"Why are you crying? I'm sorry, Sue. What did I say? I'm sorry if I hurt you. This is all my fault. I should have known. I should have done something about her already."

Sue took her hand away from her face and looked at him through tear-filled eyes. He let go of her hand, stood up abruptly, and began to pace, mumbling to himself.

"Mike, come here." Sue reached out to him, but he continued to pace back and forth.

"I should have known. It's my fault you're in this hospital. You should be at the resort, doing your work, being happy and living life with your sisters."

"Mike!" Sue used a firm voice to get his attention. For a moment, she thought they might be about to have their first fight. And it would be about her trying to comfort him so they could think about what to do.

"Do you know what she did, Sue?" Mike stopped pacing and turned to face her. She shook her head. "She downloaded my security app on her phone and deleted the footage of what she'd done. She deleted it! Right after I watched it. There was probably more I didn't see. That evil woman deleted our evidence."

Sue dropped her eyes to her legs, under the sheet of the bed. She contemplated what he'd told her, and searched her mind for any other proof they could get.

"How did she do it?" she asked.

Mike told her what he'd seen on the video, step by step. She listened, growing more fearful by the moment. Mandy was out of control. She was obsessed with Mike. That was the long and short of it.

"What are you going to do?" she asked. "You can't keep working with her."

Mike resumed his pacing, shaking his head. "No, I fired her and banned her from the bar. I told her I would have Francesco take her things to her place."

Sue raised her eyebrows. "I think you should go make sure she doesn't burn your bar down."

Mike shook his head. "She won't do that. There's no way she'd kill a bunch of people. She wants me, not to murder a bar full of people."

"I don't know about that." Sue was genuinely concerned. "You didn't think she was capable of doing something like this, did you? One of the cops that was in here earlier said he knew you. Maybe you could call him, and ask him to go check on the place, and make sure everything is okay. Maybe they'll even watch it for you tonight. I'm really worried about it."

Mike studied her face for a moment. She didn't say anything more, waiting for him to make a decision. Her heart sped up, her nervous anxiety making her jittery. She tried to control her shaky breathing. After a few minutes, he reached back and pulled his phone from his pocket.

"Did you catch the name of the cop that was here?"

Sue gave him a comforting smile. "You know a lot of

them?"

She was glad when his face relaxed, and he gave her a gentle, closed-mouth smile. "I guess I know a few. They came to investigate when my equipment went missing."

Sue shook her head, keeping her smile. "He didn't give me his first name. Last name was... Wilkins, I think? He said he was an old friend. That you're a good guy."

"Ah. Kevin. Yeah, he's a good friend. One of the best. I met him right after I moved here, before I bought the bar. He helped me get established and meet some people. It was him that introduced me to your uncle."

Sue's smile widened. "Really?"

He nodded, his eyes dropping back down to his phone. "I'll text him. No, I'll call him."

Sue held in a giggle at his uncertainty. She watched him, thinking how handsome he was, and how much she enjoyed it when he took control. She'd noticed when he set his mind to something, he got it done. His determination was strong and she admired that about him.

He held the phone to his ear, placed the other hand on his waist and turned toward the window, his eyes drifting out to the scenery. Sue waited with him for the officer to pick up his personal phone.

"He's on duty, he might not..."

She stopped speaking when Mike lifted one hand to her, saying, "Hey, Kevin. It's Mike. Yeah. You were?" He looked at Sue, mouthing "he was expecting me", before turning back to the window. She grinned.

"So, yeah, I need your help... yeah, I know who did it. It was my bartender, Mandy. Yeah. Yeah."

Sue listened to his side of the conversation, wondering what the officer was saying. Mike repeated "yeah" more than any other word in the conversation.

She could tell when the conversation was about to end, because of Mike's demeanor. He turned back to her, but his eyes were on the floor as he listened. "Okay. Yeah, that will work fine. I've got my laptop in the car. Maybe your tech people can get that footage off..." He stopped. Sue was disheartened by the look on his face.

"Yeah, you're probably right, but I'd still like to give it a try. Okay. Thanks. Alright. Bye."

He took the phone from his ear and pressed the end button. He came back to the bed, his eyes on Sue's face.

"I guess he didn't have any good news to tell you, huh?" she asked.

Mike shrugged. "He doesn't think the footage can be retrieved, because it wasn't downloaded to my laptop. He thinks it has to be downloaded to be retrieved. But the security company might be able to get it. Maybe they have it stored."

"Like a backup, in case someone accidentally deletes something," Sue added in a hopeful voice.

He nodded, pointing at her with the phone. "Exactly. I knew there was a reason I like you."

Sue stuck out her bottom lip. "You like me? Aw, I thought we'd gone past that."

Mike chuckled, reaching out to tap her on the nose. "You're cute when you're smart."

Sue giggled, delightedly. "You're cute when you compliment me. Go ahead, do it some more."

Mike's smile stretched across his face. He looked up at the ceiling. "Let's see, you've got pretty hair and a pretty smile. And you're just as pretty on the inside as you are on the outside. Oh, and you smell really great."

Sue laughed out loud. "You haven't been around me after a work-out."

Mike waved one hand in the air, dismissing the thought.

"Ah, I'm sure it's not that bad."

"I think you're probably going to find out about that." She used a teasing voice, sticking the tip of her tongue through her teeth, smiling at him.

He opened his eyes wide. "Am I?" he asked.

She pressed her lips together. "Yeah. I'm going to your house tonight, right?"

"You bet your sweet momma you are."

Sue laughed again. "I don't think I've ever heard that before."

"Well, my dad always said sweet bippy, but I think that's a little old-fashioned for the 21st century, don't you?"

She nodded. "I suppose it is. I'm glad you don't say everything is swell."

They both laughed.

"I so want to get out of here, Mike. I want to enjoy the dinner you're making, and spend a relaxing night with you."

"Uh-oh. Did I say I was *making* dinner? Hmmm."

"Oh, you don't have to," Sue hurried to say, thinking she was mistaken. "I don't mind if you order something. I just thought…"

"Hush your pretty mouth," Mike said, shaking his head. "I'm just teasing you. I'm a great cook. I'll make you whatever you want. What do you like? Please tell me you're not a closet vegan or something."

Sue shook her head, chuckling. "Not even close. Steak and potatoes for me, or something with some meat in it. Any kind of meat. I eat it all."

"Well, that sure makes it easier on me."

Sue's eyes strayed to the door, making Mike turn to look. No one entered. When he looked back at her, she asked, "Will you do me a favor?"

"Anything." He leaned forward and placed a soft kiss on her lips. "I'll do anything for you."

"Go out there and tell those doctors I want to go now. I'm fine. I don't need to wait another couple of hours. I'm not going to get better faster, just because I'm in here. This is just costing me more money by the minute."

Mike nodded, standing up. "I'll be glad to. I want to take you home. Kev's gonna make sure the bar is safe tonight, and come by the house in the morning to talk with us about what we need to do."

"Did he say whether or not there's anything we can do? Or they can?"

"To Mandy? Not yet. They can't arrest her because we say she did it. They need a reason to arrest her."

Sue frowned. "Well, that doesn't do us any good."

"We'll figure this out, Sue. I'll be right back. I'm gonna go demand the release of my girl."

A rich feeling of love swept through her. She was his girl.

She was *his girl*.

Chapter 28

When Mike pulled into his driveway, he looked over at Sue. "Don't even think about getting out first, Sue. I'm gonna help you into the house."

She lifted one eyebrow. "What are you gonna do? Carry me?"

She made it sound like a joke, but Mike was serious. He was going to make sure she had the most relaxing night of her life. Everything he wanted to do for her passed through his mind. All the way home, he'd been thinking of different things he could do to spoil her. He would run her a hot bath, add some bubbles, if he had any, light candles and place them all around. If he had roses, he'd drop petals everywhere. Women liked that kind of thing.

He mentally ran through the food he had in his fridge, pondering what he could make special for her. He was glad she was a meat-eating woman. He didn't know what he would do if he had to adjust his cooking style to suit her tastes.

"I'm thinking that's exactly what I'm going to do." He gave her a serious look. "So, don't get out."

He put the SUV in park and turned it off, giving her a stern look that made her break out into giggles.

He got out and circled the car, his chest tight, and his heart beating hard. He opened her door and held out one hand to her. "My lady."

She took his hand and swung her legs around, so she was facing him sideways in the seat. He grinned, took his hand from hers, and swept one arm under her knees. She laughed as he pulled her from the seat, exerting more effort than he needed to.

With one arm under her shoulders and the other under her knees, he lifted her out, grunting.

"My God, woman, do you have bricks in your pockets?"

Sue laughed. He knew she wasn't insecure about her weight. She was a slender woman, with curves in all the right places. He wouldn't have wanted her any thinner. She slapped him on the arm lightly, making him laugh.

"I don't even have any pockets, Mike. Don't be mean. We'll have to fight."

He gave her a shocked look, raising his eyebrows. "You wanna take me on, little lady?"

She gazed at him with love in her eyes. His heart thumped as he carried her to the door. She wrapped her arms around his neck, hugging herself to him. He was swept over with heavy emotions, as he struggled to keep her in his arms and unlock the door. She laughed, trying to hold herself against him as he fumbled with the keys in his hand.

"I need a remote for this," he mumbled, jokingly. She giggled.

"Sounds pretty high-tech."

He got the door open and passed through, kicking it closed behind him. He carried her into the living room to his right, laying her down on the couch as gently as he could. He grabbed the nearest couch pillow and put it behind her, against the arm rest. He adored the grateful look in her eyes as she laid back.

"You stay right here. I'll go get a blanket."

Sue raised her eyebrows. "Am I staying here all night?"

He looked at her, blinking rapidly. "Do you want to?"

She smiled. "Not particularly. I believe you said you have a spare room, right?"

He nodded. "I do, but bedtime is far off. I have plans for you, and going to sleep right now isn't one of them, unless you want to. If you're tired, that's okay, too."

Sue shook her head. "My body is exhausted, but I'm not tired. I just feel weak. The doctor said it would take several days before I feel right again. I tried to work earlier, but I couldn't clear my head enough to think straight." She put one hand against her forehead. "I really don't feel capable of any deep thinking right now, either."

Mike crouched by the couch so he wasn't looking down at her. "Then we won't talk about anything serious. We need to have a good night, a relaxing night, away from all the drama."

Her eyes were concerned when she looked at him. He felt blessed to have her on his couch, in his life. He took in her pale face, seeing the weariness in her eyes.

"What about your bar? And Mandy?"

Mike shook his head. "We're not going to worry about that right now. Kevin's got it covered. He'll have a couple of officers sit at the bar tonight, to make sure no one comes on the property after it's closed. And I told Becky to call me if Mandy showed up. She has my cell number."

"Do you think she will?"

He raised his eyebrows. "Call me? Yeah, I do. She's trustworthy and has no allegiance to Mandy, that I know of. They work opposing shifts. I don't even know if she's spoken to her more than a few times."

Sue dropped her gaze, nodding. "Okay, if you're sure."

Mike reached out and touched her cheek, running his fingers under her chin. "Listen to me, lovely woman. We're going to forget about life for a little while, and enjoy each other's company. If we talk about any kind of business at all, it will be our singing collaboration. How's that?"

Sue's grin made Mike's heart feel ten times lighter. He smiled back and pushed himself to his feet.

"That's my girl. You stay here… for now…" He winked at her. "I'll be right back."

He left the room in search of a blanket. There were several extras in his hall closet.

He quickly returned to her, unfolding the blanket as he walked into the living room. "Here we go. This is big and soft, and should make you nice and cozy."

He spread the blanket over her, noticing how long and shapely her legs were. He ran his eyes over her, as he pulled the blanket up to her chest. When he looked at her face, he saw her giving him a teasing look.

"I see you lookin' at me. You like what you see?"

"You know I do, darlin'." Mike winked at her. "That's a mighty nice shape you've got there."

"Well, thank you." Sue feigned haughtiness. "It's a God-given gift. I struggle with it all the time."

They both laughed.

"Tell me something, though." Sue pushed herself up a little further, leaving the end cushion open. He immediately sat down. She laughed. He gave her a confused look. His first thought was that she was going down a serious road again. He mentally prepared himself to be encouraging and supportive, no matter what she said.

"What?" he asked, innocently.

"I was just going to ask you how you were going to get comfortable, with me laying on this couch. You'd be a million miles away, sitting in that chair over there. And that whole loveseat?" She shook her head. "I just want you to be close to me."

"I want to be close to you, too." He scooted toward her on the couch, lifting her legs with one hand, and scooped under them to put them on his lap. "Let's get rid of these." He grasped each shoe and pulled them from her feet. Her socks were shockingly white. He glanced at her.

"I think your socks just blinded me. How do you keep them so white?"

"I never go anywhere without shoes on," she responded with a smile.

"I think these socks deserve some loving." He took one foot in his hand and began to knead it, gently rubbing his thumb over her toes and the ball of her foot. She moaned and laid her head back, propping herself up, with both elbows on the arm rest.

"Oh, my God, that feels great. Don't stop."

Mike held in a sigh, gazing at her face. He had never loved a woman so much before. He kept massaging her feet, then her legs, until his fingers cramped. He pulled them back and flexed them.

"Okay, I see that," Sue said, pulling her legs from his. "You don't have to do that anymore. That was so great. Thank you so much, you big hunk of love."

Mike laughed. "Let me guess. You're gonna start calling me Pookie, and thinking it's funny, especially in public, right?"

Sue shook her head. "Oh no. That's for private use only."

He gave her a pleading look. "Please don't ever call me Pookie. I'm begging you."

She giggled. "Okay."

"Promise me."

"I promise. Cross my heart and hope to…"

"Nope!" He interrupted her, raising one finger in the air and lowering his head at the same time. "Don't you dare say that." It was the last thing he wanted to hear. The thought that Sue might have been killed by the pistachios still haunted him. The last thing he wanted to hear was that she hoped to die, even in jest.

"Sorry." Sue leaned forward and touched his arm. He put one hand over hers. "Let's not get serious again. I thought you were gonna make me something to eat. I'm starving. Where's my dinner?"

"Yikes. Yes, ma'am. Sorry."

Mike pushed himself to his feet. He looked down at her slender face, gazing up at him. She looked happy, despite her weakness and fatigue.

"Steak?"

She nodded. "That sounds wonderful."

"Any particular sides you want?"

She shrugged. "I guess anything you want to make will be fine. I'll eat almost anything. Love my veggies."

"Uh-oh. No closet vegan?" He grinned wide. She laughed, sending a pleasant thrill through Mike.

"Oh, no. I'm a food person. I like food. All of it. Anything, as long as it isn't too spicy. Can't take that curry. You don't want me eating spicy curry, anyway."

Mike let out a barking laugh as he turned to go to the kitchen. "You don't want me eating spicy curry. Or anything else spicy for that matter. Not on one of our first dates."

"Thanks for the warning."

Mike laughed as he walked to the kitchen. He went through the kitchen to the door that led to the back porch. Once he was outside, he started the grill, planning his night with Sue. Neither of them needed to think about what was going on in the real world. Not tonight.

He wanted her to be happy, safe, and comfortable.

He would make sure she was.

Possibly, for the rest of her life.

Chapter 29

Sue woke up to a knock on the door. She was surprised to find herself still on the couch, before she remembered the night had stretched out long for her and Mike. She didn't even remember falling asleep. She attributed it to the wine. He'd filled her stomach with the most delicious steak she'd ever eaten, plied her with wine, and didn't even think about taking advantage of her.

She sat up abruptly, pushing the blanket from her legs when she saw Mike coming down the hallway in his robe. She was immediately impressed with his form. The robe was plush and black, with a yellow happy face embroidered over the right chest. His legs stretched out under it. She couldn't help noticing the muscles of his calves.

She wondered if he'd had to work out to make them that way, or if they were like that naturally.

Her heart did a flip when he looked at her and shook his head, waving for her to lie back down. He went toward the door, disappearing behind the wall, and she couldn't see him anymore.

She settled back on the couch, but was wide awake, her heart thumping from the knock on the door. Worry slipped through her mind. Despite their decision to keep the night relaxing and casual, Mike had left his phone on and kept it with him, just in case he got a call.

She heard the door open, and heard Mike's greeting.

"Hey. Come on in. Thanks for getting back to me so quick."

"No problem, Mike."

Sue recognized the voice, but couldn't place it, until the man came around the wall with Mike, into her view.

It was Nathan Hawke, the man whose wedding she and her sisters were planning. She smiled, and he smiled back at her.

"Well, hello there, pretty lady," Nathan said.

"Good morning, Nathan. What are you doing here? You're not checking up on me, are you?"

Nathan turned to Mike. "Am I?"

Both men laughed softly. Mike looked at her with a loving gaze that filled her heart with warmth. "No, my dear. Nathan is a good friend of mine. He's part owner of the security company keeping an eye on my bar. I called him to ask for some help getting the footage back, if it's possible."

Sue raised her eyebrows, a pleasant feeling sweeping through her. "That's great!"

"I'm sorry I woke you, Sue. I didn't know you were here."

"It's okay, Nathan. My sisters brought a bag to the hospital for me yesterday. I think I'll just take a shower and..." Sue made to push herself off the couch, but a sudden feeling of weakness covered her and she fell back with a sharp exhale.

Mike was by her side immediately. Her head was spinning. She pressed one hand against her forehead, her eyes closed. It felt like the room was spinning, even though her eyes were closed. She swayed to the side and found herself held up by Mike's arms.

"You stay right here." She could hear sorrow in his voice. She leaned all her weight on him. "No," he murmured. "I'm taking you to my room. You need a nice bed to lie in."

"You don't have to do that," Sue whispered softly. "I'll be fine. I just need to take it slow, instead of acting like I'm one-hundred percent." She opened her eyes and gazed at the floor, trying to focus, so it wouldn't spin anymore. The effect slowly wore off. She didn't push herself out of his arms until she could breathe without feeling like she was about to vomit.

She glanced up at Nathan, who had come close to the couch. He was looking at her with a deeply concerned expression.

"I'm sorry you have to see me like this, Mr. Hawke. Please, don't think it will reflect on my work for you."

Nathan frowned. "You can call me Nathan. And I know the quality of your work. If I'm right, you and your sisters already have it mostly planned out, anyway. I'm sure all that's left is the finest of details."

Sue thought of her sisters with pride. She nodded. "Yes, that's about true. I just don't want you to think bad of me or my sisters."

He shook his head. "Never. You've got my friend's heart, and that means a lot to me. Mike's a great guy. I don't want to see him hurt anymore."

Sue glanced at Mike, whose face went through several emotions as Nathan spoke. He looked flattered by the compliment, and then confused by the last portion. Nathan noticed the look, too, and shook his head.

"Don't look at me like that, Mike. You told me what's on that video footage. I've watched that woman manipulate you and ruin other relationships you've had." He turned his eyes to Sue. "Mostly friendships. He never had a chance to take it any further than that, because Mandy never let him."

"Mandy doesn't have control over me," Mike insisted. "I decided not to pursue any relationships before. I didn't meet the right woman until now."

Sue's heart did a flip in her chest. The pleasant feeling quickly disappeared when Nathan continued.

"That's bull and you know it. The only reason you broke off your friendships with other women is because of something Mandy did or said about them. Don't tell me that's not true, because I know it is. I've spoken to some of the women who were interested in dating you. It's a small town, you know. We're all friends here, pretty much. Did you know a couple of them were approached by Mandy, and she threatened them to stay away from you?"

Mike frowned. Sue watched his face. The thought that Mandy had been manipulating Mike that long made anger slide through Sue, making her chest tighten. She pulled in a deep breath and held it, trying not to cough. Her stomach was turning over, rejecting the food she'd put in it the night before.

She grabbed Mike's arm, leaning forward. "Mike. Help me to the bathroom, please."

Without hesitation, Mike slipped one arm under her knees and the other under her shoulders, lifting her up with ease. She sighed, resting her head on his shoulder. He carried her to the bathroom and set her down gently on the toilet, which had the lid down.

"Can you take it from here or do you need more help?" he asked kindly, giving her a warm look of love. She shook her head, meeting his loving eyes with her own.

"No, I can handle it myself."

"You call me if you need me," Mike said sternly. "You hear me?"

She nodded. "Yes, I will."

He gave her a long look, before turning back to the door and closing it softly after him.

Sue turned her body and slid gently onto the floor, kneeling in front of the toilet. She lifted the lid and put her hot forehead down on the cool ceramic seat. Her stomach continued to churn.

Her attention was drawn away from her pain, when she realized she could hear Nathan and Mike talking, as if they were standing just on the other side of the door. She wondered if they were. Either way, their conversation became her focus. She was grateful, concentrating as much as she could on what they were saying, taking her mind off the pain in her stomach.

"Is she going to be okay?" she heard Nathan ask.

"I don't know. I sure hope so. Mandy did a job on her, I'll tell you that. I can't believe she did this. I can't believe she wanted to kill Sue."

Sue could hear the pain in his voice. His love for her came through every word.

"Yeah, I knew she was crazy but not *that* crazy. Where's your laptop? I brought mine in case we need it."

"It's in the room. Come on, I'll show it to you."

Anxiety slipped through Sue when she heard them walking down the hallway. They had been standing outside the door. Their quiet voices carried through, until they were further down the hall. They must have gone into Mike's room and come directly back out, because seconds later, she heard their footsteps in the hall.

Sue's stomach turned over, and nausea overruled everything else. She lifted herself up, and was over the bowl just in time.

Pain split through her, tensing her muscles, ripping through her throat, making the blood pound in her head. Tears slipped from her eyes.

When her stomach was emptied and she was dry-heaving, she leaned back, grabbing a handful of toilet paper and holding it to her mouth. A thick black towel hung over a rack to her side. She reached out for it, pulling it down to her.

She tossed the toilet paper in the bowl and forced herself to lift up to flush it. She dropped back down to the floor, holding the towel to her face, pressing it into her eyes. To her surprise, she was feeling much better, now that she had nothing in her stomach.

She breathed slowly, in through her mouth and out through nose, several times, glad her stomach was settling down. She still felt weak. She stayed the way she was for a few more minutes, before pushing herself to her feet.

She looked in the mirror and was ashamed of how she looked. Her hair was all over the place, sticking up and frizzy, as if it was a rainy bad-hair day. Her eyes looked swollen and her face was as pale as she had ever seen it. There was no color to her. She was washed out and weak. She wished Mike didn't have to see her that way.

She pulled open the door and slowly left the room, letting her hand slide along the wall as she went. She could hear the men's low voices coming from the kitchen. She made her way to the kitchen door and pushed it open.

Mike got up immediately and came over to her, his caring

eyes studying her intently. "You feeling any better, honey?"

She looked up at him, honestly answering, "Yeah, I do. Tell me what you guys have found out. Anything?"

"We have." Mike smiled at her. "Nathan is a genius. He knows how to do what others think is impossible."

Nathan laughed from the dining table. "Yeah, it's more like I have the passcodes to the security system, and we keep back-ups of the videos taken for a week before we get rid of them."

"Only a week?" Mike grinned at his friend, before turning his eyes back to Sue. She felt the warmth of his love, when he took her hand and led her to the table. He pulled out a chair across from Nathan and helped her sit down. "Can I get you a drink? Some coffee or tea or something? Tell me what I can do for you."

"Right now, all I want is to see your smiling face, Mike. And I see it. So, does this mean we're gonna get justice?"

Mike sat in the chair next to her. "I guess that's up to you. I've already fired her, but I can't do anything about this. I can't press charges against her, because she didn't hurt me. That's gonna be up to you."

"Then I guess we're going to get justice."

She and Mike shared a smile.

Chapter 30

The day started with a beautiful sunrise, that Sue was awake to see. It had been almost a week since she'd been poisoned, and she was pleasantly surprised that it had been a time of peace for her and Mike. She wasn't there when the police picked Mandy up, but she was aware it had happened.

She silently wished she had been there. She wouldn't tell anyone she was that petty, though. Not even Mike.

She left her room, after primping to look as good as she could. It was the day of Nathan's wedding, and she wanted to look her best for Mike. She was pleased that Nathan was such a good friend of Mike's, and he had been invited.

Her mind went back to a funny conversation she'd overheard between Nathan and Mike. They were in the kitchen, still talking, while she was on the couch in Mike's living room.

"So, why didn't you invite me to your wedding, bro?" she heard Mike ask.

"I sent you the invite, Mike. You must have thrown it away."

"I would never!"

Sue was smiling as she remembered it, the same way she'd smiled that day. She could tell the two men were good friends by the way they talked to each other.

"Nah, you must have," Nathan had replied. "I wouldn't forget you."

"Maybe that lovely bride of yours did. I don't think she likes me much."

Nathan had laughed. "Mike, everybody likes you. Some, too much."

"All right, now. That's enough of that."

Sue walked down the hallway, their voices drifting through her memory. The resort was buzzing with sound and people, as they went about their day. She saw Lynn at the end of the hall, walking from one side hallway, through the corridor to the other side. She was staring down at the tablet in her hands, moving one finger over the surface.

"Lynn!" she called out, lifting her hand.

Her sister looked up. A smile covered her face and she turned to walk toward Sue.

"How are you feeling this morning?" Lynn asked.

Sue chuckled softly. Both of her sisters asked that same question, every morning since her hospital stay.

"I'm feeling good. I'm fully recovered. No need to worry anymore."

Lynn nodded. "Good. You're ready for the Hawke wedding today?"

"I sure am. I've got all my ducks in a row."

Lynn raised one eyebrow. "That would be a first."

Sue mocked surprise and resentment. "I'll walk with you," she said in a normal voice. Lynn stopped walking, and waited for Sue to catch up to her. Then, she turned and went back to wherever she was headed.

"How about you? You ready for this?"

Lynn nodded, her eyes steady on her tablet. "Yeah. But I'm actually having a little trouble here. I think the caterer we chose is going to be late. That's not good."

"That's their responsibility, Lynn. If they get here late, they'd better have extra workers to set everything up properly, before the reception. If they don't, well, like I keep hearing, Queen Anne is small and our business is thriving. If they want to be successful here, it kind of depends on them being reliable for us, doesn't it? All we have to do is spread the word that they are unreliable and they won't get any business at all."

Lynn glanced up at her. "And there's the Sue I know and love. You're a real hard-nose with business, aren't you?"

"Well, do they have a good excuse? It doesn't take that long to get here from town. Have they ever catered here before?"

"Sue. This is my part of the business. I'll handle it. Don't worry about it."

Sue felt the urge to pursue it, but held back. Her sister was right. It wasn't her part of the planning. Lynn could handle it.

"I'm sorry. I know you can take care of your business. I'm being pushy."

Lynn chuckled. "That's just the way you are, Sue. I appreciate your advice, though. I'll make sure they get what they deserve."

"Dang, when you say it like that, it makes me sound like a really awful person."

They continued to discuss business until they reached the end of the corridor, which turned either to the left or right. A door leading to the outside was directly in front of them.

"You know, I think I saw Mike around here somewhere, a few minutes ago," Lynn said, giving her sister a direct look. "Why don't you go find him?"

At the mention of Mike's name, Sue's heart did a double flip. She felt giddy for a moment, his handsome face coming to her mind. She could hear him whispering "I love you". It made her heart race.

"He's already here?"

Sue nodded. "Yeah. Did you know he's a friend of Mr. Hawke's? I didn't know that."

"Mike is friends with everyone in Queen Anne, and probably well beyond there. Lots of tourists come through his bar. I wouldn't be surprised if he had friends all over the globe."

Lynn laughed. "Well, you go find your man and let me get back to business."

Sue pushed through the door and into the bright sunlight, squinting and shading her eyes, so she could search the grounds in front of her. She should have asked Lynn where she'd seen him.

She turned to the right and walked down the long, wide deck, past the wicker, iron, and plastic chairs and tables. There were people wandering around, smiling at her and nodding as they passed. She thought a couple of times about asking them if they knew Mike, and where he might be, but couldn't get up the courage.

They probably knew him, but she didn't know them, so she avoided asking them any questions. She walked all the way around the building. Once she'd rounded the corner, she thought about how vast the resort was. Chances were small she would find him by wandering around.

She pulled the cell phone out of her purse and put in her passcode to open it. She pulled up her messenger and typed in a text to him.

Hey, where you at?

She lowered the phone, stopping to stand still in the middle of the deck, not seeing the people around her. Seconds later, her phone buzzed, making her smile.

I'm near the pools in the snack area. Glad you're up. Come meet me. We'll have breakfast.

She slipped the phone back in her bag, after sending '*omw*', and hurried in the other direction. The pools were on the other side of the building, toward the back. She didn't think she would get a good breakfast from the snack bar, but that's where he was, so that's where she wanted to be.

Her heart raced faster as she got closer to the snack area. The tables came into sight. She saw him sitting at one of them with Nathan. He was facing her. She wondered if he'd faced that direction so he'd see her when she got there. It was a nice thought, but unlikely. He had no way of knowing what direction she'd come from.

The moment he laid eyes on her, he stood up. Nathan glanced over his shoulder and smiled. He turned back and said something that made Mike look down at him with his own smile.

He left the table and his friend behind, to come toward her.

They met, and she moved directly into his arms, wrapping hers around him, and pressing her cheek against his chest. He hugged her back, as tightly as she hugged him. After a long, warm hug, he pulled back and looked down at her face.

"Don't you look stunning today. You might as well be getting married. You look like you're glowing."

She grinned. "If I'm glowing, it's because your love is shining off my face."

He tilted his head to the side. "Wow. That's the most cliché thing I've ever heard. Flattering, and probably true, but still… cliché."

They laughed.

"Want to spend some time together this morning?" Mike asked, turning to go back to the snack bar. "Get a nice healthy breakfast of nature bars and orange juice?"

Sue chuckled. "Yeah, I didn't think there would be eggs and bacon at the snack bar. But we have a real kitchen, and we could go there for breakfast."

Mike stopped walking. He turned to face her. "You want to cook it? Because I'm not much in the mood for cooking. It's too early in the day."

"You're right. I'm not either, and it is. Let's go get some nature bars and orange juice."

Mike gave her a pleasant smile. "Honey, if you want a good breakfast, I'll take you for one right now. I know some great places in Queen Anne."

She shook her head. "This is silly. Let's just get us something and walk around for a while. How's that sound?"

He nodded. "Whatever you want, Sue."

He turned again to continue walking, but she took his arm and turned him back to face her. She gazed up at his face, loving the look he was giving her.

"Mike, I don't want you to give up anything just for the sake of being with me. I know you're an independent man, and you have a life that has nothing to do with me. I don't want you giving up anything for me."

"I'm gonna give up something for you, whether you like it or not."

She frowned. "What do you mean?"

He chuckled. "I'm giving up the bachelor life. Thank God. You and me will be good. We'll be forever."

Sue felt her heart jump in her chest. "Forever?"

A chill passed over her when he responded with a loving gaze and a slight nod.

"Forever, Sue. I want to marry you. I want you to be my wife and take my name. I'll live here with you, if you want. Or you can come live with me. Whatever you want to do, as long as you're with me. I don't ever want you out of my protection again, not that I did a great job the last time."

"You didn't even know you needed to protect me, honey," Sue said gently. "You did try. You had me come on a night she wasn't supposed to be there. You did what you thought was right. I thought it was right, too. She's in jail now. We're safe. Right?"

Mike nodded. "That's right. Listen to you, comforting me, when it's my job to do that for you."

She shook her head. "No, it's not like that. I want a partner. I want to protect you and your heart, the same way you protect me and mine."

Mike was quiet for a moment, looking into her eyes intently. "You will marry me, then?"

Sue giggled. "Of course, I will. You are the man I want for the rest of my life. But I'm afraid I come with at least one condition."

Mike swallowed visibly and made a face, indicating he was preparing himself for the inevitable.

"Oh, Lord. What is it?"

She smiled wide. "You have to formally ask for my hand, from my sisters."

Mike laughed.

"I think I can handle that."

Epilogue

Lynn and Mari took care of everything for their sister's wedding.

Sue stared at herself in the mirror, taking in the long, white dress with pearls around the bodice and lace on the hem. It was a gorgeous dress. One of the ladies from Queen Anne's Beauty Parlor offered to do her hair and makeup. She looked like a model, and was proud of it.

She knew she would impress Mike. It was the only thing that mattered to her.

The door behind her opened. She looked in the mirror to see Lynn and Mari coming through, their faces beaming with broad smiles.

"Oh, my God, you look beautiful!" Lynn exclaimed, throwing her hands up to cover her open mouth. A tingle of delight passed through Sue. By the end of the day, her cheeks would be hurting from all the smiling she was doing.

It was the best kind of pain she could think of.

Mari came directly to her, holding up her phone. "Hold on, picture time," she said. She snapped a few normal photos before Sue began posing. "Nice," Mari said, cheerfully. "I'm going to send these to a bridal magazine. You're absolutely gorgeous."

"Thank you, girls. That's so sweet."

"I bet you're just out of your mind with excitement, aren't you?" Lynn asked, coming up behind her picture-taking sister. "I would be. I know Mari was, on her wedding day."

Mari glanced at Lynn. "I really was, wasn't I?"

Both Sue and Lynn laughed softly. Sue remembered Mari's harried behavior before her wedding. She'd run around like a chicken with its head cut off. It took everything she and Lynn had to keep the woman calm enough to actually walk, and not run, down the aisle.

"It won't be long now," Lynn said, turning back to Sue. "I can't wait to stand up there next to you and Mari, and Mike and Nathan… oh, I'm so excited!"

Sue laughed. "I think you might be more excited about my wedding than I am."

Lynn shared in her sister's laughter. "Oh, I doubt that. I'm sure your stomach is just turning over, isn't it? Butterflies and all that? I'll be so nervous on my wedding day, I'll be shaking like a leaf."

Sue could see Lynn was already shaking. She tried to keep her own heart calm. She didn't want to mess anything up. Lynn's over-the-top energy made her feel jumpy.

She turned back to the mirror. "Are you sure I look good?" she asked. She watched both her sisters roll their eyes, making her laugh nervously.

"Alright, come on, we need to have some quiet time together," Mari said in a demanding voice. "Everything's going to change after today, and I know you need to be calm and collected when you walk down that aisle."

Sue thought it was funny that Mari made the wedding about herself. She knew it was natural for Mari to demand things from her sisters. It had never bothered her before, and didn't bother her then. She nodded.

"You're right, as always, Mari. Let's have some time together."

By the time Sue found herself standing at the beginning of the aisle through the Queen Anne church, she was as calm as she could be. She looked at the front of the church, to the altar, where Mike was standing in a black and white tux. His face was shining with pride.

She chose not to wear a veil, just so she could see the look on his face when he saw how she looked. She was satisfied with what she saw in his handsome features. She calmly walked down the aisle, after her sisters and their groomsmen.

Her heart fluttered in her chest when she stepped up next to Mike. As hard as she tried, she couldn't keep from shaking slightly. Her breath was short and quick.

Mike leaned over and whispered in her ear, "You look terrified. Beautiful, but terrified. It's all right, Sue. Everything will be all right."

A feeling of great comfort slid through her, a peace she hadn't felt before. This was the man she would live with for the rest of her life. Her handsome husband. Her Mike.

"Mike Nelson," the preacher began.

The rest of the ceremony was a blur to Sue. She repeated her vows flawlessly. When the preacher announced that they were man and wife, and introduced them as "Mr. and Mrs. Nelson", Sue's heart nearly exploded.

She walked back to the front doors of the church, hand in hand with him. She felt like she was walking on a cloud, like the solid floor was no longer under her feet.

Mike leaned toward her as they left the church. He was leading her to his SUV, which his friends had attached cans to, and spray painted "Just Married" on the back.

"My friends aren't very unique," he said, chuckling. "Sorry. I'll take those cans off down the block. I don't think we want to annoy ourselves, and everyone else, all the way to the reception."

Sue giggled. "It doesn't matter to me, hon. Nothing could bother me today. This is the best day of my life, so far."

He opened the passenger door for her and helped her gather the bottom of her skirt, so she'd fit inside without crushing the fine fabric when it was closed. He held the door open for a moment, gazing at her with so much love, her heart thumped hard and she felt a bit faint.

"I hope this is the only wedding day that makes you feel that way." His voice was solemn, though his tone was loving.

She leaned back out the door toward him, saying in a low voice. "I said the best day so far, not the best wedding day. I'm sure there will be plenty more best days for me. Like when we have our first child. Or the second, or sixth. I don't know. We'll see."

Mike's eyes widened. "Six? Did you say six?" He glanced over his shoulder. "Is it too late to call this off?"

Sue gasped, with a wide smile on her face, reaching out to slap him softly on the arm. "Mike! You know I want a dozen kids."

"That's not something you mentioned to me," Mike responded seriously. "That might be a deal breaker."

Sue lifted her eyebrows, pulling back. He immediately leaned forward and grabbed her in a passionate kiss. She heard their friends cheering behind him.

When they separated, she looked in his eyes, wanting to see how much he loved her. She could see it, all the way into the depths of his soul.

"I didn't mean that, Sue. Nothing is a deal breaker between you and me. Nothing. I'll never stop loving you. I mean that."

Sue sighed softly. "I'm so glad to hear that. I never want to spend a day without you."

"We're gonna fight sometimes, Sue."

She lifted her eyebrows. "We've been together for six months, almost every single day. We haven't fought yet."

Mike snorted softly. "You haven't lived with me yet."

Sue laughed. "I've stayed over enough to know about your little functions, and all that. You're a man. I'll get used to it."

Mike shared her laugh, stepping back, holding the door to close it. He made sure she was all the way in before he did so. He went around the SUV, waving to his friends.

"Go on, get out of here! Go to the reception! There's wine there. What's wrong with you all?"

Sue leaned out the window and called out, "Hey! I almost forgot this dang bouquet! Get ready ladies! Gather round!"

Sue didn't wait too long before she tossed the bouquet in the air, toward the women who'd gathered. They all screamed and laughed, jumping for it. Lynn shouted with delight, when the flowers fell directly in her hands.

"I didn't do that on purpose!" Sue yelled out, to the laughter of their guests. "See you all at the resort!"

She turned to Mike. "Come on, husband, let's get out of here."

"You do mean the reception, right?"

She nodded. "This time I do. But in the future, when we get out of here, we're gonna do it in style, and leave everyone behind. This is our party right now."

Mike glanced at her, causing a feeling of love to pass through her. She couldn't believe how blessed she was. She said a silent prayer of thanks, scanning her man's handsome features.

"I love you so much, Mike."

"I love you, too, Mrs. Nelson."

She tilted her head to the side, giving him a soft grin. "Aw, I should have said Mr. Nelson."

Mike laughed. "I love you, Sue. I foresee a lot of years of happiness ahead for us."

"Me, too, Mike."

Sue looked forward, watching the road ahead, thinking about how every road she took in her life, from that point on, would be with Mike, the man of her dreams.

Book 3: Lynn

Prologue

Justin Brownstone pushed the door to the kitchen open, went in, and dropped himself into the chair nearest him. He hefted his backpack up on the table and unzipped one of the small pockets in the front. There was no one else in the combination small kitchen and dining room. His sister, Kathy, had gone out early that morning.

He pulled out a pack of cigarettes, took one out and propped it between his lips. Once he'd lit it, he dropped the lighter back into the same pocket before sitting back to think.

After only a moment, he looked behind him at the counter to the coffee machine. Kathy had made a pot, but he was willing to bet it was cold by now. Grumbling under his breath, he got up to stretch his muscles and yawned wide.

He turned back to lay the cigarette in the ashtray before crossing the small room to the cupboard. In only a few minutes, Justin had a cup of coffee in one hand, and his cigarette in the other. He put his feet up on the chair on the opposite side of the table and sat back to look through the window next to him.

For the life of him, he couldn't remember where Kathy had gone. All he knew was that she had mentioned Emerald Resort.

He'd never been up there. It would be a cold day in hell when he had the money for something like that. As far as he was concerned, they were a bunch of rich snobs with no respect for people who didn't have wealthy parents or a job that netted them a million a year.

He grunted, taking in the bright blue sky dotted with puffy white clouds. It was a typical spring day in Queen Anne, but Justin had nothing to do. Sometimes, he worked for Kathy in the Brownstone Deli and Catering but, typically, he just made enough to get by. He didn't have any special skills. He'd long ago decided to skate through life as best he could, just to get it over with.

He drank some of his coffee, keeping his eyes on the scene outside. The street was just outside the window. Their small front yard did not provide a great deal of space before the waist-high, white fence gave way to the road.

He wasn't very surprised to see people walking up and down and cars driving slowly by. It was warm out, and the beginning of the tourist season in Queen Anne. His little hometown in Georgia was close enough to St. Simon's Island for the tourists to come spilling in when they were done with the other coastal town.

He watched them pass by through narrow, skeptical eyes. He didn't see a reason to be so upbeat. What was there to be so pleased about? Life was boring, as far as he was concerned. Nothing much to entertain him in the little town he'd grown up in.

Queen Anne wasn't a place to raise children, in his opinion. He and Kathy were two of very few who were born and raised in the Georgia tourist town. And though he wished for more, something different and exciting, something that would lift his spirits and gave him a reason to get out of bed every morning, he couldn't bring himself to leave Queen Anne.

It was his home, and he'd just have to accept it.

His eyes focused on his sister's car when she pulled up alongside the curb, stopped the car and got out. She was looking down at some papers in her hand, as she walked, using her other hand to guide herself around the car. She glanced up when she stepped on the sidewalk, just enough to see where the gate was and reach for it.

She went through the gate and walked up to the front door, her eyes still scanning the paper in front of her. She flipped it to the bottom and studied the second one.

Justin lost sight of her when she was close to the house. He moved his eyes to the door of the kitchen.

The apartment was fairly small. His parents hadn't been a part of the wealthy elite that visited and lived in Queen Anne. Their house had been demolished in reconstruction years ago. A mini-mall was put up where it had been and was much more popular than the row of houses that had once taken up that stretch of block. It was a stone's throw from the long shore that led to the ocean and had a special road that led to the Emerald resort.

He was grateful the construction hadn't happened until after his parents were deceased. Cancer had taken both of them, making him and Kathy adult orphans at a young age, just a year apart.

Truth be told, Kathy had agreed to the sale of the house and land for the expansion, being older than Justin and having real plans for her future. She hadn't given Justin a say in the sale. Being eight years older, she felt entitled to do what she wanted. She treated Justin like her child, rather than her brother.

But her heart was in the right place, and she tried as hard as she could to keep them going strong. He wouldn't have wanted a different sister. He knew she loved him.

Kathy wanted to be a part of the wealthy elite that visited their hometown. She did her best to mix in with them all, advertise her deli and catering company, dress for success. She started the catering company with the money from the sale of their parent's house. He hadn't asked her for any of the money, though he should have. She gave him enough to buy his SUV and provided spending money every week, along with his paycheck when he worked at Brownstone Deli and Catering.

He heard the apartment door open and close. Seconds later, Kathy came around and into the kitchen. She glanced up at him from the papers in her hand.

"Good morning, Mr. Brownstone," she said with a smile.

"Good morning, Ms. Brownstone," he replied.

Kathy walked to the table and dropped the papers, sliding out the chair and sitting down across from Justin. "I guess it's not actually morning anymore, is it?" she asked with humor in her voice.

"It's not noon yet. Close but not yet."

"Did you just get up?" He could hear sympathy in her voice.

The night before had been busy. One of the locals threw a fundraiser and paid Brownstone Catering for a huge spread of good food. Kathy and her team of chefs spent the entire day cooking and prepping. That evening, Justin and the rest of the serving crew were up till almost four serving during the event and then cleaning up afterward.

It wasn't the easiest of jobs, but there was nothing wrong with it. Cleaning was the hardest part. He was always shocked by how disgusting rich people could be. It was like they didn't know how to throw away their own trash. Leaving plates, utensils and glasses everywhere was one thing. But balled up napkins, tissue papers with lipstick and God knew what else covering them, little bits of wrappers from nature bars, aspirin powders… They just left those things lying around for someone else to throw away.

They probably used the words, "it's their job" or "that's what they're being paid for".

He kept his opinion to himself. He always smiled at the guests at the events and was extremely polite to them. If there was one thing he knew how to do, it was schmooze.

"Yeah, I'm exhausted from last night."

"You've only had six hours of sleep. You can go back to bed for a few hours if you want."

He studied her face. "Thanks. I don't want to but thanks for your permission."

They both chuckled.

"Just letting you know I don't have anything else for you to do today. Or tomorrow. You can take a few days off."

He dropped his eyes to the papers. The top was graced with the name and logo of the Emerald Resort.

"So, what's up with that?" he asked, waving the hand with his cigarette clutched between two fingers. "You got some deal going on up there at the resort with the elite of society?"

Kathy grinned at him. "The Wright sisters are not part of the elite. They have the money but not the attitude. You should meet them. They're really great. I do have something going on with them, as a matter of fact. I was contacted by the youngest sister. She's the one in charge of catering. She wants to open a deli and catering shop there in the resort."

"Well, that sounds like competition to me."

Kathy nodded. "It would be, if she wasn't asking me to move my business to there. I don't have to give up the place I have now, but I imagine there are probably other people who would love to open a small restaurant or business where it is. It's in a prime spot and such a pretty little building."

Justin nodded. He wouldn't be making any decisions in the matter, as it was all Kathy's business. He rolled the idea around in his mind. Selling the store would really be a change.

He didn't know how he felt about it.

Chapter 1

Lynn walked into the small conference room and took her seat at the table. Her sisters were late. It wasn't a huge bother for her. They were always late. The resort was huge. It was common to get caught on the other side of the main building or anywhere else on the grounds without enough time to get to the conference room.

Lynn had done that herself.

She pulled her portfolio out of the thin briefcase she carried and sorted through the papers. She hadn't collated them already. She figured she'd have enough time since her sisters were late for the impromptu meeting.

Four days previous, Lynn woke up with an idea. She was in charge of all catering at Emerald Resort. For three years, the sisters had been hiring local companies to cater the weddings and events they held. It didn't make sense to Lynn. It created more paperwork and took up more time finding someone.

If she was to open a catering department on resort grounds, she could delegate the responsibilities to the manager of the department and not have to worry about it anymore. All she would provide would be the list of desired food from the client.

During the last four days, she'd prepared a package proposal for her sisters, specifically Mari, who made all the final decisions. As the eldest, the sisters agreed someone had to take charge when an agreement couldn't be met. So, Mari acted as the third vote. Whatever she wanted was the way it went.

Lynn was sure her sister would approve of the idea. She still wanted to make the best presentation possible, so her sisters would be proud of her.

Once she collated the papers, she set the two copies on the table where her sisters would be sitting. She turned and smiled when the door opened, and Sue came in with Mari close behind her.

"Sorry, sorry," both were mumbling as they took their seats

and settled in. Mari folded her hands on the folder in front of her and looked at Lynn. "This is your presentation? What are you proposing, hon?"

"I want to bring a catering department to the resort. As you both know, I'm in charge of the catering right now and with all the other duties I have going, it can be a little difficult. I've done some research, and I want to move a local company onto the grounds and give them the responsibility of making sure everything goes as it should. If you'll look in the folders, you'll see my notes and suggestions, with an outline of how much it will cost to open the department."

Mari and Sue opened their folders and pulled out the papers. Mari scanned them, flipping through the pages before looking up at Lynn, only moving her eyes. "Brownstone Catering? We've used them before?"

Lynn nodded. "They're the best catering company in Georgia, as far as I'm concerned. The owner, Kathy Brownstone, is an excellent chef with a crew that I've found outstanding in the past. I've even recommended them to others. Their prices have always been good, but it's not the price that got me. It's Kathy's style of ownership and production. She's a determined lady. I think she would be best for the job."

"Have you spoken to her about it?"

It was the only thing Lynn was a little nervous about. She'd had the meeting with Kathy that morning. She pulled in a deep breath and hoped for the best.

"I have. I actually had a meeting with her this morning. She's looking over the plans now."

Mari nodded. "That's taking initiative, Lynn. I like to see that. Welcome aboard." Mari smiled, making Lynn feel warm inside. She'd only done what she was told in the past, leaving all the brain work to Mari. It felt good to have her sister's validation of her efforts.

"Thanks, Mari. I was afraid you'd be mad that I forged ahead without your permission."

Mari raised one eyebrow. "You don't have to wait for my permission. I'm not really your boss. I just make the last decision on matters." She tucked the papers back in the folder and held it up, shaking it lightly. "This is excellent. You definitely have my blessing to go forward with this. Anything that's in your department, you have the right to change or add to. I like to know what's going on, but I won't tell you not to pursue something potentially profitable."

"I might come up with something utterly ridiculous," Lynn replied with a smile. "You never know."

Mari laughed softly. "I do know. You are too smart for that. You might be a hippy…" Mari held out her hand to take in all of Lynn, with her long flowing yellow shirt, her long blond hair and her long golden chain earrings that brushed against her shoulders. Lynn glanced down at her many bracelets and rings and her long, manicured nails.

"I've always dressed like this." She wasn't really defending herself. She was making an observation.

Mari nodded. "Yes, I know. And you look lovely. I couldn't pull off that look. But that's neither here nor there. Did you give Ms. Brownstone an end date for the proposal?"

Lynn shook her head. "I didn't think of that. But she seemed to be excited by the idea. I think she'll go for it. If not, I have a second choice lined up. I really want Kathy's business, though. I work really well with her, and she knows her stuff. I wouldn't be surprised if our event schedule filled up just because of her."

Sue, who had been quiet up to that point, spoke up. "When we added Mike as the music planner, that happened. I bet it will with Ms. Brownstone, too."

Lynn was delighted her sisters like the plan. Her smile beamed at both of them. "I'm so glad you like my idea!" she said in a high-pitched, happy voice. "I've spent a long time working on it and thinking about it. Four whole days!"

Her sisters laughed.

"After all that time spent, I hope your idea works out in your favor," Sue chuckled the words as she stood up. "If there's nothing else, I've got to get back to the music department. We've got a show coming up tomorrow night at Badlands. Are you girls coming?"

"We wouldn't miss it, Sue. Go on if you've got stuff to do."

As she passed Lynn, Sue leaned down and gave her a quick squeeze around her shoulders. She pressed her cheek against her sister's. "Good job, Lynn. Proud of you!"

Lynn lifted one hand and patted Sue's before her sister withdrew her hands. "Thanks, Sue. I took my cue from you when you proposed the music department last year."

"Oh boy, I'm an inspiration!" Sue laughed, as she left through the glass entrance door. Lynn watched her walk down the hallway. She was hurrying, which meant Lynn's impromptu meeting had disrupted something in her schedule.

"It was nice of her to take time to come today. I didn't mean to interrupt her schedule. Or yours. I just wanted to show you what I've been working on."

Mari shook her head, waving one hand in the air to dismiss Lynn's worry. "No, no. We are all in this together. We can spare some time for each other."

Lynn and Mari stood up at exactly the same time and stared at each other with big smiles. They met in the middle for a quick hug before leaving the room.

Lynn walked in the opposite direction of Mari, noticing her sister was hurrying just as much as Sue had. She'd interrupted both their days.

But she was feeling giddy over their approval. She couldn't wait for the meeting tomorrow with Kathy. She realized she hadn't told Mari about the second meeting. Though she hadn't given Kathy a deadline for her decision, the businesswoman had asked if they could speak again the next day. Lynn was fine with that but a bit curious why Kathy needed a day.

Not wanting to pry, she hadn't asked. But that meant Lynn would be wondering all the way up to the meeting the next day. It was likely Kathy would reveal why she wanted a day to think about it. In Lynn's experience, people either answered immediately or took a long time to ponder it.

Lynn figured Kathy must have a partner, someone with whom she must consult before giving an answer.

She walked down the hallway with her mind preoccupied by the new business venture. She was pulled from her thoughts by the ringing of her phone. It wasn't a call but a text. She reached into her bag and pulled the phone out to look at the screen.

It's Kathy. I was wondering if you would like to come to my restaurant for lunch tomorrow instead of the resort. I have some work which I can't leave behind. I think it will interest you.

Lynn smiled. She hadn't been to the Brownstone Deli and Catering restaurant, but she'd heard a lot of good things about it. Kathy had an eclectic menu that served odd things like Grilled Turkey Balls on bread while also having hamburgers, steak and fries on the menu.

It wasn't a deli, but Lynn wasn't going to tell Kathy that. The name was misleading. She would have gotten more business if people knew she sold hamburgers and steak.

Not that Kathy was in need of business. She had run the place successfully since buying it years ago, just after the sale of her parents' home. All her Yelp reviews were five stars with positive comments about her staff and food. Lynn had left one herself.

I'd love to come out there, Lynn tapped into her phone. *I've heard a lot of good things. I'd like to try some of the food you serve outside of catering.*

She hit send and dropped the phone back into her bag. She could already tell that it would be a productive week. Once she was back in her office, she went to the window and looked out at the tennis courts and one of the outdoor pools, which were right underneath her window.

Everything was going well in her life. The only thing missing was a man. Lynn had spent so much time working and concentrating on the resort business since their Uncle Nathan left it to them in his will, she hadn't pursued any kind of relationship.

She would be twenty-six in three months. It was time to find a man.

She giggled. She didn't really want a relationship. Like her sisters, she expected she would fall into a relationship without much effort and end up married with children.

Chapter 2

Lynn slowed the car down as soon when she saw the distinct brown and red Brownstone Deli sign. It was shaped like an arch and gave off an antique look. She couldn't believe how many times she must have passed right by, even after she'd hired them for catering at the resort events.

It wasn't surprising. She was a bit flighty and hadn't done much socializing out of the Badlands, which was owned by Sue's husband, Mike. And when she went to the Badlands, she stayed with Mari, Sue, Mike, or Becky, the bartender. She'd been hit on but never had more than a good laugh with the men she encountered. She'd felt no spark with anyone.

She parked in the slanted spaces provided in front of the building and got out of her green Dodge Charger. The one thing she'd gotten from her father was a love of muscle cars. The Charger could reach sixty in three seconds flat. Not that she needed it to.

She looked at the front of the restaurant, immediately falling in love with the atmosphere. She hadn't realized Kathy had such a beautiful creation already up and running.

There were tables set outside on a red slate floor, each one sporting an umbrella of different colors. The chairs matched the tables and looked perfect for the style Kathy had created; one of comfortable peace. That was Lynn's first impression.

Trees were planted or potted in strategic places around the deck, giving the place an outdoor look that rivaled its neighbors well.

How nice, she thought as she walked through the black iron arch, which was also covered with pretty vines and flowers.

A black chalkboard sat beside the entrance door, displaying the daily special: *Soup and salad with a turkey, bacon, and ham sandwich and fries. Only $7.99.* Lynn was impressed with the price.

She went inside the deli and was immediately met by a

breeze of cool air. The scents that filled her nose had her stomach immediately grumbling.

She giggled. She hadn't had breakfast but, even if she had, she would still have been caught by those delicious smells. A bell tinkled when a door was pushed open from the kitchen area. Kathy came out and spotted Lynn. A smile covered her face, and she waved Lynn over so she wouldn't have to call through the whole restaurant.

There were half a dozen customers in the deli. Somewhere in the back, Lynn could hear the sound of a telephone ringing incessantly. She approached Kathy while holding out her hand.

"I'm sorry. I guess I'm a little early. I thought you said you close at two for lunch."

Kathy laughed softly. "Oh no, dear, I said sometimes I take it at two but, if I get busy, I might run late. But it's perfectly fine. I wanted to talk some more with you about this idea you have."

Lynn nodded, following the woman down a small hall past the restrooms.

"Let's go in my office. I want you to meet my brother. He's got a lot to do with the success of our company."

In the small office, Lynn settled into a comfortable, red cushioned chair and looked around her. "You have a nice office. Mine's pretty plain, I gotta say."

Kathy had circled the desk and was seated at it, smiling widely at Lynn. "It's not because I'm a good organizer, necessarily," she quipped. "I have OCD so bad, it's coming out my pores. Listen, I've been thinking about what you've said, and I'm not sure I want to give up my store."

Lynn was somewhat relieved to hear that. It wasn't until seeing the deli that she realized what Kathy would have to give up. She understood now why the woman had asked for a day to give her proposal some deep thought, especially with a place that looked so beautiful.

She nodded as Kathy reached forward and shifted some

papers on her desk, fishing out the packet Lynn had given to her. Before she could go further, Lynn spoke up.

"I didn't know your place was so beautiful. I don't think you should give it up either. Maybe a second branch at the resort?"

Kathy froze, her arm still stretched out over the desk. Her eyes widened as she stared at Lynn.

"A second branch? Oh, Lynn, I don't have the money for that."

Lynn tilted her head to the side, giving the woman a quizzical look. "What would you be paying for? I'm willing to invest the money. It will come back to the resort anyway. And it will line your pockets, too. And the best thing about it is that you can go work in either place."

Kathy's eyes drifted around the room as she thought about it. "I'd have to hire a new staff."

Lynn leaned forward, clasping her hands together in front of her with her elbows on the arm rests. "I can provide a list for you. I keep track of everyone in Queen Anne in need of a job in case we have something open."

Kathy's eyebrows shot up, and she gazed at Lynn. "How in the world do you do that?"

Lynn smiled. "Inside sources." In truth, it was Mike, Sue's husband, who kept track of people who needed jobs in Queen Anne. He knew when someone moved to the little city and knew everyone in town, at least by sight. His bar and lounge was very popular among locals and tourists.

"I could use that list, thank you."

Lynn nodded. She sat back, picking up her case from the floor and setting it on her lap. She folded the lid back and took out a notebook. She flipped it open, clicked a pen and set the tip on the paper while looking up at Kathy. "How many people will you need?"

Kathy's face was thoughtful. "I'd say at least six. Maybe eight. After I run the numbers, I'll know better."

Lynn wrote down the number and made a few notes underneath.

"What will they need to know?"

"I can always put an ad in the paper and on the internet. There might be people from outside Queen Anne who would like the job."

"If you don't mind," Lynn replied, looking up at Kathy again. "I'd like to keep it to local workers unless there aren't enough skilled or qualified people to do the job."

Kathy nodded, a pleasant look on her face. "Me, too. I'm glad you think like I do. I'm hoping we can get people from here instead. It's basically just a server job, since me and my crew will be preparing the food here, and my brother will be in charge of the servers when an event is held."

It was Kathy's second mention of her brother. Lynn hadn't know she had a brother, or that he was involved in the business. She was mildly surprised and lifted her eyebrows slightly.

"I never knew you had a brother."

Kathy chuckled. "He stays by himself a lot. Kind of a loner. He's had some things happen to him that... well, it's no one's business, you know. I don't want to put his business out there to strangers..." She reached out and tapped the desk in front of Lynn. "Not that you're a stranger, Lynn. Don't take that the wrong way. He's just a sensitive guy. Of course, if you said that in front of him, it might upset him."

Lynn could hear the concern and love Kathy had for her brother in her voice. She couldn't help wondering what the man had gone through that had made him react by withdrawing from everyone.

"I look forward to meeting him," she said. "I'm sure he's not as bad as you think. You are his sister, after all. We judge our siblings a little harsher than we do others."

Kathy was quick to speak. "Oh, I don't judge him harshly. I love him a lot. He just makes a lot of poor decisions. Or, he did when he was younger."

"How old is he, if you don't mind me asking?"

"He's your age; twenty-five. I'm seven years older than he is. I've been taking care of him for a long time now, since the death of our parents when we were kids."

"To have gone through losing your parents when you were kids; that's enough trauma to withdraw from society."

Kathy tilted her head to the side, shaking it gently. "I know, isn't it? He was very close to my dad. Dad was always there to protect him and take care of him. I think he never really got a chance to think for himself. I'm afraid I'm at fault for that, too. I wanted to make his life easier after mom and dad died. I kind of coddled him. He was so young and so broken by it."

Lynn's first thought, watching her new friend's face change from casual business talk to emotional hardship, was that Kathy was too strong for her own good. She had obviously pushed through the death of her parents, so that her brother wouldn't feel the full impact of what happened.

She didn't press for more information about the loss. It wasn't her business, and she had only met Kathy for the first time the day before. If the woman wanted to give her more, she would do it on her own. She wasn't the type to pry.

To her, it said a lot about Kathy's character. She would be a benefit to the resort business.

"I'm happy the two of you are coming on board," she said when it was obvious Kathy didn't want to continue. Lynn could see it on her face and decided to change the subject. "I think this is going to be a really good business relationship."

"I think so, too."

"And I really am looking forward to meeting your brother. Everyone has issues left over from trauma they've suffered. I don't judge people that way."

Kathy nodded, a relaxed look returning to her face. "I can see that. Plus, I did my research on you and your sisters." Her voice took on a teasing tone. "I've heard nothing but good things about you all."

"That's very nice to hear." Lynn's smile matched the woman across from her. Compliments from strangers always lifted Lynn's spirits.

Kathy stood up, putting both palms down flat on the desk and looking directly at Lynn. "Now, I know you've got to be hungry. You have to try some of our food. I can take you through the kitchen and have something special prepared, or you can go out and sit at the tables and be a regular customer. It's up to you."

Lynn stood as well, tucking the notepad back into her case. "I think I'll do both. I want to order from the menu, but I think it's important that I see how your kitchen is set up and check on some of those details, too. We'll be setting up something similar or exactly the same at the resort, depending on what you choose to do."

Kathy went to the door and pulled it open, holding it for Lynn to go through first. Lynn walked out into the fresh, delicious smell of food cooking and remembered how hungry she was.

Chapter 3

Lynn decided to sit on the deck outside to eat. With a menu in one hand, a sweet tea on the table, and Kathy across from her, she could not have felt more welcome and comfortable. There was something about Kathy's style that impressed her.

She ordered the New York Strip with a baked potato and corn on the cob.

"You realize this isn't delicatessen food, right?" Lynn asked as she handed the menu to the server, who bowed, smiled and left the table.

Kathy chuckled. "Yeah, I started the place with deli foods—sandwiches, chips, pickles, that sort of thing—but... well, to be honest, my brother is an avid meat eater. He can barely live without having a steak or two a week."

"I'm like that, too!" she exclaimed, laughing as she picked up her sweet tea and emptied a third of the glass. When she lowered the glass, Kathy was giving her a surprised look. Lynn had to ask, "What?"

"I wouldn't have guessed you would be a meat eater from the way you dress."

Lynn looked down at herself. She typically wore tight fitting clothes like tank tops and leggings with a long, lightly woven fabric sweater with three-quarter sleeves. She'd been called a hippy many times and was often asked if she was a dancer. She wasn't much of a dancer. She'd taken ballet and tap as a little girl, but she didn't think that qualified her as a dancer in any shape or form.

"You think I look like a vegetarian?" she asked, amused.

Kathy grinned. "Only because you're so slender, and you look healthy and all that."

Lynn laughed. "You think being a meat eater doesn't make you healthy?"

Kathy shook her head, chuckling. "Please don't think that.

It is almost offensive to think I would push a vegetarian lifestyle. I'm no hypocrite. I love steak and beef and even hot dogs."

The two women looked at each other and said the same thing in chorus. "Not meat."

They both roared with laughter, Lynn throwing her head back. Her voice echoed up through the trees. When her laughter died down, she gazed up at the clear sky. The clouds from the past few days had passed, not that they'd produced any moisture.

It was often hot and muggy in Georgia, but Queen Anne was so close to the coast, they were more likely to feel the cool breeze of the ocean air than those who were deeper in state.

"It's so beautiful out here," Lynn mumbled, dropping her eyes to Kathy's face. She wasn't a young-looking thirty-two. Whatever she'd been through made her look closer to forty than thirty.

"I know." Kathy agreed with a nod.

"But I don't just mean here in Queen Anne," Lynn sat forward, gazing at the friendly woman across from her. Kathy's brown eyes sparkled in the sunlight when she shifted her position and left the shade of the umbrella for a few brief seconds. "I mean your little place here. You've got great style, Kathy. I'm really impressed. I'd really like you to do this same kind of thing at our resort."

Kathy tilted her head to the side, looking confused. She crossed her legs and leaned forward with her arms folded in front of her. "It looks like this because it's a restaurant, though. The kitchen can look the same as the one we went through, but I didn't think I was putting a restaurant there, too. I don't have the money for that, that's for sure. And I can only imagine… wow, we'd need a lot more people."

"I think a restaurant in our food court would be a really good idea, Kathy. But I think we'll have to make it more of a steak restaurant, though. I'd love to invest in it."

Kathy looked blown away by the thought of a second restaurant.

"You might also want to consider franchising. I think you can find someone who would like to buy into the company."

Kathy sat back, resting her elbows on the chair's arm rests. She had a dazed look on her face.

"Wow. I can't imagine. I can't think of that right now. It's blowing my mind."

Lynn chuckled.

"Kathy," a male voice said from behind Lynn.

They both looked up, and Kathy pushed her chair back, as a smile crossed her face. "Justin! Come here. You've got to—"

"Kathy, I need to speak to you," Justin said, stepping up to the table. He looked down at Lynn. She looked up at him. Their eyes met.

Lynn tried not to let her shock show on her face. She tried not to stare, but she was sure he had caught her. She pulled her eyes away from him, as her cheeks flushed with embarrassment.

Justin and Kathy Brownstone may have been siblings, but they looked completely opposite. Kathy had long brown hair that fell softly over her shoulders and big brown eyes. She was shorter than Lynn, which had to make her about five feet tall. Justin wasn't exceedingly tall. He was taller than either of them, probably nearly six feet tall but not quite there. His hair was shockingly blond, and his light blue eyes were filled with emotion as he gazed at his sister. He looked troubled by something.

"What is it?" Kathy didn't call Justin out on interrupting her and neither of them introduced him to Lynn. She lifted her hands and placed them on Justin's arms. "You look upset. Sit. Talk to me."

Justin hesitated before going around Kathy and sitting in the chair nearest her at the round table. "I think someone is stealing from us."

Kathy's face paled. Her eyes flicked to Lynn. "Oh, that's not possible. How can that happen? What do you think was taken?"

Lynn could tell Kathy thought, if they were being stolen from, it would look bad for her business. Seeing her look, Lynn shook her head reassuringly.

"The margarita mix is at least a dozen bottles short," Justin continued, crossing his arms in front of his chest. "And there are some other bottles we're missing, too. But random items like that bottle of grenadine we had mysteriously disappear. We found out that Josh dropped it and didn't think to tell anyone."

"So, you think the dozen bottles were actually stolen and something happened to the others?"

Justin nodded. "Yeah. That's what I think."

Kathy took her cell phone from her back pocket and pressed the screen. Lynn and Justin glanced at each other while his sister dialed and then held the phone to her ear.

"Lacey..." Kathy said when the line was picked up. "Justin says we're missing a dozen bottles of margarita mix. Do you... Oh?" She stopped and listened. "Okay... yeah, I'll tell him. Thanks for telling me... Okay. Thanks. Okay. Yeah."

She finally pressed the end button on her phone and looked at Justin. "Lacey says there were rodent droppings in the box which the mix came in, so she sent them back for fresh replacements."

Lynn cringed and glanced at Justin to see his upper lip curl.

"That's gross," he said, still holding his arms crossed in front of himself. He looked less upset to Lynn but still, the unease on his face was prominent. He looked directly at Lynn. "Who's this fine lady?"

Lynn chuckled. "Careful, I'm the same age as you."

Justin gave her an amused look. "I didn't say you looked old."

"You called me a lady," Lynn responded, laughing. "We haven't officially met, yet you called me a lady. If you knew me, you might not call me that."

Justin ran his eyes up and down her entire body. He gave her a skeptical look. "I called you a lady because it's a term of respect. Anyone who looks at you can tell you are a lady of class."

A slip of delight passed through Lynn. She looked directly at Justin, taking in the look in his blue eyes. He looked back at his sister, his eyes sparkling in the sun. Lynn continued to look at him, studying his profile. His blond hair wasn't curly or long like his sister's brown hair. He had it cut short on the sides and longer on top, coming down his forehead in a sweep. He was of average weight, not muscular but not skinny by any means.

Lynn could see he had a bit of a belly going on. After he'd found out where the bottles had gone, he had relaxed even more over the last few minutes. Lynn admired every degree of his relaxed state.

"That was nice, Justin," Kathy said, smiling at her brother. She gave Lynn a friendly look.

"It was," Lynn nodded. "Thank you, Justin. My name is Lynn Wright. We're just talking about opening a new restaurant at the resort. And take the catering up there, too. New kitchen, new staff, new restaurant completely. How does that sound to you?"

Justin's eyebrows shot up, and his eyes returned to meet hers. "Sounds like a lot of work to me."

The women laughed. He moved his eyes between the two of them. "What? I'm just telling the truth here."

This made both Kathy and Lynn laugh more. Lynn realized as she was laughing that she was highly attracted to Justin and would have to be careful with her words and actions. Suddenly, she was self-conscious. Her mind went to thoughts of whether or not he noticed her; whether he thought she was pretty, smart, funny… He would only form an opinion of her looks so far since they'd barely even spoken.

Clearing her throat and trying to gather her thoughts, Lynn said, "I'd be glad to have the two of you up to the resort for something other than business. Have you gone swimming there at all? Used the tennis courts? Eaten at the restaurants in the food

417

court? Anything?"

Both shook their heads. Lynn was a little distraught that there was anyone in Queen Anne who hadn't had the privilege of visiting the resort. It was the pulse behind the little community, and everyone knew it. It drew customers to the stores and eateries and put money into everyone's pockets. Just because the Wright sisters' coffers were full already didn't mean there wasn't more to be made.

"That's so disappointing. I'm going to have to change that."

"You should have a community day," he said softly. Lynn's body lit up with chills. She hid it as best she could, as his deep and smooth tone continued, "Open the resort and have discounts and stuff like that for people who can't afford the high prices."

Lynn's heart warmed over. It was such a compassionate idea. She grinned widely. "I'd like that, Justin. I'll bring it up to my sisters. We're going to implement that. Would you like to be involved in the process?"

"Me?" Justin asked, one eyebrow raised and motioning to himself with a finger at his chest.

"Yeah." She nodded. "Kathy tells me you manage her serving department of the restaurant here."

"And the catering," Kathy interjected. "He's in charge of all the servers throughout the company."

Lynn nodded, having already understood that. She moved her eyes back to Justin's handsome face.

She waited patiently for Justin's answer and smiled when he said in an incredulous voice, "Yeah. That...that sounds good. I'd like that."

Chapter 4

Lynn left the Brownstone Deli feeling happier than she had in years. Justin stayed with the two women through the rest of lunch. The food Lynn ordered was delicious. She'd been served extra rolls and had her tea refilled three times. She felt as full as she could ever be.

As she walked to her car, she thought that she might have eaten too much. She didn't want a stomach ache. She planned to go for a walk around the court when she returned to the resort.

She got in her car, feeling almost like she was walking on a cloud. She replayed the lunch, hearing Justin's deep, smooth voice in her mind. Butterflies fluttered in her stomach. She hadn't felt like this since she crushed on a boy as a teenager in high school.

She giggled. At twenty-five-years-old, she was crushing on a boy again. The thought sent her into giggles that made her grip the steering wheel and try to keep the car in between the lines.

The drive back was peaceful, and the scenery around her was beautiful. She couldn't wait to get back and tell her sisters what had happened.

At the end of the lunch, Kathy had insisted they all take a picture together on her cell phone. At a stop light, Lynn snatched her cell phone from her purse and texted Kathy quickly, requesting a copy of the picture.

She heard her phone ding several times before she made it to the parking lot of the resort. She was anxious to see what Kathy was saying, but she refused to text and drive.

She sat in the car while reading the texts. After the photo, Kathy sent one very long message that came through in four parts. Some of it was about the restaurant at the resort, asking for time to come up with details about its inclusion in their new project together. The last two messages were about Justin.

Lynn's heart thumped hard in her chest when she read it.

I could see you like Justin. I want you to know I'm not

419

against something growing between you two, but I feel I should warn you. He was hurt by the only woman he cared about when he was nineteen. I haven't seen him with a woman since. He's not into men, so don't think that. He's just very sensitive and is hurt easily. I want you to know so, if he rejects you or doesn't notice your attraction, it isn't your fault. I love him, but he's pretty broken inside. I've never been able to heal him. Maybe you can. It would be nice to see him smile and be happy again.

Lynn was sympathetic to Justin's pain. Everyone their age had gone through some kind of breakup unless they were completely out of the dating scene as teenagers. She didn't know anyone that had dated no one.

She also felt Justin wasn't old enough to be set in his ways. His pain could be healed.

If enough love was shown to them, that kind of pain could be healed regardless of age.

With a sense of determination, Lynn stepped out of the car, and then scrolled up to see the picture of the three of them outside the restaurant. Justin's smile was closed-mouthed but pleasant. He was leaning his head slightly in her direction. She was standing in the middle. She remembered feeling his hand lightly touch her back. Her skin tingled at the memory.

It's the first time he touched me, she thought. *Hopefully, it won't be the last.*

Lynn walked up the steps, a little worried about herself. She had just met him. She had to be cautious that she didn't make a fool of herself by giving her heart to the first man who really sparked her flame.

She pulled open the door to the business building. Her eyes were still on her phone, specifically on his face.

"Miss Lynn," A voice made her eyes dart up. She was staring into the eyes of the security guard, John, who was about to leave. She'd almost run into him.

"I'm so sorry. I wasn't paying any attention at all, was I?"

"It's okay, Lynn. I can see you're a little preoccupied. You ladies stay busy, don't you?"

Lynn smiled. "We do. Everything okay today?"

"Everything is fine here. In fact, I'm not sure I feel comfortable taking your money for this job when I never do anything but hang around and look at people. I mean, I spend some time on my phone, you know; social media, looking at You Tube, and all that. You pay me for that. You realize that, don't you?"

Lynn laughed. "You're telling on yourself. Don't do that. You might not keep a job in the future."

John chuckled. "Are you kidding? Like I'm ever going to leave this job. But you're right. If I want to keep getting paid to do nothing, I should just keep my mouth shut, huh?"

"I think that would be best."

John's expression turned very serious. He gazed intently at her, as his voice dropped lower, "We never had this conversation."

She pressed her lips together to keep her laughter inside, then responded in a similar low voice, "We never had this conversation."

He nodded without smiling and passed her by, mumbling just loud enough for her to hear, "I didn't know the Jedi mind trick was real. Cool."

Lynn spun around to watch him leave and caught his eye when he glanced down at her. His face lit up with amusement.

She turned away from him, laughing as she walked down the hall toward her office. It was turning out to be such a good day.

When she got to her office door, she passed it by but glanced in through the window at her desk. The same papers were scattered over the top. Nothing looked changed. It never did. No one ever went in her office except her sisters, and they were allowed.

She went to the next office and looked in. It was Sue's. She wasn't there. That wasn't surprising. Since her marriage the year before, Sue was only at the resort when she needed to be. She'd trained to be a bartender at her husband's bar and found she had a real knack for splashing out cocktails. She'd also realized she had a passion for it and had spent a lot more time there than at the resort for months.

Lynn and Mari never discussed Sue pulling away from the resort. They were handling things well and had an incredible crew of over three hundred employees, with managers of each department who had hiring and firing capabilities.

Queen Anne was small for a modern city. Its citizens were all friendly and carefree. There was so little crime, there were only four police patrol cars and the courts and municipal building made up almost all of the government buildings. They were three stories high—the largest buildings in the city—and located in the downtown square. They were the buildings that looked out of place rather than the older, antique-looking buildings, shops and homes.

Regardless of the low crime rate, Mari had insisted on precautions at the resort. Her point was that there would be so many wealthy clients and guests coming through, they deserved to know their safety was important.

Uncle Nathan had thought so, too, but he only hired one security guard for the entire resort. For a place that covered such a vast space on the coast, the guests deserved more than that. She'd hired on an entire crew, so that there were casual and uniformed guards in every part of the resort. The main hotel was huge. Mari put three guards in that building to make everyone feel more comfortable and safer.

The next office was Mari's. She was seated at the desk pouring over papers spread out in front of her. She was holding her forehead with one hand, her eyes moving from one side to the other.

Lynn lifted her fist and knocked lightly on the glass. Mari waved her sister in. Lynn entered and immediately asked, "Hey, Mari. You look like you're really busy. You have time for a quick chat?"

Mari nodded, pushing her papers away from her and

dropping the pen in her hand on the desk top. She reached to the side and tapped a button on her computer, changing the screen from one Excel file to another.

"Feel free. I could use a break. This is nerve wracking."

Lynn looked at the papers, which had a lot of numbers in a row. She was glad she didn't have to do that kind of work. She'd rather talk to people any day of the week than run numbers. That was usually Sue's job.

"You gotta take a break sometimes."

Mari looked at her. "You're my break. So, speak. You've got..." She glanced at the computer screen in the lower right corner. "14 minutes left."

"I'm on a time limit? I better hurry, then."

Her sister's humorless grin let her know she was only kidding.

"I think I've found someone." Lynn's voice came out nervous, which surprised her.

Mari's confusion almost made her laugh.

"You've found someone." Her voice was flat and blunt, and her expression was neutral. "For what?"

Lynn giggled. "A man. A man I'm interested in."

Mari's eyebrows shot up. "Say what? When did this happen?"

Lynn's heart hammered in her chest, seeing Justin's handsome face in her mind. "I just met him today. Here. This is his picture."

Lynn turned her phone around and showed Mari the picture from that afternoon.

Mari pulled her glasses down from the top of her head, where she'd propped them when Lynn came in the room. She peered at the picture, then sat back and looked at her sister.

"He looks really young, Lynn. You better be careful."

423

Lynn turned the phone back to herself to look at the picture. She hadn't noticed that Justin looked about nineteen or twenty years old.

"He's not young. He's my age."

"No, he's not," Mari said. "No way. He's twenty five?"

"He is."

"Where did you meet him?"

Lynn sat forward with her phone in her hand. She pointed at Kathy, showing her to Mari. "That's Kathy Brownstone. She's the owner of Brownstone Catering. She runs a fake deli in Queen Anne, too."

Lynn enjoyed Mari's look of confusion. "A fake deli?"

"Yeah," Lynn laughed. "She sells steak and burgers, too."

Mari joined her in laughter. "That's not allowed at a deli."

"I know, right?"

The two sisters laughed for a few minutes.

"So, he's her brother," Mari said when their joviality died down.

"Yeah."

"Is he involved in this deal, too?"

"Apparently he is in charge of all the servers for both the catering and the deli." Lynn used air quotes when she said the word deli. "He's a real quiet guy, totally laid back. I think he's cute."

"He's the one, huh? You're going to join us in married land?"

Lynn widened her eyes. "Whoa. I met him today. I'm not marrying him tomorrow. Slow down."

Both women laughed again.

Chapter 5

Justin lifted a pan and inspected it for spots. It had just come out of the huge washing machine for all the pots and pans. It wasn't usually his job, but he felt the need to do something, to get moving, and he had nothing to do.

Sitting in the dining room after Lynn left, he'd discovered how incredibly bored he was. The woman was vibrant and full of energy, making him feel refreshed. Suddenly, he didn't want to just sit around and mope. He wanted to get his hands into something.

"Mr. Brownstone?" He heard behind him. He looked over his shoulder at the kitchen manager, Chris. "Is everything okay?"

He could see the confusion on Chris's face and felt like a fool. He put the pan back down.

"Yeah. Looks like the washer is doing its job."

Chris's eyes moved to the washer and then back to him, his confusion unsatisfied. "Yeah. We haven't reported something was wrong. Did someone say it was broken?"

"No. I'm looking for Noah. He around?"

A look of understanding covered Chris's face. "Oh. Yeah. He's in the back in prep. We didn't have much for him to do today. I told him to go through the prep station because someone called in today."

Justin nodded. "Okay, thanks."

He moved away quickly, feeling like an idiot for picking up the pan like he knew anything about the kitchen work. He hurried to the door of the prep room and pushed the swinging door open, going through into a room filled with busy workers.

The bustle caught him off guard. The only time he went to the prep room, it was usually empty when he and the servers were getting all the food to load on the trucks and take to events.

Although he'd been to the resort for events in the past, he'd never met any of the Wright sisters. Now, he regretted his inattentiveness. Lynn wasn't just a beautiful woman; she was sharp as a tack. It was a little intimidating, but he was thinking about her more than any other woman he'd met. Especially in business dealings.

Noah Campbell was his best friend, the only person in Queen Anne with whom he got along well. It wasn't that he wasn't friendly. He just wasn't a social person. When he was in with a crowd, he could handle himself, but he didn't actively seek out that kind of atmosphere.

He spotted Noah at the salad counter, chopping up lettuce heads with a huge knife. His friend lifted the knife up in the air and brought it down on the head with great force, as if he was chopping up a body.

Justin chuckled, amused that was the first thing that came to his mind. He wasn't a violent man in any way. He wanted the least amount of drama in his life he could possibly have.

"Noah!" he yelled out over the crowd of talking people. His voice brought an immediate silence to the room that lasted just long enough for everyone to turn to him and recognize who he was. The voices rose again, as they all resumed their work. Except Noah.

He was waving the knife in the air as Justin approached. "Hey buddy. How you doing today?"

Justin shrugged. "Kinda bored. You got time to take a break?"

Noah set the knife down on the cutting board, pulled on a second glove over his cutting glove, and swept the lettuce into a large bowl.

"Yeah, let me clear this off. I can take a break if the boss lets me." He grinned at Justin. "And you're the boss, so I guess you're good with it."

"I'm good with it, yeah. Come on, hurry up. Who taught you how to prep? A sloth?" Justin teased, looking at his best friend with a half-grin.

426

Noah reacted by slapping a top on the bowl and scurrying to the refrigerator. He yanked the door open, tossed the bowl on top of a matching one and slammed the door shut.

"Hey!" one of the other staff members called out. "Watch out. The boss will see you, and you'll get in trouble.

Tittering laughter went through the room, as Justin grinned at them. He and Noah walked out together, passing through the front kitchen. Justin led Noah to the deck to sit in the same place he'd been with Lynn and his sister.

The sun was dipping down in the West when they stepped outside. The sight of the beautiful woman sitting with his sister popped into Justin's mind. He shook the memory away. It was too soon to be feel anything. He just met her.

"Hey, Becks!" Noah called over his shoulder to the server setting napkin with folded utensils on each of the six tables on the deck. "I'm dyin' of thirst. How about a beer?"

He glanced at Justin. "You want a beer? You mind if I have one? I'm on the clock, but I'm not really supposed to be here today. I was just bored."

"Really?" Justin raised one eyebrow. "I came to get you because I was bored. Go clock out. Take the rest of the day off. We'll go up to Emerald Resort and mess around."

Noah stared at him. "Mess around? At Emerald Resort? Have you lost your mind?"

Justin shook his head. "I haven't lost my mind. Nah, I'm not serious. But yeah, go clock out. We'll hang out today."

Noah looked skeptical. "I kind of need the money. I'm getting time-and-a-half today, you know."

Justin reached into his pocket and pulled out his wallet. He took out a fifty and handed it to Noah. "Will this cover the next couple hours? You can work tonight, if you want, too. I shouldn't have to pay for my friends to hang out with me."

"Friend," he said. "I'm pretty sure I'm you're only friend."

"Don't rub it in, Noah. Come on. Hang out with me."

Noah shook his head, pushing Justin's hand away. "I'm not takin' your money. Put it away. I'll go clock out. I don't need the money that bad. I was just messing with you."

Justin held in his anxiety, as he sat down and waited for Noah to come back. A minute or so after Noah went back inside, Becky brought two beers to the table. She knew what kind he liked, so he picked it up and tilted the bottle in her direction. "Thanks, Becks."

"You're welcome, Justin. You doing okay today? You look a little tired."

"Do I? That sucks. I'm sorry."

Becky furrowed her brows and let out a sharp laugh. "Don't apologize. Just get more sleep. We're all concerned about you. When you go without sleep for a while, we can tell."

An uncomfortable surprise drifted through Justin. He suddenly felt like everyone was looking at him, judging him by his appearance each and every day.

"I hope you guys don't think that about me all the time," he mumbled.

Becky gave him a sympathetic look. It was a look he hated. But he knew it was coming from a good place, so he said nothing.

"Of course not. The reason we get worried…" She leaned down close to murmur into his ear. "The reason is because you're usually so good-looking. When you look tired or sick, we notice."

A slice of resentment split through Justin. He had never considered himself to be good-looking, though he had his days. He'd been complimented on his smile many times, but it was usually followed by *you should do it more often.*

Maybe he didn't feel like smiling. Did they ever think of that?

He gave Becky a smile that didn't reach his eyes but was as genuine as he could muster.

"Thanks, Becks. I appreciate the compliment."

"You should come down to Badlands sometime, Justin," she suggested. "Hang out with the rest of us rats. You and Noah."

Justin nodded. "Sounds like fun. I met the sister of the wife of the owner today."

Becky chuckled. "Mari or Lynn?"

Justin stared at her in surprise. "Lynn?" he said in a questioning tone. She laughed again.

"Do you even know?"

"It was Lynn." He nodded, feeling a little foolish. "I just didn't know they were well known."

"They are if you go to Badlands. Ever since Sue and Mike got married last year, the sisters are there frequently. Lynn more than Mari. I'm surprised you haven't been there. You've been here for years, and you like beer."

"I like beer," Justin confirmed. "Not bars."

"It's one of the best I've ever been in. Never any drama, no hook ups, no loud, crazy people. I like it."

"I'll check it out sometime."

If Lynn was there often, he would definitely show up.

Noah returned and sat down at the table, grabbing his beer and tipping it up, drinking the entire thing. He slammed it back down on the table, grinning at his friends. "Well, that hit the spot! Didn't know how much I wanted that until I saw it. Thanks for telling me to clock out, man. You're a great boss!"

The three of them laughed.

"You guys want something to eat?" Becky asked. "I know you don't need a menu."

Justin nodded, glancing at Noah. "I'm hungry. You hungry? Free food. Don't pass it up."

"Free?" Noah asked. "I don't have to pay my half? Fifty percent discount is all we get, you know."

"Not when the boss is buying. Shut up and take my free food."

Noah laughed deep in his throat and moved his eyes to Becky. "I'll take a Philly Cheesesteak, no mushrooms, extra green peppers, and light on the onions."

Justin raised his eyebrows. "Picky much?"

Noah shook his head. "Nah. Allergic to mushrooms and too many onions will make my breath smell bad. I don't want Anna getting mad and not kissing me. That would be the worst!"

Justin smiled up at Becky when she gave Noah a serious look and said, "You do need to make sure of that, Noah. You couldn't live a day without a kiss from your woman."

"You're only saying that because she's your sister," Noah responded.

"You're right," Becky said, grabbing the empty bottle from in front of him. "I'll get you another and put that order in." She turned to leave.

"You're not gonna take my order, too? Special privileges for the guy dating your sister, huh?"

Justin gave her a wide-eyed look, crossing his arms in front of his chest when he spoke.

"Oh, Cam! I'm so sorry! Of course, what would you like?" Becky asked, using a shortened version of Cameron, his middle name.

"I'll have the same but put it all on there. And heavy meat for us both. And bring some chips and some rolls, too."

"You got it, boss." She gave him a smile and wink as she turned away.

Once she'd gone inside, Justin looked back to see Noah grinning at him.

"What?" he asked, unfolding his arms and picking up his beer bottle for a drink.

"I think she likes you. How cool would it be if we were

430

dating sisters. Think about it. Double dates and all that? Would be cool, wouldn't it?"

Justin chuckled. "It would be. But Becky doesn't like me like that."

"I think she does. Did you see that wink?"

Justin shook his head. "Doesn't matter. I've got someone else in mind."

The look of shock that covered Noah's face was amusing. Justin pushed his tongue into his cheek and briefly lifted his eyebrows. "What do you think of that?"

Noah swallowed visibly and shook his head. "I think I came close to fainting. Haven't ever seen you dating or interested in anyone. Who is it? Tell me, tell me. I gotta know."

A sense of nervous anxiety flooded Justin, but he did his best to push it away. "One of the Wright sisters."

Noah resumed his shocked look. "There's only one that isn't married. I hope it's not one of the married ones. Is it Lynn?"

Justin was once again taken by surprise that the Wright sisters were so well known. Everyone used their first name when they spoke of them. He nodded. "Yeah. Lynn. Met her today."

"You met her today, and you're interested in her? I don't think I've ever heard you say that before." He sat back, staring at his friend. "Congratulations, Cam. This is a day to be remembered. I'm wishing you luck. Lynn is awesome. I've met her at Badlands. She's not one of those bar babes you meet in big cities. She's a classy lady."

Justin was glad to hear Noah call her classy. It confirmed his opinion and lifted his hopes.

Chapter 6

Lynn forced herself to wait three days before she went to Brownstone Deli to catch up on progress with Kathy. She wished she had taken Justin's cell number. She had Kathy's but she wasn't about to immediately throw personal stuff into the mix. Her business with Kathy was just that… business.

She made sure to look her best when she went to the restaurant, hoping to see Justin at some point.

She got to the restaurant at the perfect time, in her opinion. First, she found a parking spot directly in front of the deli and saw Justin sitting at a table on the deck. He had his feet up on the chair opposite him, and his face was buried in his phone. He looked completely engrossed and bored at the same time.

Her heart did a little flutter, as she stepped through the gate, but her eyes remained on him. He didn't look up, even at the sound of the gate's movement. She stood there for a moment, debating whether she should go over and talk to him. She couldn't help thinking how good he looked. The first thing she noticed about men was their eyes. The second thing was their hands. She'd taken some time at their first meeting to look at his eyes. This time, she looked down to study his hands.

To her, it looked like Justin hadn't done a lot of work with them. He didn't look like a construction worker anyway. His hands gave away that he was part owner of this business.

When Justin still didn't look up, she made a quick decision and crossed the deck to stand next to him. As she approached, she said, "Hello."

He glanced up at her. At first, his face showed disinterest, as if a stranger had approached him with an odd question. When he saw it was her, he smiled. Lynn's heart practically thumped out of her chest. It was a welcoming smile, unlike the one he'd given her the first day he met her.

"Lynn!" He pulled his legs off the chair and shot to his feet, making the seat tilt back and almost fall to the ground. He twisted

432

and snatched it with one hand, never taking his eyes from Lynn. She was impressed. Her cheeks were starting to hurt from smiling the way she was, so she pulled her lips together and pursed them.

"It's good to see you again, Justin," she replied. "Mind if I sit for a minute?"

"Not at all." He moved around the table and pulled the chair out for her. He was a gentleman. The act took her by surprise and made her feel warm inside. "Haven't seen you for a while. Did you come to talk to Kathy?"

"I sure did." She sat down, placing her bag on her lap and folding her hands around it. "We have a few more things to talk over, and I wanted to see her progress on hiring new employees for the resort."

"Sounds good," he said, as he sat back down. He was almost immediately back up on his feet. "Can I get you a drink? What can I get for you?"

Lynn shook her head. "I can't stay long. I have to talk to Kathy and then get back to the resort. I've got a lot of work to do. But it's good to see you."

"You sure?"

"Yes, thanks."

Justin sat back down, his eyes on hers. "So how have you been?" he asked. "It's been a couple days."

"I've been good." Lynn was enjoying the small talk, happy that he was being so friendly to her. "Since proposing this idea to your sister, I've had so much planning going on, I haven't had time to do anything. Tonight, I'm going to Badlands. My sister and her husband are doing a duet. They do that all the time."

Justin nodded. "I've heard a lot of good things about that place. Especially since you talked my sister into this business venture."

Lynn's eyes widened. She could see on Justin's face she'd taken what he said the wrong way. He shook his head.

"I didn't mean you talked her into it. I meant you…brought it to her attention. You know…that it was a good idea. Good job opportunity. I mean…"

Lynn giggled when he trailed off. "It's okay, Justin. I know what you meant."

He visibly relaxed. "Good."

He said nothing more. Lynn could tell he was uncomfortable. She hated to see the uneasiness on his face and tried to think of something to say that would ease his tension. She'd already been warned about his social anxiety due to his break up.

"You want to come see them on stage? They're really good. I think Kathy might come." Sue felt foolish, mentioning that his sister might come. She hadn't even invited the woman. She just wanted Justin to feel more comfortable. The mention of his sister didn't have the effect she was hoping for.

He looked more irritated than ever. She sensed he was shutting down and desperately wanted to avoid that from happening. But she had no idea what to say or do to stop it.

"I'd really like it if you came," she said softly.

He gave her a skeptical look. "Oh yeah?"

She nodded. "Yes, I really would. I…I get lonely sometimes in there. Lots of people mingling around, drinking, talking to each other. I'm not a huge fan of bars but, with Sue playing there and being married to the owner, I kind of feel obligated, you know?"

He nodded. "I know what you mean. I don't care for bars either. That's why you haven't seen me in there. I heard you go there a lot."

Butterfly wings flashed to life in Lynn's stomach. If he'd heard anything at all about her, it was probably because he'd asked. The thought left her hopeful. She took in the soft curve of his jaw, noticing the little dimple in the middle. Without thinking, she bit her lip.

He was gazing at her when she did it. She looked away, her cheeks flushing.

"Yeah," he said in a smooth voice. She turned her eyes back, smiling wide. "I'd like to go. I guess I can handle one night in a bar. Since you asked. You know, it's not like I haven't been in bars. I traveled a lot about five years ago with a band I was in."

Lynn tilted her head and gave him a quizzical look. "You were in a band? What did you do?"

"I was the drummer. I am a drummer. But I'm not in a band. Haven't been since I was twenty-two. I miss it. It's only been three years, and I'm itching to get behind a drum kit. Don't think it's gonna happen, though."

Lynn curiosity took over. She'd dated a drummer in high school. That boy had been her favorite boyfriend through her teenage years. Not that she had a lot of boyfriends.

Her train of thought brought the color back to her cheeks. She chuckled softly, covering her mouth with her hand. His face took on a serious look. She could tell he didn't know why she was laughing.

"I'm sorry," she said, cheerfully. "I just...I dated a drummer in high school. He was a really cool guy. I loved hanging out with him."

An immediate smile burst across Justin's face. "Yeah, drummers are really cool. There's just one problem with being a drummer."

"Oh? Just one?"

They both laughed.

"Well, one of the problems. I guess I could think of one or two more. But I'm only twenty-five, and it's hard for me to hear. All that loud music."

"You said you traveled with a band?"

"Yeah, we had gigs up and down the east coast. I was in that band for about four years. Had the time of my life."

"I'm sorry, I never saw you play. Did you put out any demos?"

Justin shook his head. "Nah. It was just a playing band. We made some good money on the road. But I couldn't do it anymore. Needed more stability. Decided to quit and come back here where my sister is."

"So you've gotten to see a lot of places, then."

He nodded. "Yep. Been to New York City and down into Florida in Miami. We even played at the Outer Banks once."

Lynn was impressed. She thought it must have been a powerful urge to come home to quit a band that gave him playing gigs.

"I liked it a lot," he continued, his eyes drifting off as he remembered. She watched his face, admiring the glint in his blue eyes. "It was fun. Wish I could go back. But I won't leave again. I don't like traveling. The van was always stinky. Men." He shook his head.

Lynn laughed out loud, covering her mouth with her hands and squinting her eyes. His returned smile made her heart sing.

"Oh, my goodness," she said. "That must have been horrible."

He laughed with her. "It was. It was hell. Hell on earth. I promise you."

They both laughed a bit longer. Finally, Lynn pushed her chair back, reluctant to leave but anxious about her schedule.

"So, I'm going to see you tonight at Badlands?" she asked, stopping next to his chair.

He looked up at her for a moment before standing up. He was close to her, less than a foot away at most. She didn't back up and neither did he. She gazed up at him, hoping that the look she saw in return was what she thought she saw.

She saw a sparkle in his eyes and for a moment, she thought he might bend down and kiss her. Her heart hammered, her blood racing through her veins.

When he didn't do anything but stand there, looking at her, she nodded and turned halfway from him.

He caught her arm, and she stopped.

"I'll be there," he said, his eyes warm on hers.

Chapter 7

Justin lifted the box and put it on the dolly with the others. Noah was behind him, sorting through the other prep boxes for the charity event they were catering that night. He had his tux pressed and ready to go for the evening, hanging on a rack with the other uniforms but put to the side so it wouldn't get mixed in with the rest.

He ran through his meeting with Lynn from just an hour before; seeing her smile, hearing her laugh. Could he consider that a date? A quickie? He grunted a laugh.

He hadn't been on a date in more than six years. He'd never been asked out and wouldn't bother asking a woman out. He'd convinced himself long ago that he had no game. He didn't want to waste a woman's time.

But the way she'd looked at him…it was different from any woman he'd encountered. His sister certainly didn't look at him that way. Lynn acted like she was conversing with a celebrity who she adored.

That word—adored!

He didn't see how any woman could adore him that way. Knowing Lynn wanted to spend time with him literally scared him to death. The only thing he had to offer anyone was music and money. And he didn't want a woman who just wanted him for money. Lynn hadn't even seen him play, so music was out of the equation.

What did Lynn see in him when she didn't know him at all?

It didn't matter, he thought to himself. She was interested.

But in what?

"Man, you are really lost in thought," Noah said, coming up next to him. Justin looked over at him.

"Yeah, thinking about Lynn. Can't get her off my mind."

"Ask her out!"

438

Justin gave him a side-long glance before shaking his head. "I don't think I can."

"Oh, you can, and you will. I know you like her. Just give it a shot!"

Justin thought about it for a moment before shrugging. "Maybe I will ask her out."

Noah grinned. "I'm proud of you, man! Stepping outside your comfort zone. This could be a great adventure for you!"

Justin chuckled. "You think?"

"Hell yeah, I think! You kind of look different, too." Noah turned his head and called to the other worker helping them load the truck. "Hey, Matt. Don't Justin look different to you?"

Matt, a tall, bearded man with sleeve tattoos and a shaved head looked over at the two of them. "Huh?"

"I said, doesn't Justin look different today?" Noah slapped a thick hand on his friend's shoulder. Justin tried not to wince from the heavy touch.

Matt stared at Justin for a minute, looking him up and down. He shook his head. "I don't see a difference."

Justin made an exasperated but humorous sound, waving one hand in the air.

"Ah, what does he know. You do look different, Cam. You look happier."

Justin glanced at Matt, who just shook his head and continued what he was doing. He moved his eyes back to Noah, who was grinning from ear to ear.

"Look, just because I said I'd think about asking doesn't mean anything's going to happen between us."

Noah shook his head and laughed. "I know exactly what's going to happen."

Justin raised one eyebrow. He leaned to pick up another box. "Oh yeah? Do tell."

439

Noah continued working while he talked. "Since you've got so little experience in the dating world, Lynn is gonna take you and make you the best boyfriend ever. You can resist all you want. But that's a strong woman you're dealing with and, if she decides you're hers, I think you're gonna give in and fall in love."

His last words sent a streak of terror through Justin. Falling in love was too much for him to think about. Relationships brought unwanted drama and stress. He shook his head, thinking it might not be a good idea to ask her out, after all.

"I don't know, man. Maybe I shouldn't get into this. Lynn is really popular, I guess. Every time I talk to someone, they know her."

Noah looked confused. "You're upset because people know the woman who owns one of the biggest resorts in Georgia? Come on, Cam. Don't be ridiculous. Of course, she knows people. I can tell you, though, I've never seen her with anyone but her sisters at Badlands. Like I said, she's not a bar babe. She's a lady with class and self-respect."

"Yeah, maybe that's exactly why I shouldn't do this," Justin responded, not looking at Noah as he sorted the boxes in the truck to make the most room possible. He climbed up in the back and began to stack the boxes, Tetris-style. Justin watched him work, leaning on the side of the truck as he talked. "I mean, that woman is way out of my league, don't you think?"

"Nope," Noah said it without inflection. "You're a fantastic guy. She's gonna love you. You've got nothing to worry about."

Justin smiled up at his friend. "This is why you're my friend, Noah. You're just so darn supportive. What would I do without you?"

Noah climbed out of the van, chuckling. "You'd be all alone with just your sister to tell your problems to. You'd love that, huh?"

"That's a definite no." Justin tilted the dolly back on its wheels and placed one hand on the top box to steady it as he pushed it up the ramp and into the van. He circled around the dolly

440

and started to unpack it. When he was done, he grabbed it, tilted it back and started to push it to the ramp.

He lifted his eyes and froze when he saw Kathy and Lynn come into the large storage room. She was gazing around at the shelves of food products and the refrigerators and freezers lining one wall before taking in the other workers in the room.

His eyes dropped to Noah, who was just coming up the ramp with a box in his hands, and was telling him, "…is one of the cold platters that…"

Noah stopped talking when Justin's gaze moved back to Lynn and Kathy. Out of the corner of his eye, he saw Noah turn to see where he was looking. His heartbeat sped up and nervous anxiety slid through him, as Noah turned back with a big smile.

"Well, look at that. Your woman has come to see you."

Justin felt a little irritated. "She's not my woman."

Noah snorted. "Not yet. I'm betting that's gonna change."

Justin sighed heavily. "Out of my way, man. I gotta put this dolly back down there."

Noah stepped out of Justin's way, giving him an intense look as he murmured, "Go get her, tiger."

Justin shot him a side glance, as he pushed the dolly down the ramp. He tried not to look directly at Lynn but flipped his eyes up every few seconds to see if they were looking at him. When he saw Lynn glance in his direction, he lowered his eyes quickly and hoped his cheeks weren't flushed. He couldn't think of anything more embarrassing than being caught blushing which threatened to make him blush even more.

With his heart hammering in his chest, he turned away from the women. He heard Noah stomping down the ramp and, when his best friend raised his voice to greet them, he felt an anxious chill run through him.

"Kathy! Lynn! How great to see you both in here with us men. Refreshing. You never come down here, do you? You should more often."

"Down here?" Kathy laughed. "I don't need to. Justin takes care of all this. He doesn't need me breathing down his throat. Do you, Cam?"

Justin felt like a rat in a trap. He was being forced to confront the situation whether he liked it or not. He grabbed a box and looked over at the women, lifting his chin. "Yeah, I can handle this place. As long as my workers actually work instead of talking to visitors all day."

Noah laughed. "All day? Man, you're crazy."

It had the effect Justin wanted. Noah came back over and took the box from his hands.

"Go over there and talk to her!" he mumbled just loud enough for Justin to hear.

Justin gave Noah a frustrated look before wiping it from his face to approach the ladies.

"I'd say long time no see, but I just saw you an hour ago." He hoped his anxiety wasn't coming through in his words. He smiled at Lynn. When she smiled back, his mood lifted and some of his anxiety slipped away. He'd never had that happen before and wanted to feel that way much more.

"You guys saw each other earlier?" Kathy asked.

Justin wondered why Lynn hadn't mentioned it to Kathy. He moved his eyes to the woman's face to gauge her reaction. Lynn shook her head, not taking her eyes from Justin's face.

When neither of them answered, Kathy covered her mouth and coughed a laugh. Both looked at her smiling face. Justin realized what had happened and knew he couldn't keep from blushing. He felt a bit of relief over Lynn having the same embarrassed blush coloring her cheeks.

She looked so beautiful in that moment, Justin had to resist the urge to grab and kiss her. He didn't know if he'd ever be brave enough to follow through with something like that. Even if they were dating. He had no game.

"Okay, enough of this awkwardness!" Noah called out.

"Boss, we do have a job here. Come on, enough flirting for this afternoon."

For once, Justin was glad for his friend's interruption, even if he did point out how Justin was feeling in such a blunt way. After smiling warmly at Lynn, he spun around and went back to the stack of boxes that needed to be loaded.

He kept the memory of her returned smile in his mind, as he attempted to ignore that the women were still in the room. He could hear their conversation behind him. Kathy was telling Lynn how their process worked when they were heading to a job.

"It wouldn't be the same there, though," he heard Lynn say. "Everything will just be put on golf carts and moved to the event room where the reception or banquet takes place. We'll have to put together a new process once we start up."

"We can do that. No problem. Maybe Justin can work on that with you, since this is part of his job. He'll need to train the people he hires. I think, if he creates the process himself, he'll know exactly what needs to be done and how he wants it done."

Hearing himself being discussed in business terms made Justin feel like he'd won some kind of prize. He was being given responsibility he hadn't had before. He'd never offered to do anything extra for the business, figuring Kathy would ask if she wanted help. She had the business head in the family, but he had skills to offer, too.

It made him proud to hear Lynn agreeing with Kathy's ideas for his future. She thought he was worthy of the extra opportunities. His spirits were lifted, and he smiled, carrying another box up the ramp and into the truck.

Chapter 8

Lynn followed Kathy around the storage room. She could barely pay attention to the woman's words with Justin working in the room. She wanted to turn to see what he was doing, to see if he was looking at her.

"These are the refrigerators we use. You can see they only have a few shelves in them. Each one is designated for certain foods. This one, you see, has all the fixings for a salad and, that one there holds all the fruit. Any condiments that are needed for these ingredients is on the shelves. These are the different salad dressings we offer. We've got a pretty good variety." Kathy looked up at her when Lynn's eyes had drifted to the men working at the truck.

Lynn became aware that Kathy had stopped speaking. Her eyes darted back to the woman's face and she grinned sheepishly. "I heard what you were saying, Kathy. The condiments are on the door, this is salad stuff, that is fruit."

Kathy chuckled. "You don't have to prove you were listening, Lynn. If you want to talk to Justin, you can. In fact, you'll have to. You need to discuss the serving details with him. Like I said a few minutes ago."

Lynn nodded, feeling like a silly teenager with a crush. "I know. I'm just...let's keep going. I see what's in here. I suppose the other refrigerators are the meats?"

Kathy took her around the rest of the storage room, pointing out how their current system worked. Lynn saw a lot of potential for the resort and mentioned it to Kathy frequently, so the woman would know she was paying as much attention as she could.

But her mind continued to wander. She was planning to ask Justin about the show that night at the Badlands. From the way he'd been looking at her, she was pretty sure he was looking forward to going.

She wondered what it would be like sitting with a man,

talking with him, flirting with him. She wasn't a heavy drinker, and she was a little worried about whether she would be able to control her behavior. The last thing she wanted to do was make a fool of herself.

She could hear him and Noah joking around, as they loaded the remaining boxes on the truck. Once the last box was in the vehicle, both men went up the ramp and began to count and compare their numbers to the paper on a clipboard Justin was holding. She saw him checking off each box as Noah read the label.

"Each time a truck is loaded, they double and triple check to make sure everything is correct. We've never had an instance where something that was ordered didn't show up at the event."

Lynn nodded. "You've never let us down at the resort. It's kind of nice to see behind the scenes. I didn't really think about what it took to prepare for something like this. I just call up and place orders and follow up to make sure everything is right once it's there."

Kathy nodded, running her eyes around the room. "It is a lot of work. But I love it." She turned to Lynn and smiled. "They're almost done. Do you want to go over and discuss business with my brother?"

Lynn's lips twitched, and she pressed them together to stop the motion. She nodded. She could see Kathy trying to keep her amusement to herself. Without another word, Kathy began walking toward the truck. Lynn followed close behind, her eyes on the handsome man who was in the vehicle checking off sections on his clipboard.

Justin looked up and saw them coming. Lynn would have sworn the look that crossed his face for a moment was one of utter terror. It amused her, making her smile wide. The look disappeared when he saw her smile. His face relaxed along with his body. He'd been standing in a rigid position, his brow creased as he stared at the clipboard.

He came down the ramp in a bouncing motion, his eyes directly on her. It made her feel tingly inside. Noah came down the ramp behind him, his eyes moving between the three of them before settling on Kathy.

They all met at the bottom of the ramp, and Kathy spoke up.

"Justin, if you would be so kind as to discuss the needs of the servers once you get to the resort, that would be great. I, uh, I think Noah and I have something to do…somewhere else…right, Noah?"

Noah had no trouble catching on to Kathy's intention. His jovial face filled with humor. "Yeah. That thing we need to do. Somewhere else. We should…go…now."

He moved around Justin, giving him a look Lynn found amusing. Kathy was giggling, as she and Noah moved off, talking to each other in low, excited tones. Kathy glanced back several times, giving Lynn a quick wink before turning to hurry away.

Lynn watched them for a moment before looking back at Justin. Their eyes met and both of them started laughing.

"Let's go outside and talk," Justin said.

Lynn nodded. She resisted the urge to touch him, just to rest her hand on his arm or his back but she could think of no good reason to do so.

The two went back to the table they'd been sitting at before her meeting with Kathy and sat in the same chairs.

"You know," Lynn started the conversation. "I was really amazed by how big your restaurant is inside, considering how small this front looks. It's just like a little delicatessen." She grinned. "Even though it's not really a deli. You don't serve steak and burgers at a deli."

Justin grinned at her. "I hear you. I've been telling Kathy for ages that the name needs to be changed to Brownstone Restaurant and Catering or something like that. But she doesn't listen to me. She never listens to me. She's my older sister by quite a few years, so she thinks she's my mom."

Lynn chuckled. "I can understand that a little. Probably not

446

as much as you, but my sister, Mari, does that to me. She's kind of controlling. I don't really mind, though, she has my best interests at heart. I know that sounds cliché, but it's true. She cares, and I know it."

Justin nodded, sitting back and folding his arms over his chest. Lynn admired how relaxed he looked. She was reminded how she'd thought earlier that he was extremely laid back. She wondered if he ever stressed about anything. He seemed so well put together, so confident in himself.

His light blue eyes sparkled at her. His grin made her heart pound. She knew she was already done for when it came to him, so she indulged in the pleasant feelings.

"So, about the servers." He sat forward now, folding his hands on the table and giving her a serious business-like look. "It's true I'm in charge of the staff that does the serving but, as a manager, I don't really do a lot. I don't plan out anything or contact the ones who are working the event. I really only show up. I look different from the other servers, and it's the clients and customers who come to me if there's a problem. I take that problem to Kathy. She's always there on sight, watching over everything. I'm kind of a glorified crew member."

Lynn was a little confused by that. She wondered why Kathy wouldn't give Justin the authority he deserved for being a co-owner in the company, even if Kathy was the majority stockholder.

She tilted her head to the side and gave him a quizzical look. "So the servers don't come to you when something is wrong?"

Justin shook his head, sitting back again. "No. They go to Kathy."

Lynn licked her lips and chewed gently on the bottom one as she thought. "How strange. I wouldn't have expected Kathy was like that. She has enough to do without taking on every responsibility, doesn't she?"

Justin shrugged. "That's just the way she is. She's

447

controlling, and she likes it."

"But how does that make you feel?" Lynn knew if Mari or Sue tried to take away her responsibilities and not give her any authority at the resort, she would be angry and hurt. Justin didn't look either. He looked content, as always, casually brushing off the obvious slight.

Justin raised his eyebrows briefly. He shook his head. "I don't care. Less I have to deal with."

Lynn thought about that for a moment. She couldn't imagine feeling like she was only there to be a face for the customers and nothing else. She would feel like she didn't belong, wasn't a member of the family. He was a co-owner.

"So you don't want any more responsibility than what you have?" She knew her tone came out surprised. She could tell by the look on his face that Justin thought he'd said something wrong.

"It's not that I don't want any more. I'd just rather not have a confrontation with my sister about it. It's what she wants, so I give it to her. It does mean less work for me, but she's willing to take on all that stuff. If she was to turn around tomorrow and tell me that my responsibility from now on was to deal with any and all of the servers' problems, I'd do it."

Lynn felt a bit of relief slide through her. For a moment, she thought Justin didn't want any responsibilities because he was lazy. She didn't want a lazy man, no matter how cute he was.

"I see."

"You know that old phrase; I'm a lover, not a fighter? That's me, though I'm not loving on anyone right now. My sister is the last person I want to fight with, especially when I know I'm trying to take something from her which she really likes to do."

His eyes darted away from her face when he said that, causing a tingle of pleasure to slide through Lynn. It almost felt like a lie; that maybe he was loving on someone right now. Someone sitting across from him at that very table. She kept herself from giggling. She didn't know his thoughts. It was dangerous to assume he was feeling the same way she was.

"So, about the show my sister is putting on tonight at the Badlands," Lynn rushed to say the words before she lost her courage. "How do you feel about joining me? And do you want to meet me there or go together?"

Justin's eyes widened, flipping back to her face and then away again. He shifted in his seat. Lynn couldn't tell if she'd made him uncomfortable or not, which made her nervousness skyrocket.

"I...I am looking forward to going, Lynn. I've never been to the Badlands. I hear it's a great place for a drink and some good food."

Lynn nodded. "It really is. I can't wait for you to see my sister and her husband sing. And we'll have some time to get to know each other. We'll be working together, after all, right?"

Justin grinned at her. "Yeah. I suppose we will be."

Chapter 9

Justin sat silent, staring down at the plate Kathy set in front of him before sitting down herself with her own. She looked up at him. He could feel her eyes on him. He was nervous about going to the Badlands that night, and he hadn't told her about it yet.

"So," Kathy said after picking up a French fry and popping it in her mouth. "What's on your mind?"

He looked up at her innocently, wrapping his fingers around the burger she'd made him. She knew exactly what he liked. His mouth had been watering while it was cooking.

"I don't know what you're talking about," he finally said.

He deliberately pushed the burger far in his mouth and took a huge bite. It was almost too much, but he was determined not to choke, so he chewed vigilantly while staring at her with amused eyes. She gave him a sardonic look, as she sat with one elbow propping up one arm of the chair. She continued popping fries into her mouth and chewing them, not taking her eyes off him.

"I think I knoooowwww," she sing-songed the words, giving him a closed-mouth grin to hide the food in her mouth.

"Don't talk with your mouth full." Justin replied with food still in his mouth. He covered it with his hand, trying not to choke and feeling like an idiot. At least it was just Kathy. He wouldn't try that joke with Lynn. The last thing he wanted was a first kiss that involved giving CPR.

Kathy, who had swallowed all her food, started laughing softly. "Methinks you should listen to your own advice."

Justin waited till he swallowed before he spoke again. "Look at you, being all proper. You going to meet the Queen of England?"

"Just tell me, Cam. You know you're going to anyway."

He narrowed his eyes at her. "I have no idea what you're talking about."

Kathy snorted, good-naturedly. "Yeah, right. Just tell me, Cam. Tell me. Tell me, tell me, tell me."

Justin sighed heavily. She was going to drag it out of him anyway, but he really didn't want to talk about it. On the other hand, he figured he might as well get it over with.

"You want to know about Lynn, right?"

Kathy's grin widened. "Of course, I do. Are you going to date her?"

The mention of the word made Justin's chest tighten with anxiety. He looked back down at his plate, deciding the fries needed to be eaten before they were cold. He ate half the portion he had before answering. Kathy was surprisingly patient, picking up her burger and consuming a few bites.

"I don't know. There's really not a lot to tell."

"You two were out there bonding for three hours!" Kathy said, surprise in her voice.

He furrowed his brows. "Three hours? No, we weren't."

Kathy's response was to snicker under her breath and look down at her plate. A chill ran over his body. Had they really talked that long? He thought back to their conversation that afternoon.

He realized much of what was said after she asked him to come to the Badlands was a bit foggy. He remembered she loved the smell of lilacs and vanilla. How had that even worked itself into the conversation?

All he remembered, through the whole time he was with her, was that he felt good. He felt lifted somehow, as if his spirit had been given a boost in the right direction. That was what he wanted from a woman.

That's what he'd had with…

His mind automatically reversed, pulling back to Lynn. He knew Kathy was watching his face. He waited for her to say something. When it didn't look like she was going to, he said, "I don't think it was three hours. Maybe two. An hour-and-a-half.

451

She left before I came back in, you know. I wasn't done resting."

Kathy rolled her eyes and shook her head, picking up what was left of her burger. Before she shoved it in her mouth, she said, "It was three hours, and she only left a few minutes before you came back in. It's okay if you want to date her, Cam, but be cautious about dating the boss. Sometimes, it isn't a good thing. Doesn't turn out like it should."

"All relationships turn out like they should," Justin replied. "In the end, what was said and done was supposed to happen. That's just the way life works."

Kathy looked up at the ceiling as she chewed. When she was done, she said, "I guess that's right. Just keep it in mind, okay? If you see any red flags because she's the boss, pull away quick. Okay?"

"I got you," Justin said. A thought came to mind and he continued, "Besides, she's not my boss. You are. Always have been."

Kathy laughed, holding a napkin over her mouth. "You're right."

She wiped her mouth and finished off her fries quickly. "Well, that went quick. I guess I'll have some chips and salsa for dessert and sit on the couch in front of the TV."

"When are you going to find someone?" Justin asked curiously, looking directly, at her as he picked up his cold can of Coke. "You're all up for me dating, but you don't even have a boyfriend."

Kathy smiled. "I'll find someone someday. But, how about, since Lynn is here right now and you have this chance…and since you've never really shown much interest in anyone else since…for a long time…now is your time, Cam. It's your time now."

Justin grinned. "You think so, huh. You think Lynn might be that one girl that takes this heart."

Kathy nodded. "You keep saying stuff like that and it's a win. You should write poetry."

Justin shook his head. "Poetry is for the birds."

Kathy looked at him, surprised. "What are you talking about? You've been writing song lyrics for ages. You know Lynn's sister is the one performing tonight at the Badlands, don't you? They like music. You should talk to her about playing down there sometime."

Justin thought about his guitar. He hadn't picked it up in three months. Going from every day practicing to once every three months was disheartening. He loved playing, and he was good at it, judging by the bands he'd been in. But his heart was with the drums, but he couldn't go down to Badlands and play the drums for 45 minutes.

He chuckled. It was a funny thought.

He shook his head. "Let's just see how tonight goes first."

Kathy fell quiet. He looked up at her.

"What's tonight?" she asked breathlessly. "Are you going on a date, Justin Brownstone? Are you seriously going on a date with Lynn?"

Justin gave her a half-hearted, nervous smile. "Yeah, I guess I'm going to the Badlands. Lynn asked me this afternoon if I wanted to meet her down there."

Kathy straightened her back and clapped her hands excitedly. "Oh my God, Cam, that's great news! I know you'll have a good time. I think she really likes you."

Justin tried to feel more positive, listening to Kathy's excitement and seeing the obvious joy on her face. He felt a little better inside, knowing his sister was on board with him seeing Lynn.

"Well, go get ready, then," Kathy suddenly stood up, pushing her chair back with her legs. She reached down and picked up both their plates.

"Hey!" Justin grabbed the last three French fries off his plate and shoved them into his mouth. He chewed and swallowed as he got up and pushed the chairs under the table. "I'm going outside to smoke. I'll get ready after."

Kathy gave him a small frown, as he pulled out the pack of cigarettes from his pocket. "I wish you'd stop that nasty habit."

Justin shrugged, lifting his lighter and lighting one before he left the room.

He could hear her call after him, "You could at least wait till you are out of the house before you light it."

He felt bad. He should have waited. He usually did but he was extra nervous because it was coming down to the wire. He had avoided dating again for so long. Lynn was so pretty and gave him such a warm feeling. If he'd really been talking to her for three hours, he had a lot to remember.

It came to him in bits and pieces. He would remember saying something that made her laugh. The sound had sent a pleasant tingle through him. She agreed with a lot of things he said and, if she didn't agree with him, she'd either ask him to explain or tell him why she didn't agree. Her voice was so smooth and pretty. He could listen to it all day.

She seemed like the very talkative type, too. She had a smile for everyone who passed and seemed very animated. It was nice not to be expected to talk all the time. When he did talk, she actually listened. She looked right at him while he spoke.

Another thing he remembered that hadn't seemed like much at the time but was so important to him now; she hadn't once pulled out her cell phone. He distinctly heard a notification sound several times but couldn't quite place what the sound was.

He now realized she had ignored the messages, so she wouldn't look rude in front of him. She *wanted* to talk to him and listen to him.

He stood outside their small apartment on the border of Queen Anne and stared out at the sun, as it crept across the evening sky. The colors of the sunset were just beginning to grace the blue in the sky, as if God had just started a new painting. He stared as the colors became more intense the lower the sun went behind the horizon.

He was going to have a good time with Lynn. He would make it happen. He would impress her and not embarrass himself at all.

Doubt slipped into his mind and his will weakened. What would she think of him? What if he said something completely stupid?

He shook his head. He would be fine. He just had to be positive and confident. He could take a lesson from Lynn. She exuded confidence. He didn't get the arrogant vibe from her, though he didn't think he would fare well having her as a boss. She seemed like the type that was good at telling people what to do. She was polite but firm.

He grinned. Good qualities for a woman in business. But in a relationship?

He looked down at the end of his cigarette, noticing the orange in the sky was the same color. He moved his eyes above him, taking in all the colors, from the grass on the newly cut lawn to the red of the fire hydrant at the end of the street.

The colors on earth were just as beautiful as the ones in the sky.

Chuckling at his thoughts, he turned to go back inside and get ready for his date.

Chapter 10

Lynn was reeling from her afternoon meeting with Cam. She was over-the-top excited that he'd agreed to coming to the Badlands. She couldn't wait.

During their conversation, she'd realized he was a fountain of information when it came to music of all kinds. He'd mentioned several bands she enjoyed and told her about going to see them in concert. They never came to Queen Anne, he said, unless they were on vacation.

They'd had a good laugh trying to outdo each other on who had met the biggest star and when. He had to give in, telling her that working at the Resort gave her more access to the rich and famous than his catering shop did.

"The only elite that come into this deli aren't here to be friends. They're already with friends, and they're eating."

They'd had a laugh about that.

Lynn was sure she hadn't met such a gracious and calm-looking man in her life.

Another thing she liked was that his best friend, Noah, and his sister, Kathy, seemed to approve. If you have the approval of the people closest to the person you were interested in, it was so much easier.

She stepped out on the tennis court for her afternoon session with Sue and walked over to the gazebo where her sister was waiting for her.

She lifted her racket in acknowledgement and Sue waved back, lifting up from the seat.

"Don't get up yet," Lynn called out. "I've gotta change into the right shoes and all that."

Once she got to the gazebo and the table where Sue was sitting, she set her bag down and slid onto the arched bench seat that surrounded the round table.

"I'm actually surprised you wanted to keep our date today," she said, unzipping her bag and pulling out a different pair of shoes. They were much more comfortable than the ones she was wearing. At least to play tennis.

"Oh? Why would I back out?" Sue gave her a quizzical look.

Lynn shrugged. "With your show and all, I just thought…" She let the sentence trail off, looking up at her sister as she slipped off one shoe and put the other one on. "It's okay with *me*. I'm taking the rest of the day off. I'm coming to the show."

Sue nodded, glancing down at her phone. A new message had come on the screen. Lynn could see it since it was lying flat on the table.

"Who you talking to?" Lynn asked, looking down to tie her shoe.

"It's nobody. I'm planning something for Mike tonight. I think he's going to really like it."

Lynn smiled. "I'm sure he will. No matter what it is, a surprise for Mike is always a good thing."

Sue laughed. "Not always. When he had all that equipment stolen, it came as a real surprise to him."

"I suppose it did. I stand corrected."

"But yeah, he usually loves surprises. Especially when I plan them for him. I know him so well."

It was Lynn's turn to laugh. "I hope you do. You've been married to him for *so* long now. What's it been—a whole year?"

"Stop it," Sue said in a contrite tone. "I know you're teasing, but I love him to death, you know."

Lynn wanted the kind of love her sister displayed for her husband, too. Justin's face crossed her mind, and a sensation of warmth flooded through her. It was such a nice feeling, she wanted to feel it again, so she pictured Justin in her mind and smiled softly.

457

"Well, I can see you've got your eye on someone, too. What's up? Is it that Brownstone guy? What's his name again?"

"Now you are teasing *me*. I know I've mentioned Justin before."

Sue's face lit up. "So it *is* Justin Brownstone. Wow, he's that young guy, right?"

Irritation split through Lynn. Sue's tone of voice made it sound like Justin was just a teenager and not her age.

"Cut it out, Sue. I don't like it when you say that. I'm not a cradle-robber, and I don't like little boys. Not like *that*, anyway."

"I'm glad you're meeting him at the Badlands," Sue changed her tone. "I want to meet him. I've seen him a few times. I like his look. He looks… nice."

Lynn nodded. "I think so, too. I spent practically the whole afternoon, just sitting on the deck outside the restaurant talking to him."

"That's so cool," Sue said, smiling. "What did you talk about?"

"We talked a lot about music. He likes music."

Sue chuckled, giving Lynn a direct look. "Most people like music. I don't know anyone who doesn't."

Lynn scrunched up her face, picking at her tennis racket with one finger as she spoke. "You know what I mean. We like the same kind of music. Stop picking."

They both laughed.

"You want to do this or not?" Lynn asked, gesturing toward the court with her racket. Sue moved her eyes out to the court, slowly lifting her energy drink and taking a big swallow. She moved her eyes to Lynn, and she shook her head.

"Not really. I'm gonna be on stage for hours tonight. This might make me really tired."

Lynn nodded her head, exhaling a laugh. "That's why I said I was surprised you'd want to do this today. You usually rest before a show. And you might use up all your voice talent screaming when I beat you."

"Enough of that," Sue said, snickering. "I will beat you, and you know it."

"Now don't be like that," Lynn raised her voice to a high pitch and looked haughtily at her sister. The look didn't last long before she smiled and laughed. "It's okay if you don't want to play today. We can just sit here and talk for a while, if you want."

"You gotta tell me about your new boyfriend," Sue said, sipping from her energy drink before holding it between her hands and leaning forward over the table. "Come on. Tell me what Justin is all about. Besides the bands you both like."

"He likes steak, too, made the same way I do. I found that out when I asked about the chefs at Brownstone restaurant and if they were good at their jobs. Justin told me nothing but the best for them. I did some research and called all the references and didn't find anyone who had anything bad to say about their restaurant. Even the staff are ultra-friendly."

Sue nodded. "It's like that at the Badlands, too. Have you noticed?"

Lynn raised her eyebrows, giving her sister an approving look. "Yes, I've noticed. Ever since that old manager stopped working there, the place has gone way up in quality."

"Thanks."

Lynn nodded. "Oh, you've been a great influence on Mike. I know he was struggling a little before you started dating him, but you really pulled him out of the fire with that loan you gave him. I'm glad Mari didn't object. Look where you guys are now."

Sue's face was beaming from her sister's compliments. Satisfaction swept through Lynn. She was proud of her sister and Mike. They made a good team running the bar and grill.

Lynn hoped she and Justin would work well together when they brought the Brownstone Catering Company into Emerald Resort. She was aggressive in her business so that things would run smoothly. The least amount of drama, the better. That very fact was probably one of the things that kept her from seeking a relationship until this crush fell in her lap.

She longed for a relationship but desired it to be drama-free. In her experience and, from watching others go through various stresses, she knew that would be impossible. Even Sue and Mike, who were the perfect couple in Lynn's eyes, argued every now and then.

It was okay to argue. She didn't have a problem with that. But she didn't want other people interfering, no exes coming into the picture, nothing like that.

From the way it looked, she didn't think she had to worry about exes and Justin. He was more of a loner than anything else. She wondered if she would be able to break down the walls he'd built. It was obvious to her Justin hadn't been dating for a while. He was a good looking man, to be sure.

Lynn thought back to when she first met him, remembering the very moment she felt that spark of love light up inside her. It was just a crush, it probably wasn't true love, but it was strong and something she wasn't likely to forget anytime soon, if ever. If they stayed together, she would remember it for the rest of her life as the first time she felt the strong desire to be with him every minute of the day.

In her heart, Lynn knew, if she truly fell in love with Justin – or with any man – she would give her life for them. It was a bone of contention with her sisters, since they knew her so well and loved her so much. She was a giver, they'd told her in the past. If she wasn't careful, she would be stomped on and taken advantage of. Men were like that these days, they'd said.

But that was before they found and married their husbands.

Now it was Lynn's turn. The youngest of the three, going in succession just the way it was meant to be.

"Lynn?" Sue got her attention, snapping her fingers in front of her sister's face. "Where'd you go?"

Lynn chuckled softly. "I'm sorry. I was thinking."

Sue grinned. "About Justin, no doubt."

"Yes, I suppose so," Lynn replied breathlessly.

Sue shook her head. "My goodness, it looks like you're already head over heels in love with this guy. You don't even know him."

Lynn pulled in a long breath and let it out, her smile dissipating. "I know. There's just...something about him." She shook her head. "I don't know what it is. I feel so strongly about him. Like..." She looked away from Sue, knowing what her sister's reaction would be. "Like it was meant to be or something."

Sue nodded, pulling the corners of her lips down in an understanding way. "I know how you feel, Lynn. And as much as Mari and I have warned you, if you feel that much about him, there must be a reason. Have you felt like this before?"

Lynn shook her head. "Never. He makes me feel like I'm in high school again. But with maturity on my side."

Sue gave out a single laugh. "That's a nice feeling. Mari and I want you to be happy. We just worry that you'll give your heart to the wrong man. You never know these days."

"I hope you and Mari will give Justin a chance. I...I really, really like him."

Sue's pleasant smile made Lynn feel better. Her voice was soft when she spoke. "I can tell, honey. And we'll give him a chance. We love you bunches. And you're not a child. But if we see him doing something that might hurt you, we're going to say something. Okay?"

Lynn gave her a half-grin. "Okay."

Chapter 11

Justin looked up at the sign when he got to Badlands. His heart thumping nervously. He hesitated, standing outside the bar near a corner where it was dark. He lit a cigarette and looked down at the ground, willing himself to go inside.

He'd looked around the parking lot when he pulled in but didn't know what car Lynn drove so the effort was somewhat wasted. He pulled in a deep breath of fresh cool air in between puffs on the cigarette. Usually the effect of the nicotine would calm him down, but it wasn't working this time. It had been so long since he'd been on a date, he wasn't sure what to say.

He chided himself silently. He'd already talked to Lynn so many times. They had that long conversation…

He sighed. He needed to get himself together. The last thing he wanted was for Lynn to see him nervous and scared.

I'm not scared, he told himself, *I'll be just fine.*

His internal words of encouragement weren't serving him as well as he would have liked. He leaned back against the wall, his eyes still focused on the ground in front of him, though he couldn't see it since he was standing in the dark.

The door to the bar opened, and a woman came out. She turned in his direction, and he glanced up to see if it was Lynn, somehow knowing he was standing out there.

It wasn't Lynn. It was her sister, Sue. He cleared his throat, so she would know he was standing in the pitch dark before she passed by. He didn't want to scare her.

His attempt didn't work because when he cleared his throat, he saw her stop, jumping slightly.

"I'm sorry," he said, immediately. "I didn't mean to scare you. I was just…smoking before I went in."

Sue smiled at him and then crossed into the darkness. "I will never understand why Mike put the garbage dumpster in the dark. Unless it was so customers didn't have to see it. But you're

462

standing so close to it, how can you not smell it?"

Justin smiled. "I have no idea."

Sue passed him, still grinning. He watched her shadowed form lean back and toss the bag she was carrying into the large dumpster which he hadn't realized was just a few feet from him. When she came back, she stopped just on the other side of him, so half her body was in the shadow and the other half was in the light.

"Aren't you coming in?"

Justin shuffled his feet slightly, dropping his eyes back to the ground. "Yeah, eventually."

"What's keeping you?"

Her voice was kind and soft. He could tell she was Lynn's sister. He recognized the same caring nature. His mother had been the same way. She seemed to know every time he or Kathy had been down about anything, anything at all. As if being their mother had made her psychic.

"I...I'm just smoking. I'll be inside in a minute. Is Lynn in there yet?"

Sue's smile seemed to grow larger. "She is. She's really...looking forward to seeing you. You know, when it's not business you're talking about."

Justin chuckled. "Yeah, I kind of feel the same way."

Sue tilted her head to the side and gave him a contemplative look he could only see half of. "Can I ask you something, Justin?"

His heart immediately went into overdrive. What did she want to know? He braced himself.

"Sure," he said.

"Do you really want to be a part of your sister's business? I only ask because she's bringing this to us saying that you will be in charge of the catering for the Resort. Lynn has a lot of confidence in you, even though she just met you. She's a smart girl, very intuitive. So my sister and I do trust her. But we don't know you.

You know what I mean?"

Justin nodded. "Of course. I understand completely."

He turned toward her and tossed the cigarette into the flower pot ashtray sitting near him.

He tried to quickly think of a response for her that wouldn't be discouraging. Working in the deli and catering business wasn't his dream. It wasn't what he wanted to do with his life. But it was what he was doing right then. He needed to do it. For Kathy.

But could he tell Sue that? Was it enough to satisfy her?

He doubted it.

"I do want to run the catering business at the resort," he said finally, moving toward the door to go inside. He stopped next to her and looked out over the parking lot, gathering his thoughts. "I really didn't think about something like that before. I mean, I've never thought about it…the resort…it just kind of fell on us, I guess, with Lynn deciding she wanted to propose the idea to Kathy. I don't mean to sound confused or anything. I'm just…this isn't…"

"What you planned for your life?" Sue supplied, raising her eyebrows.

Justin sighed. "I guess not. I do this because it's what Kathy wants me to do. Otherwise, I guess I'd just be bored, sitting around doing nothing with my life. I don't want that. I'd rather be working and making money."

"Of course. That's why everyone works." Sue's smile comforted him. It looked a lot like her sister's, and he was crazy about Lynn's smile. "I think you'll do fine, Justin. I want you to know that Lynn really likes you. I don't want to see my sister get hurt."

Justin shook his head. "I won't hurt her, Sue. Not on purpose."

"Well," Sue said, gently. "As long as it isn't on purpose. I'm married, you know, and Mike hasn't hurt me on purpose either. But that doesn't mean he hasn't made me mad."

Justin chuckled. "I'm sure. I've never even contemplated getting married. Why would I want to? It seems like a piece of paper that makes people act differently than they normally would. I don't want to change because of a piece of paper."

Sue raised her eyebrows again. "It isn't just a piece of paper, Justin. Some people might think of it that way but for me—and for my sisters—it's not. It's a commitment. It's giving yourself to the other person completely. For the rest of your life. We don't..." Sue stopped abruptly, looking up into his eyes. He could see the similarities in her face to Lynn's.

He stared at her while she was silent. She blinked a few times and continued, "I'm sorry, Justin. I don't want to put pressure on you. She just really likes you and your company...I mean being with you, not Brownstone Catering."

They both laughed softly.

"I know where you're coming from," he said. "It's okay."

"No, I shouldn't be bringing up marriage when this is pretty much your first official date with Lynn. That's jumping the gun, don't you think?"

He chuckled again. "Maybe a little." The thought of being pressured into marriage made Justin's stomach churn. If that was what Lynn was pushing for, he would have to take a step back. But Sue was right, it was their first date. Maybe Lynn wasn't thinking about that already. He hoped not.

"You, uh, you don't think she's thinking about that now, do you?"

Sue shook her head vigorously. "Oh no, Justin. Don't go in there thinking she's going to expect some kind of proposal. I bring it up because Mari and I are married so that's where our minds are, you know? But not Lynn. She's..." Her grin widened. "She's probably as nervous as you are."

He gave her a half-grin. "Is it that obvious?"

"Oh, I can see that you're nervous," Sue replied, nodding. "Tell you what. Let's get you loosened up before you go in."

Justin drew his eyebrows together in confusion. "What do you mean?"

Sue touched her upper lip with her tongue before reaching out and grabbing both his wrists. She lifted his arms and flapped them both with hers, tossing her head back and forth, making a strange noise as she did so.

Justin felt like a complete fool until she stopped doing it. She dropped his wrists and grabbed both his upper arms, proceeding to shake him lightly back and forth.

He started laughing, shaking his head. "What in the world are you doing?" he asked as she continued shaking him.

She grinned. "Making you laugh, of course. There's no better relaxation than to laugh. I hope you like my show tonight. I think you will. You have to come out and tell me what you think after. I'll be watching you." She pointed two fingers of one hand toward her eyes and then turned them toward him. "I'll be watching you for more than one reason."

Justin couldn't help laughing some more. "I'll be a good boy, I promise."

Sue pursed her lips. "You better be. Lynn is a sweet girl with a big heart. We don't want her hurt."

"I don't want to hurt her, either. I like her, too. We get along well."

Sue raised her eyebrows, nodding. "I know. You like steak and potatoes. There's no faster way into my sister's heart than to feed her steak and potatoes."

"Sweet," Justin replied. "You serve steak and potatoes here?"

Sue's grin stretched from ear to ear. "We sure do. And our cooks are the best in Queen Anne."

"Oh, I don't know. We've got some pretty good chefs at Brownstone, too."

"I'm sure you do."

Sue grabbed his arm and gently pulled him toward the entrance. "Now you just make sure you keep your business talk to the minimum. In fact, don't say anything at all about business. Talk about yourself. Ask her questions. But don't talk about business. Think you can do that?"

"I know I can do that, Sue. I'm glad you came out and talked to me. I was feeling pretty nervous."

Sue looked up at him, circling her small hand around his elbow. "I could tell. Sue doesn't smoke, you know."

Justin nodded. "I noticed. I haven't actually smoked in front of her before. I hope she isn't turned off by it."

Sue had a thoughtful look. "I don't know about turning her off, but you should probably ask her what she thinks of it before you light up in front of her. Have you considered quitting?"

"All right, Sue," Justin said lightheartedly. "I've already got one sister scolding me about that habit. Not married to your sister yet but let's just stick with Kathy getting on my back about that, okay?"

Sue laughed, nodding. As they went inside, Justin realized he'd added the word "yet" to his sentence.

Chapter 12

Lynn was watching the door, waiting for Justin to come in. She tried not to look conspicuous, like she was actually waiting for him. But she was. She was anxious, nervous, and just a tad giddy. She'd been picturing him in her mind all afternoon, wondering what he would wear, if he would really show up, if they would have a good time.

When she saw him come in with Sue on his arm, a smile on both their faces, she was overcome with an intense feeling of desire. He looked so handsome, though he was just wearing a regular t-shirt and jeans. His blond hair was swept back from his face. The moment he entered, the variety of colored lights above them caught his eyes, making them sparkle.

He looked like he'd just been laughing. Standing up to wave at them both, Lynn was grateful to her sister. Justin's grin widened when he saw her. Sue released him, giving her sister a teasing grin and a wink, as she walked over to the bar.

"Lynn," he said, coming over to the table. "You look great. I hope you haven't been waiting too long."

Lynn shook her head. "Not at all. It wouldn't matter anyway. I'm at home here."

"I bet." He pulled out the chair to the side of her instead of across and sat down when she did.

"Thanks, by the way. You look great, too. You look comfortable."

He raised his eyebrows, glancing down at himself. "Is that a compliment? Not too casual, I hope."

Lynn laughed, a pleasant feeling filling her. "Of course not," she said. "This is a bar. You're supposed to be casual here."

"Cool." Justin relaxed in the chair, resting one arm on the table in front of him, putting the other on his thigh, splaying his fingers out and looking toward the bar. "I could use a beer, though."

Lynn leaned over the table, looking into his eyes. "Are you nervous?" she asked in a teasing voice. He moved his blue eyes to meet hers. The feeling she got when their eyes met almost took her breath away. He was more handsome than she remembered. Or maybe it was the light. Or the two beers she'd already had.

She decided it was neither. It was just because he was that good-looking. She wanted to grab him and pull him into a big kiss.

Too soon, she thought with an internal giggle. *Gonna scare him off.*

"You want me to get you one?" she asked, pushing her chair back.

He shook his head, tapping his fingers on the table in front of him. "That's my job. I'll get our drinks."

"Well, I get a discount but if you want to get them…"

He laughed. "Hey, I'm not one to turn down a discount. If you can get it cheaper, I'll bow to your authority."

She joined him in laughter, shaking her head as she got up and trotted over to the bar.

She leaned on it, catching the eyes of Francesco, the bartender on duty that night. "Hey, I'm gonna get a couple more. One for me and one for my friend over there." She turned and pointed at Justin, whose back was to her. He was looking around him, taking in the bar atmosphere.

Francesco gave her a knowing, teasing look. "Is that your new man, girl? He looks nice."

Lynn nodded. "I know right? He's cute as a button."

"Don't let him hear you say that." Francesco set about pouring beer into two tall glasses. "Men hate that, you know."

Lynn nodded. "Yeah, that's what I've heard. But if he's cute as a button, he just is."

Francesco laughed, setting the beers down in front of her. "Yeah, he is, I got to admit that. You know what I mean. I can't really tell with guys."

Lynn laughed, picking up the glasses and taking them back to the table. When she got there, she noticed he had set two napkins down, one for her and one for him, coating the top with salt to keep the glasses from sticking.

She lifted her eyebrows and set the glasses down on the napkins. "I see you know what you're doing," she said.

He nodded. "I guess so. Thought that was common knowledge."

"It is if you've been to the bar a lot," she said, sliding into her chair. "I've never seen you in here before."

He chuckled. "This isn't the only bar in Queen Anne."

"True," Lynn replied, reaching for the straw sticking out of her empty beer glass. She plucked it out and slid into the new glass. He watched her with amusement. She noticed and tilted her head to the side. "Yeah, I use a straw. What of it?"

They both laughed.

"This might not be the only bar," she said, after taking a sip through her straw. "But it is the best one. And the biggest."

He nodded, taking a drink from his glass. "And the most popular, too. But what can I say? It's just not my style. I don't like bars much. I know this trick from drinking at the Brownstone."

"That's not a bar."

"I know. But it's where I live and work and eat. And we do sell a few beers, you know."

Lynn shook her head. "I actually didn't know that. I don't see it on your menu."

He nodded. "It's not on the board over the ordering station. But if you look at the catering menu..." He pulled his brows together, taking another drink from his glass. "Wait a minute, shouldn't you know what's on our catering menu?"

Lynn nodded. "I really should, shouldn't I? But no, I haven't had time to memorize it all. Probably never will. Not my job, you know?"

He chuckled. "No, I suppose it isn't. But yeah, we have the liquor license and serve beer or mixed drinks, cocktails, you know. Lots of weddings and receptions and events like that have an open bar. We have to appeal to all types, right?"

Lynn turned her head to the bar, where Sue was motioning to her. Justin turned and looked behind him to see what she was looking at. Lynn tilted her head, trying to figure out what Sue was saying. She was pointing at Justin, then her and back again.

"What in heaven's name is she saying?" Lynn asked softly, squinting and focusing on Sue's lips.

Justin stayed where he was for only a moment before turning back to her. She felt another wave of adrenaline rush through her when her eyes met his. Her heart beat hard in her chest and her stomach fluttered. "I think she's telling us we aren't supposed to talk about business. That's what she told me before I came in here. I guess I gotta entertain you with my wit and charm. I don't know if that's gonna fly, though. I don't have much game."

Lynn laughed, shaking her head. "You don't have to have game with me, Justin. I already like you."

Justin grinned. "That's good to hear. I like you, too."

"I think we'll get along just fine then. But how did you know what she was saying?"

Justin shrugged. "I can read lips pretty well."

Lynn raised her eyebrows. She was learning more about him by the minute and was enjoying it thoroughly.

"So what kind of music does your sister do with Mike? Don't tell me its country."

Lynn huffed, pretending to be offended. "What's wrong with country music?"

"Oh nothing," Justin said hurriedly, lifting one hand in the air. "If that's your thing, that's your thing. I'm just saying..."

Lynn laughed. "I'm just teasing you, Justin. They don't play country. I don't think I've heard anyone here play country

471

music. Sue and Mike play original music. His stuff. Mostly soft rock."

"How long have they been together?"

"They've been married a year. I guess they were playing together about six months before that."

Justin looked over his shoulder to where Sue was leaning over the bar talking to a customer with a big smile on her face. "She's really nice." He turned back to look at her. "Like you. You're nice. I think."

Lynn lifted one eyebrow. "You think?"

She could see his lips twitching as he tried to hide his grin. "Well, I don't really know you that well."

"But you think Sue is nice..." She couldn't help keeping the teasing going. "Thanks a lot."

He laughed. "No, my dear, I do not think she is nicer than you. I look forward to finding out a lot more about you."

Lynn gazed at him softly, her eyes filled with admiration. His use of the term of endearment flooded her with warmth. He was definitely a southern boy. She imagined he called lots of women "dear" and "honey". She hoped he would mean it more for her, though. Eventually. "I feel the same way, Justin."

He nodded curtly, as if that's what he expected. "I'm glad to hear that."

Lynn saw his eyes lift up and look over her shoulder. The room went dark and suddenly lights burst onto the stage, lighting it up in blue and red. The crowd was decent for the show, and Lynn joined the rest of them as they clapped. She didn't need to turn around to know her sister and Mike were heading to the stage.

She grinned at Justin. "You're gonna love this. I know it."

His returned smile made her stomach feel jittery. She had to look away from him, so she turned her eyes to the stage. Movement made her glance back at him. She had to control her breathing. Justin had scooted his chair closer to hers and was leaning on the table close enough to touch her arm with his.

Throughout the show, Lynn found it incredibly hard to keep her mind off him. He was so close, and she wondered if he was brushing against her on purpose. Every time he moved, she glanced at him. Several times, he was looking at her instead of the stage and, if he wasn't, he turned his eyes to meet hers.

It was the first time Lynn wanted the show to be over quickly. She wanted to talk to him privately. He got up twice to get beer from the bar. The first time, he came back with two beers and leaned over to speak directly into her ear, so she would hear him. His breath on her skin gave her tingles.

"They gave me your discount. I gotta come here with you more often."

He pulled away with such a big grin, Lynn found it almost impossible to resist the love struck look she knew she had to have on her face. She tried not to feel like a fool, but she did anyway. She'd fallen for him, and there was nothing she could do about it.

She bit her lower lip, nodding and taking the glass from him as nonchalantly as she could.

Her head was spinning when the lights in the bar came back up full. The sound of clapping around her made Lynn's head spin. She leaned back in the chair, looking at Justin.

"What do you think?" she asked, grinning.

Her heart did a flip when he answered, "I think I'm looking at the most beautiful woman in Queen Anne."

She giggled and winked at him. "See, Justin? You do have game."

He laughed delightedly.

Chapter 13

Lynn's phone vibrated, making the top of her desk rattle as it slid to the side. She snatched it up and looked down at it. It was a text from Justin. An immediate smile came to her face. She leaned back in her chair, picking up the piece of pizza she was eating for lunch and took a bite while she read the text.

Can't wait to see you for lunch.

It was amazing how one simple sentence from him could put her in such a good mood. A call was always nice, but his texts could be saved and read over and over again. She didn't have to feel like a stalker. The relationship was developing nicely, and she couldn't wait to see what happened next. They still had yet to share a kiss. It was getting more and more difficult for her to resist it.

She didn't really know what was keeping him from taking another step. But no matter what, she was willing to wait. He was worth it. She'd discovered a sweet, gentle soul that fit well with hers.

She would wait.

She looked up when her door was shoved open and Sue came in, looking agitated and worried. Without saying anything, she marched to Lynn's desk and set her tablet down firmly.

Confusion ran through Lynn and she stopped chewing. "Sue? What's wrong?"

Her sister looked like she was trying to hold something back but wanting desperately to say it at the same time. "Just look at this, Lynn."

Lynn didn't want to look at the tablet. From the look on Sue's face, whatever she saw wasn't going to please her. She hesitated for as long as she could, swallowing her pizza, reluctantly dropping her eyes to look at the screen.

She ran her eyes over the spreadsheet document. The numbers she read made her frown. It was a list of supplies, as noted by the heading at the top of the sheet. She'd been in charge of catering for long enough to know the shorthand her sister used for the budget sheets and knew what each symbol and letter meant. The numbers looked a little high to her, but she didn't know what the worry was.

She looked back up at her sister. "What's this? Am I supposed to be worried? What does this mean?"

Sue leaned forward, her eyes directly on her sister's. "Lynn." She leaned forward and tapped the tablet, bringing up the properties of the document. "Look at this. This is where it was created and who created it. These documents show that these supplies were transferred at a much higher rate than they were supposed to be."

Lynn frowned, scanning the document after closing out the property window. She shook her head. "This doesn't make sense. Brownstone Catering doesn't send them supplies. They buy them."

Sue nodded. "I know. But this shows the companies overcharging when the companies themselves have set prices and don't overcharge. The extra money has been moved somewhere. The company was charged more than they should have been but only on paper."

Lynn's chest tightened and her heart went into overdrive. She shook her head again, shoving the tablet back toward Sue. "This is wrong. There's a mistake."

Sue shook her head. "Lynn, I've been doing this for a long time now. I know what I'm looking at. The only way to access these accounts is with a passcode and the only two people with passcodes are Kathy and Justin." She reached forward and tapped the tablet. "This is Justin's passcode. There is no mistake. I've checked it, double-checked it, triple-checked it. This shows…you know what it means, Lynn."

Tears threatened to rise in Lynn's eyes. It was Justin's passcode, according to the file. His name was right there in plain sight.

She swallowed hard and tried not to look at her sister. She didn't want to believe it. It couldn't be true.

"This has to be wrong," she breathed softly. "It has to be. He's not extorting money from his sister. He's not like that. He wouldn't do that."

Sue gave her a sympathetic look. "I know you like him, honey. But…"

Lynn shook her head again. "No. You're wrong. It can't be true. He's not like that."

Sue sighed. Lynn hated the look on her sister's face. It made her angry. She stood up, shoving her chair back with her legs. "I don't believe this. It has to be wrong. It can't be Justin. He's…he's too…"

She didn't know what word she wanted to say. She couldn't get a handle on her feelings. She was confused, because the passcode showed it was Justin's work.

"How do you know it isn't him? Kathy wouldn't do this. It would destroy her company, and she has no reason to do it at all. She makes good money. Brownstone has a good reputation. We can't work with people who extort money, Lynn. And if Justin is doing this…"

"He's not!" Lynn slammed her hand down on the desk, making Sue jump. She felt confused and hurt. "This is not his work, and I'm going to prove it. He's not hiding money. Where is it going anyway?"

Sue shook her head. "I don't have access to those kinds of files, Lynn. I only know what I've been given access to by Kathy. If she was the one responsible, she wouldn't have given me these files. I wouldn't have been able to track this. The companies are providing the supplies and equipment at the normal rate, charging what they've charged us and others for as long as they've been in business. And Brownstone has been paying out more. The money is being withdrawn from the accounts mid-way and diverted to somewhere else."

"Where?" Lynn demanded.

"I don't know. I told you. I can't access that file."

Lynn was having trouble breathing. She pictured Justin in her mind, his gorgeous blue eyes sparkling at her, the touch of his hands and the warmth of his hugs. She refused to believe he could be greedy. He wasn't a criminal. There was no way.

She snatched the sweater from the back of her chair and stomped around her desk. "He's not responsible. And I'm going to prove it. You'll see. I'm going to prove him innocent."

Sue jumped to her feet, following her sister as she stomped out her office door.

"Lynn! What are you going to do? You aren't an investigator. If you go and talk directly to Justin, you know he's just going to deny it."

Lynn spun around and glared at Sue. "Of course, he'll deny it! He's innocent! Do you expect him to just say, oh yeah, my bad? He's going to deny it because he didn't do it."

With a thumping heart, holding tears back, Lynn went quickly down the hallway to the front door, Sue close on her heels. What if she was wrong? What if Justin was responsible for the theft?

"No," she said aloud to her own thoughts. "No, he's not like that. Why would he want money anyway?"

"Lynn, wait, wait!" Sue reached out and grabbed Lynn's arm, spinning her around to face her. Lynn was surprised to see tears in Sue's eyes, as well. "I know you want to prove him innocent. I understand that. If it was Mike, I would be doing the same thing. But you don't know how to investigate something like this and…"

"So, what, you're going to call the police? Have some detective investigate this? Someone who doesn't know Justin at all?"

"Lynn, you barely know Justin. Kathy told us he never wanted to be a part of the company. He had bigger dreams, he had things he wanted to do with his life. Maybe he's just saving up for that."

"By stealing from his sister?" Lynn curled her lip, unable to keep her anger from boiling over. "That's ridiculous! If he wanted out of the company, he wouldn't have agreed to take the resort job."

Sue shook her head and gave her a doleful look. "Maybe he just agreed to that so he could get close to you."

"He didn't volunteer to be in charge of the resort catering," Lynn replied. "He was asked to do it and he said yes. Why would he do that if he was stealing her money? Wouldn't that risk exposure?"

Sue looked doubtful, but Lynn knew it wasn't for the reason she wanted it to be. "Maybe he thought no one would find out. Maybe he thought it would be a good opportunity to double his income."

A cry of aggravation flew from Lynn. She turned around on her heel and shoved the door open, nearly hitting one of the housekeeping staff as she went out. When she didn't apologize, the employee turned to give her a dazed look. Sue went past him, apologizing for Lynn, who turned an angry look back at her sister.

"Don't apologize for me! You are wrong, and I'm going to make sure of it. Justin doesn't need to steal money. He's got enough. Kathy would let him go wherever he wants, whenever he wants. He knows that. He has no reason to steal."

"I don't know. I can only tell you what is shown on these papers here. He has to have known about the theft, even if he didn't perpetrate it."

"Oh? And why is that?" Lynn's tears were coming to the surface again. She couldn't picture Justin in jail. She couldn't picture him anywhere but, in her arms, kissing her, loving her. The only man she'd ever felt this strongly about. He couldn't be a criminal. He couldn't be.

"Because he has to look over these accounts sometimes. It's his passcode. No one else knows it."

"How do you know that? Someone could have gotten it from somewhere. You have it, don't you?"

"I don't have access to his files. I only know the two passcodes but not any of the other information that's required to open all of them. Kathy gave me my own passcode so I could access certain things. But nothing else. Only what I needed so I could verify the security and legitimacy of the Brownstone Corporation."

"I'm telling you, he's innocent, and I'm going to make sure you know that."

She spun around again, so that her sister wouldn't see the tears she was unable to stop. She wanted to work closely with Justin. She wanted Brownstone Catering at the resort now more than ever, if only to prove that Justin could be trusted. But once Sue told Mari about the misappropriated funds, she would never allow Brownstone to join the resort.

She ran to her car, yanked the door open, and slid into the driver's seat.

"Don't go to him yet, Lynn! Think about it! He's not going to tell you the truth!"

She could hear Sue's remarks as she called out, her hands cupping her mouth. She ignored her sister, threw the car into drive and squealed out of the parking lot. Her heart was thumping so hard in her chest, she wondered if it might jump out all on its own.

Chapter 14

Noah grinned at Justin as the two of them bit into their sandwiches. "I love eating here for lunch," he said. "The best food in Queen Anne."

They were walking together down the hallway at the warehouse for Brownstone Catering. There was a line of offices at the end of the long hall, where the accounting and human resources offices were.

"You think we should just go in those offices with these sandwiches?" Noah asked, looking down at the one in his hand as if he hadn't seen a sandwich in years and was in love with the one he had.

Justin drew his brows together, giving Noah a side glance. "Why not?"

Noah tilted his head, shaking the sandwich at his friend, making the top and lower bread pieces flap like the mouth of a Muppet. "Because these people haven't had good food in years, of course. We're gonna tempt them too much. They might have to spend their money where they work."

Justin snorted. "If they want delicious food, that's what they should be doing anyway. No one is better than Hettie with these things." He took a huge bite from his sandwich as if to prove his point and chewed with a large closed mouth grin.

"Nah, man, let's finish before we go in. Seriously."

Justin's confusion returned and began to nibble on the edge of the sandwich bread. "I'm eating as fast as I can."

Noah shook his head. "No, man. I mean, it's just not professional to go waltzing into business offices with some of the best sandwiches in town. You'll make everyone jealous, then they'll try to kill you for yours. No win, my friend. No win."

"The win is in the sandwiches," Justin responded with a laugh. "Don't get me started. We'll be fine. Not like we can get in trouble.

Noah grabbed Justin's arm to keep him from going into the accounting office. "Wait, really. Can we just finish these first? There's..." Justin raised his eyebrows, looking down at Noah's hand on his arm. He moved his eyes back up to his friend's face with a questioning look. Noah looked uncomfortable; a look Justin couldn't remember seeing before.

"What's going on?"

Noah winced and said in a low voice. "Anna and I broke up. I didn't want to say anything, and please don't tell anyone. Anyway, there's a girl in there...a woman. She...I like her. I've been trying to get her attention. I just don't want to go in there looking like some kind of...I don't know, Cookie Monster or something."

Justin couldn't help laughing. Noah grabbed him by the shoulders, looking anxious.

"Don't laugh so loud, she'll hear us. She'll know!"

Justin shook his head, still laughing. "Dude! If you like her, you need to say something!"

Noah pulled back one side of his lips and narrowed his eyes. "Oh, like you told Lynn? Or any of the other women you've been interested in? You just went up and told them, right? I don't think so, Justin. You're more shy than I am! Come on. I'm your best friend! Do this for me. Let's just eat these real quick before we go in there. Man, I can't have her seeing me stuffing my face."

"So you don't want her seeing you stuff your face, but you're wanting to take her out on a date. Where are you gonna go? The bowling alley?" He shook his head. "Nah, I'm teasing you. Sure, we can finish first. Don't got much left anyway." To prove his point, Justin shoved the last of his sandwich in his mouth.

He waited patiently for Noah to finish, amused by the way his friend took a bite, chewed furiously, swallowed and took another bite. "Whoa, you're gonna choke if you keep that up," he said, shaking his head. "Slow down. Last thing you want to do is throw up all over her desk, right? Who is this chick anyway? What's her name?"

Noah raised one eyebrow, swallowed, and said, "Are you kidding? Don't you know any of your employees besides me?"

Justin gave him a skeptical look. "Are you kidding *me*? Why would I? Kathy does the hiring and firing. This isn't my company, it's hers. She just put me in charge of Emerald Resort. That's why I even have to come here. I gotta talk to human resources about hiring some new staff and talk to accounting about rerouting some of the funds from a couple different places into the pay for the staff and the new equipment. If I didn't have to be here, I wouldn't be, trust me. Besides, there's three women working in accounting. And a guy but I'm assuming since you said woman, you weren't talking about him."

Noah shook his head. "I wasn't talking about him. I was talking about Sarah. Sarah Levingston."

Justin nodded. "Oh, the blond." He knew he was right by the look on Noah's face. The man was already enamored. He wondered if he looked at Lynn that way. Probably not.

Thinking about Lynn distracted him from what he was doing. He pictured her in his mind, a warm feeling flowing through him. He'd been wanting to kiss her for a week. Since that night at Badlands, he'd barely been able to resist himself. But he couldn't. Not yet. It was too soon. He was afraid he'd be too forward. If she rejected him, or turned her head away, he didn't know if he could handle the humiliation. What if she didn't like the way he kissed? What if he bumped her nose or bit her lip?

"Hey, hey." Noah snapped his fingers in front of Justin's face, bringing him out of his thoughts. "Where'd you go? Thinking about Lynn, aren't you? All right, I admit, I sent you down that road. But I'm done now, let's get our business done here."

Noah pulled open the door, grinning.

"Yeah, yeah. You gonna ask her out today? I'll leave you in the office with her if you want me to." Justin raised his eyebrows.

"Maybe," Noah replied. "Maybe. I'll let you know."

"How? Bird call?"

They both chuckled, walking down the short hallway to the two doors opposing each other. One said HR on the door in gold letters. The other had a simple A on the door.

"You know, we could always cut this down and you go in one and I go in the other."

Justin shook his head. "Can't. I have to talk to them both. But I'll tell you what. Let's go to accounting first. When I'm done in there, I'll go to HR and you stay in accounting and talk to Sarah. How's that sound?"

"I like the sound of that."

Justin shrugged. "Well, you're only here to keep me company anyway. What other motive could you possibly have to come along?"

Noah grinned. "Boredom?"

"Now that sounds right." Justin tapped his knuckles on Noah's chest and flicked his fingers toward the Accounting door. "Go on. Open the door."

Noah chuckled, reaching out to turn the knob and push the door open. "Entre, boss." He held out one hand for Justin to go in before him.

The room consisted of three desks and more filing cabinets than Justin had ever seen in his life. His eyes widened. He had only been in the room once before and it was when they had one accountant, not three. Everything was tripled but for the life of him, he didn't know why they were still using paper logs.

The room held three desks, one directly in front of them and one on each side. There was only one person in the room, and it was Sarah. She was sitting at the desk in front of them, one hand plunged into her hair, her eyes on the tablet which was lying flat on her table. The computer next to her was open to a spreadsheet document, and she appeared to be comparing what was on the tablet to the screen. She was using a stylus to move the page on the tablet up.

She looked up when they came in. Justin thought she

looked distraught for a moment but, when she saw them, it disappeared, and a bright smile covered her face. He noticed that she didn't look at Noah. She was looking directly at him. She pressed the button on the tablet to turn the screen off.

It didn't surprise him that she was staring at him. He was her boss, after all. But as they walked toward the desk, she didn't look at Noah even once.

"Sarah," he said, leaning over to shake her hand. She stood up to take it. Her hand was firm on his, and she pumped it twice before letting go.

"Mr. Brownstone. Good to see you. What…what can I do for you?"

"I need to talk to you about the resort job. We're going to need to move some funds around."

Justin was surprised to see the woman's face soften. He glanced at Noah, who was looking as distraught as Sarah had when they'd come in.

"You, uh, you know Noah, right? Seen him around?"

Sarah glanced quickly at Noah before moving her eyes back to Justin. "Hello. What areas did you want to move, sir?" She sat back down, looking at her computer and tapping on the keyboard. She pulled up a screen and turned the monitor toward him. He leaned forward and looked at the screen. It looked like gibberish to him. He pulled a paper from his back pocket and unfolded it, laying it flat on her desk.

"These are the departments Kathy wants defunded or reduced. I need to have the printouts on my desk by noon tomorrow, so we can start getting everything together. We'll have to hire a new staff for the place and that means advertising in all the papers we can and online. I know that's not your department, but you'll need to allocate some of the funds to that department, too. I'm sure Kathy has everything written here you need to know."

Sarah nodded. "Yes, I recognize these anagrams. I know what she wants to do." She looked back up at him, a tiny smile

484

crossing her lips. "Will you need an accountant on site there?"

Justin tried not to look surprised. "No, they do all that themselves. What we have...that is, who we have here should be enough."

Sarah nodded. He couldn't help thinking she looked disappointed. When he glanced at Noah, his friend had the same look on his face but for different reasons. Things weren't going the way Noah wanted. Justin had Sarah's full attention. She never took her eyes off him.

It made him feel uncomfortable, as if she had been stalking him for years, and he was suddenly confronted with her drooling all over him. His chest tightened, and he suppressed a sigh.

"I think we'll let Noah handle some of this, too," he said. "He knows what we need. He's been in supplies longer than I can think of."

Noah gave him a grateful look, but Sarah didn't take her eyes from Justin. "If that's what you want, Mr. Brownstone."

He sensed she wanted him to respond in a friendly way, telling her to call him by his first name or some such nonsense. He wasn't about to do that. He'd finally found someone he really wanted to be with. He wasn't going to jeopardize that now.

He hadn't gone years without dating, so he could screw it up in the first month.

Chapter 15

When Lynn passed through the Brownstone Catering entrance, her eyes moved all around the interior, hoping beyond hope she would not see Justin. Her eyes were swollen from crying on the drive over. She couldn't believe how much her heart hurt. Three weeks felt like an eternity to her. It was as if she'd known and loved Justin for years.

Her plan wasn't to confront him. She wanted to talk to Kathy. No one knew Justin better than Kathy. She wished she'd gotten the tablet from Sue before she stormed out of her office, but she wasn't thinking straight.

Before she went in, she'd turned the rearview mirror to look at herself and wipe her eyes. She didn't want to look as devastated as she felt.

Her heart thumped, as she passed the customers in line and walked confidently into the back rooms. The employees didn't pay any attention to her. They'd probably gotten used to seeing her there. She hurried to Kathy's office door, knowing she would have to go by the door to the office Justin rarely worked in. When he told her he had an office, she was amused and asked if he'd ever actually done any work in there. He said he wasn't interested in a desk job and liked to work hands on in the warehouse with Noah and the other employees.

Remembering that gave Lynn some hope. She tried to push her doubts away and focus on what she needed to say to Kathy. She would know if Justin was capable of embezzling from his own sister.

She raised her hand to knock on the door but hesitated, pulling in a shaky breath.

She opened the door when Kathy said "Come in" in response to her knock. Kathy was at her desk. She did a double take before standing up.

"Lynn. I'm sorry, did we have an appointment I've forgotten about?"

Lynn shook her head and crossed the room to sit in the chair in front of the desk. "I think we have a serious problem, Kathy." She hated the sound of her whimpering voice.

The concerned look on Kathy's face made her feel even worse. What she was about to tell her would make her just as sad as Lynn felt. She was sure of that.

"Please tell me what it is," Kathy said. "I'm sure we can work it out. I don't want to lose this opportunity with Emerald Resort. Let's try to work it out together."

Lynn swallowed, dropping her eyes to her folded hands in her lap. She pulled in a deep breath.

"Sue came in my office earlier. She showed me something on the files you sent her, the accounting files."

Kathy nodded, staring intently at Lynn, waiting for her to continue. She had her hands clasped on the desk in front of her. Lynn noticed they were clutched firmly, as if Kathy was bracing herself.

Lynn sighed. "Kathy," she said in a low voice, leaning forward. "Sue has evidence that money is being embezzled from your company. It's hard to tell how long it's been going on from what we have."

She stopped talking. She could see Kathy needed a moment to process the shock. She sat back, staring at Lynn as if she was crazy. Lynn was covered in chills, detecting anger on Kathy's face.

"You're wrong," Kathy said, shaking her head. "There's no way anyone can do that. Only Justin and I have passcodes to get into those programs. Everything else is done by handwritten memo."

"You have accountants, don't you? They're in charge of this kind of thing."

Kathy nodded. "Yes, but they don't have full access. Only Justin and I can get into..." Kathy narrowed her eyes. The anger Lynn had detected was now obvious on her face and in her voice. "Wait. Wait a minute. Are you saying Justin is stealing from our company? Is that what you're saying?"

Lynn was struggling to hold back her tears. She hated confrontation, especially when she'd invested so much of her heart into the relationship that she'd built both with Kathy and Justin.

"I don't want to say that, Kathy. You…you have to know how I feel about him. But the numbers don't lie, and it was his passcode used to get into the system and divert the funds."

Kathy closed her mouth. Lynn could see her clenching her teeth together. She leaned forward even more, putting both arms up on the desk.

"Please, Kathy, don't think bad of me for delivering this to you. Sue and Mari won't continue with our business contract or put Brownstone Catering in the resort if there is money being diverted. You must know how this looks to them."

"You need to leave," Kathy's voice had dropped several octaves and degrees. She sat back, glaring at Lynn.

Lynn shook her head. "I can't. I can't leave until we figure this out. Please, if you'll just pull up your records and have a look yourself, you'll understand. The changes are subtle, and you'll need comparison sheets, like the ones Sue used to show me, but I can point it out to you for now." Her voice turned desperate when Justin passed through her mind, making her heart ache. "I don't want to believe it was him. There must be some other way this has happened, some other person who is…maybe close to Justin that could do this. Or it could be one of your accountants. Really, it could even be a hacker who's gotten into your system. Though it's not likely, since Justin's passcode was used."

Kathy leaned forward again, the angry look still burning on her face. "So, you think my brother is stupid enough to steal from me and leave his passcode on there? If he's smart enough to doctor the numbers, don't you think he's smart enough not to use his own passcode?"

"What other passcode could he use?" Lynn asked. "There's only the two, right? Your accountants don't have it. Unless he's gotten drunk and told one of them…" It was an offhand comment that slipped out of Lynn's mouth before she could bite it back. She sucked in a deep breath when Kathy's anger turned to fury.

"So now you think my brother is a raging drunk that sleeps with our accountants? What's wrong with you? I thought you really cared about him."

"That's not what I said," Lynn responded, flustered, shaking her head vigorously. "I mean, I didn't mean to…"

"I see your true colors now. Get out of my office, Lynn Wright. I don't want anything to do with you or the resort. You can't come in here making accusations without proof. And my brother? Really? Just leave."

Lynn stood up and leaned over the table, her own anger catching up with her sadness and anxiety. "I am not leaving until you help me sort this out. Money is being stolen from you, Kathy. And I don't want to believe it was Justin. If you aren't going to help me figure out who's stealing from you, you are ignorant, and I really don't think you are."

Kathy sucked in a deep breath, her eyes widening. Lynn could see her trying to control herself. The two women stared directly at each other. Finally, to Lynn's relief, Kathy dropped her eyes.

She stared at the table in front of her, and Lynn felt comfortable enough to sit back down. She waited with an anxious heart for Kathy to say something.

After a few moments, Kathy stretched her arm out over the top of her desk and tapped the top with her fingers. "You really don't think he's done this?" she asked, her voice still deep and disturbed.

Lynn shook her head. "I don't want to believe it. Justin isn't the type. You've known him all his life. There's no one who knows him better than you. What do you think?"

Kathy moved her eyes to meet Lynn's again. "My brother is not guilty. I have complete trust in him. He is not greedy or selfish. He is not the kind of man with the fortitude to be a thief."

Relief flooded Lynn from the moment Kathy began talking. She nodded. "I knew you would say that."

"I'm not just saying that because he's my brother," Kathy said. "It's the truth. He really isn't that kind of man. He lives with me. I would know if he had a secret like this." She sat back, shaking her head and crossing her arms over her chest. "It can't be true. No. It isn't true."

"I agree." Lynn pictured Justin in her mind. "But what do we do? Should we go to Justin with this now? Or should we figure it out first? I don't want to go to the police. And I don't think my sisters will without talking to me first."

Kathy's face fell. "You don't really think they would, do you? Oh, I hope not. This is really something I should take care of. It wouldn't be fair to report this before we figure out what's going on."

Lynn shook her head. "No. They wouldn't do anything without talking to me. I know it. Sue was trying to keep me from even coming here. But we have to do something because they aren't going to allow us to bring Brownstone Catering into the resort. Not until we figure this out."

Kathy shook her head. "I'm going to get the paper copies and receipts and look at the signature myself. These are photocopies. Maybe they've been doctored somehow."

"Maybe. What should I do?"

Kathy pulled in a breath, keeping her eyes on Lynn. "Do what you think you should do. If that's asking Justin about it, you are free to do it. He's supposed to be in his office in about a half hour. You can wait in the lobby, if you want. Have…a drink or a sandwich on me."

Lynn nodded and stood up. Kathy did the same. The worried look on her face matched the feeling in Lynn's chest.

"I'm sorry I flew off the handle like that," she said, concern in her voice. "Let's figure this out. Are you going to talk to Justin?"

"If you don't mind. I think I will. I'll get a sandwich."

"Will you let me know what he says?"

Lynn nodded. "I will."

Lynn turned and left the office. Kathy went around her desk and followed her to the door, leaving through another door at the end of the small hallway that led to the warehouse.

They turned in opposite directions without a good-bye. Lynn's anxiety had peaked. She ran through her memory of the time she'd spent with Justin, looking for any sign she missed that he could have been deceiving her.

She didn't trust herself. He was already too important to her for any common sense to be left where that was concerned. Hopefully when she talked to Justin, she would be even more confident of his innocence.

She dropped onto a stool at the tall bar lining the window and turned to watch the people passing by outside. What would she say when she saw him? How was he going to react?

She clasped her fists in front of her mouth, propping her elbows on the table.

Chapter 16

Justin stepped out of his jeep and onto the pavement, slamming the door shut. He pushed the lock button on his key fob to lock the car. The first thing he saw when he lifted his eyes was Lynn's face in the sun, on the other side of the window. She was waiting inside.

She was waiting inside.

His heart did a flip in his chest and he halted in place. She looked beautiful. The sun glinted off the blond in her hair. When she turned her eyes, the rays made them sparkle. An intense desire filled him with warmth.

He pushed the gate open and went past the outside tables without looking at any of the customers. A broad smile was on his face, as he passed through the entrance. He went directly to her table but stopped a few feet away when she turned and looked at him.

She didn't look as pleasant, as she usually did. In fact, she looked much more worried than anything else. He lost his smile and stepped up to the small round table. "Lynn. What's wrong?"

She blinked at him. As she responded, he slid onto the stool across from her and leaned forward on the table.

"I have to ask you something. I need you to be a hundred percent honest with me. Can you do that?"

He could tell she was nervous asking the question. It confused him. He leaned forward even more, sliding his hand over hers.

"You can tell me anything you want, Lynn. I won't tell anyone. I promise."

She looked like she was about to cry. He hated that look on her face. He would do anything he could to make it go away.

Lynn looked around them. He did the same because she did, looking for someone she might recognize. He didn't realize what was going through her head until she spoke again.

"I think we should go in your office where we can be alone."

Justin's heart slammed in his chest. What did she want to talk about? Wasn't that the dreaded phrase, that they needed to talk? That meant something bad was going on. The kind of drama in a relationship that motivated him to be single for such a long time.

They were about to have their first argument. He could feel it.

His stomach churned as he said in a low voice, "We can go in my office. It's back here across from Kathy's."

Lynn nodded. "Yes, let's go in there. We might need your computer, too."

Her words confused him more. He realized her worry must have something to do with business. Something had gone wrong, and she thought it was important enough to come over instead of just texting or talking on the phone.

He slid off the stool and moved toward the hallway, waiting for her, as she grabbed her bag and came after him. He led her to the door of his office and opened it, sweeping one hand inside so she would go in before him.

She did and he followed, doing his best to take in her beautiful shape in as respectful a way possible, in case she turned around. It was hard to keep his hands off her.

He rounded his desk on the other side and sat down, only to stand up again. He moved his eyes to the second chair next to the one Lynn had taken. This was too formal. He didn't want to be on the other side of the desk if she needed consoling of some kind.

He didn't even know what to do if she did need consoling. Was he expected to kiss her? Hug her? Hold her somehow? What if she didn't want him to touch her at all?

He looked at her. When she moved her eyes to the chair across from her, he took it as a sign that's where she wanted him to sit.

493

He rounded the table and dropped down in the chair, his knees pointed in her direction.

"You look really worried, Lynn. Tell me what's on your mind."

"Okay. I...I was in my office earlier and Sue came in. She had some documents on a tablet that showed...that showed..."

Justin was more confused than ever. Lynn looked only seconds from crying; her face was strained, and her eyes were misty.

"What is it?" he asked anxiously. "Just tell me, for Christ's sake."

Lynn nodded. "I'm trying. They showed your signature on some documents that show embezzlement of funds. Even down to the bank account transfers. They were done under your passcode in the security system."

Justin was completely confused at that point. Most of what Lynn had just said was gibberish to him. He had a passcode to the complete business files and transactions in case his sister needed to use it for some reason. It was a backup security measure only. He never used it and didn't know what to do or even how to use it.

He shook his head. "Documents I signed? What are you talking about?"

Lynn was quiet for a moment, studying him. He didn't understand the look on her face. Was she accusing him of something? She tilted her head to the side.

"The misappropriation of funds. It's a crime, Justin. It shows you've been stealing from the company."

A shock wave ran through Justin, making him tingle. He shook his head again, this time more vigorously. "Oh, no. No, no. I don't think you've got the right Justin on this."

"Your passcode was used," Lynn repeated.

Anger split through him. Did she not think he heard her the first time? Or maybe she thought he was too stupid to have

494

understood the first time. She *was* accusing him of something, after all.

"I don't know what you're talking about. Why don't you spell it out in layman's terms, so I'll know what you mean."

"Justin, your passcode was used to overcharge Brownstone Catering when buying supplies and equipment and somewhere in the middle, the overages were split off and sent to a bank account somewhere."

"Where was the money sent?"

Lynn fell silent again, studying him. After a moment, she said, "You don't know?"

He shook his head. "I barely understand what you're talking about. It sounds like you think I forged some documents and made my sister pay more than she was supposed to so I could skim off the top and steal it off into a bank. Is that what you're saying?"

"That's it in a nutshell, Justin," Lynn said, firmly, scanning his face.

Justin felt like a rock had formed in his stomach. He pushed one hand over it as it turned over and sent bile up into his throat. It burned and he swallowed vigorously. He raised his other hand to put over his mouth. He coughed as the feeling settled back down.

He shook his head. How could this have happened? For the first time in so long, he'd found someone to spend his life with, that just might love him as deeply as he loved. There shouldn't have been anything that could come between them. He'd spent so long making sure no drama came into his life.

Life's timing was awful, he moaned to himself.

An ache formed in his chest.

"Do you think I stole money from my sister?" he asked, dropping his voice to a deep tone.

Lynn just looked at him with that intense look of hers. The green and blue in her eyes mixed with a soft mist of tears. Finally, she shook her head, sending relief flooding through him. He moved his eyes away from her.

"That's good to hear," he said. "I wouldn't do something like that. Why would I do it?"

"Your passcode was used, Justin," Lynn said softly, leaning toward him, closing the distance so they were a few inches away from each other. "Tell me how that happened."

Justin shook his head, unable to take his eyes off hers. "I don't know. I really don't know."

"Have you ever told anyone what it was?" Lynn asked, looking afraid for a moment.

He wondered why she would be afraid. The only reason she could possibly look that way was if she genuinely cared for him. She might even love him.

He struggled to comprehend that. He'd spent so many years alone. So many years doing and thinking only about and for himself. Lynn was the first woman to ever make him want to change that about himself. He wanted to share his life with her in a way he never had with a woman before. He trusted her.

He trusted her.

The thought raised goosebumps on his arms.

"No, Lynn," he responded seriously. "I've never told anyone the passcode. I barely remember it myself."

Lynn raised her eyebrows, her eyes suddenly clearing a bit. "Do you have it memorized?"

He nodded. "Of course." He wondered where she was going in her thinking.

"Well, do you have it written down anywhere?"

"I'm sure I do somewhere."

Lynn's shoulders visibly relaxed and her face turned gentle. "So, you're telling me you've got the passcode to the entire security system just written down somewhere and you aren't sure where? Anyone might have access to it, where you put it, if you can't even remember where it was."

Justin felt a streak of humiliation pass through him. He drew his brows together and pulled away slightly. "I don't think I'd be stupid enough to do that. I'm sure I put it somewhere safe. Like in a safe. Or something like that. I wouldn't just leave it lying around."

Lynn reached out and rested one small hand on his cheek. It sent a chill down his spine.

"That mistake might be your saving grace, Justin. Don't be embarrassed. I have to use only one or two passwords on everything, or I'll definitely forget what it is. If someone got access to your code, you're innocent and we need to move past that and look for the person who did this."

Justin turned his eyes to the door, another wave of anxiety sweeping through him. "Does Kathy know? Did Sue tell her or Mari? What are they saying? What do they think?"

Lynn laid it out for him clearly. He listened to the soft tone of her voice, heard a sweet drawl he was beginning to love and lost concentration twice staring at her lips. But he got the gist of what she was saying. Her sisters were unhappy. They were ready to pull the plug on the whole operation. They wanted nothing to do with someone who would steal from his own company.

"So, we need to find out who did this so you can still come to the resort and…"

Justin shook his head, feeling like a door had just been slammed in his face. "They'll never agree to it now," he said forlornly. "That opportunity was just blown out of the water."

"You don't know that yet," Lynn retorted in an insisting voice. "You need to wait and see. We'll figure out who did this and everything will go back to normal."

Justin's heartbeat sped up when he looked in her eyes. He sensed the longing she was feeling. He reached out and put his arms around her, coming off the chair, pulling her to him. He pulled in a deep breath when she hugged him back, standing up so they were pressed together.

He could hear her shaky breath in his ear. He pulled away slightly and looked down at her. She turned her face up to him, and he lowered his head on instinct, pressing his lips against hers.

Chapter 17

Lynn left Justin's office determined, feeling like she was walking on a cloud. His kiss had been warm and passionate. There was no way he could have kissed her that way if he didn't have real feelings for her. It was so spontaneous, so sweet.

She felt a little dizzy.

By the time she got to her car, she had to sit in the driver's seat and gather herself together. It was sure to be the first of many. And she couldn't wait for the next one.

For now, her plan was to go back to the resort and talk to Sue and Mari together. If they put a hold on the progress of the addition, it would give her time to prove Justin's innocence. She couldn't imagine them not giving her some time. It would be completely unlike them.

She rested her forehead on the steering wheel, a smile bursting across her face. She giggled, a new sensation flooding through her, pleasure sliding down her spine, when she remembered the kiss.

She let herself enjoy the feeling for a few moments before harshly getting herself back to reality. She would have plenty of time to make new memories with Justin after she proved his innocence.

Lynn pulled the car out of the parking lot and headed in the direction of the Resort.

What if they couldn't find evidence proving Justin was being framed?

A thought came into mind, and her eyes widened in alarm. She took her eyes from the road long enough to glance in the direction of her purse. She reached out, looking out at the road again, unzipped and shuffled through the contents without looking.

She felt in the upper right hand pocket for her cell phone and struggled to pull it out of the small space. She glanced down at it quickly, searching her contacts for Kathy's name. She pressed the button and held the phone up to her ear while it connected.

Her heart thumped, as she waited for Kathy to answer. It seemed to ring a few times before it was answered. Lynn prepared herself for the voicemail, but it was Kathy's voice.

"Hello, Lynn," she said, as if she'd been expecting Lynn to call.

"Kathy, I just thought of something. Have you already talked to your accountants?"

"We have one that works offsite, but I don't think it's him, so I'm not bothering with that."

"Why don't you think it's him?" Lynn asked. She wasn't sure it was wise to rule anyone out."

"Because he's never met Justin and runs a business that takes care of accounts for a lot of clients. He's barely involved in our everyday business. He's more of a consultant. Did you talk to Justin? Is that why you're calling?"

"I didn't call because of that but yes, I did talk to him," Lynn responded. "He says he's innocent, and I believe him."

"I'm sure it didn't take much convincing," Kathy said, a trace of her old humor coming back for a moment.

Lynn let a smile flicker across her lips. "No, probably not. But listen, if you go to the accountants and tell them what's going on, it's going to warn them. Someone is going to go in and wipe the information."

"I thought of that," Kathy responded. Relief flooded through Lynn. She closed her eyes briefly but opened them up just as quickly, to look at the road in front of her. "I didn't say anything about these files. I went in on one of their computers, I don't know where they were, but they weren't in the office. Maybe lunch. I did a little searching but didn't see anything I thought was suspicious in any of their desks."

Lynn listened as Kathy related the story of her adventure in the office, feeling like she was doing something wrong, looking over her shoulder constantly, hoping no one came in while she was in there.

"So, you don't suspect any of them?" Lynn said, disappointment in her voice.

"On the contrary," Kathy's voice sounded electronic in her ear for a moment. "I suspect *all* of them. Nothing stood out to me specifically, but that's just one brief search. I'll have to talk to Justin. We might be able to get the money put in the bank accounts transferred. Then we will use it as we see fit."

"When are you planning to talk to Justin?" Lynn asked. She suddenly noticed the phone was hot against her face.

"In a few minutes. Are you going to talk to your sisters?"

"Yes. I have to convince them to give me time before completely pulling the plug on the operation. I want your company to open a new addition in the resort, and I want Justin in charge of it. It's a great opportunity which I don't want him to lose."

Her brow creased.

"Kathy," she continued. "Do you think this is what he really wants to do? Doesn't he have other things he's more interested in?"

A surge of adrenaline swept through her when Kathy hesitated before she answered. She hated that intense feeling of doubt.

"I think even if he does have other aspirations, he wouldn't commit theft to get it. He would either work for a while and save the money, or he'd ask me for a loan or part of his inheritance money. It's not like he doesn't have a trust."

Confusion filled Lynn. "Wait a minute," she said. "He has a trust fund?"

She heard Kathy chuckle on the other end. "Of course, he has a trust. We both do. Except what I've kept, and I'm building up for retirement. Justin's money has just sat in the bank, waiting for him to be interested in using it for something."

The skin on Lynn's arms tingled. She didn't know Justin

501

already had money. That was more proof he wouldn't commit embezzlement, at least in *her* mind.

"He never mentioned that."

"Yeah, he doesn't care a lot of about it," Kathy replied.

"How many people know about the money in trust?" Lynn narrowed her eyes, seeing the entrance of Emerald Resort approaching in the distance.

"No one. That's our private business."

"So, your accountants don't know about it either?" Lynn pressed on.

"No," Kathy's voice had become confused. "Why are you asking about it? What relevance does it have?"

"I just think it goes to prove he wouldn't have a reason to steal, like you said, and if the accountant or the person who is doing this didn't know about the trust, they wouldn't realize he couldn't be framed. Does that make sense?"

Kathy chuckled. "I think it does in your mind, Lynn. But I get what you're trying to say. Why frame a man with theft if he already has thou…a lot of money he's sitting on."

Lynn noticed the abrupt shift in Kathy's words and grinned. "You don't have to worry about me wanting Justin for his money, Kathy," she said lightheartedly, feeling better knowing this new information.

Kathy chuckled again. "Oh I know, Lynn. You have plenty of your own, that's for sure. I would never have told you about Justin's money. That's his business and I would have left it up to him to say something under normal circumstances. But this seemed like something you should know."

"I'm glad you told me, Kathy. And I'm sure he'll tell me eventually. Maybe he wanted to make sure I didn't just want his money."

They both laughed at that. She had no doubt Justin knew full well she didn't need or want his money. It was *him* she wanted. And now, after the kiss, she wanted him more than ever.

She went through the entrance gate to the resort and drove up and around to the offices. Both her sisters' cars were still there, which was to be expected since it was the middle of the day. Whether or not they were in their offices was something else, though.

She jumped out of the SUV and jogged up the path to the glass doors.

She pulled them open and a fresh breeze of air conditioning swept over her, blowing up the ends of her blond hair. It was a good feeling in the hot muggy Georgia air. She took off at a fast walking pace down the hallway, her eyes focused on the next hallway, where she would turn to get to the offices.

Her heart beat anxiously as she went. She wanted her sisters to be there and hoped they would listen to what she had to say. She was certain they would. They had never been unreasonable before.

And they'd both been in love before. They knew that desperate feeling of wanting everything to be perfect, no mistakes, no hiccups. Just love and peace and the thrill of a new relationship.

She stopped outside Sue's door first. She pulled in a deep breath before opening it. She stuck just her head in. Sue was seated behind her desk. Lynn's eyes slid up and over Sue's shoulder, where Mari was bent over, one hand on the back of Sue's chair and the other flat on the desk in front of her.

Both women looked up when she entered.

"Lynn," Mari said, her voice stern. "We were just talking about you."

"And Justin?" Lynn asked, regretting the resentful tone of her voice. "I mean, I'm sure you've told Mari about the...issues we're having, right Sue?" She tried to end using a friendlier tone. She didn't want to upset them right off the bat. She wanted them to listen to her and that wasn't the way to get on their good sides.

Sue nodded. "I told her. We're actually looking at the

documents right now, trying to compare Justin's signature with some others on the documents, but a lot of them are digitally signed and without paper copies. It's hard to judge his signature. These are all photo representations."

"I talked to Kathy," Lynn came in and dropped into the chair in front of Sue's desk. She perched on the edge anxiously, her back straight as a board. "She doesn't believe this is Justin's work either. She is looking through the actual paper documents, probably right now. I think she'd trying to be discreet. It might take a while. I'd like to look through those documents myself but…well, I guess I might have to ask Justin if he wants to go on a late night excursion with me."

Both Sue and Mari gave her confused looks, their brows drawn together, making them look almost like twins if their coloring was different. Lynn hadn't noticed before how much the two looked alike. She wondered if she had the same facial features, too.

"I want to go when the offices are closed and look through the paper files," Lynn explained.

The looks of confusion cleared up. She grinned when Sue did.

"Oh, you're going to do a little investigating, are you?" Sue asked.

"Yes," Lynn answered.

"I hope you find the proof we need, Lynn," Mari said seriously, causing a chill to rise up through Lynn's spine. "Because we can't do business with them if you don't find out the truth soon."

"How long are you willing to wait before you put the kibosh on our plans?" Lynn asked.

Mari gazed at her for a moment and then shook her head. "I don't know. A while. I know how you feel about him, Lynn. So just do what you can. As fast as you can. Okay?"

Lynn nodded, feeling more determined than ever.

Chapter 18

Justin couldn't believe this was happening. He'd pull up documents on the computer but how was he to know what he was really looking at? He didn't know accounting. What did he have to compare the numbers to? He'd have to go through documents he doubted he'd even be able to find. He didn't know about accounting.

He didn't know anything about it at all.

He ran one hand over his mouth and chin, sighing and sitting back in his chair. The next moment he sat forward and propped his elbows on the desk, running his hands through his wavy blond hair. He stayed that way, staring down at the top of his desk.

His looked up when his door opened, and Kathy looked in.

"I thought you were still here," she said.

He gazed at her, lacing his fingers together and tapping his lips with them. "Yep. Still here. You talked to Lynn, right?"

Kathy came in and sat in front of him in the chair. The only person who'd ever sat in that chair before was Noah. No one else ever came to Justin's office to visit him. He usually wasn't there if they did.

"I don't know what's going on, Justin. But if there's something you need to tell me, you should do it now."

Justin felt an ache slide through him. Kathy didn't trust him. She thought he was guilty. He sat back, looking at her with chagrin on his face. "You think I did this? You think I'd steal from you?"

Kathy shook her head quickly. "No. I don't. I just want you to tell me you had nothing to do with it. I'll believe you if you do. Tell me, Justin."

He sat forward again. "I had nothing to do with this. I don't need to steal from you. I have enough money. I don't even touch what I do have." He pulled his eyebrows together, unable to get rid

505

of the feeling of hurt. "I can't believe you wouldn't trust me. How could you even ask?"

"I don't think you did this, and I want to find out who did. Lynn believes in you, just like I do. I just had to ask. I had to hear it from you."

"Well, I'm telling you right now. I didn't do this." Justin moved his eyes to the computer screen, where several documents were displayed in smaller boxes so more than one could be seen at a time. He waved his hand at the screen. "I pulled up this information. But I don't know what I'm looking at."

Kathy sat forward, leaning one arm on the desk and looking at the screen sideways. He reached out and turned the monitor so she could see easier. "I had the passcode in my wallet, tucked in behind a couple cards. No one has ever gone in my wallet. The passcode has never been anywhere else."

"Did you look at the signatures on the papers?" Kathy asked. "Do they look like yours?"

Justin nodded. "They do look like mine, but I don't sign most papers in person. And the electronic signature always looks the same. Whoever did this had to know all my personal information, too. Social, birthdate, all that stuff, so they could open an account to put the money into. That account probably has a different password, something I wouldn't know. Security questions I wouldn't be able to answer."

"We'll figure that out," Kathy said in a determined voice. "In the meantime, we should narrow down who might have done this."

"I still don't know how the passcode got into someone's hands."

Kathy gave him a direct look. "Are you sure you didn't give it to anyone? Mention it to anyone?"

He shook his head.

"And you never changed it to something you'd remember, did you? Like, when we were given our original numbers, you kept the one you were given."

Justin nodded, picturing the scrap of paper in his wallet. "It's a set of random numbers. That's why I keep the paper, to remind me. It's not my birthday or something that would be easily guessed."

He narrowed his eyes, flipping them between the computer screen and his sister. "You don't think someone could use a random number generator to get it, do you?"

Kathy appeared to be thinking about it.

"I mean, if someone in HR is responsible, they would have my personal information on file."

"Well, most of that is common knowledge anyway, like your birthday," Kathy reasoned.

"Yeah." Justin nodded. "But not my social. And you can't open a bank account in someone's name without a social. Just like a credit card can't be taken out. That's identity theft."

"Well, yeah, Justin, whoever did this *did* commit identity theft. *And* embezzlement."

Justin sighed. He knew some of the people in HR and accounting. But none of them were close to him. Noah was the only person he hung out with on a regular basis.

He frowned. "There is a girl in accounting who was acting strange with me a couple days ago."

Kathy raised her eyebrows, giving him an intense look. "Oh? Like how strange?"

Justin shifted uncomfortably, remembering how he'd tried to get out of the room and leave Noah in there to flirt all he wanted. "It's the woman named Sarah. She looks about my age, maybe a little older? I mean, she was just flirting, but it seemed strange to me."

Kathy gave him a doubtful look. "It was strange for her to flirt with you? She's never done that before?"

"I don't think I've met her but once or twice before. I went

507

in there with Noah. He likes her. Tried to get her attention the whole time, but she was concentrated on me. I had to leave him in the room with her so he could do his thing."

Kathy shook her head. "Do his thing," she repeated. "Anyway, what do you think? Could she be the one?"

Justin pulled back one side of his lips. "I just don't know. I don't know why she'd do something like this and frame me for it."

"You and I are the only ones with the passcodes to the entire set of business files. If this person did it on any other level, it would have been picked up by the other accountants."

Justin nodded. "Or HR."

Kathy nodded back. "Someone would have discovered it. I'm ashamed I didn't."

"You had no reason to double check. When was the last time you signed in under my passcode to see what I was doing?"

Kathy chuckled without humor. "I've never checked your passcode."

Justin nodded and shrugged. "Why would you? You've always trusted me. Haven't you?"

"Of course, I have. You're my brother. I love you. I know you."

Justin was relieved and sighed heavily. "Good. I hope Lynn feels that way, too." The kiss swam through his mind and his body tingled with leftover excitement. His heartbeat sped up just a little. He couldn't help the tiny smile that lifted the corners of his lips. He couldn't wait to do that again.

Lynn would be lucky if he didn't smother her with kisses every time he saw her.

His attention came back to where he was and what he was doing when Kathy lifted one hand and covered her smiling mouth with it. He narrowed his eyes.

"What?"

"I've never seen you in love before. It's cute."

508

"Don't start with me, Kathy. I'm not in the mood."

"Sure you are," his sister replied. He lifted his eyebrows, already feeling a bit more light-hearted. He had his sister on his side. The woman he loved believed in him. He would do anything he could to keep that, to keep Lynn's love and trust. Something like this happening as soon as he found her made him feel like the world was against him, like maybe Satan was out to get him. Hadn't he suffered a depressing life long enough? Hadn't he been alone long enough?

"You just keep thinking about Lynn, Justin," Kathy continued, her tone just slightly cheerful. He could tell she was trying to be encouraging. "She believes in you. I know she does. I think she's fallen for you pretty hard."

Justin's heart skipped a beat. A pleasant tingle flooded through him. He didn't know why Lynn would care about him so much, but the thought made him feel like shouting from the rooftops.

"You think so?"

Kathy lifted one eyebrow. "Of course, she does. You can't possibly be wondering about that."

"I really don't want to screw this up. I really don't."

Kathy slid forward more in the seat until she was on the very edge. She leaned both elbows on the table, laying her arms flat in front of her. "Justin. I can see it all over her face. She's head over heels. You've already got her heart."

Justin sighed. "I know. That's what I'm worried about. You know how long it's been since I've been in a relationship."

Kathy met his eyes with hers and let them linger for a moment. "I don't remember you ever being in a real relationship. You've gone out with girls, at least when you were a teenager. I don't remember anyone for at least the last five years. Not even one." She drew her eyebrows together and gave him a concerned look. "I wish I'd noticed that before. You've been so lonely for so long."

Justin shook his head. "You don't have a boyfriend. Are you lonely?"

Kathy grinned. "I have this business. And I have dated. I just haven't found the right man for me. I went out just a couple weeks ago with someone staying at the hotel. Very nice man, a marketer for…Oh, I don't want to talk about that right now. I doubt I'll ever see him again anyway."

"Why not?"

Kathy chuckled. "He was just passing through. I'm afraid what he really wanted wasn't something I was about to give."

"Say no more," Justin lifted one hand in the air in a "stop" motion. "I don't want to hear about it. I probably would have gone over and smashed his face in if I'd known."

Kathy nodded. "Precisely why I didn't tell you, my brother."

They both laughed.

"Well, you've proven your point that you've gone out and I haven't. But I haven't really thought of it as lonely. I was just waiting. I wanted to be with a woman I think mom would have liked. And I think she would have liked Lynn."

Kathy's face softened, her gaze resting on him gently. He knew he'd touched her heart. It was the truth. He held his standards by the mother he still had in his memory, a dear woman who had taken good care of him until her death when he was young. Kathy had filled in well as a parent figure.

"Mom would have approved," Kathy said, softly, nodding her head. "She would definitely have approved."

Chapter 19

As he was leaving his office to go to the warehouse where Noah was waiting, he thought about what his sister had said. He wondered what Lynn was doing right at that moment. He pulled out his cell phone, as he walked down the hall, deciding to get a drink and have a smoke on the deck outside at a table before he went to the warehouse.

Just as he stepped out into the lobby of the deli, he bumped into a woman coming out of the bathroom. He almost dropped his phone but caught it in midair before looking up to see who he'd run into.

"Oh, sorry!"

He looked up to see Sarah smiling at him, one hand over her heart.

"I'm sorry, Justin! I wasn't expecting to see anyone on the other side of the door. You aren't stalking me, are you?"

The teasing sound in her voice would have been cute if it was Lynn speaking to him. But it wasn't. And his suspicion of Sarah made it hard for him to respond in the friendly, polite way he wanted to.

"I'm sorry about that, Sarah," he said quickly. "It was my fault. Won't…won't you let me get you a drink before you leave work? I guess that's what you're doing?"

Sarah nodded, her eyes directly on him. He was a little uneasy under her gaze but made sure his face was neutral. He didn't want to give himself away, in case it *was* Sarah responsible for the theft and embezzlement.

Why would she want to frame him, though?

"I would love that, Justin. Thank you!"

Her smile beamed at him. He noticed she was attractive, with straight auburn hair falling softly over her shoulders and bright green eyes the color of emeralds. If he'd noticed her before, he might have been attracted. But his suspicion of her made him

511

think of her differently. That in addition to the fact that his heart was already taken.

"I wonder where Noah is?" he said offhandedly. "I haven't seen him for a couple hours."

"Noah?" Sarah asked questioningly.

Justin nodded. "Yeah, the guy I was with the last time I came in there. Didn't you two have a chance to talk after I left?"

"Oh him," Sarah said the words dismissively, giving Justin a disheartening feeling. The next moment he was glad she wasn't interested in Noah. There was a good possibility she was a criminal. He wouldn't want his friend falling for a woman like her. "Yeah, he stayed for a minute while you talked to them in HR."

She fell silent. Justin walked to the bar with her, going through the small door and fixing them two beers. He lifted his glass to her with his eyebrows raised to see if that was what she wanted, too. She smiled and nodded.

He brought the glasses out, handing one to her. "I got it for you, but I'm not carrying it for you. Here you go."

"Oh, I thought the man was always supposed to carry the glasses," Sarah giggled. He gave her a direct look.

"That's only on a date. I'm not really available right now."

He caught the look on her face. He recognized it as one of instant jealousy. He could see she was trying to hide it. He didn't know if she realized she wasn't succeeding at all.

He pushed open the door and held it open, so she could go out on the deck.

"You want to drink out here?" Sarah asked, staring at the outside tables. There was only one available, so Justin went straight to it and sat down, setting the beer glass down, as he pulled out his pack of cigarettes. He hoped silently that Sarah was against smoking, and it would make him less attractive to her.

"Yeah, I like it out here," he answered, as he lit the cigarette with a lighter from his front pocket. "Plus, Kathy doesn't allow smoking inside. And I need a cigarette for what I'm going through."

Sarah plopped down across from him and gazed at him intensely. "What's going on? If you don't mind me asking."

Justin turned over responses in his head. There was absolutely no reason to be honest with this woman or give himself and his suspicions away. He wasn't even really sure what he was doing with her at that point. He didn't want to be where he was and couldn't imagine how he could glean any information out of her.

"I'm sorry you didn't seem to like my friend," he said, changing the subject abruptly. He turned his eyes away from her disinterestedly, hoping she would get the point.

The more he thought about it, though, the more he wondered if getting on her good side was the way to go. If she thought he was interested in her, he might be able to get her to tell *him* what was going on. She might even confess.

He chided himself silently. He didn't have the charm to make a woman confess her sins to him. Especially not when it might be him that is implicated by what she was doing. She'd be a fool to say anything to him about it at all.

And he'd be a fool to tell her.

"I...I think he's a really nice guy," Sarah said, falteringly. "It's just...I have my eye on someone else. And...well, I don't really care for the way he slinks around."

Justin frowned, his eyes darting to her slender face. "What? What do you mean; slinks around?"

"Well, he's around the office a lot, even when no one is there. We know because he's there sometimes when we come back."

"He's in the office? In your office? At someone's desk?"

Sarah shrugged, her eyes moving to the side, as she appeared to remember. "I think a couple times he might have been behind a desk. Like, looking at a computer, you know. But usually, he's just standing in front of my desk, looking at the file cabinets and stuff."

Justin was becoming more confused by the moment. It could have been that Noah was trying to find a way to endear himself to Sarah. But what if it was something else? Had he revealed his passcode to Noah? He tried to remember. Even if he'd been out drinking with Noah, which he had on several occasions, he wouldn't have told him that passcode. And Noah would never ask.

Justin's chest tightened with apprehension. He didn't want to suspect Noah. He didn't know whether to believe Sarah's story or not. Maybe she was trying to deflect attention from herself.

But the way she flirted with Justin didn't imply she was trying to divert any attention. She *wanted* Justin's attention, that was clear. Maybe she was just an employee with a crush on the boss.

He felt a heavy burden on his shoulders. He didn't want to suspect Noah.

"Why would he be in your office? Was he leaving you notes or something?"

Sarah frowned in confusion. "Leaving me notes?"

"Yes. He's got a crush on you. Don't you know that?"

Sarah lifted her eyebrows. "I didn't know that. He doesn't act like he does. He's never asked me out or anything. Besides, like I said, I've got my eye on someone else. I think he must know that. If he's been trying to get my attention, he hasn't been doing a very good job."

"I'm surprised you didn't know," Justin replied. He was back to not knowing whether he could trust her or not. "He's a pretty outgoing guy. I would have thought he'd have asked you by now."

Sarah shook her head, lifting her beer glass and tilting it back to swallow a quarter of it in just a few swallows. She set it back down and smiled at him, wiping her mouth with the back of her hand.

Justin grinned. "I see you like your beer."

She tilted her head to one side and straightened it immediately. "Sometimes. I have to be in the mood."

He offered her his pack of cigarettes. "Smoke?"

She shook her head. "Nah, I'm quitting. Well, I might if I have another one of these. Or two." She giggled, tilting the beer glass back and forth. "I only smoke these days when I'm drinking. And I do neither of which very often, so I'm glad to say I don't have a problem with it. I used to…" She used a confessing voice, moving her eyes reluctantly away from his face. "But I've been abstaining for a while now. It makes me feel like crap the next day, and my throat burns because, if I drink a lot, I smoke a lot."

"I've heard that's a common problem. My sister's been trying to get me to quit for years. I want to, I guess. Especially because the woman I'm interested in doesn't smoke. I don't want to turn her off, you know?"

Sarah nodded. The look on her face had changed to something Justin couldn't decipher. She didn't give him that longing look, and it wasn't quite jealousy he saw. It was something in between. He wondered if he was actually missing out on a good friendship. If it was possible for a man and a woman to be friends. He'd never had a platonic relationship and didn't know anyone who did.

"So, I'm sorry you have bad stuff going on," Sarah said. "Anything I can do to help?"

Justin contemplated the idea of bringing Sarah in on the investigation. But she was still a suspect, even if he was beginning to feel differently about her. He shook his head.

"No, not really. Just business stuff. Karen and I will figure it out. We've got that new business going into the Emerald Resort, as you know, and that puts a lot of stress on us. We'll get it figured out."

Sarah nodded, drinking another large portion of her beer. It was nearly empty when she set the glass down. "I know that's a lot of work. It seems like it to us, too. We've been crunching numbers for you for weeks now."

Justin turned his eyes away from her. She was gazing at him directly. He thought she'd done a good job directing the conversation back to the problem he was having. He wondered if it was simple curiosity that made her do that or if she was prying for information.

He didn't want to give anything away. He shrugged.

"You don't have to worry. We'll get it worked out. We just have to find the money to make sure this works out the way it's supposed to. You know I'm going to be in charge over there. I don't want anything to go wrong."

Sarah's eyes softened and the look of desire was back. Justin looked away.

"I know, Justin. But you'll do just fine. I know you will. I have a lot of confidence in you. You're so smart. I think you could accomplished anything you set your mind to. I'm sure of it."

Chapter 20

Justin tapped his fingers on the surface of the table, consciously keeping himself from grinding his teeth in frustration. He swept his eyes around the deck, looking at the patrons, vowing not to make himself noticed by any of them.

His instinct was to get up and find Noah, question him about his supposed trips to the offices. But he knew what his friend would say. He would reiterate his "desire" for Sarah and act offended that Justin could even suspect him.

But he did suspect Noah. Sarah was a good candidate for suspicion, and she definitely wasn't off the hook. If Noah had been skulking around, as Sarah said, that changed his outlook on the whole thing. It didn't have to be Sarah.

No matter who it was, he still didn't know how either could have gotten his passcode.

Frustrated, he turned his attention back to Sarah, who was gazing at him with pure admiration. He had to look away, his sense of unease rising.

"I can see you're troubled about something," she said in a soft voice meant to attract him. He knew flirting when he saw it. "I wish you would tell me. I'm here to listen to you, Justin. I wouldn't say a word to anyone. I really wouldn't."

The urge to spill it all swept through him again, but he shook his head, clamping his mouth shut. He wasn't going to compromise their investigation by revealing everything to a prime suspect.

"It's really not something I can talk about freely," he said, gently. "Sorry. My sister and I need to take care of it."

"Well, if it has something to do with money, you know I can help. I'm a certified accountant, you know."

Justin sensed she was prying, doing her best to get more information from him. He wondered why she was so interested. He thought quickly, formulating a plan in his mind. He would have to depend on Lynn for it to work but he couldn't wait to consult Lynn in person. He had to put it into action now, while he had Sarah where he wanted her.

He reached into his back pocket and slowly pulled his cell phone out. He didn't lift it above table level. If it worked the way he wanted it to, he could send a text without Sarah noticing.

He tapped out a few sentences, glancing down every now and then and motioning with his thumb as if he was just scrolling through social media.

Lynn, with Sarah now from accounting, need to talk to you, meet me here in half hour?

He hit send with his thumb, lifted his eyes and pretended to focus his attention on Sarah. He narrowed her eyes, which got her attention and she stopped talking.

"Will you do something for me, Sarah?" he asked, sitting forward and lowering his voice in a conspiratorial manner.

He saw her face light up with excitement. "Sure," she said quickly, matching his low tone.

"I want you to buy the supplies for the resort business, but I want you to keep it private. Don't let Noah in your office. Will you do that for me?"

He didn't know if he liked the slow smile that spread on her face. He would have sworn he saw traces of satisfaction there, too, but it could have just been his wishful—or rather hopeful— feelings. He didn't want Noah to be the guilty party. But, if he got Lynn on board, and they had Sarah do the ordering, chances were good she would do one last heist, since the spotlight had now fallen on someone else.

He wouldn't be surprised if he started finding all kinds of clues leading to Noah as the guilty party. Lynn had copies of the papers the way they were already. It was too late for Sarah to change them.

He had already decided she was guilty. That probably wasn't a good thing. But he couldn't help himself. Noah was too good of a friend. Nothing would make him believe he could do something like that.

"When do you want to go over the paperwork?" Sarah didn't look in the least bit nervous. Justin wondered if she was so cold, so callous that she would show absolutely no sign of what kind of person she really was.

He hoped his thoughts weren't reflected on his face. He forced himself to smile, wishing fervently that Lynn would text back just when his phone buzzed in his hand. He tapped the screen and glanced down at it. It was a message but information about it was hidden.

He swiped the screen with his thumb and pulled up the message. Lynn had written back to him.

I'm here with Kathy. Going over some things. Where are you?

He typed in Outside on deck as quickly as he could. He hit send and looked up at Sarah.

"I'm sorry, did you ask me something? Just tending to some business here." He lifted the phone, pressing the power button so the front would go black, twisting it back and forth in the air in front of him.

Her eyes dropped to the phone. He studied her face, watching for a reaction. He saw nothing. She lifted her eyes back to his face, giving him an expectant look. "I asked when you want to go over the list of supplies. I can look them all up. I very often do price checks for Kathy. I think we can get some really good deals. It's a shame prices have been going up across the board but with the new business at the resort, I think you'll make up all the money you've lost recently."

Justin felt a strange sensation slide through him. He felt like he'd just listened to her confess what she'd been doing. He calmed the anger that split through him a second later. If she *was* responsible, that meant she was willing to let everyone think *he* was stealing *from his sister*. He couldn't think of anything more damaging to his reputation in Queen Anne. That was the ultimate act of greed, in his opinion.

He tried giving her a grin, but it was difficult. He didn't want to tip her off. In the back of his mind, he was waiting anxiously for Lynn to come out. Maybe she would assess the situation and give her opinion of Sarah. As long as she believed he was innocent. The plan wouldn't work if Lynn had any doubt in him whatsoever.

Sarah was smooth and looked believable. She had an innocent look about her. Justin would have to depend on Lynn's feelings for him and the smarts God gave her.

"We'll have to get with Lynn Wright, the owner of the Resort, too. She might want to amend the list. But try not to let anyone else see the list. It will just be the three of us on this project, okay?"

Sarah grinned at him. She winked and nodded. "Yeah, I know what you're saying, Justin. I know who you need to keep it from. And don't worry, I'll make sure he doesn't come prowling around this project."

Justin nodded, giving her an approving look. He could see her drinking it in, her eyes growing softer the longer she looked at him. The uncomfortable feeling was rising in his stomach again when her eyes shifted to the entrance of the deli behind him. He turned his head to see Lynn coming out.

She held the door open for a moment, running her eyes over the people sitting at the tables around the deck. When she got to him, she stopped. It looked like she wanted to smile but didn't on purpose. Her eyes flipped to Sarah and then back to him.

"There's Lynn right there," Justin said, as if surprised by her presence. He glanced back at Sarah to see how she was reacting to it. The expression on her face hadn't changed but her eyes narrowed slightly, taking in Lynn as the woman approached.

Lynn stepped up to them, crossing her arms in front of her belly, taking hold of her elbows with the opposite hand.

"I thought I heard you were out here, Justin," she said in a neutral voice. "Did you have something you wanted to talk to me about?"

"It's about the resort," Justin said, standing halfway and holding his hand out to an open chair at the table. "Please, sit. This won't take long. I'm sorry if this is a bad time for you."

Lynn frowned slightly, moving her eyes between Justin and Sarah.

"It's not a bad time. What did you need?"

Justin kept his voice as calm as possible, trying not to let on that he wanted to grab her and kiss her and never let her go.

"I just told Sarah here that we need to go over the list of supplies for the resort business. She needs to order them. We have a suspicion that someone on the inside might be sneaking around." He looked directly in Lynn's eyes, hoping she would understand there was more to this story.

"Someone on the inside?" Lynn asked, her voice tepid. Justin didn't know whether she was acting or if she was genuinely upset. "Are you sure you should be telling everyone our business? I don't think that's a good idea at all." She leaned toward Justin, giving him a direct glare.

Justin's chest tightened. His thoughts turned dark and he immediately chided himself for making a stupid plan and following through with it before he had a chance to talk to Lynn about it. He didn't see a way to let her know what he was doing.

"I think it might be someone I know," he said defensively.

"And what if it's not who you think it is?" Lynn asked, hotly. "What if someone in this company is doing something criminal and you just want to involve all kinds of people?"

Justin wondered if Lynn was being real. He couldn't tell. He threw his hands up in the air, deciding that he would play along and hope she wasn't being serious.

"I trust Sarah. I don't think she will betray our behind-the-scenes work." He turned his eyes to her. "Will you? You won't tell anyone about our business, right?"

Sarah shook her head vigorously, giving Lynn an innocent look. "No, I really wouldn't, Miss Wright. You can count on me. I don't have a criminal bone in my body, I promise you."

Lynn stood up, kicking the chair back with her legs. She glared down at Justin, whose stomach was churning painfully.

"If you want to trust anyone and everyone, that's your business, Justin Brownstone. I don't see why I should trust anyone with my money when you think someone is doing something criminal. I'll give you a little time to think about it. You come to me when you have a better idea than trusting anyone." Lynn turned her narrow, seething eyes in Sarah's direction. "And everyone, apparently."

Lynn spun on her heel and stomped toward the front gate. Justin felt nauseous. He turned his eyes to Sarah, who looked just as stunned as he felt.

He jumped up. "I'll be right back," he mumbled, dashing after Lynn.

Chapter 21

Relief flooded through Lynn when Justin came up behind her beside her car and grabbed her arm. She turned to look up into his blue eyes, her heart pounding like a bass drum.

"Justin," she said immediately. "I'm not mad at you. I wanted her to see you stand up for her. You think she's the one doing this?"

Justin's shoulders visibly relaxed and he sighed heavily. "I thought you were mad at me. I don't want to see you like that again."

Lynn couldn't help grinning. "If we decide to be a couple, Justin, you will probably see that a lot more. That's what happens when two people get comfortable with each other."

"You sound like you've been through it before," he said, a teasing lilt in his voice.

Lynn chuckled, shaking her head. She pictured her sisters in her head. They were her point of reference whenever it came down to living with other people. Everyone was different, with their own set of rules. It took a lot of forgiveness and adapting to live as an adult with other people, spouse or not.

"I've lived with my sisters all my life. And now I live with their husbands sometimes too, when they stay at the resort in our house. It takes some work."

Justin came a little closer to her, looking down into her eyes. "You're looking nice today," he said in a low voice that sent a chill down Lynn's spine. She felt herself falling into the sky blue of his eyes. Her eyes dropped to his lips, anticipating they would soon be pressed against hers.

Instead, he inhaled sharply and pulled away from her. The moment was broken, and she was left feeling disappointed. He turned his head and looked through the trees to the deck. The table he'd been sitting at was hidden from their view.

He rested one hand on top of her car and looked down at

her.

"Come to the deli tonight," he said softly, leaning close to her again. Her heart raced once again but he didn't kiss her. Twice disappointed, she nodded, stifling a sigh.

"What time do you want me here?"

"I'm thinking about 10. That will be late enough for no one to be here. Cleaning crew leaves at 9 every night. They don't come back till about 6 in the morning."

"What are we going to do?" Lynn turned her eyes toward the deli, looking for anyone who might be listening. No one was. She didn't know why she would have thought anyone cared what they were talking about.

"We're going to go through the computer system and see if there's any other clues we can find. I want to know how the thief got hold of my passcode. The only thing I can think is that she downloaded some kind of algorithm generator and put it through until she got it. Maybe we can find it on her computer."

"Do you think she'd be stupid enough to leave it on there if she did?" Lynn asked. "It might be hidden, like from being deleted. If she's done that, we could probably get Sue to go through it and find it. She's a whiz when it comes to stuff like that. Mari can undelete stuff from the computer, too."

Justin's eyebrows shot up. "I don't know anyone with those kinds of skills. Sounds good."

"I'll come back tonight. In the meantime, I'm going to find my sisters and tell them what's going on. But Justin." She grabbed his arm when he turned away from her. He looked back, his eyes so soft and warm that Lynn felt a streak of desire slide through her. "If you have to be nice to Sarah so she isn't suspicious...don't be too nice. You know what I mean?"

She grinned at him.

He raised his eyebrows, the corners of his lips lifting in a slight grin. "You don't have to worry about that, Lynn. I'm not a cheating man. Never in a million years. I promise you that."

Lynn felt strangely comforted by his words. They were the same that any man would say, she was sure. But when Justin said them, she believed him without a shadow of a doubt. She could see he was telling her the truth.

"Why do you think this girl is guilty of doing all this?" she asked, glancing toward the deli again, even though she couldn't see Sarah. "She looks like a nice young woman. Is it because she has a crush on you?"

Justin frowned. "How did you know that?"

Lynn giggled, the sight of Sarah's adoring gaze floating through her mind, making her feel grumpy and amused at the same time.

"A girl can tell, Justin. It seems to me a girl can't look at a man like that unless she harbors some attraction to him. Why would she do that to someone she obviously adores?"

"I don't know. Maybe she thought she could get all that money together, and I'd run off with her, leaving my sister high and dry. After all, that really sounds like something I would do, right?" The sarcasm in his voice made Lynn chuckle.

"Do you think we should argue or something? Make it look like we aren't..." Lynn stopped herself. She'd been about to say, "falling madly in love with each other". Regardless of his obvious attraction to her, Lynn wasn't sure those were the words she wanted to use so soon in a relationship. It was equivalent to talking about marriage on the second date.

She pressed her lips together, returning his expectant gaze. He lifted his eyebrows.

"I don't really want to argue with you, Lynn," he said, his voice thoughtful. "Just a few minutes ago, I felt what it would be like to have you angry with me, and I don't really like it. I don't even want to play at being mad at you. Like you said, if we do get into a long-term relationship...if we date for a while, we're going to end up getting on each other's nerves then. Let's keep it light and civil as long as we can, right?"

Lynn didn't want to think about that, even though she knew

he was right.

"I think you're right, Justin. Let's reserve the fighting for a long time from now when we're old and gray and..." She stopped again. No matter what she said, it seemed it could be taken out of context. She was terrified she'd push him away if she was too aggressive. He was such a laid-back guy.

"So, I'll see you tonight then?" he said in a quiet voice.

She nodded. "Yeah. I'll be here about ten o'clock. You gonna meet me out here?"

"Come around back. There's a drive that goes all the way around the building, and a door that lets in the warehouse workers early in the morning. I'll be back there. I'll leave it unlocked, but I'm gonna come out and wait for you anyway."

Lynn reached down and took hold of the door handle. Before pulling open the door, she looked up at him, relishing the sensation of pleasure that slid through him when their eyes met.

"I'm going to convince my sisters you aren't responsible for this, Justin."

She felt an intensity emanating from his body, as if he was hugging her with his spirit. Another tingle slid through her. Gazing directly into his eyes, she wished he would wrap his arms around her and hold her close against his broad chest.

"Thank you for believing in me, Lynn," he breathed in a smooth voice. "It means more to me than you know. I've been accused of things in my life and...well, let's just say those things didn't turn out in my favor."

Lynn frowned. "I'm sorry to hear that."

He shook his head and added quickly, "Nothing like this. You don't have to worry about a pattern of behavior here. I have never been accused of stealing anything before. Nothing in my life. And I sure wouldn't start by stealing from my sister."

Lynn nodded. "I know you wouldn't. I believe you completely. I'm going to make sure my sisters do, too. We have to find out who's doing this, so don't let up because I sure won't until we're sure we have who's responsible. "

"I'm so glad to have you on my side. It means everything to me. I've…" Justin hesitated, his face turning light red. Lynn's heart beat with warm affection for him. "I've never really had anyone do that for me except my sister. Never had a woman in my corner before." He smiled at her. "Feels nice."

"I'm happy to be the one doing it for you, Justin," Lynn said. She didn't know how much longer she could stand the intense desire flowing through her. She yanked the door open and slid into the driver's seat before she lost control of herself and grabbed him for a kiss.

She immediately rolled the window down and pushed the key into the ignition quickly. She looked up at him, smiling.

"Ten o'clock," she said brightly. "I'll be here."

Justin leaned over the car, resting both hands on top of it and gazing in the window at her.

"You be careful, Lynn. I don't want anything happening to you between now and then."

She nodded. "Fortunately, we're not dealing with a murderer."

She was amused to see him close his eyes and shiver briefly. "Don't even say that. I don't want to be stumbling on any dead bodies."

"No, that would be awful. I'll text you later after I talk to my sisters. The plan is to have Sarah order the parts, and we'll follow the paper trail if she skims money off the top?"

He nodded. "Yeah, we can catch her red-handed."

"What if she doesn't steal anything from this deal?"

Justin glanced up to look over the top of the car before dropping his eyes back to meet hers. "If she's as greedy as she seems to be, she won't be able to pass up a big deal like this. You pick out the supply company. Tell her you want to use your own people, but she's responsible for getting quotes. In the meantime, you go ahead and get quotes of your own. I'll set it up and tomorrow we'll go over it all and order it. Let's see what numbers she shows us."

Lynn nodded. "So why are we meeting tonight if she isn't going to order the stuff until tomorrow?"

"We'll have to meet tomorrow night, too."

Lynn raised her eyebrows in confusion. She gazed at him openly for a few seconds before realizing what he was doing. She sucked in a breath quickly. "Oh. Oh, we do need to meet tonight, don't we?"

He nodded. "Yeah, we gotta search the offices. Tonight. Alone."

"Just you and me?"

He grinned, sending a swift sensation of pleasure sliding through Lynn. She was suddenly anxious for the rest of the day to pass.

Chapter 22

Justin leaned back against the exterior wall beside the entrance. It was partially hidden by a short wall that served no purpose other than aesthetics, as far as Justin could tell. It also offered a place to hide in the dark.

Not that he needed to hide. No one came around the back entrance at this time of night. He'd stayed and watched for Sarah to leave in particular. When he saw her little Ford pull out of the parking lot, he'd gone back inside with the specific intent on going through the entire accounting office, not just her desk but the other two desks that were used in the room. The more he thought about it, the more he realized everyone in the accounting office was probably smart enough to hack their security system.

Kathy didn't hire them because they were idiots, after all.

He pulled the pack of cigarettes from the pocket of his long shorts and lit one with a flick of his lighter. The flame burst up into his face briefly, making him squint. The trails of smoke rolled up around his head as he took the first puff.

At the last minute, he decided to wait for Lynn. He went to the dining hall and looked through the leftovers, making himself a sandwich and sitting at the bar to eat and drink a Coke. It was remarkably quiet in the deli when no one else was there. He was glad they closed at seven. Their staff spent time with their families.

Sometimes, Justin ate after everyone left. It was usually what he preferred. Eating with his sister was okay, but his preference had always been to eat by himself, in peace, not worried about entertaining or talking to someone else. He was content to talk to himself inside his head.

But it didn't feel the same anymore. He didn't want to sit alone and eat. He wanted to sit with Lynn. Even if they didn't say anything—and he imagined if they stayed together long enough, they would indeed run out of things to say to one another—he would be happy just to be in her presence.

She was the least annoying person he'd found. He wasn't

529

sure if that qualified her as the one he wanted to spend the rest of his life with, but it was pretty darn close.

He blew smoke out into the darkness around him, watching it float in the ray of the street lamp nearby. He could hear cars in the distance on the other side of the building, as they went down the street. It wasn't the most popular road in Queen Anne, so they weren't bothered by heavy traffic. By 9:30, the streets of Queen Anne were usually dead quiet.

He'd enjoyed many nights on the deck of the deli, stretching back in one of the chairs, staring up at the bright starry sky. He was always amazed how many stars that could be seen in the Georgia sky. There was very little pollution in Queen Anne. That left the beauty of nature plenty of room and time to show off.

He was deep in thought when he heard a noise come from inside the building.

He frowned, spinning around and looking at the window to his left. He couldn't see in it without going to it and peering through, which he had no intention of doing. If someone was prowling around in the building, he wasn't going to give away his position.

He looked over his shoulder, hoping Lynn wouldn't pull in right at that moment.

Justin hoped it wasn't Noah in the warehouse. If it was, he was going to be really upset. It would ruin his trust in friendship altogether. The only person he'd ever trust again was Lynn...and his sister, of course. He couldn't not trust Kathy. His sister never had anything but his best interests in mind. Even if her idea of what was right for him might not be what he wanted. Her intentions were always good.

He saw no headlights coming down the slight hill from the alleyway.

Justin moved around the short wall and walked to the doorway. The only way to gain access was to slide a card through the reader. When the light turned green, the person was allowed entry. Lynn wouldn't be able to come in if he went in first and the only thing he could do was prop open the door. He didn't want to do that. Anyone could come and go, and that would defeat the purpose of their little sting operation.

He pushed himself against the wall and slid to the side until he was directly next to the window. He peeked around it enough to see a flashlight bobbing up and down. It moved as if whoever was holding it was walking around the room casually.

Justin frowned in confusion. He looked back at the door, wondering if he should just go in. Waiting for Lynn was probably the better idea. He didn't want to go in alone. If it was Sarah, she could say anything she wanted about their meeting. She'd be believed long before he would if she decided to say he'd harassed her in any way. No one had ever believed Justin before. He didn't know why they would start now.

The only one who would believe him would be Lynn. Of that, he was certain. He didn't know what he did to deserve her belief in him, but he was grateful for it.

It had always only been Kathy. His sister was the one who kept him going through the years of depression and darkness after their parents had died. He didn't know where he'd be if it wasn't for her.

He glanced down at his phone, bringing up the screen, so he could see the time. It wasn't even 9:30 yet. He wished he'd told Lynn to come earlier. He debated texting her and asking her to come now.

But could he tell her he wanted her to come, so he wouldn't have to go in alone? Chances were Sarah was the one in the building. Lynn would understand why he had his concerns. She wouldn't think bad of him.

Insecurity rose up in Justin. His chest tightened along with every muscle in his body. He gathered his courage and rested his hand on the door handle. The latch wouldn't lower until he slid his access card anyway.

He stood for a moment, blinking, trying to decide what to do when the door was taken from his hand. It swung open, seemingly all on its own.

He was staring at Sarah's shocked, yet curious face.

"Oh my...Justin! What are you doing here?"

He frowned. "I could ask you the same thing, Sarah. I own this place. That's my excuse. I can sleep here if I want to."

Sarah giggled, seemingly unaffected by his sour nature. He stared at her, wondering what excuse she could possibly give him.

"I'm just working late, boss," she said, grinning and dropping her eyelids seductively. "That should make you proud, considering you are my boss, right? Are you proud of me?"

"You were working late?" Justin couldn't keep the doubt from his voice. She nodded, raising her eyebrows.

"I was. You asked me to work with you on a big project. Selecting all the equipment and getting the best prices. It's an important job! I'm glad you gave it to me. I take it very seriously."

"Do you now?" Justin couldn't help the skeptical tone of voice. He didn't believe anything she said.

"I truly do," she said, nodding. "And since you're here, even though it's so late, you can come in and see what I've done if you want."

"What were you doing coming out here?" Justin pursued. He didn't want to go in the building alone with her. He would refuse that until Lynn got there and just hope Lynn wasn't upset that Sarah was there, too. He didn't want her thinking he'd invited Sarah to their private investigation party.

"I usually park in the back," Sarah said quickly. She glanced around him. "I don't think I parked back here tonight though."

Justin drew his eyebrows together. "Do you usually come here after hours?"

She shrugged, giving him a casual look, stepping out of the doorway and leaning against the door jamb. "Sometimes, when I have a lot of work to do. The business is thriving. Even with all of us in accounting, there seems to be something to do every minute of the day."

"You enjoy your job enough to come in at all hours?" Justin forced surprise in his voice. Casual conversation wasn't on his list of favorite things to do, especially when he didn't trust the person he was talking to.

Every time he thought about her willingness to destroy him, he had to keep his temper down and remember who he was. He was calm and collected. That's what Kathy told him. The most calm, collected man she'd ever met.

He'd covered his temper most of his life. Holding it all in had made him bitter about a lot of things.

Besides, he couldn't be a hundred percent sure she was guilty. It was all really just his gut telling him something was wrong.

"I love my job here," Sarah answered him, watching as he took a last drag from his cigarette and threw the butt in the large pot ash tray beside the door. "I feel like I can really progress. I will have plenty of money to retire on and, in the meantime, I can enjoy the work I'm doing and the money I'm making for you. That's my ultimate goal, you know. To make money for you."

"I guess as an accountant, you're really good with numbers," Justin prolonged the conversation, wishing Lynn would hurry up and get there. But he'd told her ten and hadn't had an opportunity to text her to come earlier. He regretted not sending a quick message to her.

He wanted desperately to look at the time on his phone but thought it would be rude of him. It would also reveal he was waiting for someone.

Sighing, he tried to think of something more to say to Sarah to keep from having to go inside with her. He focused on her relaxed stance and realized she was in no hurry to go in. His suspicion of her rose back up and he made a move toward the door.

"Let's see what you've been working on," he said abruptly, abandoning his plan to avoid her. She might have left something in plain sight. And she wouldn't have time to get anything off her computer she didn't want there.

He pushed open the door and walked past her, taking quick, long steps so she would have to hurry to keep up with him. She did a remarkable job doing just that, speed walking so she could pass him and go in the office first. It amused him on one hand. On the other, his suspicion mounted.

Chapter 23

She rounded her desk, immediately pushing papers together and stacking them in a pile. There weren't many, but her desk wasn't as messy as some Justin had seen. She reached out and turned her monitor, so he could see the screen.

She tapped a kay to bring up what was on her screen when she left.

Justin was slightly disappointed but not surprised to see a plain Windows background with icons lining the left hand side. She'd left nothing open, but it didn't surprise him.

"This is what I was doing," Sarah said, moving the mouse, so the cursor fell on one of the folders. She brought up an Excel book and tapped through each page, telling him what each one was. There were different categories and numbers written down each page.

Chills ran over Justin's arms, looking at the numbers. Sarah was the lead accountant, apparently, and had her fingers in every financial part of the Brownstone business. He chided himself silently for not paying more attention to the details. He wondered how so many months could have passed without Kathy noticing something was wrong.

"Did you ever receive access to the highest security level clearance?" he asked, feeling like he was in the CIA. Sarah shook her head. He turned his eyes from her innocent-looking face to the computer screen, wishing he knew more about the field, so he could make a better assessment of what he was looking at.

"No, no one has access to that level except you and Kathy. Why? Has something happened?"

Justin tried to decide if the question came from curiosity or if the person responsible was trying to find out how much he knew.

He shook his head, keeping his face neutral. "No, nothing you need to be concerned about."

Sarah leaned over the desk, giving him a close look. "Do

535

you think there's a mole in the pot?"

Justin frowned, staring at her. "A mole in the pot?"

Sarah giggled, covering her mouth with one hand. "Oh, I can't remember the right phrase. It's something I saw on TV. Boss starts acting weird, showing up when he isn't usually there, asking probing questions…I watch a lot of true crime. I guess I thought maybe you're having some trouble. You know, the *business* is. Not you *personally*."

Justin tried to make sense of Sarah's rambling. When her words trailed off and she gave him a sheepish look, he said, "It's really nothing you need to worry about. All I need from you is to go over the list of supplies and order them, take care of that part of the Resort contract. Can you do that?"

Sarah's eyes widened a bit and she straightened up. "I can, yes, of course."

He nodded. "Good. We're just waiting for the supply companies Lynn wants to use. Once we have that list, or rather, you have the list, you can start calling them to make the orders."

Sarah's smile was back, spread across her face. Her straight teeth were brilliantly white. So much so, Justin noticed and wondered how she managed to get them so white. "It's so exciting, isn't it, Justin? Expanding and now you'll be in charge of your own deli. Well, sort of, I guess."

"I'll be in charge," he said, nervousness building in him. He wasn't nervous at the thought of being in charge. Not now. That might have happened a few months ago but now…Lynn had given him confidence he hadn't known he had. She made him feel better than he ever had in his life, as if he could accomplish something and be proud of himself for it.

He was nervous now because that opportunity might be taken from him. He had it in the palm of his hand until Sue found the embezzlement documents. Now he felt the urge to fight desperately to redeem himself and prove he wasn't guilty of the crime. At the same time, he would be catching someone who'd been stealing from his sister and framing him for it.

"I think you'll be wonderful at it. You know, if you need someone to come there and work in the office area...I can do that. I don't mind transferring. I've only been up to the resort a few times, but it's so pretty. I like it there. Would love to work there. Almost like a dream come true, really."

Justin could tell by the dreamy look on her face Sarah was imagining working in an office at the resort. Lunch breaks would be fantastic for her.

He shook his head, moving his eyes over the surface of her desk, not bothering to hide that he was taking in everything he saw. "I don't think we'll have an office over there. Some storage units and a kitchen with refrigerators for the cold stuff. Bakers on hand, chefs, but not office workers. That's all staying here. No need to muck up the works, right?"

She smiled at him. Her eyes turned to look over his shoulder, and he spun around.

Lynn was standing in the doorway, looking unhappy. He swiveled his eyes back to Sarah, who looked like she was trying desperately to look friendly, rather than angry. But her narrow eyes and the blazing look she was giving Lynn spoke volumes.

"Lynn. I'm glad you're here."

Lynn came through the door and stepped over to him, then leaned toward him and placed a kiss on his cheek. It sent a shiver of surprise through him. A smile burst across his face. He reached up with one hand to touch her elbow.

"I'm glad to be here," she said, looking directly at him. He could tell she was purposefully avoiding eye contact with Sarah.

"Sarah just happened to be working late," Justin said, feeling foolish for justifying why his accountant was there and, at the same time, knowing the woman might be guilty of a terrible crime. "I don't think she expected the boss and his woman to come knocking, did you, Sarah?"

Sarah gave him a warm, fake smile as she rounded her desk.

"I'll leave you two to your business."

"Sarah, before you go…" Justin reached out as she went past, taking her arm but letting go almost immediately. She turned the upper half of her body toward him and gave him an expectant look. "Do any of your coworkers come in late at night like you do? Have you seen anyone doing anything strange around here?"

He watched as a remarkable change came over Sarah. She turned her body back toward him and smiled, moving her eyes between him and Lynn. "So, there is something going on! I knew it. I haven't seen anyone really doing anything suspicious, Justin, but if I do, I'll let you know. You can trust me. I wouldn't do anything to hurt you or your sister's business. Ever."

She spoke in a fervent tone. For a moment, Justin doubted she could be the one stealing from Kathy. She looked almost excited that there was something clandestine going on behind the scenes. Could it be she was just a bored, lonely, single woman who had nothing to do with her time, so she spent it in the office?

Justin turned questioning eyes to Lynn, who had a similarly confused look on her face. He thought quickly, deciding that he would tell Sarah something but continue to watch her. Maybe if she was comfortable and believed he trusted her, she would slip up and expose herself.

If she was guilty.

It could be Noah.

Justin turned his mind away from that. Noah hadn't acted any different earlier in the day when they'd met in the warehouse. He was his normal self through and through. Justin still didn't tell him about the embezzlement. Just in case.

But he refused to believe Noah could be responsible for it. He wasn't a computer whiz. He didn't know how to hack into systems or break password protection.

Sarah probably did. Or one of the other accountants.

"Justin." He came out of his thoughts when Lynn said his name. He looked down at her. "You zoned out for a minute," she said, affectionately. When she smiled at him, he saw the obvious warmth and attraction, unlike Sarah's cold, fake smile.

"I was just thinking," he said in the smooth voice of a possible double-agent. "that maybe we should let Sarah in on our little secret."

Lynn stared at him. He wished he could send her his thoughts. He could only rely on her reading his eyes and playing along.

"You...you do?" she asked, tilting her head to the side and sliding her eyes toward Sarah. The young woman looked like she was about to jump up and down with excitement. Justin almost didn't want her to be the guilty party.

He nodded. "Yes. I think we can trust her. Who better to know about this kind of thing than our head accountant?"

"I would love to help you, Justin!" Sarah exclaimed. "Just tell me what I need to do."

"I think someone has hacked into the system using my passcode," Justin said, praying and hoping he was doing the right thing. "And I think they might be changing some things, maybe stealing some money. Some of the records aren't coming back correct. I think that's something you might know a little about."

Sarah nodded, her smile fading a little. "Yes, that's my department. But if someone was taking money, I would have seen, wouldn't I?"

Justin shook his head. "No, it might not be accounts you take care of. And you can't get to my level of security. Whoever did this is the one who knows what's really going on. It would have gone right over your head, so to speak."

Sarah moved her eyes away from him, staring off into space, a thoughtful look on her face.

"So, someone might be stealing from you. Do you want me to find them?"

Justin nodded. "That would be ideal, yeah. I think it's something that should be stopped, don't you?"

Sarah gave him an innocent look. "Oh yes, definitely. But...won't I need access to your files to be able to check?"

Justin could see Lynn's curious look, as she moved her

eyes between Sarah and him. He couldn't wait to talk to her when Sarah was gone.

"Yeah, we will. But we're not doing this tonight. We'll all get together in the next week or something and go over some of the files in there. That should tell us what's going on. You're knowledgeable. You'll be able to spot what we don't see. Right?"

Sarah nodded. "Yes, I can do that. I know what all the numbers mean."

Justin could see her brain working, as Sarah thought about the task.

"So, we'll see you tomorrow then, and I'll send you a text or an email about when we'll do that."

"And I'll send you the list of suppliers through email," Lynn added. Justin felt a streak of pride.

"I'm glad we can trust you with this, Sarah," Justin said, adding a bit of extra warmth to his words. "It means a lot that we have good employees like you working here."

Justin had to bite back a laugh when Lynn was struck by a quick coughing fit that made her turn away from them both and put one fist up to her mouth. He kept his eyes on Sarah, who had the grace to look concerned for Lynn.

She looked back at him, nodding. "Yes, that's fine. I'll see you both on Monday, then."

Justin grinned. "Yeah, tomorrow's Saturday, isn't it? Do you have plans?"

Sarah looked surprised by the question. She raised her eyebrows and hesitated before saying, "No, not really. Just sitting around with my cat watching TV, I guess."

"Ah." Justin nodded. When he didn't say anything more, Sarah laughed uncomfortably and turned away

He couldn't have been more relieved when Sarah finally went out the door, closing it behind her.

Chapter 24

Justin wasn't the only one relieved when Sarah left the room. Lynn's heart was racing when she walked in and saw the two of them together alone. She had never felt such jealousy in her life. She knew there was nothing between them.

Justin went to the door and stood there for a moment, his hand on the doorknob. He turned to look at her. The blue in his eyes was so bright, Lynn felt her stomach fluttering. She wanted him as close to her as she could get him.

He smiled, giving her a warm rush of pleasure. She smiled back.

He waited another moment before opening the door and looking out. He closed it and turned back to her.

"She's gone."

"What was she doing here this late to begin with?"

Justin walked back to her. Her eyes were glued to him as he approached, taking in his handsome face, his crooked smile, the way he looked at her like any moment, he would wink. That simple move would probably weaken her knees.

She giggled at herself. She was crushing on him like a schoolgirl, feeling just a bit insecure that he might kiss her, and she might make a fool of herself somehow.

"What's so funny?" he asked softly, gazing down at her. She bit her lips together, trying to contain her attraction to him.

"Nothing," she replied in an equally low voice. "I was just thinking…how good you look. You are very cute, you know that?"

He grinned wide. "Cute, huh? Yeah, I guess I've heard that a few times. From my sister."

They both laughed. He shook his head, moving so he was even closer to her and sending a thrill of excitement through her. If he kissed her, she would surely faint.

He was so close to her; they were practically touching. She

541

was having trouble breathing, looking up at him. She swallowed, waiting for him to make the next move.

"I don't know why she was here," he murmured, tilting his head to the side slightly and leaning toward her. Her breath caught in her throat when the edge of his lips brushed softly against hers. "But I know why you are."

He whispered the words just before pressing his lips against hers. Lynn's body lit up in flames. She pressed herself against him, her hands on his chest, the warmth of his passion sweeping over her. He wrapped his arms around her and held her close to him.

The kiss didn't last nearly long enough for Lynn. He pulled away first, resting his forehead against hers and breathing heavy.

"I've been wanting to do that for a long time," he said softly. "I'm so glad you let me."

Lynn felt a giggle in her throat. "You don't know how much I've wanted you to do that," she replied, pushing her hands through his jacket and holding him against her. He let go of her face and put his arms around her head, holding it against his chest.

She felt him kissing the top of her head and petting her hair, which made her giggles return. She pressed her cheek against him, listening for his heartbeat. She wanted to know if his was pounding as hard as hers was.

She was delighted to hear its rapid beating bouncing against her ear. She squeezed him and was rewarded by the sound of him chuckling. She pulled away slightly and looked up into his shining blue eyes.

"So, if I squeeze you, you giggle?" She hugged him tight again, making him laugh in response. "Oh, it does work! Shouldn't you be a little bit heavier than you are though? I can't call you the Pillsbury Dough boy when you're skinny."

His laughter continued. "I don't think I'm gonna gain weight so you can call me that, hon. But you can squeeze me anytime, and I'll laugh if you want."

Lynn was pleasantly surprised when, in the middle of her

laughter, he grabbed her cheeks and placed another firm kiss on her lips.

"You are such an angel, Lynn," he said, his voice dropping into a serious tone. "I promise you, I'll never hurt you. Not ever. Not on purpose. I'll never do anything to betray you. I'm so glad you believe in me. Kathy's the only one I've ever had believe in me before. Never a woman."

"I'm glad I'm the woman, then," Lynn replied, softly, gazing at him. "I guess we should see if we can find some evidence to clear your name, so you can work at the resort, huh?"

He nodded but didn't let her out of his arms. She didn't really want him to let go anyway. She was perfectly content to stay exactly where she was and receive many more loving kisses from him.

He sighed, his eyes studying her face. Being under his scrutiny made Lynn wonder what he was thinking about her. Was he admiring her? Was he noticing all the flaws on her face, the scars or early wrinkles?

Whatever he saw, it didn't stop him from looking. She enjoyed the way the corners of his lips were pulled up in a content grin.

"So..." She smiled wide, gesturing with her head toward the desk. He reacted as though he was coming out of a daze.

"Oh, yes. Of course. All right. Work. Okay."

She laughed when he pulled away but, the moment he wasn't close to her, she felt a sweep of cold air rush over her. She wanted to be back in his arms. She wanted to feel his touch and his passionate kiss.

Gathering her wits, Lynn leaned over the desk while Justin went around to the other side.

"I was thinking," he said in a business-like tone that immediately made Lynn miss his fun side. "It might not be Sarah. But I told her I trusted her with the hope that we could actually keep a better eye on her. She seemed trustworthy there at the end.

Makes me think maybe I've just been pre-judging her because I want someone caught. I know someone else is guilty, and it's making me mad that I don't know who."

Lynn nodded, leaning down and holding herself up by her elbows. "I understand. What made you suspect her in the first place?"

Justin's face turned dark for a moment, as if he was thinking something unpleasant. He hesitated before he answered, which gave Lynn pause. She stared at his face. He was looking at the computer screen when he answered.

"She's been showing me a little too much attention, I guess. I'm…not used to getting attention like that. And I think she might have been doing it to get closer to me so I wouldn't suspect her."

"Do you think she realized she was going to be found out?" Lynn moved her eyes to the computer screen, watching Justin navigate through files. She wondered if he knew what he was doing or just pulling up anything he thought might be relevant.

"I guess it's a possibility." Justin's voice trailed off. Lynn could tell he was interested in a file he'd found. She moved quickly around the desk and came up behind him, leaning over his shoulder to look at the screen. "Look at this." Justin said, turning his face up to her briefly. He ran the cursor over a folder before clicking it twice.

It brought up a program called Intoworx. Lynn frowned. She'd never heard of it before. She shook her head.

"What is it?"

"It's a computer hacking software program," Justin replied, triumphantly. Lynn was overcome with awe, looking down at him.

"Whoa, I'm impressed. How did you find it so quick? How did you even know about it?"

Before she could think of it, he said, "Don't you go thinking I put this on here and knew it was there, Lynn."

She scowled at him but relaxed when she saw him grin.

"I'm teasing. I know a little bit about computers. I did some research on hacking software and what to look for. Mostly what to guard against and how to find programs that have been installed."

"So, you think she used this program to get the passcode to your security level?"

Justin nodded. He backed out of the folder and sat back in the chair, his jacket pressing against Lynn's hand. She pulled it out and rested it on his shoulder. A thrill ran through her when he lifted his hand and placed it on hers, his eyes still on the computer screen.

"I'm not going to open it up. I'd like to see if there's a record of what codes were decrypted but if she's as good as I think she is, she'd notice the program was recently used and know we found it."

Lynn frowned. "Won't she think that anyway? I mean, she did leave us in here alone with all her files and information."

Justin shook his head. "I'm going to act dumb. We're both going to act dumb. She won't even know."

Lynn pulled in a deep breath, chewing on her bottom lip. "So, you don't think this program is enough for us to just pin it on her? Doesn't it prove she's guilty?"

Justin lifted one hand and placed it over his mouth and chin, still staring at the computer screen with a thoughtful look. "I...I don't know. If I open the program and it doesn't show a record of being used, we've let her know we are on to her, and we're left with no proof she's guilty of anything."

Lynn nodded, impressed by how smart Justin was. She would probably have given herself away by now.

Justin spun around in the chair and looked up at her with a smile.

"She's going to be on our side, Lynn. We'll find a way to make her confess or something. We'll get the evidence we need. Right now, I'm just glad you're here with me, you believe me, and you trust me."

"I do trust you, Justin," Lynn said, a rush of adrenaline moving through her body. She bent over and pressed her lips against his. Tingles ran through her body when he returned the kiss with as much passion as he had the first time.

Lynn wanted many more kisses. She turned her body and dropped down slowly on his lap, wrapping her arms around his shoulders. When his hands touched her waist, her thighs lit up, sending a tickling sensation down her legs.

"I don't think this is what we came here for, Lynn," Justin said in a quiet voice. "But I'm glad I finally got to kiss you. You're a really good kisser."

Lynn giggled, gazing into his eyes. "Thank you. You are, too. I think I want to do that some more. For a long time."

He chuckled. "We gotta breathe sometime. Just letting you know. If I pull away, you know, it's not because I don't want to kiss you. I'm just trying to survive over her. You know how it is when you're a human being and you just want to breathe to survive but someone…"

Lynn cut off his teasing words by pressing her lips to his. Her passion for him was spilling through her like hot lava.

Chapter 25

The sun was just getting ready to set when Justin stepped out onto the porch. Noah had just pulled into the parking area and was waving at him from his jeep. He'd taken the top off and was standing up, yelling at Justin.

"Hey! You ready? Let's go! The ladies are waiting!"

Justin laughed, jumping down the steps. "Ladies? What ladies? I'm meeting Lynn, who you got? You get her to bring someone for you?"

He pulled himself into the passenger side of the jeep, smiling at his friend, who plopped down and grinned back, as his hands gripped the steering wheel.

"Nah, it's a bar, man. There will be plenty of ladies there for me to talk to. I've been to Badlands before, you know. They love me there!"

"Huh. I never took you for a bar kinda guy." Justin sat back in the seat, prepared to enjoy the cool summer breeze as the jeep sped along the scenic Georgia roads. His day had been made when he received the text that morning from Lynn asking him to come to Badlands and bring a friend with him. He'd been expecting not to see her for the weekend.

After their encounter Friday night at the deli, Justin was sure of Lynn's feelings for him. She was attracted to him and more than that, she trusted him enough to believe fully that he wasn't responsible for the theft of his sister's money. But still, he'd been afraid to ask her if they would see each other over the weekend. He didn't want to push her away by being clingy.

So, when he received her text, he was thrilled and had been skating on cloud nine all day. He was excited and nervous, jubilant and carefree, and his soul sang like he'd grabbed a live wire. Nothing could wipe the goofy grin off his face. He was positive that he felt everything he'd never expected to feel. Lynn made him feel better than anyone he'd ever been around.

As the jeep sped along, and Noah rambled about some

woman he'd been talking to online, Justin tried to keep his thoughts away from the embezzlement and his suspicion of Noah. The only reason he had any suspicion at all was because of Sarah. She was the one who accused Noah of being in the office when he wasn't supposed to be.

In reality, Noah was never supposed to be in the office. He had no business there at all. He was a warehouse worker.

But there was always a chance Noah was never in the office, and Sarah was just making it up to divert suspicion from herself. When he'd clued her in to what he and Lynn were doing, she hadn't mentioned Noah at all. His "involvement" must have slipped her mind.

Realizing the embezzlement was *all* he was thinking about, Justin envisioned Lynn in his mind concentrated on the warmth of his attraction to her which never stopped flowing through him. He sighed, glancing at Noah, who was laughing about something he'd said. He laughed, too, to be polite, but he hadn't been listening to his friend at all.

He vowed not to think about any of it the entire night. He would devote all his attention to making sure Lynn knew how beautiful and wonderful she was; his angel.

His heart beat hard in his chest, his muscles tightening.

"You anxious about something?" Noah asked, glancing over at him. Justin grinned, shaking his head.

"Not really anxious. Just...I haven't had a girlfriend in...man, I can't remember the last time I dated someone. It's been years."

Noah shook his head. "Don't know how you've managed to kick it solo this long, my friend. I'd have been goin' crazy years ago."

"I don't know." Justin tried not to feel ashamed of his natural instinct to keep to himself. Until Lynn came along, he hadn't met a woman he wanted to give up his single life for. He'd given up hope of finding love in Queen Anne. It was small and, though there were plenty of locals and residents—some of them very beautiful women—Justin had felt no interest in seeking them out.

If it hadn't been for Lynn showing him attention, he would probably have stayed single his entire life.

"You think Lynn's the one, do ya?" Noah sounded genuinely interested.

Justin glanced at him and shrugged. "I don't know. I think she might be. I know I've never felt like this about a woman before. This isn't even like a crush you have in school. It's…I don't know. Deep and passionate, I guess."

"Uh oh, somebody's gonna start reciting poetry now," Noah teased. "You gonna get all mushy now? Start talking about her all the time? Asking her permission to go out with your friends?"

Justin laughed, shaking his head. "Somehow, I don't see Lynn doing that. And if she did, well, you know I know how to be single. I can do it again."

Justin didn't even like saying the words. Now that he found Lynn and was having these feelings, he didn't want to be single again. He would miss her too much. He'd already surrendered to the feelings. No going back now.

They pulled into the Badlands parking lot. Justin was surprised to see it was full. It took a minute for Noah to find a parking spot.

"What's going on tonight?" Noah asked curiously, craning his neck to look at the sign outside the venue, displaying the night's events. He groaned but with a smile. "Oh, it's karaoke night? Oh my God, don't even think about it, Justin. I'm not doing karaoke. I sing like a frog in heat."

Justin laughed, raising his eyebrows at his friend as he stepped out of the jeep. "Are frogs ever in heat? I don't think that's the right expression, Noah."

Noah waved his hand in the air dismissively. "Whatever. I'm just warning you now."

Justin shook his head, still laughing. "I don't do karaoke. I'm only here for my girl."

Noah nodded approvingly. "That's right. You keep up that thinking, Justin my boy, and you'll keep her to the end."

"That's the plan."

The two men crossed the parking lot, passing several people standing outside smoking cigarettes. Justin was tempted to stop for one himself but decided he wanted to be fresh and smoke-free when he saw Lynn. Noah pulled the door open and swept his hand in front of him.

"Age before beauty," he said, grinning at Justin. Justin halted before walking in, glaring at Noah.

"I'm pretty sure I'm younger than you."

Noah laughed and grabbed Justin by the shoulder, shoving him gently into the bar. "Just go on, ya fool."

Justin searched for Lynn as soon as he entered, his eyes moving first to the table she typically occupied when her sister was on stage. She wasn't seated there. In fact, there were no empty tables in the bar at all, and Lynn wasn't at any of them. He turned to look down the length of the bar when he heard the faint sound of what he thought was his name being called out.

He grinned wide, seeing Lynn standing up on the lower rung of the stool she was sitting on, waving frantically at him. She had a big grin on her face. He wondered how much she'd had to drink so far. It wouldn't matter. The few times he'd seen her a little drunk, she'd been nothing but funny.

He looked over his shoulder to make sure Noah saw where he was going. His friend had already moved off toward the bar on the other side, apparently seeing someone he knew. Noah turned back once to lift his hand in the air and call out, "I'll see you in a bit, buddy!"

Justin nodded and hurried to Lynn. He felt complete when he was standing next to her. He leaned over and kissed her cheek after she sat back down.

"It's packed in here tonight!" she called out over the chatter and the sound of music playing over the loudspeakers. "It's karaoke night, so it's usually like this for a while. Everyone will clear out about nine or ten. That's when it's over."

Justin looked around and shook his head, leaning toward her, so she would hear him when he spoke. "It's okay! Bunch of people having fun! Nothing wrong with that."

Lynn smiled wide, sending a thrill through him. He couldn't help wondering what a classy, beautiful woman like Lynn could possibly see in someone like him. Until he met her, he hadn't really had much ambition in life. He got up, worked, ate, slept, and existed. That was it.

Until he met her.

Now he wanted to really live. He breathed in fresh air every morning and didn't wake up wanting to go back to bed. He pictured her smiling at him when he woke up and thought about her until he fell asleep. She completely occupied his mind to the point that he was sometimes relieved when he had work to do. It was the only thing that distracted him from thinking about her.

He put his arm around her shoulders and stood next to her rather than taking the stool. He just wanted to touch her.

"I'm glad you're here, Justin," she said, looking up at him, sending adrenaline rushing through his body. "I've been thinking about you all day."

"Have you? I can't imagine why." He grinned, hoping she would think he was teasing. He really didn't know why.

She laughed and slapped his arm lightly. "Oh, you know why. Last night...I, uh...really enjoyed myself. I hope we get a chance to do that again."

He laughed, hoping it didn't sound as nervous as he thought it did. "What, kiss? I'll kiss you. All day, every day. Just gotta let me know you want me to."

She bit her bottom look, her eyes soft and seductive. He couldn't resist the urge and bent to press his lips against hers. She responded with great passion. His heart slammed in his chest the entire time. He pulled away when he thought he might not be able to stop. He really could kiss her all night.

She was smiling from ear to ear. "You really are good at that, you know."

He gave her a stiff bow from the waist. "Why thank you, my lady. I…" He laughed abruptly. "I haven't had much practice, I gotta say."

She laughed with him. "A girl likes to hear something like that. Your guy friends might want to hear about all your exploits, but I'd rather not."

He shook his head. "No exploits here. I haven't really gotten out much. Like…ever."

Lynn nodded, to his surprise. He pulled his eyebrows together curiously until she continued. "I know. Your sister told me you haven't. She said you really haven't gone out very much at all."

A rush of understanding swept through him. Of course, it was Kathy. His sister wouldn't say anything bad about him, but she didn't mind talking about him, either. Or maybe it was just to Lynn because she knew he was interested in her.

Whatever the reason, Justin could forgive Kathy. She never meant him any harm. Which made the thought of him stealing from her all the more ridiculous. He loved his sister. He would never hurt her or their business. Ever.

He wished he hadn't thought about the embezzlement mystery. The feeling doubled when he heard a familiar voice behind him.

"Well, hello! Fancy seeing you two here!"

He turned, feeling a little sick, and looked down at Sarah's smiling face.

Chapter 26

Lynn's stomach turned when she looked around Justin to see Sarah standing there. The girl obviously changed her style completely from work to casual. She was dressed in a tight tank top, black leggings that hugged her curved hips and long legs, and a black and white over shirt that almost came to her ankles. Her feet were strapped in extremely high heeled sandals, exposing her brightly painted toenails.

She tried not to react to the toe ring.

She pulled her eyes forcibly back up to Sarah's face, noticing the girl wasn't smiling at her. She was smiling at Justin. Very purposefully.

She hadn't seen Sarah in the bar until that very moment, but Sarah's eyes looked glassy, as if she was already well into a few drinks. She wasn't quite swaying, but Lynn thought she looked a tad unbalanced.

"I didn't know you came here," Justin said, glancing back at her. She wondered if he was expecting some kind of reaction from her. Did he want her to act a certain way because it was Sarah? She was confused for a moment and then chalked the feeling up to being a little tipsy herself.

She'd come to Badlands early to have a few before Justin got there. Her anxiety was through the roof, since their time together the night before. He was respectful, didn't pressure her to go further than she wanted. She enjoyed his kisses and the warmth of his arms around her. He didn't seem to mind taking it a little slow. In fact, she got the impression that's what he wanted, as well.

The alcohol didn't exactly steady her nerves, but it gave her the courage she needed to control herself when he came strolling in. She was worried she would somehow look like a fool in front of him. If he ever laughed at her and walked away, it would break her heart into a million pieces. She wanted to impress him, make him laugh, see him happy. It was all she wanted.

"I usually don't," Sarah was replying to Justin's remark.

553

She finally glanced, at Lynn but it was only for a moment before her eyes were concentrated back on him. Lynn felt a twitch in her chest and consciously controlled her temper. "I just came tonight to see what all the fuss is about. I've heard a lot of good things about this place."

Sarah had to lift her voice high for Justin to hear her. She leaned toward Justin, and he leaned back, tilting his head slightly so his ear was closer to her. A streak of angry jealousy split through Lynn. She wanted to leap off the stool and shove Sarah away from Justin as hard as she could. The next moment, Lynn was chuckling at herself, picturing what it would be like if she really reacted that way.

It wouldn't be funny at the moment, but it would be something to tell her kids about someday.

She let the fantasy slide through her mind, telling herself it was a natural instinct to lean toward someone when you couldn't hear what they were saying. Justin wasn't trying to get closer to her. He was just acting like a normal human being.

After she talked herself down, Lynn refocused on what the woman was saying. She was gesturing with one hand, a mixed drink in the other. She pointed to the place where she was standing. Lynn strained to hear what she was saying. Her voice mixed in with the sounds around her and, when Justin turned to look at her, she shook her head.

"I can't hear her," she said, making sure to mouth the words, so he would understand even if he didn't hear her. He nodded, put one hand on her shoulder and leaned close enough for his lips to touch her ear.

"She's just talking about coming here tonight because someone said the karaoke is bangin' or something like that. She's not saying anything important. I'll try to get rid of her."

He pulled away from her, his eyes on her face. She nodded, and he turned away.

Lynn picked up her drink and sipped it, thinking about how quickly the two of them had become comfortable with one another.

He wasn't just her love interest. In just a short time, he'd become her friend. She'd noticed little things about him. The way he tapped his fingers on desk tops when he had something on his mind. The little snort that almost always accompanied his laughter. The way his eyes shone bright sky blue sometimes and stormy blue when his mood was low.

She wondered what kind of little things he'd picked up about her. She hoped he liked whatever it was that he noticed. She hoped she didn't do anything embarrassing.

He turned back to her, interrupting her thoughts of love. His expression changed a little when his eyes settled on her face. She wondered what he saw there. She probably looked completely love struck.

Her cheeks flushed, and she dropped her gaze to the floor to hide her blush.

He took her chin in his hand and lifted her head back up, so she was looking at him. He leaned in and touched his lips to hers for just a moment before moving to speak into her ear again. "I don't know what you were thinking," he said in a voice that sent chills through Lynn's body. "But if you ever want me to do anything for you, all you have to do is look at me like that again."

He moved back, looking into her eyes again. He shook his head softly, gave her another kiss and slid onto the stool next to her so that he was between her and Sarah.

Lynn was only slightly annoyed that Sarah was still there. The feelings Justin had sent through her for the past ten minutes were enough to last her a year. Her body felt hot. She thought it might be a good idea for her to get some fresh air.

She took the napkin out from under her beer glass and waved it in the air in front of her face. It made for a very poor fan. It was flimsy and didn't provide any wind at all.

She wanted to go outside for just a moment. But she didn't want to leave Justin inside with Sarah. She didn't trust the woman as far as she could throw her. And she highly doubted she could do more than pick Sarah up off the ground a few inches.

She rested one hand on Justin's back and then leaned forward, so she was sprawled across him, looking over his shoulder with just her eyes. He twisted his neck to look down at her, a big grin on his face.

"What's up, Buttercup?" he asked cheerfully and loudly.

She pulled back just enough to say in an equally loud voice, "I love that movie. That was a great movie. Wasn't it, Sarah? You saw that movie, didn't you?"

Lynn hoped Sarah had never seen the *Princess Bride.* To her dismay, Sarah's smile grew wider.

"Oh, yes! I love that movie. I really don't know anyone who doesn't."

Lynn hid her disappointment, turning her smile to Justin. "Are we going to sing together tonight?"

"Oh, I'd love to sing with you, Justin!" Sarah blurted out, tilting forward in her chair and nearly sprawling into Justin's lap. Lynn felt him push back toward her when Sarah came close to him. He looked over his shoulder, his eyes meeting hers. The intensity of the look that passed between them was something Lynn wouldn't soon forget.

It was as if she'd known Justin all her life, like he saw into her soul and knew everything about her, like he could read her thoughts and knew every feeling she was having.

She was almost overwhelmed with the feeling and struggled to keep herself under control. She'd quit drinking for an hour or so. The alcohol wasn't helping her deal with the level of feelings she was having.

She hung onto Justin's back while he helped Sarah sit upright. She could tell he was trying to avoid touching her more than he absolutely had to. It made her giggle. She pushed away from him and sat in her chair, holding onto the back and the side of the bar, watching him deal with the drunken Sarah.

"I'm not…I'm not going to sing," Justin said, pushing Sarah's shoulder slightly to keep her from falling over. She shook her head and looked at him, narrowing her eyes.

"I think I shouldn't have had that last shot…"

Justin shook his head. "No, you probably shouldn't have. You look like you're gonna be sick."

"I…I think I might be. Help me, Justin. Help me!" Sarah grabbed Justin's arm with one hand, clamping her fingers around his jacket and slapping the other over her mouth. She shot to her feet and began to drag Justin away from the bar toward the front door.

Lynn frowned, watching the scene play out. Justin turned and gave her a reluctant look, lifting his hands up in the air before turning back and hoisting Sarah up, practically carrying her to the front door.

Lynn's chest squeezed tight. Her frown deepened into a scowl when Sarah plowed through the front door, Justin right on her heels, holding her up on her feet. Lynn turned toward the bar and pulled her feet up on the bottom rung of the stool. She lifted the beer glass to her mouth. Why shouldn't she keep drinking? She might as well, if she would have to deal with that woman going off with her man in tow.

"What was that?" She heard Sue's irritated voice right behind her. She turned to see her sister staring at her, both hands placed firmly on her hips.

"What was what?" she asked, a feeling of calm sweeping over her.

Sue held one shaking hand out to the front door. "That was Justin, wasn't it? Going out with some other girl on his arm? What's going on? I'm not having that cheating, lying, thieving…"

"No, no…" Lynn shook her head. "No, you don't understand. It's what I told you before. He's being framed. And, well, that might be the thief right there."

Sue gave Lynn a skeptical look. She took a step closer, so she didn't have to talk as loudly. "What? That girl looks too innocent for something like that. There's no way."

Lynn shrugged. "Looks are deceiving. You know that. It's like when you and Mari said Justin was too young because you thought he was a lot younger than he is. She looks innocent. But believe me, she's as rotten as they come."

Lynn couldn't help sneering. She didn't want to picture Sarah outside with her man, his hands on her as he tried to help her not be sick. Sue was right to be outraged. The whole thing wasn't sitting well with her, either. But she didn't want Sue thinking bad of Justin. It was bad enough they needed him to prove his innocence before they reported it to the police.

"They sure can be," Sue said, nodding.

Chapter 27

Justin tried to keep his disgust to himself. When Sarah walked over to them, she hadn't seemed nearly as drunk as she was now. She couldn't stand up on her high heels. He thought it wasn't a very wise choice to get drunk in shoes you couldn't stand up in.

"I'm sorry, Justin…" she whimpered, still holding onto his arm, leaning over the railing of the deck in front of the Badlands. He expected her to vomit, but she didn't. She just stood there, gripping the railing while her head hung down.

She reached up and swept her dark hair behind her ear, looking sideways at him. "Thank you for coming out here with me."

Justin frowned. He didn't see that he had much choice, considering she dragged him out with her. He wanted to say what he was thinking, but he was fairly certain in her current state, she would start an argument with him. He didn't have the time or energy to spend arguing with someone he cared very little about. He didn't want to argue with Kathy, much less an infatuated employee.

If that's what she was.

He glanced over his shoulder at the front glass of the Badlands. He couldn't see through to the other side because of the words painted on the window. His heart thumped in his chest nervously, and he pulled in a deep breath. He took a step closer to her and reached out to push her hair over her shoulder. He leaned in close, taking in her face.

"Are you feeling any better?" he asked, keeping his voice low. He hoped Lynn wouldn't come outside. He didn't want her to see him that close to Sarah.

When she turned her head to look at him, he was washed over with the scent of heavy liquor. It was like Sarah had done a few shots back to back. He hadn't seen her but had the sneaking suspicion that's what she'd done to get the courage to come over to him and Lynn.

559

"I do feel a little better," she said, her words slurring slightly. "I don't know what came over me."

"I think it was probably all that liquor you had," Justin said matter-of-factly. "Did you take a couple shots back to back?"

Sarah grinned wide. "Yeah, I guess I did. I think...yeah...vodka? Or...tequila?" Her face scrunched up as she tried to think. Justin clenched his jaw, bracing himself. He had to be nice to her. He might be able to get a confession out of her. If she was guilty.

If she wasn't...he was just leading her on. He was washed over with a feeling of guilt. He didn't want to hurt Sarah's feelings. He didn't want to hurt anyone's feelings.

His eyes flipped to the front door of the Badlands again. He and Sarah weren't the only ones on the deck. There were pockets of people all around them, smoking cigarettes. He thought it sounded like a good idea and pulled the pack from his back pocket.

Sarah's eyes lit on them as soon as he pulled one out. He stuck one between his lips and held the pack out to her. She smiled gratefully and slid one out for herself.

"I really shouldn't," she said, giggling. "I only do this when I'm drinking, you know. I just can't stop."

Justin nodded, flicking his lighter in front of his cigarette and breathing in slightly. Sarah was gazing at him expectantly, so he held the lighter under hers, as well, bringing the flame to the end of it.

She smiled seductively, narrowing her eyes when smoke curled up into them from the cigarette which was held dangerously close to her hair.

Justin watched her gesturing, wondering if a slight breeze might lift up the dark strands of Sarah's hair and land them directly on top of the lit end of her cigarette. He found it so distracting he could barely focus on what she was saying. He moved his eyes back to her face when she asked him a question.

"What do you think of that? Would you ever do that?"

Justin searched his brain quickly for clues to what she was talking about. He hadn't been paying any attention but seemed to remember hearing the words "ghost" and "hunting" used together, so he pieced a response together as quick as he could.

"I've always been interested in stuff like that, sure," he said, hoping it would fit with what she was saying. Her grin told him he'd said the right thing.

"Me, too!" she exclaimed enthusiastically. "I like it when things are hidden away, and they're only discovered years and years later in old abandoned places." She scooted closer to him. When she took a puff off her cigarette, the smoke she blew out came up directly into his face. He turned away, curling his nose. Stepping away from her a little didn't help. As soon as he moved, she moved with him, sticking to him as if she needed him to keep her warm.

Her closeness was starting to annoy him.

"You know, I've heard of one of those places around here. Out near St. Simon's Island."

"Oh yeah?" Justin had to lift his arm and hold his head up to take a puff from his cigarette. She'd pushed herself into the crook of his arm where he'd had it stretched out on the railing. He switched the cigarette to his other hand, so he wouldn't have to reach above her. He felt like it made him even closer to her, which was not what he wanted.

She seemed to be enjoying it thoroughly, though. She snuggled up against him like he was her long lost lover.

"Yeah. Maybe you'd like to visit there sometime." She looked up at him. "With me."

Justin couldn't take any more of her flirtation. He tried not to let his voice sound too stern. "I'm not really free right now, Sarah. You know that. I'm dating Lynn."

Sarah nodded, her face taking on an innocent look. "Oh, I know. I know. I'm just saying…you know, in the future, if you…you're ever free…or maybe if I get someone and we can all go together, the four of us. Wouldn't that be fun?"

Justin nodded. "Oh yeah. It's something to keep in mind."

Sarah seemed satisfied with his answer. She snuggled back against him, smoking her cigarette in silence for a few glorious moments. Justin looked around at the other customers. He hoped none of them were watching and, if they were, that they didn't know Lynn. The thought of her coming out and catching him with Sarah so close to him made his stomach turn.

He kept his eyes focused on the door, which was now brightly lit with the outside multicolored lights. His heart was pounding hard, his body tingling with nervousness almost to the point of shaking.

"Hey," Sarah's voice dropped, and he felt her press herself against him. He looked down at her. "I wanna show you something. Can…can I show you something?"

Justin's eyebrows shot up, and he gave her a quizzical look. "That really depends on what it is, Sarah. You're pretty drunk. I don't want you doing something you'll regret." *Or pin on me,* he added in his mind.

Sarah shook her head sloppily, closing her eyes for a moment. "No, no, it's not like that. Nothing like that. I've…I've been doing something in the secret…just so no one will know but me. And I want to tell you about it because…well…I just want to, that's why."

Justin tilted his head to the side and gazed at her. She couldn't be so drunk that she'd tell her own boss what she was doing with his own money…could she?

He hoped she was. He didn't want playing along with her, but he didn't know any other way to get her to tell him what was on her mind.

"You gotta come with me, though." Sarah pulled her clutch bag around to the front and unzipped it. She shuffled through it as if it was a mile deep. "Where's my keys? Where…where…"

Justin reached out and put one hand over hers, stopping her drunken motions. "Oh, honey, you aren't driving anywhere." The instant it came out of his mouth, he regretted it. She looked up at him with dreamy eyes, slumping forward a little, so he had to catch her and hold her up.

"Oh, Justin," she purred. "Do you want to drive us? I can tell you how to get there. I think you know, though." She laughed. "I know you know." She poked his chest with one finger, wiggling it and giggling at the same time.

"I don't have any idea, Sarah," Justin said. "I don't know where you live. I've never been there."

Sarah gasped as if shocked by what he said. She left her mouth gaping just a little and then grinned. "Oh you! Where is your mind? I wasn't talking about my apartment. But we can go there if you want. I'd love that."

Justin shook his head, feeling foolish and humiliated. "No, no. I thought that's where you meant. Where are you talking about?"

Sarah's eyes half closed, and she seemed to doze off while standing up for a few seconds. She blinked and looked at him. "Oh, the office, of course! Where else would we go to look at my retirement fund."

Justin's skin lit up with chills. "Your what?"

Sarah pushed herself up against him, forcing him to take a step back before he could steady himself and her at the same time.

"*My retirement fund,*" she repeated, overemphasizing and poking him in the chest with each word. She looked up at him, reaching up with the same finger and tapping him on the chin. "I want to share it with you, Justin. I know you're not all about money. I know it. I…I've heard you say it a bunch of times. That's why I know you'd be perfect to share it with."

Justin inhaled slowly, unable to believe what he was hearing. He wished Lynn was standing next to him, but if she had been, Sarah wouldn't have said any of it.

"You want to share your retirement fund with me?" he repeated.

She giggled, nodding. She was walking her fingers across

his chest, seemingly unaware that he was a bundle of angry nerves.

"Show it to me, Sarah," he demanded, grabbing her by both arms and looking into her eyes. "I want you to show it to me, right now."

She gasped, giving him a shocked look before collapsing into a fit of giggles again. "Okay, okay, you don't have to get rough. Not here anyway. But you know…"

She tapped him on the end of his nose, which sent a jolt of rage through him from his head to his toes. He gritted his teeth to keep from saying something he might regret.

He grabbed at her clutch bag and pushed his fingers through it for her car keys. "Which one is your car? We'll take that. I came with a friend."

"Yeah, that guy Noah," Sarah nodded, pointing into the parking lot. "It's that one. Right there. You see it? Red. Toyota. Camry. Right. There."

She stumbled off the deck area of the Badlands and into the parking lot, going toward her car. She was only a few feet away from him when she spun around, grasping in the air. He reached out and stopped her from toppling over face first.

"You shouldn't drink so much so fast," Justin scolded her, walking with her toward her car and helping her in the passenger seat. Before he slipped into the driver's seat, he looked over the roof of the car at the bar, wishing he could let Lynn know what he was doing.

Feeling like a fool, he suddenly remembered he had a phone and could text with it. He pulled it swiftly from his back pocket and sent her a quick message.

Meet me at the BC office. She's gonna confess.

Chapter 28

When Lynn's phone buzzed, she snatched it from the top of the bar and thumbed it until she could read what Justin sent. Relief ran through her when she saw that the message was from him and that he wanted her to meet him.

Her eyebrows drew together when she read the last sentence. Was he serious? Sarah was going to confess? What had he done? What had he said that would make the woman want to do something like that? She had to have hundreds of thousands of dollars stashed away. And she was just going to confess?

It was too easy. Something was wrong.

Lynn shot off the stool, slapping the bar top to get Francesco's attention. She told him quickly that she would be back to pay her tab later. He waved her on and focused on another customer.

She hurried toward the front door, grabbing her purse from under the bar. She was stopped halfway by a large body in between her and the door a few feet away. She looked up, irritated, into the eyes of Justin's friend, Noah.

"Hey!" Noah said, cheerfully. "I'm sorry. I didn't mean to startle you or anything." He waved his hands in the air, giving her a big smile. "I saw you with Justin. You, uh, you wouldn't happen to know where he is now, would ya? I kinda lost him."

Lynn tried to focus on him. He had always seemed like a friendly man, intelligent and hard-working. Justin told her Sarah had tried to put some attention on Noah, but he didn't believe his friend would do such a thing.

In just a few seconds, Lynn analyzed Noah and decided he was exactly what Justin thought he was, a big, friendly man with only good intentions.

"I do know where he is," she said in a clandestine way. She leaned toward him, cupping her hand around her mouth. "We're going to catch a thief. You want in on it?"

A smile grew slowly on Noah's face, and his eyes sparkled in the moving lights inside the bar.

"Now that sounds like an adventure. Yeah, I'm in. Where are we going?"

"We're going to work."

Lynn enjoyed the confused and amused look on Noah's face. He said nothing, just followed her to the door. He reached in front of her and held it open so she could go through.

She scanned the parking lot but didn't see Justin's car.

"So, is Justin back at work? And is this going to be some kind of work adventure or something? I've taken working vacations before and let me tell you, there's no vacation in a working vacation. It should be called a working work. Only difference is you're in some foreign place in a hotel where…"

Noah stopped talking when they got to Lynn's vehicle. He whistled, pulling open the passenger side door. "Is this your ride? I like it. Nice. I bet you get pretty good gas mileage for an SUV. It's light weight. I bet you zip around in this thing, don't you?"

Lynn glanced at him after getting in and pulling her seat belt across her chest. She'd never heard anyone talk so much in her life. That had to be why him and Justin were such good friends. Justin was much more of a listener. She could only imagine the hours Justin must have sat, just listening to Noah talk.

"Justin is back at the office," Lynn said, trying to edge the conversation away from her, her vehicle, or her driving. "Did he tell you someone has been stealing money from the company?"

Noah's face paled. He stared at Lynn. "You're kidding me. How did you find this out?"

"My sister found a mistake in the records. She did some digging and discovered there was some embezzling going on. Skimming off the supply orders."

Noah turned his eyes and stared out across the road, as they pulled out onto the main street. Lynn hadn't noticed it before, but she did like to zip around town in her little SUV. It had amazing maneuvering capabilities.

It was late and dark. The streets of Queen Anne were bare. They were leaving the downtown/partying district and heading back into the business district, where everything was closed down for the weekend except for one Amazon distribution center.

"So, you and Justin, huh? I'll tell you what, I've been working with that man for a lot of years now, and I've been waiting for some woman to come along and grab his heart. Never thought it would happen though."

Lynn looked over at him. His face was at once light, then dark, then light again as they passed under the street lamps.

"You didn't? Why not?" Lynn couldn't help her natural curiosity.

"Well, he's a good lookin' guy," Noah said in a conceding way, waving one hand in the air. "I'm sure you know that, and I don't mind sayin' it, though I'm straight. He's a good lookin' guy, looks younger than he really is. He's smart. Got a lot up here."— he tapped his temple—"And he's got a good heart, too. Saw him helping out this couple that, I guess, lost all their money somehow, or something...I don't know the details. But he helped them out, gave them some money, food, gave 'em money for a hotel. In fact, I think they might have come up and stayed that night at the resort. They kept trying to give some of it back, but he kept insisting they take it."

Lynn's heartbeat sped up at the thought of Justin's true good nature being noticed by someone else. She was willing to bet he didn't even realize he was being observed that way.

"That's really nice of him," she breathed softly. She saw Noah glance at her in the corner of her eye and turned her head to look at him. He gave her a closed-mouth grin.

"You really like him a lot." It wasn't a question. Noah was stating it as a fact. Lynn looked back at the road in front of her, nodding slowly.

"Yeah. I really do."

"Good. I think he likes you the same. And that's really an accomplishment, Lynn, I gotta tell you." Noah shook his head. Lynn couldn't get over the amazement in Noah's voice. It was as if he couldn't believe Justin could be in love. She tried not to let her thoughts turn negative, but they did anyway. Nagging doubts ran through her. Maybe he was just bored of his single life. Maybe he was just using her to have some fun for a little while.

She frowned, upset with herself for thinking that way.

"Aw, now what are you thinking?" Noah asked, clucking his tongue at her. "You women. Always overthinking. You like him. He likes you. I'm glad for both of you because I think you're both amazing people."

"You don't know me," Lynn pointed out gently.

He shrugged his broad shoulders. "I don't have to really. I've read so much about you and your sisters, I feel like I do know you. You're like a local celebrity. Everyone likes you and your sisters. I figure everybody can't be wrong. Right?"

His grin was contagious. Lynn couldn't help returning it. She could see why Justin hung out with Noah so often. The man was like a firefly enjoying life to the fullest, buzzing around, lighting up everyone's day.

"So, this plan of yours, to catch this thief," Noah said, changing the subject abruptly. "Is there gonna be some danger involved? I wasn't really prepared to get in a fight. I was in wrestling in school, though. I did pretty good for my weight division. I was a scrawny kid. It was either scrawny kids or overweight kids. They were the only people on our wrestling team the whole time I was in junior high and then, like, freshman and sophomore years. My dad was heartbroken. Was a big time wrestler when he was in high school and wanted me to carry on that legacy. I was the only boy, you know. I have three sisters."

He glanced at her. She wondered if he needed to take a breath, but he continued without skipping a beat.

"Yeah, three sisters. Two older and one younger. By only a year. We're all crunched up together in a span of five years. I'll tell you what, you ever need someone to braid your hair, you give me a call." He wiggled his fingers in the air. "I'm a master. A grandmaster. I am the Grand master of Women's Braids. All because of my sisters."

He laughed.

Lynn didn't know whether she was grateful for or irritated by the distraction of his talking. She didn't have even a moment to think about where she was going, what was happening there, whether or not Justin was in any kind of danger.

Until Noah mentioned it, she hadn't given danger any thought at all. It was Sarah, after all. She was a five foot three inches, barely a hundred-pound woman who wouldn't be a match for Justin. He could outwit and outmaneuver her any day of the week.

Nevertheless, her fingers gripped the steering wheel, and she inadvertently jerked it several times while making a turn which made the car jolt in the street. Noah called out "whoa girl" each time, followed by a nervous laugh. He'd ask if she was okay and she'd say yes.

But she was a bundle of nerves. They were going to find out if Sarah was the thief. Justin's assumption that she was going to confess seemed much too convenient for Lynn. She had a feeling something else was going on. Sarah was planning something. She'd gotten drunk much too easily and much too quickly.

They were close to the Brownstone warehouse doors when Lynn was covered with a terrified sensation. Her breathing became raspy, and she swung into the parking lot behind the big building, slamming on the brakes.

She bent over the steering wheel, trying to catch her breath. Her eyes opened wide, and she grabbed out at Noah, who took her hand in both of his and squeezed it.

"Calm down, Lynn. Calm down. Everything is gonna be all right. Don't worry. You'll be all right."

Lynn looked up at his smiling face. It was the last thing she saw before she blacked out.

Chapter 29

Justin drove to the office, listening to Sarah's heavy breathing. She passed out as soon as they got on the road. He didn't know if that was a good thing or not. If she wasn't as drunk, she might not confess to embezzling money and framing him; all disguised as her *retirement savings*.

They pulled into the parking lot of the warehouse, and he stopped the car in a spot near the door. He reached over and jostled her awake. She gasped and opened her eyes, looking frantically around her. Her eyes settled on him, and she visibly relaxed.

"Oh, Justin. We're here. Whew. I shouldn't have drunk so much. Come on!" She was suddenly excited, grabbing the car door and shoving it open. "I want to show you! You're going to be so happy with me!"

Justin turned the car off and pocketed the keys before stepping out of the carto follow her. Full of energy, she bounced to the door. She giggled and grabbed his arm, as he pulled the key card from his wallet and slid it through the security slot next to the door. It buzzed, so he pushed the door open.

Sarah went in first, flipping the light switch which flooded the hallway with bright white that reflected off the light blue tiles on the floor and walls. Before following her, Justin pushed a small door wedge in place to keep the door from closing and locking. When Lynn got there, he wanted her to have an easy way in.

He turned to see Sarah had made it halfway down the hallway already. She spun around just as he started after her. She was laughing and waving her hands in the air, motioning for him to hurry up.

"Wait till you see, Justin!" she called out, excitedly.

By the time he got to the office and went in, she was on the other side of the desk, hovering over her computer, her eyes squinting as she stared at the monitor.

"Okay, let me see here..." she mumbled. She stuck her tongue out slightly and squinted even more, as if she was seeing double. Justin wouldn't have doubted if she *was* seeing double. Maybe triple.

He stepped to the other side of the desk and leaned over, flattening his hands on the desktop. "What is it, Sarah? What are you trying to show me?"

Sarah pushed her chair back abruptly. "Oh! I almost forgot!" She jerked on the drawer in front of her, the lowest one on the right side. It was deep but filled to the top with tiny little bottles of liquor. Justin's eyebrows shot up.

"Oh my God," he mumbled. "Are those...do you..."

Sarah looked up at him, laughing. "This is my private stash. I couldn't get through the day without a couple of these. Here! We have to celebrate!" She snatched up two of the bottles, handing him one and clutching the other one to her chest as if it was sacred. "Today...today is the new day. Everything will change after today."

Justin couldn't have agreed with her more. He held the bottle up to her, twisted the top off and drank the shot. He dropped the bottle on the desktop and looked her squarely in the eye. "Tell me what we're celebrating, Sarah. Tell me the details. I want to know. Why am I going to be so happy?"

"Because you get to be with me!" Sarah replied, delightedly. "You'll get to spend all your time with me, and you won't have to work another day in your life! We'll spend it on some beautiful island somewhere, basking in the sun and having the time of our lives!"

She tipped her head back, dumping the shot of liquor down her throat. Her smile was almost too big. Justin shook his head, not liking the effect of the alcohol on his brain. He regretted taking the shot, but it was too late to worry about it now. Lynn would be there soon enough. His back up. His woman.

Sarah slammed the drawer shut and turned back to the computer.

"Let's see, let's see..." she mumbled, tapping the keyboard. She moved the mouse and brought up a folder, opening it to see the documents. "See here? See this? This is what I've got saved right now. That's going into my bank account in a few hours. See?"

Justin stared at the screen. Sarah had skimmed over half a million dollars from his sister. Chills covered him from head to toe as anger spilled through him. He failed to keep the frown from darkening his features.

"What is that?"

Sarah laughed. "That, Justin Brownstone, is my retirement fund. I'm happy with how much I have now, so I think I'm going to retire early."

Justin slid his eyes to her face. His chest was getting tight, his muscles felt stiff. He leaned forward, staring directly at her. "When are you planning to retire?"

Her smile looked frozen on her face. "Tonight."

Justin was having trouble thinking. His mind was jumbled as he searched for the words he wanted to say. "I...I'm not going with you."

Sarah laughed again, shaking her head. "Of course, you're not going with me. Why would I want to take the person who's funding my retirement *with* me? No, I've got a better plan. A better man. It's never been you, Justin. Are you kidding?" She snorted, running her eyes up and down his body, settling on his face. She tilted her head to the side, giving him a sympathetic look.

"What's wrong, Justin? Aren't you feeling all right? Do you feel like sitting down? You probably feel like sitting down. Here, let me help you."

Sarah stood up and walked around the desk. Justin knew she was moving, but it seemed like she was going in slow motion. Either that or he was. He tried to react to her coming close to him but could barely lift his hand. He tried to speak but the words didn't form in his mouth. He felt almost paralyzed.

"What...did you...do to...me?" He managed to get the question out before he fell backwards directly onto a chair which

Sarah had slid behind him.

"Whew, that was close!" Sarah came around to stand in front of him, bent at the waist, so she could look into his eyes. "Don't worry, Justin. You're gonna be fine. You just have to watch while we take care of our business here first."

Justin was facing her desk, his back to the door. He heard when it opened and was stunned to hear a voice he knew very well.

"He out?"

He felt an ache in his heart like he'd never felt before. It was Noah's voice. He closed his eyes, not wanting to believe his friend would betray him. For money and a woman. He should have known.

"Nah, he didn't pass out. At least, not yet. I guess. He's still looking around, trying to talk and all that."

"Good. I didn't put enough in that little bottle to kill him. Don't want him dead. We'll be long gone by the time he or she can do anything about it. They'll be incapacitated for at least a couple hours."

"I don't know if we should leave them behind."

Justin's ears had perked up when Noah said *she*. From the sounds they were making behind him, he pictured Noah dragging someone in, probably Lynn, and propping her up in a chair behind him. He felt his arms being pulled back and something being wrapped around his wrists.

He tried to keep his head steady, but it flopped from side to side as he was jostled around. He concentrated hard on what they were saying, vowing to remember every word. If he got out of this situation, he would hunt them down and make sure they got everything they deserved.

"Lynn…" He grunted out her name, hoping one of them would come around and talk to him, tell him if Lynn was really okay. He wondered what Noah had done to her to knock her unconscious.

"He's not out," Noah said sternly.

"I told you he wasn't," Sarah retorted, hotly. "I said he's still moving around. You want to tell him what's going on, or should I?"

"I don't care. Doesn't matter to me at all."

Justin tried focusing his eyes, but his brain was too foggy. His face was grabbed by a strong hand and moved, so he was looking forward. He tried to keep his eyes open. Noah's face bobbed in front of him.

"Hey!" Noah called out in a voice Justin had never heard before. "Hey, you in there! Rich boy! Gonna take a little bit of what you got here, right? What do you care? You never cared about money, right, rich boy? You can just sit back on your lazy butt and do nothing all the time if you want to. You got your prissy sister to take care of you, right?"

Justin hated the ache he felt inside. He had trusted Noah. He'd always trusted Noah. The man knew things about him no one else knew. He didn't stop his eyes from fluttering closed. If he could have, he would have squeezed them tightly closed. He didn't want to look betrayal in the face.

"Well, now it's time for you to get something you deserve for your lazy attitude. I've worked all my life, and I never got no trust fund or savings account. I worked! Worked hard! So now, I'll just take a little of what you've got. You won't miss it."

"All right, all right," Sarah's whining voice pierced the room. "Thought you didn't have anything to say. Thought you didn't care. Come on. Let's get the documents printed and get out of here."

"Make sure you do it right this time," Noah said. "I don't want any of those signatures coming back on me."

"You're gonna be with me anyway, Noah," Sarah said, chiding him. "You're the one who says we can't get rid of these two. If we can't get rid of them, they're gonna tell and we're gonna be fugitives. Kind of wish we'd held out for one more job. The one at the resort would have gotten us another quarter of a million easy."

"Well, we don't have a choice. I told you something was wrong. I knew someone would catch it sooner or later. Just be glad with what you got."

Now, Justin didn't have the strength to open his eyes. He kept his ears alert, though, trying his best to remember everything he was hearing.

After a lot of shuffling and finger-tapping on the keyboard, the printer hummed and came to life.

"You were right, you know," Noah said, his voice amused.

"Oh yeah? About what?"

"She didn't even notice when I put that in her drink. You told me to go up behind her when you got Justin to follow you out. You said she'd be so concentrated on the door. She wouldn't notice her drink at all. Perfect. You're perfect."

Sarah giggled. The sound made Justin's stomach turn.

Chapter 30

Sound filled her ears slowly, as if she was coming to the surface after being deep underwater. Lynn sucked in a deep breath and lifted her head.

"Looks like someone else is awake," she heard behind her. She looked around, trying to remember where she was. She recognized the office of the Brownstone warehouse. Her memory flooded back, and terror struck her heart.

Her arms were pulled behind her, and her wrists were tied with what felt like some kind of cloth. She stretched her fingers out, touching what someone else's fingers from behind her. She craned her neck to see Justin's arm and shoulder just behind her. His back was to her.

"What is going on here?" she demanded, narrowing her eyes. "What...wh—"

She stopped, knowing full well what was going on. Noah had drugged her. Sarah had drugged Justin. They were being held captive.

Fear nearly paralyzed her. She heard shuffling behind her and looked sideways to watch Sarah move around her and Justin. She bent over directly in front of Lynn to look her in the eye.

"Okay, honey, here's what's going to happen. Noah here says we can't kill you two. So we're going to transfer our money over to a bank where you'll never find it. We're going to get out of town, and you'll never see us again. We worked hard for this money. We deserve it."

"Way more than rich boy over here," Noah called out from behind Lynn. Sarah's face crumpled into an ugly sneer that she turned in Noah's direction.

"Oh, shut up, Noah. So tired of hearing you call him rich boy."

"Well, that's what he is, right?"

"That's not the point! I'm just tired of...oh, whatever.

Never mind." Sarah shook her head, turning her eyes back to Lynn. "So anyway, what I'm trying to say is that you and your boyfriend here are just going to sit tight until we're long gone. Someone will find you, I'm sure. I know it's the weekend and no one ever comes to this office on Sunday, but I'm sure you two will be good company for a day. You might get a little hungry, though."

Sarah tilted her head sideways, sticking out her bottom lip. "I'm so sorry about that. We all have to make our sacrifices, right? For the greater good."

Lynn wanted to say something back. She wanted to make a smart remark. But she was too stunned to think of anything to say. If she threatened to go to the police, Noah might change his mind, forcing Sarah to kill them. If she played along, the two would get off scot-free with all Kathy's money and Justin would be held responsible.

She was being held captive by a crazy woman and a greed-driven man. From the way Sarah was acting, Lynn wasn't sure what her next move might be. What if she lost it completely, found a gun, and shot them both?

What if she shot Noah, too, just so she could have all the money she'd stolen to herself?

From the tapping of the keys, Lynn decided Noah had his hand far in the pockets, too. Sarah hadn't done this all by herself. Noah knew more about computers than anyone thought.

Sarah straightened up, her focus directed somewhere behind Lynn who quickly realized Sarah was watching Noah. She moved out of Lynn's eyesight, giving Lynn a deep sense of relief. It also gave her time to think. Her mind was surprisingly clear considering it was obvious she'd been drugged somehow and had already been drinking before Justin got to Badlands.

She stretched her fingers out and tugged on Justin's, hoping her touch would revive him. His head was hanging down. The only reason he wasn't slumped completely forward was his elbows and upper arms, which were behind the chair.

Lynn tried to turn in the chair as subtly as she could, just to

577

get a glimpse of him. There was no way for her to see his face but turning let her see more of the desk and the two people staring at the computer screen. She saw Sarah reach out and point at something on the screen. Noah nodded and looked down at the keyboard, tapping on the keys.

Lynn dropped her eyes to get as much of Justin in as she could before she had to turn away to relieve the uncomfortable position. Her body ached for a moment, as the muscles and bones readjusted and relaxed.

She didn't want to twist around like that again. She was afraid she would injure herself. She thought for a moment. They could do something to get out of the situation. But she needed Justin's help. He needed to wake up.

She pushed the chair slightly back, trying to move closer to Justin's seat. Noah's fingers on the keys paused for a moment, but neither of her captors said anything. When the keystrokes resumed and their mumbling continued, Lynn stretched her arms back and pushed her fingers out toward Justin's. She was close enough to almost take his whole hand in hers. She stroked his fingers and tugged on them.

When the gentle approach didn't work, Lynn ran her finger up his palm and dug down into his skin with one of her fingernails. She hated hurting him, but she couldn't think of any other way to get him to wake up.

His gasp sent a rush of relief flooding through her and she almost cried when his fingers closed around hers.

"Great, now they're both awake," Sarah grumbled.

"Just ignore them. We only have a little left to do here anyway. Then we'll be long gone. Gone on our long honeymoon. Long gone on our long honeymoon."

"Yeah, yeah, let's get on with it," Sarah replied grumpily.

Lynn wondered for a moment why someone with a vibrant personality like Noah's would want to be around someone as bitter as Sarah obviously was.

Lynn could only hope Justin would catch on to her thoughts if she gestured the right way. She tapped on his hand and pulled on his fingers until he tapped hers several times. She took that to mean he understood she was trying to communicate with him.

She moved her hands over his slowly, trying not to make visible movements with her shoulders. She couldn't rely on an assumption that Sarah and Noah was not watching her because she was unable to see what they were doing. She felt along Justin's hand until she reached the fabric tying his hands together. It was a loop from the curtains on the wall. The fabric was thick and not very good for keeping someone tied up. Lynn worked as quickly as she could, untying Justin's wrists.

"Noah," Justin said as soon as his hands were free. Lynn was proud of him for staying in the exact same position.

"What?" Noah asked, absentmindedly.

"How could you do something like this to your best friend?" As he spoke, Justin returned the favor and untied Lynn's wrists. She was relieved when the pressure was off but a little surprised how hard it was to keep her arms held back as if they were still tied.

Noah snorted. "Best friend? I've been listening to you whine about your petty problems for years when you don't know the first thing about trouble. You don't even have to look for a woman. She just falls right into your lap."

Justin grunted. "Yeah, after what, ten years of being alone?"

"You chose that, buddy," Noah said, his voice disgusted. "You got to choose that. Lots of us don't get to choose that. For most of us, nobody wants us."

"I want you, babe," Sarah said in a seductive voice.

"Yeah, yeah, I know," Noah said dismissively.

Lynn wanted to turn around so badly. But she stayed where she was, waiting for Justin to make a move.

"You're nothing but a coward, Noah," Justin said, his anger

579

seeping through his words. Lynn hoped she would never hear him talk that way again. He was boiling with rage. She could hear it. "You got me all tied up because you don't have the guts to fight a man. You just steal and run off like a coward into the night. You make me sick."

"I might make you sick, buddy," Noah said. Lynn heard him push his chair back and stand up. She sensed him walking around the desk. He would soon be standing in front of Justin. She felt Justin grasp at her fingertips, warning her that he was about to make a move.

She braced herself.

"But if you only knew how…"

That was as far as Noah got before Justin flew off the chair and tackled him. Lynn shot to her feet, spinning around to find Sarah. She wasn't about to let the woman get away or interfere with Justin and Noah. Sarah had come running from the other side of the desk, shrieking like a banshee with her arms flailing out from side to side.

Lynn shoved the chairs they'd been sitting in to the side and leapt across the room, grabbing Sarah by the shoulders. She wrestled the woman to the ground, trying desperately to get Sarah's arms behind her back. She was still holding the cloth that had been around Justin's wrists. If she could get it around Sarah's wrists, the woman would be helpless.

She almost lost all the breath in her lungs when Sarah's arm darted forward, then swiftly back—right into Lynn's stomach. She struggled to catch her breath while, at the same time, holding onto Sarah. She wrapped one slender arm around Sarah's neck and leaned back.

Sarah's hands flew to Lynn's arm. She slapped at her, gasping and scratching Lynn's skin; trying everything to release her neck from Lynn's grasp.

Finally, she weakened, and her hands fell to her side. Lynn let go of her and stared down at her face. When she was satisfied that Sarah was just unconscious, she quickly wrapped the fabric around the woman's wrists and tied it tightly.

Finally, she looked up to see that Justin had made short work of Noah. He was sitting on the chair he'd been tied to, breathing hard, looking down at Noah, who was unconscious at his feet. He glanced over at Lynn.

"Nice work, toots," he said, grinning.

She laughed. "I'll say the same to you. But I don't know the equivalent to the word toots."

"There isn't one." He got down on his knees and crawled toward her. Her heart fluttered in her chest when he crawled directly to her and pressed his lips against hers. He pulled away and looked into her eyes. Her blood raced through her as her heart pounded. "Mighty fine work, though. Really. I'm glad, if I had to be in this situation, it was with you."

He shook his head, looking down at Sarah.

"You're really amazing, Lynn. Amazing."

"I knew you were innocent from the very beginning," she said, her breath steadying some. He looked at her, his blue eyes shining.

"I know, babe. I know."

He leaned forward again. This time, after kissing her warmly, he pitched forward, so he was almost lying on top of her. His head was rested on her chest. She wrapped her arms around him, flattening her hand against his head and holding it against her. She kissed the top of his head, her love for him washing through her like warm water.

Epilogue

Justin hopped over the little garden wall. His heart was light and happy. He spotted Lynn and the rest of the women in the distance, standing around each other at the long snack table. He chuckled. Of course, they were at the snack table. He'd never seen women eat as many snacks as the Wright sisters.

Their husbands didn't exactly discourage them either.

He jogged over to them, anticipating the warm greeting he was going to get.

"Here he is!" Mike, Sue's husband and the owner of Badlands, called out, lifting one hand high in the air. He brought it down in a hand slap with Justin, laughing uproariously. "It's good to have you in the family, Justin! Real good!"

Justin nodded, his return grin as genuine as his new brother-in-law's. "Thanks, Mike. I'm glad to be here with you guys. And my lovely wife."

Lynn giggled when he put his arm around her, snuggling up against him. He looked down and caught her winking at his sister. Kathy laughed.

"You two. I just can't be happier, looking at the two of you."

"We do make a cute couple, don't we?"

Lynn reached up and grasped his chin gently, turning his head and puckering out his lips. She did the same with her own, matching his look. He jiggled his face to release it from her grasp.

"I don't want to look like a fish, Lynn," he whined, pretending to sulk and be annoyed. He furrowed his brow and looked away from them.

"Aw, come on now, Justin," Kathy teased. "You look so cute like that."

"That's what I thought!" Lynn said, laughing. "But he didn't believe me. He says he looks like a pucker fish."

"Well, he kind of does. When he does that." Mari spoke up, tilting her champagne glass in Justin's direction. "But normally, no. Normally, he just looks like a man." She nodded vigorously. "A handsome man." She turned her eyes to her husband. "Not as handsome as my husband, of course. But handsome. Yeah."

They all laughed. Justin put his arm around Lynn's shoulders and watched them all, as they picked through the snack offerings.

He looked down and caught Lynn gazing up at him. The love in her eyes made him feel warm all over.

"What are you thinking about, my dear?" he asked.

She sighed softly, a sound he'd come to adore. "Oh, just how we might not have been here if we didn't trust each other so much. From the very beginning. I don't know how that happens. I really feel like I was blessed. Like God told me I needed to be with you. You've had such a lonely life, so isolated. I know you did that to yourself kind of but…well, I'm so happy to be the one to bring life to…to your life."

She smiled up at him. She was right. She was the one who had brought him out of his darkness. He'd never considered there could be anything more than the dreary existence he'd been living. He never would have guessed one of the richest ladies in Queen Anne would give her heart to him.

"Let's walk around and mingle," Justin said, turning his head toward the pockets of people all around the courtyard. Lynn scanned his profile, admiring the glint of the sun off his blue eyes.

"Actually," she said, softly, getting his full attention. "I'd rather go for a walk with you. Down there. By the creek."

She pointed to a wooden bridge at the bottom of a nearby slope. It crossed over a bubbling creek that followed a trail around the outer edge of the larger golf course. The area was filled with tourist attractions that Lynn still found fascinating, even though she owned the property and had lived there for years.

Instead of responding, he steered her gently in that direction and walked with her, keeping his arm around her shoulders. She felt a warm tingling flow through her.

"It's so beautiful here," she murmured, comfortable to tell him her thoughts. "My uncle designed this, you know. He's the one who picked out all these gorgeous decorations and fountains and all of it. I think he might have even designed the golf course himself."

Justin nodded, sliding his arm down her back side and slipping his fingers through hers. Her entire arm lit up with chills when he touched her. She couldn't believe she was married to him. She would enjoy his touch for the rest of her life.

She pulled in a contented sigh when he lifted her hand and kissed the back of it.

"He was a brilliant man," Justin said. "He had to have been, to leave this massive wealth to his beautiful nieces."

He smiled at her.

They'd reached the bridge. Justin stepped back to let her go in front of him. She walked carefully, sliding her hand along the arched railing. She stopped when she got to the very middle and turned to look out over the water running along below her. It was so clear she could see the rocks lining the bottom, and the small fish swimming this way and that.

Her body lit up in flames when she felt his hands slide around her waist and his body press against hers. She turned her head to the side, closing her eyes and drinking in his musky scent. He wore the most delicious cologne. She made a mental note to find out what it was so she could keep buying it for him.

She felt that same pleasant tingle when he leaned over and murmured in her ear. "You are the most beautiful thing on this land, Lynn. I'd apologize to God, but He made you, too, so…"

He chuckled.

"You say the sweetest things, Justin," Lynn murmured, turning around to face him, pressing her back against the railing. She put her hands up on his chest, gazing into his eyes. "I'm so glad I found you. Life was really boring before I met you."

He grinned. "I don't know if I can keep up the level of excitement that brought us together, Lynn. I'm sorry."

She giggled, shaking her head. "No, I don't want that. I don't want any more danger. That kind of excitement is better left for people on TV."

"I agree. Let's keep it to a minimum. How about the most dangerous thing we do is...say, go hiking on a high ridge."

Lynn shook her head. "No heights. That's out."

Justin frowned. "Oh no. No heights? How about roller coasters? Can you do that? If not, I don't know. Might be a deal breaker."

Lynn gasped, grinning wide. "Hey! It's too late to back out now. You already put the ring on my finger."

Justin raised his eyebrows, giving her a sly look. "Oh, a man can find a way out if he really wants one."

Lynn cried out, slapping him playfully on the arm. He laughed and pulled her into his arms, hugging her against him.

"I don't want to find a way out!" he exclaimed. "You've got me hook, line and sinker, baby. I'm not going anywhere."

"You better not. I don't want to be the spinster sister. I had to get married sooner or later. Might as well be you."

They both laughed.

When their joviality faded, Lynn found herself content to gaze up at him. His eyes were so filled with love and admiration. She had never felt so loved before in her life. She wanted it to last forever.

It would last forever.

She would make sure of it.

"I can do roller coasters," she said softly, lifting up on her tip-toes to place a warm kiss on his lips. "I'll do anything for you. Even the Ferris wheel."

"What's wrong with the Ferris wheel?" Justin asked before

quickly nodding his head and adding, "Oh yeah…heights."

She nodded. "Yeah. It's not that bad. Maybe I'll get over it."

"Would you try, baby?" Justin's voice was smooth and soft. Her heart pounded as he leaned closer to her. He was going to kiss her. She hoped it would always feel so wonderful, so loving, so passionate. "Would you try for me? So, we can go hiking on a dangerous ridge somewhere?"

The last part of his sentence came out while his lips were pressed against hers. The sensation of him talking, his lips moving against hers, sent a thrill through her nerves and made her shiver with delight. He pulled back a little and looked into her eyes.

"I think I like that reaction," he said softly. "I want to feel that again."

He moved to kiss her lightly, but she pressed against him, wrapping her arms around his neck. She relaxed her body onto his, so he had to put his arms around her to hold her up. Her eyes were closed, but she could feel his smile as she kissed him.

"You're a crazy woman, Lynn Wright Brownstone. Crazy. But, I love it!"

Sweet Clean Romance Box Sets by Morris Fenris

Home To You: The Complete Series Box Set
ASIN: B07HRY3R21

Forever Christmas Box Set
ASIN: B077MG4JJ2

Christmas Wish Box Set
ASIN: B077L52RQH

Christmas Tale Box Set
ASIN: B077L1STMC

Healing Her Heart Box Set
ASIN: B076HF86VY

Healed By Love Box Set
ASIN: B075PN8T1Q

Second Chance Romance: Complete Series Box Set
ASIN: B075BLV48L

Three Brothers Lodge - The Complete Series Box Set
ASIN: B074RFJ9BW

The Cold Happy Magic Box Set

ASIN: B074KX21GX

Between Love and Honor Box Set

ASIN: B016OXY5SE

Christmas Promises Box Set

ASIN: B00O3NFQJU

Christmas Reunion Box Set

ASIN: B00PVCLLT6

Season of Wonder Box Set

ASIN: B00GHPFYO4

Home For Christmas Box Set

ASIN: B00G1XIORG

Love Came Just In Time Box Set

ASIN: B077HZCKP1

Thank You

Dear Reader,

Thank you for choosing to read my books out of the thousands that merit reading. I recognize that reading takes time and quietness, so I am grateful that you have designed your lives to allow for this enriching endeavor, whatever the book's title and subject.

Now more than ever before, Amazon reviews and Social Media play vital role in helping individuals make their reading choices. If any of my books have moved you, inspired you, or educated you, please share your reactions with others by posting an Amazon review as well as via email, Facebook, Twitter, Goodreads, -- or even old-fashioned face-to-face conversation! And when you receive my announcement of my new book, please pass it along. Thank you.

For updates about New Releases, as well as exclusive promotions, visit my website and sign up for the VIP mailing list. Click here to get started: www.morrisfenrisbooks.com

I invite you to connect with me through Social media:
1. Facebook : https://www.facebook.com/AuthorMorrisFenris/
2. Twitter: https://twitter.com/morris_fenris
3. Pinterest: https://www.pinterest.com/AuthorMorris/
4. Instagram: https://www.instagram.com/authormorrisfenris/

For my portfolio of books on Amazon, please visit my Author Page:

Amazon USA:
amazon.com/author/morrisfenris

Amazon UK:
https://www.amazon.co.uk/Morris%20Fenris/e/B00FXLWKRC

You can also contact me by email:
authormorrisfenris@gmail.com

With profound gratitude, and with hope for your continued reading pleasure,

Morris Fenris
Author & Publisher